THE WHIRLWIND

THE WHIRLWIND

An Historical Romance

BEING THE STORY OF THE FRENCH REVOLUTION AS IT WAS SEEN BY RENÉ DE MASSAC, DEPUTY TO THE NATIONAL ASSEMBLY AND GENERAL OF THE REPUBLIC

By

WILLIAM STEARNS DAVIS

Fredonia Books
Amsterdam, The Netherlands

The Whirlwind:
An Historical Romance

by
William Stearns Davis

ISBN: 1-4101-0801-5

Copyright © 2005 by Fredonia Books

Reprinted from the 1929 edition

Fredonia Books
Amsterdam, The Netherlands
http://www.fredoniabooks.com

TO MY NIECE
REBECCA GIFFORD
CHILD OF MANY HOPES

TO THE READER

RENÉ DE MASSAC, the chief figure in this narrative, was apparently permitted to be an actor in some of the most important events of the French Revolution. He was present at the assembling of the States General at Versailles, the capture of the Bastille, the storming of the Tuileries, the decisive battle of Wattignies, which saved France from Austria, the death of Danton, and finally at the overthrow of Robespierre. Unlike many more conspicuous figures in the Revolution, he had the somewhat singular good fortune to survive the Reign of Terror.

Readers of a speculative cast may perhaps think of him as becoming later Marshal Massac, Duke of Caravelto, reckoned among the most humane and honorable of the Napoleonic commanders.

In any case, the pictures here presented of such personages as Louis XVI, Marie Antoinette, Danton, St. Just and Robespierre, seem to be in strict accordance with their acts and words as conveyed to us in more formal history.

W. S. D.

Exeter, New Hampshire.

CONTENTS

BOOK I. THE GOOD OLD TIMES

CHAPTER | PAGE
| I. | MAJESTY ARISES | 3
| II. | THE PRISONER OF VINCENNES CHATEAU | 24
| III. | VIRGINIE DURAND | 37
| IV. | ABBÉ VERNET'S DISCRETION IS TRUSTED | 47
| V. | THE AVOCAT FROM ARRAS | 58
| VI. | ABBÉ VERNET BURROWING | 70
| VII. | THE DEPUTY FROM ARD | 82
| VIII. | THE PALAIS ROYAL | 84
| IX. | THE GRAND COUVERT | 96
| X. | WHAT ANDRÉ TOLD | 110

BOOK II. "LIBERTY"

| XI. | A CHAPTER OF HISTORY | 127
| XII. | THE VOICE OF MIRABEAU | 132
| XIII. | THE FOREST LEAVES HAVE EARS | 144
| XIV. | THE LONGEST ROAD TO PARIS | 157
| XV. | NEARING THUNDER | 169
| XVI. | THE LIGHTNING | 182
| XVII. | CRUMBLING SPLENDOR | 196
|XVIII. | THE GREAT FEAR | 207
| XIX. | THE CHATEAU DREADS THE HOVEL | 221
| XX. | THE TRICOLOR | 240

ix

BOOK III. "EQUALITY"

CHAPTER		PAGE
XXI.	SEPTEMBER HUSH	259
XXII.	THE PRISONERS IN THE TUILERIES	262
XXIII.	THREE KINDS OF PATRIOTS	275
XXIV.	THE DAUPHIN'S SAND PILE	289
XXV.	THE KING'S STRONG BOX	301
XXVI.	THE PACKET TO AUSTRIA	314
XXVII.	THE MARSEILLAISE	328
XXVIII.	THE TWILIGHT OF THE KINGS	331
XXIX.	THE VOICE OF DANTON	348

BOOK IV. "FRATERNITY"

XXX.	HOW A SONG WENT FORTH TO BATTLE	353
XXXI.	THE NEW PARIS	375
XXXII.	THE GODDESS OF REASON	388
XXXIII.	THE INCORRUPTIBLE	401
XXXIV.	ST. JUST	415
XXXV.	SATURN DEVOURING HIS CHILDREN	427
XXXVI.	VERNET AGAIN BURROWING	433
XXXVII.	THE FESTIVAL OF THE SUPREME BEING	442
XXXVIII.	"NECESSARY SACRIFICES"	457
XXXIX.	NEARER THE UTOPIA	472
XL.	"A BAS LE TYRAN!"	488
XLI.	WHEN THE DREAMER WAKES	504
XLII.	THE LAST TUMBRILS	521

BOOK I
THE GOOD OLD TIMES

BOOK I

THE GOOD OLD DAYS

THE WHIRLWIND

CHAPTER I

MAJESTY ARISES

THE gray morning light was very cold, but the apartment was magnificent. The pale bars were slanting in through the windows upon a gaudy frieze of cupids in gilt stucco. Everything, in fact, seemed to be of gilt: the woodwork of the plush upholstered chairs, the doors and casements, the wainscoting, the chandeliers, the frames of the huge sombre pictures, all were gilt; unmistakably, however, they were not gold, and, truth to tell, were a little tarnished. As the light strengthened, one could see that the largest picture was a canvas depicting His Most Christian Majesty Louis XIV, semi-nude as "Apollo," and with a quantity of mundane and fleshy princes and princesses as scantily clad gods and goddesses arrayed in phalanx around him.

It was a morning early in December, 1788. In the corridor outside the Oeil-de-Boeuf, this anteroom of the King's chamber at Versailles, the four tall, resplendent Swiss guardsmen on duty stopped in their slow pacings, set down their halberds and punctiliously blew upon their fingers to warm them. Simultaneously from the further corner of the anteroom arose a series of grunts and mutterings behind a tall screen, followed by the sound of some one drawing on heavy boots. More grunts and grumblings; then the screen suddenly collapsed, and before it could be replaced revealed momentarily a low truckle-bed. Before the screen there now stood forth yet another tall Swiss, in white and gold braid so decorative as to vie with the chandeliers and the cupids.

The new apparition was not merely tall, he was gigantic enough to play Goliath the Philistine. Half of his face was hidden by an outstretching blond mustache, the remainder was overshadowed by a large white wig, which he was still adjusting over both ears. A last twitch—the apparatus was complete. Monsieur Hübli Kistler, First Porter-in-Ordinary to royalty itself, began with professional calmness to survey the chilly reaches of the ante-chamber, then to cast his eye upon a certain glass door, to see if there were signs of the removal of the curtain which prevented a view inside.

Monsieur Hübli was alleged to eat and sleep in the Oeil-de-Boeuf. Nothing could pry him away from his citadel of vantage, which brought him a greater flow of crowns, louis and even greater fees than were enjoyed by any other door-keeper in Versailles. Young Body Guardsmen indeed vowed that Monsieur Hübli was a greater potentate than the Prince of Condé or the Controller of Finance himself. Did not his smooth, sonorous voice make marshals and cardinals obey him like lackeys? Only twelve words apparently in his vocabulary, but what words they were! "Pass on, Messieurs, pass on!" "Messieurs, the King!" "Retire!" And last, but not least, "No admission, Monseigneur." The greatest of subjects would then halt before the master of that door knob, behind which lurked the hopes and fears of all Versailles.

But the apartment as yet was cold and empty. Monsieur Hübli rubbed his chilly hands and lolled beside the glass barrier with his standardized smile, until the door was quietly opened, and a gentleman sprucely clad emerged softly in his slippers, then closed the door not so tight as to squeeze it hard upon a cord of red silk which was looped over his shoulder and which ran back into the room.

"Still asleep?" inquired Hübli in polite undertone.

"Still asleep, thanks to that heavy supper. We may have to wake him." The First Valet-in-Ordinary adjusted his lace cravat. "His appetite continues as good as ever."

"Remember that night after the Diamond Necklace business exploded," continued the porter, "how none of us could eat a chicken-wing nor sleep a wink? *Heiliger Gott!* How many pâtés de foies gras didn't he tuck away then; and his snores you could hear clear out in the guard room!"

The valet straightened his silver shoe buckles. "Peace of mind is a royal virtue," he remarked officially, then bestowed two polite nods. "Ah! my dear Valby and my dear Crebron. Well, it doesn't seem to grow any warmer."

The newcomers were both men of well-fed bulk, dressed in austere black save for the exquisite lace at their wrists and necks and the silver hilts of their toy-like walking swords. Both also rejoiced in bag wigs of unusual size and intricacy.

"*Peste,* no," responded Valby, the First Physician-in-Ordinary. "The winter gets steadily worse. Bread riots in Paris already."

"As I was just saying," interposed Crebron, the First Surgeon, "I wish all that Paris *canaille* were quietly starved and frozen and sent to the devil; but what I *am* concerned with is that I had my second snuff-box picked from my pocket at the Queen's faro table last night."

Valby's laugh was condescending. "My dear colleague, you must not let so commonplace a happening spoil your humor. When you've held office here a trifle longer, you'll play the philosopher. Bear witness—I haven't complained and yet last night I lost two hundred louis, and that too with nasty thoughts of foul play."

"At whose table?" quickly demanded the valet.

"Guess whose?" returned Valby, snapping his spectacle case.

"Didn't I see you at the Polignac's?" queried Crebron.

Valby's smile became enigmatic. "My friend, Mme. de Polignac is a great lady and a still greater friend of the Queen. I never discuss great ladies. But I may politely remark this—she is remarkably fortunate at cards."

Before this profitable exchange could continue, the group was suddenly joined by a younger man. His countenance was extraordinarily pink and white by the grace of cosmetics; his puce and silver-gray garments a triumph of tailoring; his wig craped to the last hair; his golden shoe buckles sparkled with diamonds as did his long and delicate hands. Under his left arm he crushed a beribboned hat, and in his left hand bore a tall white staff tipped with a silver ball. This stranger approached across the sheeny, parquet floor at something so close to a run that the others all raised their eyebrows.

"My dear Marquis," began Valby, "when M. de Dreux-Brézé, Grand Master of Ceremonies, enters with such haste, I am permitted to say, 'Something extraordinary has happened.'"

"Yes, yes, something extraordinary," burst from all the others.

Dreux-Brézé leaned on his staff to draw breath. "It's true. Massac has done it," at length he puffed out.

"Massac has done it," echoed the four as men stunned, and Valby added, "Then that absurd rumor of yesterday is actually confirmed! Impossible!"

The Marquis still panted, but began speaking rapidly. "Yes, it's all true. Massac's own colonel has told me. He's thrown up his commission and will banish himself from court. He swears he will marry the girl."

The First Physician cupped his hands over his ear. "*Marry?* Do I hear aright—*marry?*"

"Yes, M. de Valby. I used the right word—*marry.*"

The First Physician, a notorious sceptic, mechanically crossed himself. "*Ma foi!* We live among miracles. I've seen the Montgolfier balloon; we'll soon be breakfasting above the clouds. But this surpasses everything. A Massac *marry* an innkeeper's wench!—Incredible!"

"I've heard of his infatuation," announced the valet, "but who could take the story seriously? They say the girl would make a charming mistress—but for a Mme. de Massac!—Are the Alps and Biscay going next to change places?"

"Merciful God, is he sane?" Valby continued, groaning.

"In charity I say that he is not," rejoined the Marquis, but Crebron laid a finger on his shoulder.

"My dear Master of Ceremonies, you know that I have not enjoyed the honor of my appointment here at court so long as have some of my friends. Who really *is* this amazing René de Massac? His title is only 'Chevalier,' and his name is not Rohan or Soubise or Bouille. Why, if some young nobleman makes a fool of himself, should the whole royal chateau be agog? Pray enlighten."

Dreux-Brézé, quite in the mood now for a speech, began by clearing his throat: "My dear First Surgeon, many have wondered like you about this chevalier and his march to favor. Now I still call myself his friend, although he has outraged me exceedingly, both by his present madness and by wearing ribbons instead of buckles in his shoes at the last *grand couvert*. There's something winsome about the rascal, I won't at all deny. Well, here's a bit of the story. As you say, the Massacs are not a princely house, but back in old Philip Augustus' time, one of them saved the King's life on the Crusade; stopped a Saracen arrow aimed at the

King on his own breast, or something like that. How could the King reward the brave squireen? 'By permitting me never to have any other over-lord, barring God, saving your Royal Grace.' So since then, though the Massac seigneury has been small enough, its head has been the direct, mind you, the direct vassal of the King himself. Few enough nobles, barring Princes of the Blood, can really say that. The Massacs have sometimes had to rusticate with their few peasants and boarspears in their dungeonous old chateau, but no one has dared to asperse their high noblesse. Dukes gladly intermarry with them when it's not a matter of dowry. They have always had a fine entrée at court. The head of the house, however, calls himself plain 'Chevalier,' because of their pride! 'We aren't rich enough to be princes, and our blood is too blue to be anything else.' "

"Yet there's a Comte de Massac and his son, the Vicomte?" interposed Valby.

"Very true," instructed Dreux-Brézé, "but they are always 'younger sons.' Well, the father of this René served in America; was a friend of Washington, they say; doubtless picked up disgustingly Republican notions, and corrupted his son. But soon after the late Chevalier returned to France, his old Yorktown wound went back on him. He presently died, left a brother who is the Count, a nephew, Laurent, the Viscount, and more especially a son—our Chevalier. Friends of the father got the young René a lieutenancy here in the Body Guard, and then his own fetching ways soon won him a stock of favor around the Trianons which gave other young nobles with deeper purses the very megrims of jealousy. If ever a lad had roses and silk all before him, that lad was René! We all said, 'He'll marry a Broglie and end up as a Marshal of France.' And now—pouf——!"

"What precisely has happened?" demanded Crebron, bending nearer in his interest.

"Not Cupid's darts, I swear, but Hecate's infection. Of course, I always considered René to be a law unto himself. Not a spark of ambition, although after his success in the last theatricals he could have driven hard for a big pension. Presently he began to talk strangely. I suspected something bad, after that dinner at the Contis, when he actually gainsaid our delightful friend Talleyrand, the Bishop of Autun, when he was arguing most wittily against the existence of a God."

"All sensible men nowadays are atheists," remarked Crebron in correct disgust.

"So we all flung at Massac, but he held out stubbornly. The worst case of Rousseau and his piosity in all my experience. After that, of course, I was ready to hear that René was hanging around coarse bourgeois salons in Paris where they discussed every vile doctrine and even questioned the desirability of kings."

"But I am perishing to hear about the girl," urged the First Valet.

"Well, hear then, wonder, yet believe. Two generations ago, upon the Massac lands near Ard in Picardy, there was an innkeeper and withal a malcontent fool and an upstart. He was almost a serf, mind you, of the old Massac seigneurs. Well, this lout, named Durand, must needs get tired of his cannekins, sold out his inn, went to Lyons, speculated in silk, made some money, married a bourgeois girl a bit above him in station. They next had a son who fiddled with—what d'you call it—chemistry, in a smart mechanical way. After that this brat must needs wheedle himself into the graces of a M. Lavoisier."

"Something of a clever chemist or apothecary, I've heard," sniffed the First Physician.

"Probably some kind of a glozing pill-roller," continued
Dreux-Brézé, "never mind. In any case young Durand in
turn married the daughter of a still bigger bourgeois, kept
a tolerable house, elbowed himself even into some bourgeois
salons. Finally this younger Durand had a daughter, who,
for an innkeeper's slattern, might be decidedly worth
intriguing."

"Ah! I begin to comprehend," observed Valby, polishing
his glasses.

"René met the girl in some fat Farmer General's parlors.
Of course she was knowing, took him on his weakest side.
Sentimental, romantic, talked like Julia in *La Nouvelle
Heloise*—affinity of souls and all such balderdash. Alas,
poor René!"

"And then," completed the First Surgeon gravely, "instead of genteelly corrupting the girl, as any man of breeding might have done, he actually proposed marriage."

The Marquis wrung his delicate hands. "What a tragedy,
my friends! Better—what a suicide! René is hopelessly
caught in her hideous spider webs. 'What is rank and blood
if I truly love her?' His talk simply turned my stomach.
Vainly we treated it as a monstrous jest. Then what did
he do? Of course, he knew he could not remain at Versailles.
Last night he took the plunge, threw up his lieutenancy in
the Body Guard, although a lieutenancy there outranks a
colonel in the line."

"The devil eat the trollop!" anathematized the First
Valet, his mouth in a pucker. "Of course, she knew her
victim. 'Marriage or nothing, Monsieur.' But has our poor
René no friends, no kinsmen? Has nothing been said and
done?"

"Said and done!" groaned Dreux-Brézé. "Do you suppose
his uncle and aunt haven't been on their very knees to him?
That Mme. de Condé hasn't wrung his hand, 'Spare the
honor of your family!' Hasn't René's colonel, the Duc de

Luxembourg, pleaded, implored, threatened? Hasn't the Shepherdess herself told him of the career he was throwing away? Even she might better have besought a horse-block. He swears that he'll marry the Durand hoyden in these six months. 'A fig for rank and family. I wed Virginie and not her ancestors. We'll make our own rank and family.' There's no way to stop him."

Valby drew himself up, coughed, then let his voice fall to a studied whisper. "No way? There is still the Fat Boy."

The others all nodded, and Dreux-Brézé's nod was a trifle cunning: "Perhaps you are right. The Fat Boy *may* be appealed to."

Before the others could answer a smart pull on the cord was felt on the valet's shoulder. "*Gratias Deo!* He's awakened of himself," announced that functionary, and he pushed back the glass door. Instantly the porter and the Master of Ceremonies stationed themselves like rigid sentinels on either side of the portal, while the physician and surgeon disappeared inside, following the valet. Already a group of brilliantly appareled gentlemen was gathering—yawning, shivering, adjusting their clothes, at the lower end of the antechamber.

"His Majesty has graciously awakened," boomed the deep voice of the Swiss. "The First Physician and First Surgeon are inquiring as to his royal health. The first entrée will be admitted speedily."—Whereat the ever-increasing throng of courtiers began to resolve itself into a number of platoons drawn up at decorous intervals before the magical door, while Dreux-Brézé's cat-like gaze went over every ruff and knee buckle like a drill sergeant before a review.

All of the crowd were smiling, all were laughing, all were talking loudly; for the first thing learned at Versailles was to raise your voice; otherwise nobody would hear you. An usher in a corner kept droning, "Quiet, Messieurs, quiet!" The buzz, nevertheless, continued just the same.

The bedchamber, like the antechamber, was lofty, magnificent, chilly. From the walls a St. John by Raphael and a David by Domenichino looked down upon a very ornate bed with an equally ornate counterpane, depicting "The Sacrifice of Isaac." Upon this bed lay a man with a large nose under a night-cap; while some dozen persons were pushing back the heavy curtains and elbowing one another for a chance to talk to him.

The "Family Entrée" of Princes of the Blood had already slipped by Monsieur Hübli's relentless scrutiny. Now it was the "Grand Entrée" of the second order of magnates that was buzzing around the bedside. Orders of St. Louis, of St. Michael and of the Holy Ghost shone on titled breasts like refulgent stars. There were diamonds enough in the room to replenish Golconda. No one, not excluding two purple-clad bishops, was present who could not meet every test for a great noble—"a man who sees the King, who confers with his ministers, and possesses ancestors, debts and pensions."

The man who lay somewhat impassively upon the huge bed possessed, in addition to his Roman nose, blue eyes that opened in a kind of dull stare, a round forehead, nostrils flaccid and large, thick lips and a florid, loose skin. The mouth at least was benevolent and carried a touch of plebeian bonhomie. If its owner was bored by the din about him, he seemed almost too phlegmatic to show it. When he spoke, it was in monosyllables in a very monotonous voice.

The Maréchal de Broglie had said something, the Grand Chamberlain had said something, the Duc de Penthievre was saying something, when elbowing through the press came an elderly gentleman in a pea-green coat with an unusual quantity of gold lace. His wig was actually awry, and his sword knot was slipping asunder. With a bare show of courtesy he forced his way to the bedside and scarcely waited for the Duke to finish a banal remark about "good hunting weather."

"What possesses Villars?" queried Crebron, as he now stood a little apart with Valby, surveying the reception.

"The Count seems on fire; Paris may be in revolt." The newcomer had in fact plunged down on his knees by the bedside, and almost dragged the royal hand from under the coverlet in order to press it to his lips.

"Oh! Sire, I cry your mercy. It is seldom, you will graciously condescend to recall, that I have made bold to ask a favor."

The thick lips on the pillow tightened a little, but the hand was not withdrawn.

"Well, M. de Villars, what is it? Another pardon?"

"I rejoice, Sire, that this month I have no mercy to ask for scapegrace cousins. Something delightfully different. Your Majesty may not have heard;—my butler told me fifteen minutes ago;—the Bishop of Monay has died this very morning."

"Ah!" This comment from royalty reverberated like an echo from every corner of the room. Five dignitaries present darted glances of rage toward Villars, and silently vowed vengeance upon *their* butlers for having failed with the same precious tidings twenty minutes earlier. Villars instantly charged home with his advantage.

"You will graciously recall, Sire, that I am blessed with a nephew in holy orders, the Abbé Clairaut, the inventor of those admirable charades so acceptable to Her Majesty. His pensions are very small, his establishment expensive. Alike, because of his merits and the credit it would reflect upon myself, I entreat you to consider for the vacant bishopric——"

The figure on the pillows rose partially, the company held its collective breath. "But M. de Villars, it is notorious that your nephew the Abbé, when he preached before the court, seemed master of every science barring the single one of theology. Besides, there are still those who say that a bishop ought at least to believe in God."

"Alas! Your Majesty, how my nephew has been slandered! A most pious youth. Consider his talents. Consider the injury done my reputation if, after proffering this small request, it should be denied. Villars is an ancient house, Sire, and of late we have received very few favors."

Au audible sigh rose from the bed. "Well, M. le Comte, we ought not to grant this; we must consider, we must consider. Remember, Monay's death is not confirmed yet. Still you have claims——"

The petitioner, in a transport, covered the royal hand with kisses. "Oh, Your Majesty! What condescension! What generosity!" And Villars retreated decorously from the bed, to be promptly congratulated by the five rivals who had just turned green with jealousy. "'Ask and you shall receive,'" quoted a cynical nobleman at Valby's elbow. "'Consider' spells 'Yes.' I tell you, my friends, success at Versailles lies wholly in this—the art of *asking first.*"

. . . The Third Entrée and the Fourth. The bedchamber is ever more crowded. The magnates of the wardrobe have their toes trodden on by the officers of the Body Guard, the Swiss Guard, the tables, the hunt. The Grand Wolf-Huntsman has just backed a lieutenant-general into a corner, when the white wand taps sharply.

"The King arises, Messieurs."

Majesty sits in his night gown on the edge of the bed,

and the First Gentleman-of-the-Wardrobe holds before him
a silver basin of holy water. Majesty crosses himself and
murmurs a short prayer. Majesty next receives his slippers from a marquis, his dressing gown from a duke, and
lets a baron set the chair whereon he seats himself to put
on his clothes. The Very Christian King is about to array
himself for another day wherein to appear and delight his
people.

A hush pervades the chamber. Enemies stop glaring at
Villars; Villars bows his head as if in chapel. Few acts of
religion are more solemn than the vesturing of the Lord's
Anointed.

The awesome ceremony proceeds. The King has dipped
his hands in a silver bowl. Two pages of Crusading ancestry remove his slippers. The Grand Master of the
Wardrobe draws off Majesty's night shirt by his right arm,
the First Valet of the Wardrobe by his left. Deeper the
hush. The Second Valet draws near with something
wrapped in white taffeta. The climax approaches. Noiselessly now the glass door opens for the last entrée of courtly
initiates into their Holy of Holies. Majesty is about to
put on his shirt.

The dressing gown falls. Majesty appears before his
dutiful subjects very much as God has made him. The
morning (we repeat) is cold, and Majesty casts certain
shivery glances of royal impatience. The Grand Chamberlain nods to the Second Valet. The shirt is unwrapped.
Majesty surveys it longingly. The Grand Chamberlain
holds it ready when the glass door swings aside. In high-
born haste there enters a gentleman before whom all give
way, the Prince de Condé, in proper person. The Grand
Chamberlain bows to his higher dignity, hands the shirt
back to the Second Valet, he to the First Gentleman, he
with another bow to the Prince.

The Prince smiles and begins drawing off his gloves. Majesty watches sadly and sneezes. But again the glass door opens. A second gentleman and more very respectful bows. It is the Comte d'Artois, the King's youngest brother. Condé proffers the shirt to him with a profound salutation. Artois smiles most correctly, and begins most correctly to remove *his* gloves. But here he catches the appealing gleam in his royal brother's eye. Majesty sneezes again—very loudly. Etiquette is shattered by that sneeze. Majesty receives the shirt from his brother, but with the latter's gloves actually upon his princely fingers. Dreux-Brézé and his assistants are completely desolated.

The toilet continues. The Second Valet holds the mirror while Majesty's hair is combed. The Grand Master of the Wardrobe assists with the vest and small clothes. The Third Valet brings in a basket of cravats from which Majesty deigns to select one, which the Second Master arranges around the royal neck.—So to the end. Hat, gloves, handkerchief and cane all are proffered and accepted. The King kneels by the bedside. The Third Almoner recites a prayer.—The Latin ceases and Louis XVI, King of France and Navarre, clad now in his customary gray silk and satin slashed with silver, stands clothed and in his right mind before his loyal nobility. The pontifical is over.

"Retire, Messieurs," booms from the glass door.

. . . The King watched the cohort bow itself backward from his presence. His own gesture of farewell was friendly but awkward. The best tailor in France could not conceal the fact that he was a very stout as well as muscular man. His movements were quick, jerky; he had a manner of shifting from foot to foot, as if habitually ill at ease. "A gentleman, perhaps; but a prince, never;" so the unenlightened might have described him. For a moment decidedly rare in his normal day, it chanced that Louis XVI was now almost alone; that is, a single gentleman-in-waiting was standing near, and this individual now approached his master somewhat diffidently.

"Well—what is it?" The King's voice was brusque, yet kindly.

"Please, Sire, M. Necker prays that you be gracious enough to attend the Council this evening. The ordinances summoning the new States General; he says that matters of great importance——"

The King sighed. "Always the States General. When can we be well rid of it?—I had promised the Queen, but what must be, must. Say that I will attend."

"And this afternoon, Sire?"

"The hunting, of course. I hope it's not too cold for flushing partridges."

"I hope not, Sire; whom will you honor by commanding to join you?"

The large nose had dropped in deliberation when the glass door reopened. A slim young officer in the red and white of the Body Guard strode up to a respectful distance, then gave a military salute, and uncovering, pressed his hat to his breast. The King seemed a trifle surprised.

"You come from the Queen, Lieutenant de Rions," spoke Louis. "What message can she be sending me?"

"Please Sire, Her Majesty begs for a special word with you before you take your breakfast and your promenade. Even now she is waiting in the antechamber."

The awkwardness of the King seemed to increase. He shifted from one foot to another rapidly.

"Some request, of course. What can it possibly be?"

"I do not have the honor to know, Sire, but Her Majesty seems very anxious to see you."

Louis' sigh was audible. "Some new request!—Of course, I'll have to grant it after that favor to Villars. God grant it's nothing amiss!" Then aloud, "Escort Her Majesty in."

The glass door clicked. The Swiss' voice rolled, "Her Majesty the Queen," and the monarch stood very uncomfortably facing not one, but three women.

Three they were, but the one who walked slightly ahead of the others would have been marked as their leader had her dress been blue kersey instead of rosy silk. Her full garments floated about her like an evening cloud. She approached with an indescribable gliding motion, the expression of the animation and grace diffusing from the whole of her tall, perfectly supple body. Out of its mass of lace shone her neck, delicately carved, upbearing a head with features not perfectly regular, but charged with a perfect zest for life and alert intelligence. The brown hair (that morning without powder) was long and silky; the forehead high and slightly projecting, the eyes clear blue like her Austrian Danube, the nose aquiline, the mouth a trifle too large for formal beauty, the countenance oval and glowing with warm color. These were a part merely of the catalogue. There were only a few golden pins in her hair; her perfectly modeled arms bore each a single bracelet, curiously carved. In short, step, poise, gesture spoke clearer than a herald, "Here is the Queen of France."

The other two women were older and appeared as admirable foils for their royal mistress. Louis recognized them as the Duchesse de Polignac, a noblewoman who was the chief familiar of the Queen, yet, nevertheless, the center of many strange stories, and the Comtesse de Massac, a lady less conspicuous at court, although of much fairer reputation.

A master painter might have limned the curious contrast of the ungainly, half-bashful man standing uneasily, and of the airy, incomparably feminine creature that was now gliding up to him with an enrapturing frou-frou of her garments. The Queen and her companions approached within four steps, then all congeed with studiously graceful courtesies. The King pushed his hat clumsily under one arm and bent forward awkwardly, while his face set itself in a slightly forced smile.

Etiquette compelled him to speak first: "Good morning, Madame; and you, too, Mme. de Polignac and Mme. de Massac. You favor us early to-day. No misfortune brings you, I hope." The effort to seem gracious was painfully apparent.

"No misfortune at all, Sire" (the Queen's French was tuneful and faultless, but the accent bore the least touch of German); "that is, if the King will be good enough to avert it."

"Alas, Madame, if only I could avert all the misfortunes in France! Does this one lie in my power?" The smile had become even more uneasy.

"Wholly in your power, Sire." The Queen beckoned with inimitable grace for the Countess to come forward. "Mme. de Massac is in distress. We all are in distress. _I_ am in distress. You will listen to Mme. de Massac, Sire?"

The Countess did not courtesy again, but immediately fell on both knees, and seized the King's hand, despite a polite effort on his part to make her drop it and rise.

"Oh! Sire, pardon the agony of an aunt. It is for René, for my nephew, that I am pleading. To save him from worse than death—the horror of his folly—the disgrace——"

The King looked painfully bewildered. "I do not understand," he almost stammered.

"Surely they have told you, Sire," interposed the Queen. "It is the Chevalier René, _our_ René, whom we all like so much. Such a fine young man! Such prospects! Now such a misfortune!"

Louis used his free hand to rub his jaw. "Why, last night Artois did say, 'I fear young Massac has been playing the ass.' A bad run at cards, I suppose."

"Cards, Sire!" almost screamed the Countess. "Holy Virgin! If it were only cards. Any gentleman can ruin himself most respectably at cards. But this—this!"

The Queen gave a half perceptible sign; the Countess arose and released the royal fingers.

"Tell the King what has happened," commanded Marie Antoinette; "then let him judge for himself."

Whereupon, with tolerable coherency, despite much of "anguish," "agony" and "desolation," and many invocations of heaven, the Countess repeated essentially the same story of the infatuation of René de Massac wherewith Dreux-Brézé had regaled his companions earlier. When she had ended her breathless protestations, the Queen looked at the King inquiringly.

"Well, Sire?"

Louis seemed utterly distressed. "Well, Madame? And what can I do about it?—Reason with the Chevalier?"

"Reason?" The shapely foot of the Queen stamped hard; "Reason? Do I hear the King of France speaking thus, with one of his own household threatening everything but suicide!"

"But, indeed, Mesdames," confessed the King, shifting again from leg to leg with increasing rapidity, "a misalliance with a Paris bourgeoise is not by law a felony. Of course, Massac will have to leave Versailles; but he is of age, and——"

"Oh, the shame, the shame!" burst from the Countess. "His uncle the Count, and I, his aunt, are disgraced before the court; his cousin, my son Laurent, before the entire Body Guard. Never in six hundred years has a Massac contaminated his blood. If he were only honorably dead!"

Regardless of royalty, the old Countess burst into tears, while the King, more discomposed than ever, cast upon his consort a glance which said better than words, "Let us end this scene. What do you want of me?"

Quite abruptly Marie Antoinette drew from her bosom a paper. "Pray sign this, Sire." And she held it toward her husband. Louis gave the document a long glance and then did not conceal his frown.

"You will not press me to sign this, Madame?" he asked.

"And why not, Sire?" The Queen took a step nearer. "Why should not this hoodwinked boy be forced to reflect awhile in one of your fortresses upon his infatuation? Every noble family can rightly demand this protection from its sovereign."

Louis' eyes dropped and he did not answer the Queen directly. "Why was not this *lettre de cachet* taken to my proper ministers? They have power to sign.—Why to me? —Now?" His voice had begun firmly. It trailed off into perplexity.

"Alas, Sire," bewailed the Countess, "they were appealed to; they refused. The Lieutenant of Police said, 'The unpopularity of these orders is becoming too great.' M. Necker said, 'We must not do something sure to be condemned when the States General meets'—Oh! what discouragement when René is about to disgrace his kinsfolk forever."

"Then," spoke Louis slowly, looking not at Mme. de Massac, but at his wife, "you ask the King to do what his ministers refuse?—Yet they are in the right. It was urged strongly at the last council that no more orders of arbitrary arrest should be issued. 'Conciliate public opinion,' every one told me."

The Queen flipped at the paper with her long fingers. "Then, Sire, René will marry that Durand wench, and the lowest turnspit in Versailles will say that the opinions of your ministers will be the only consolation for the rejected petition of (her voice caught delicately)—of your wife."

The blue eyes were close to the King's. He could not avoid them. After a tense instant he gave a jerk of sheer helplessness and rattled the paper. "Well, have it over with; but no such request again."

"A pen," commanded Marie Antoinette of the gentleman-in-waiting. A pen and ink horn appeared. The King signed hastily. He appeared deaf and blind to all of Mme. de Massac's torrent of gratitude, but when the Queen began thanking him, he bent his ungainly body and lifted her hand to his lips. "My will is always your pleasure," he said with a notable attempt at gallantry.

The Queen's smile was beatific. "Then, Sire, I will reward the granting of one favor by asking yet another. Be present at the theatricals to-night and see if I have learned my part."

The King looked again bewildered. "But, Madame, I have just promised M. Necker to attend the Council."

The Queen answered by facing the gentleman-in-waiting, while waving the paper triumphantly. "Tell M. Necker it will be impossible for His Majesty to attend the Council until to-morrow.—Till to-night then. Adieu, Sire. Come, my friends!"—And the musical rustle of her gown faded away in the antechamber.

The King stood for a moment half stupidly, then recollected himself and began to name certain noblemen to be invited to the hunt that afternoon. The gentleman-in-waiting (silent listener to the dialogue) presently departed with the list, ruminating, "So René de Massac will have to make a little trip to Vincennes." Then he began to hum under breath a ditty very popular just then with all the court, barring, indeed, its royal master and mistress:

"The shepherdess of Trianon
If you say '*Oui*,' won't answer '*Non*,'
Yet 'ware her thrust and parry!
She guides by arts kept all her own,
The nice fat boy upon the throne:
    The good fat boy,
    The nice fat boy,
She's had the luck to marry." [1]

[1] The French original is of no higher poetic merit than this attempt at translation.

CHAPTER II

THE PRISONER OF VINCENNES CHATEAU

January, 1789, and still very cold. Great fires were kept burning before the aristocratic mansions of Paris to give poor loiterers a chance to get warm. From the country came stories of wolves chasing children right into the villages. Around Vincennes chateau, four miles from Paris, the wind whistled over the ancient fortifications and particularly around the great donjon of the central keep.

Vincennes once had been a royal residence. St. Louis, Henry V of England, Charles IX, Cardinal Mazarin all had honored it with prolonged sojourns. Now it was only a prison fortress, a place of detention for those unlucky persons who had fallen under the Most Christian King's high displeasure.

Once admitted inside, a stranger was led up a gloom-wrapped staircase by the gleam of sepulchral lamps. Stones, stones on every side, often scratched with such pious inscriptions as "Blessed are they who suffer persecution for righteousness' sake—for theirs is the Kingdom of Heaven." Other scribblings were witty, satirical or profane. Mounting higher, the loopholes became a trifle wider, the air (although cold enough) less damp and benumbing. At last there was reached a narrow landing from which several chambers seemed opening. A wooden scaffolding covered the stone. There was even the crackle and warmth of a fire in one of the apartments, while at the head of the stairwell a turnkey dozed, fumbled his keys and dozed again, never

24

heeding if the occupants of the chambers visited one another.

Above the door of the chamber blessed with the fire, some one had lately scratched, *"Carcer Socratis, templum honoris."* A glance inside disclosed harsh mortared walls, a plain deal floor, a truckle bed, two straw-bottomed chairs and a black oak table. Upon this table were scattered books and pamphlets, as well as the dishes from a very simple meal. Upon the chairs were two young men in deep conversation.

The light from the grated windows brought into clear relief the features of one of them—the features of a pagan god, a profile young, regular as a chiseled Mercury, gracing a face of fine oval. The beauty was almost unearthly, albeit it was the beauty of enameled steel. The head was crowned with a mass of fair curly hair, now tumbling disordered upon the shoulders. The form beneath them was slim and held the wondrous head stiffly. Its owner seldom stirred the latter, even when the discussion glowed and his hands flew in quick gestures. His costume, as disorderly as the hair, was in a disarray not wholly due to prison hardships, and the hands would sometimes clutch at the neckband as if clothing were donned only to be cast aside. An intruder might have gazed fascinated, then whispered, "Here is no common man."

The second speaker was a trifle older. His frame was shorter, shoulders more military. His dress was of genteel quality and, even in prison, kept with scrupulous neatness. No fine cut Mercury was his profile, but it was honest, frank, irregular enough for a Scipio, and with a certain ardent quality about it which bespoke the possessor as being blessed with two inestimable gifts—a love of the romantic and a sense of humor. His hands were white enough for a woman's and bore several admirable rings. His steel black hair was neatly dressed and tied with black ribbon. "Another uncommon man," an intruder again might have whispered.

The two prisoners had been talking long and intently. The younger was now delivering himself with unwontedly vigorous gestures.

"I tell you, René de Massac, we approach the Utopia, but it is to be through blood and fire. We can discard old superstitions, but must cling fast to Purgatory. Only our Purgatory must be in this world, not in the next. The evil outweighs the good. No matter. When the dross is burned away in the terrible heat, mankind will emerge without defilement."

"What is left of mankind, you mean, Antoine Louis St. Just. Build your Utopia, but pray let enough of humanity survive to people it. Mankind by nature is good. Mankind by nature is virtuous. God desires us to live together in liberty, equality and fraternity."

"Liberty? We are in Vincennes chateau!—Bah!"

"Good fellow," protested the older man, "don't get sour. What has happened to us? Nothing very terrible to disciples of our immortal Jean Jacques Rousseau. How does he begin his greatest book? 'All things are good coming from the Author of all things. Everything degenerates in the hands of man.'—To-day we are victims of the artificiality of society. Speedily we shall be released, then we can witness the peaceful redemption of humanity by its return to nature. Do not complain of your fate. Let me rehearse your story to show that you should not get too angry. You are the son of a respectable army officer and a Knight of St. Louis. You have been educated by the Oratorians at Soissons. Later you have studied law at Soissons. The law has not pleased you. Wishing to see Paris and your mother opposing this, you have taken and sold for your expenses some of her silver plate. Your mother has caused the Lieutenant of Police to imprison you for a few months here. I have greatly enjoyed your company. We have talked philosophy, politics and religion together. I think I have somewhat improved your mind. When you are released you will be near Paris, the very city you desired to see, and I engage to provide you then with friends and delightful company.—Now in the state of nature——"

St. Just made a sign of disgust. "And again I tell you this explains nothing. We are in a cold prison and not under the trees, eating bread fruit in Otaheite. I prefer realities. You say mankind is degenerate, yet deny that regeneration can come save by fire and punishment. Very illogical. I cannot follow you. Take your own case. You quarrel with the world over a mere trifle—an unequal marriage. The world claps you in Vincennes chateau."

"The world, my friend? No, not the world. The artificially created master of the world, the King, or rather those who control him. Give the virtuous multitudes one brief release from their chains, give them one long breath of vivifying freedom—behold! in a trifling span of years the face of society is transformed. Brotherhood replaces hatred; enlightenment disperses error; pure religion without dogma will lift bloodless altars. The executioner's sword will rust——"

"Return to earth, Massac. I have heard your raptures before. Next you will begin again on 'the transports of love' and talk very wildly about Virginie Durand. To anticipate your star-stuff I will say I have been born with an eternal aversion to all women. I should become a monk; the vow of celibacy would cost me nothing. If a woman has a noble soul I will call her 'Sister'—nothing more. Let us, therefore, resume the argument. I say that I believe in the Utopia as much as you do, but it will come not through sentimental love, but by ruthlessness, pitiless cruelty for the moment, in order to achieve the eternal uplift of mankind."

They had talked thus for two hours; for two hours more they might have spun their spider webs, when the turnkey rose suddenly with a clatter of keys and stood at attention as the sub-governor of the chateau appeared and passed him, followed by two deeply cloaked gentlemen, whom he conducted directly to René's chamber. The young prisoners sprang to their feet as the official nodded affably. "My errand is to you, Chevalier," spoke he. "Permission is granted that you receive these visitors."

St. Just vanished into his own cubicle. The sub-governor with a military congé also disappeared, while the two gentlemen swung back their cloaks. As they turned toward René, the family resemblance was unmistakable. The elder stranger was a man beyond fifty, his companion of nearly the same age as the Chevalier, but both alike displayed the square build, the dark hair, the rugged features of a Massac, although the elder visitor, clothed in a severely plain and elegant habit of soot-color, had also the heavy wrinkles and ruddy cheeks and nose of a man of the world. The younger, who boasted the brilliant uniform of a lieutenant in the Body Guard, carried a flippant, dare-devil expression wholly lacking in the prisoner, who was presumably his cousin. The two gentlemen deposited their cloaks on the low bed and then glanced about the bare apartment a trifle awkwardly, but René, who had taken his stand with his back to the fire, gave the elder a bow faultless, even if somewhat ironical.

"I congratulate myself, *mon oncle*," he observed, "for this unexpected pleasure of thanking you for my enjoyment here of the past six weeks. Dare I ask you to transmit my dutiful thanks also to my aunt, who, I expect, had an even greater part in this service. My cousin Laurent, I rejoice to see, is well; let me beseech him that when he next is admitted to the Queen——"

The Comte de Massac muttered inaudibly, then seated himself on one of the chairs; his son, the Viscount, with a deprecatory gesture at his unwonted surroundings, smilingly flung one leg over the table; René continued standing.

"Let us come to business, unfortunate boy," the Count began. "We are prepared for your bravado. You have enjoyed six weeks of this kind of royal hospitality. We have come to inquire how long you wish it to continue?"

"My uncle," said René in a very mild voice, "my present hotel has indeed certain inconveniences, but as no small offset I have been permitted to devote myself unremittingly to the study of politics and philosophy—something infinitely profitable and, as I discover, far more entertaining than even the Comédie Française."

The Count, without rising, thrust at the books and papers upon the table with his gold-knobbed cane, and his voice grated.

"What have we here?—Helvetius, Montesquieu, *The Social Contract*, and faugh!—English books—Shakespeare, Locke!—I thought, Sirrah, you had been committed to a prison, not to a seminary of sedition. Whence came all this?"

"My uncle," spoke René, still very gently, "the King commanded that I should be confined, not that I should be starved alike in mind and body. The Governor of Vincennes chances to be an old comrade-in-arms of my father. He has the humanity to see to it that my quarters and food are tolerable, and that I am not denied the books in his library."

The oldest Massac delivered himself of a shrug. "If your father were living, Monsieur, I would speak to him about his son with the plainness of one brother to another. Would to heaven he had never gone to America.—Cursed folly for the King to abet those Republicans!"

"Before my father died," observed his nephew again softly, "he gave me his badge of the Cincinnati and charged me always to wear it with honor. I have talked with M. de Lafayette and M. de Rochambeau——"

"Two more seditious asses never pretended to nobility in France. Yet even they have not married beneath their station. But——" the cane stirred over some sheets of manuscript, "what have you been writing now?"

"Simply, my uncle, in a pamphlet I have been attempting to set forth the necessity that the coming States General should abolish all the privileges of our so-called nobility, which violate those principles of brotherhood, that hereafter must rule an enlightened and enfranchised world."

The guffaw from the guardsman on the table blended with the snort of fury from his father. The Count made a dart toward the offending papers, only to have them rescued by a more sudden movement of the prisoner. The oldest Massac's face glowed with sheer rage.

"Accursed fool!—*You* a Massac!—If you hadn't our nose and mouth I'd say something about your mother—I hope your vile rubbish will at length find print, if only that next I can see it burned at the Palais de Justice by the common hangman like other criminal libels."

"I share your hope, uncle." René's eyes were beginning to twinkle faintly. "To have his book publicly burned is the dream now of every author in France; it insures colossal popularity."

But here the guardsman slipped from the table, his own lips struggling with merriment, and placed himself between the others.

"I say, father," he began in a loud boyish voice, "we

aren't taking the quickest way to do what we came for—
to get René to put two grains of sense in his head and let
us take him away from this hardly jolly place."

The Count ceased slapping the table with his cane. "You
are right, Laurent. I will control myself." He affected to
eye the prisoner with greater benevolence. "My poor misguided lad, let me speak as tenderly as possible. Whatever
your devastating theories, your actual condition must surely
have come home to you. I have the word of your friends at
court—your *very highest* friends, understand, that on your
mere pledge of honor to dismiss thoughts of this so-called
marriage, all will be forgiven and forgotten. Indeed, some
consolation in the way of a pension——"

René's form stiffened instantly; again his eyes were
bright, but not now with drollery. "Monsieur, remember
you talk to a Massac. Pray omit the 'pension.' "

This reference, however, to the family sent the Count's
brief urbanity up the chimney. "You a Massac? Would
that it were a lie! No Massac has ever defiled his blood
before."

"No Massac, Monsieur, has ever been conscious of the
equal laws of Nature before."

Again Laurent flung himself between uncle and nephew.
"In God's name, father, if René is mad, let's not make him
our example. Let me talk to him." And with an apologetic
grimace, he approached his cousin. "Hark ye—dear fellow.
I'll not call you names, whatever father and mother may do.
Of course, we've fought all over your romance many times,
but haven't you found Vincennes a poor enough change from
Versailles to let me talk reasonably?—I won't say how
devilish awkward it's going to be for your uncle and aunt
and also for myself. 'Poor Laurent—how I pity him.'
Princesse de Lamballe said that behind my back only yesterday. Think a bit. Let's grant that your low-born

Pamela is all virtue and sensibility. She can't be received at court. You can't show her to your old friends. You blight your own career—and she—after the moonbeams and confectioner's sugar have disappeared, will be very unhappy. They say that her father is tolerably off, but he's not a great 'Bourgeois of Paris' who can give a big enough dowry to cover up any pedigree. You can't 'manure your acres,' as we say, by a very wealthy marriage. Think of the future, yours and hers—be rational."

The tone, more than the words, was winsome and conciliatory. The angry glitter passed from René's eyes.

"Dear old Laurent," he rejoined with a rising earnestness which at length passed into raptures, "if uncle will never pass for a tactful ambassador, you at least are more tolerable. I'll answer you clearly. Upon my honor I am not mad. Virginie's father, as any but purblind noblemen like ourselves would say, is a scientist of fame, the friend of the first savants of Paris. He is moderately rich. His daughter has received the best education which the nuns of St. Joseph Bellechase could impart to her. Doubtless she won't be received at court. Very well. I'm not the first man to tire of our old *levers* and *couverts* and all that children's pother. Why take such pride because we have taken the trouble to be 'born noble?' The time is soon coming when the question won't be, 'Who's your father?' but 'Who are you yourself?' Virginie Durand and I were made for each other. The Versailles pageant will fade like a miasmic mist. Sensibility and love will remain. Like Greek philosophers we shall spend our lives in converse with the True, the Beautiful and the Good——"

"Father," thrust in Laurent, with a wry grimace, "we beat our heads on iron. Six weeks have not cured him."

"Six years then can be more effectual," completed his parent grimly; but with the word, the door opened for the

governor of the chateau himself, an erect old soldier, his
medals shining on his breast. In his hand was a document
with dangling seals. He bowed cordially toward the prisoner, but regarded the two guests with a degree of uncertainty.

"Chevalier," René returned the bow, "I have here an
order which you will hardly regret. And I trust (with a
questioning emphasis) that the pleasure of your honorable
kinsmen may be equally complete. The Minister of Justice
transmits to us this order ratified last night by His Majesty
in the Council, whereof these are the significant words:
*'Inasmuch as grave complaints have arisen from all parts
of our kingdom, it is our royal pleasure that until we have
ripely consulted with our loyal deputies to the States General no more lettres de cachet be issued under our hand,
and that all persons held in confinement under such letters,
except as they may be actually guilty of great crimes, be
forthwith set at liberty.'* You will, therefore, my dear
Chevalier, along with M. de St. Just, cease immediately to
be a guest of Vincennes. I hope you will be witness that
you have been treated with humanity at the hands of men
of honor."

The response of René was lost under the explosion from
the Count: "Release? You will turn loose this mad man to
destroy himself? Can I trust my ears?"

"I regret your vexation, Monsieur," returned the governor
stiffly. "Here are the King's orders—not to be questioned."

"The King's?" roared the old nobleman, red enough for an
apoplexy. "Of all the unstable clowns in France, the
greatest weathercock now lives in Versailles! To listen to
that glozing money bag, Necker! To betray a noble
house!——"

"A truce to disloyal sentiments," ordered the official, his
hand upon his hilt. "The King is not to be denounced in

his own castle. I do not share your family quarrels, Monsieur, but speaking as a French officer, I rejoice in the disuse of orders of arbitrary arrest long subject to gross abuses.—Chevalier de Massac, I would also tell you that there came with the royal messenger a servant of yours calling himself Arnaud. He waits below. Doubtless you will gladly see him.—And you other gentlemen"—his gesture toward the Count was nigh contemptuous—"I wish you a safe return."

"A thousand devils!" swore the Count. "Even the army becomes infected. The kingdom's lost. Come, Laurent——" But although the Count had flung out of the chamber in so black a rage that he barely saw stair or staircase, Laurent lingered to grasp his cousin's hands and speak words of deep feeling:

"Dearest fellow. You know I think you are throwing your life away, but I am desperately resolved not to quarrel with you."

"Dearest cousin," the clasp by René had affection behind it, "we shall remain forever the best of comrades though we differ upon every subject in the world. We were boys together, went to Court together, fought one another's duels, raced one another's horses, and now——"

"I swear that no lace-bonnet, peasant, bourgeoise or noble shall ever come between us."

Whereupon, after the manner of their land and age, the two young men kissed and embraced heartily.

"You have only to meet Virginie," began René once more. "Then you will understand everything."

"Faith, give me time," cried the Body Guard. "No doubt you are even ready to cultivate the droll middle-class virtues of actually loving and living with your wife—so banal at Versailles! But what plagues me is that the Shepherdess gives 'The Village Soothsayer' next week—and that a wonderful part could be waiting you.—Now what must I say to my friends?"

"That René de Massac merely craves for them a share in the same peaceful felicity which he sees opening before all mankind. The victory of enlightenment; a world set free; the peasant exalted among the kings; the kings made happy by becoming virtuous peasants——"

The speech ended with Laurent's hand set firmly upon his cousin's lips. "Don't sky-rocket higher among the clouds. The crash will be too dreadful. Enough if I can say 'The Chevalier having firmly resolved to commit suicide, let us wish him all prosperity if not in heaven at least in "Another World than Our Own!"' "

After that there were more embracings, with more vows that friendship should remain eternal. Then the few effects of the late prisoner were gathered and leave was taken of several jailers who had melted to their charge's friendliness and grace. A more ceremonious parting took place with St. Just, who seemed stoically indifferent to his own sudden release, but who promised to visit the Chevalier at first opportunity; and next the governor himself escorted the released captives to the great outer gate. A clang of bolts and bars, a "You are free" spoken behind him, and René de Massac stood on the snows outside the fortress, the last of the winter sunlight streaming over his black hair, and gilding the frowning turrets.

"Six weeks!" came from him as he stood drinking in deep cool breaths. "Six weeks—or was it a dream!"

But here in his apostrophe his hand was wrung or rather slobbered over by a great burly creature in a bearskin coat, who let forth his joy by a series of grunts, growls and almost yelps, and then began dragging his master toward a trim two-horse curricle that stood awaiting.

"*Mon enfant! mon enfant!* How have they fed you?

How have they treated you?—We thought to get you out yesterday. M. Durand has done everything. He has besieged M. Necker. He has besieged all the Farmers-General. We knew the decree would be signed. All your friends were in an agony. I raced hither behind the King's messenger. Who but Arnaud should drive you back?"

"And Virginie?"

"She is more beautiful than ever. She cried to me as I set forth, 'Every moment is an eternity until you bring him.' "

"Away then—do not spare the whip."

But while the old servant slapped out the reins, Laurent, who had mounted a horse held by an orderly, swung up beside the carriage. "A word, cousin, before you are off. I have a wager with Dreux-Brézé. You alone can settle it."

"What is it—be quick!"

"Do you seriously and in very truth believe in God?"

"In very truth—upon my honor."

"Oh, you droll fellow. Then it's just as well that you're quitting Versailles!"

Away tore the Body Guard, pounding down the icy Charenton road, while under a ruthless lash the curricle flew toward the eastern barriers of Paris.

CHAPTER III

VIRGINIE DURAND

The Rue St. Honoré was narrow and tortuous. Footpaths at times were lacking; its channels down the middle were often masses of filth; its projecting upper stories, tall gables, swinging signboards alike spoke of remoter days. For all that it boasted the pretentious shops of the chief artery of Paris. Before their rich show fronts there shuttled incessantly the blue blouses, black coats, and the white caps and aprons, broken now by the plodding sedan chairs, the lumbering coaches or whooping, reckless gigs of the rich and mighty.

St. Honoré itself was mainly surrendered to commerce, but away from it northward, and away from the Louvre, the Tuileries and the Champs Elysées, ran a whole network of residential streets of prim respectability. The whole quarter in fact was ultra-respectable. St. Jacques, St. Antoine and other faubourgs, might have their fetid slums and brawling ragamuffins. No matter. The St. Honoré region was a world unto itself.

Somewhere between the Palais Royal and the Church of St. Roch the Rue St. Leonard sent its twisting way before gabled fronts of undeniable gentility. Here at "Number 11" on a certain January afternoon decently dressed guests were entering. The big knocker was of spotless polish. If you tapped it gently, the heavy door opened with barely a sound and one of those quiet, attentive, eternally old men-servants

who fit perfectly with such a mansion, took your hat, cloak
and cane and ushered you into the salon of M. Edmond
Durand.

The salon was not large but the tall mirrors, heavy furniture and rugs were admirable. The wall paper showed a
good Swiss landscape pattern, the hanging fruit-and-flower
or genre paintings were by Chardin or La Tour. André, the
major domo, had just entered with cat-like tread and lighted
all the glass and gilt sconces, and their shimmer now was
falling upon René de Massac, dressed in his best fawn color,
seated comfortably upon a sofa, and holding (be it confessed), even more comfortably, five soft, warm and pleasant fingers belonging to Virginie Durand.

For convention's sake a discreet aunt may have been
in the background, but for essential purposes the lovers were
alone together waiting their guests. René had been released
for several days. Just now Virginie was trying to look hard
into the firelight; René was trying not to look into his
beloved's eyes. All that did not remove them from a foolish
state common to certain young mortals since the sons of
Adam wooed the daughters of Eve.

Virginie Durand would never have made a model for
Fragonard or Greuze, nor have made Louis XV forget La
Pompadour. Her hands were a trifle too large ("Peasant
blood!" Dreux-Brézé would have scorned); her feet and
ankles hardly faultless; her mouth could have been smaller;
the Queen's corsetière would have disapproved of her waist.

What thought her lover of all that? All he knew (happy
scoundrel) was that this face was lighted by a glowing
vitality, an alert, enthusiastic intelligence. The light brown
hair was heaped in just the right degree of disorder. The
deeper brown eyes were very large, very ardent, very
dreamy. The complexion shone with health if it lacked the
cosmetic triumphs of the Chateau du Roi. The dress of

pure white was studiously simple, its only ornament the roses just brought by her betrothed.

Virginie Durand was, in fine, in her seventeenth year. She had read omnivorously and had received the best education open to a girl of good middle-class family. If her mother was now two years dead, her father had never been too concerned with his test tubes and his crucibles to devote himself to the culture as well as to the happiness of the light of his eyes.

How René met her at the liberal Noailles salon, where the "advanced" noblesse and still more "advanced bourgeois" commingled freely, how the conversation of a girl, the like whereof he had never met in Versailles, had fascinated him, how he had beaten down the resistance of the girl herself, and (more stubborn) that of the prudent and worldly wise M. Durand—this we may omit from our history. Everyone knew that the great savant Edmond Durand's father had begun life as an innkeeper on the Massac estates, and had probably been horsewhipped if not clapped in the stocks by René's grandfather. Everyone knew that never before had a Massac wedded save into nobility of at least sixteen quarterings.

The arrest of the reckless suitor and his incarceration in Vincennes (*lettres de cachet* could no longer be kept as state secrets) had been buzzed over in all the cafés around the Palais Royal. Perhaps, after that, great financiers had said plain things to the King's ministers about the difficulties attending a most necessary loan "if such absurdities are to continue in this enlightened Eighteenth Century." The news of the release of the Chevalier had in any case been received with hand clappings at fifty ultra-respectable dinner tables. If Versailles had its own opinion, Paris had its opinion also. And Paris—financial, legal, scientific and philosophical— said that this betrothal of a Massac and a Durand was a delightful augury "for the era of equal rights and of peaceful regeneration directly before us."

That had been the background; and momentarily now without a cloud upon their hearts there the two lovers sat, with their temperamental, flighty young heads crammed with *Clarissa Harlowe* and *Sir Charles Grandison*,[1] with *Emile* and all the tomes of Voltaire, with "Philosophy" and "Natural Rights," and all those other delightful sentiments and formulas by which the riddles of existence were being solved—almost. They had been conversing in that romantic, overwrought vein which another age would hold in derision; which their own found spontaneous and affecting.

"Oh, my beloved," René had just finished declaiming, "when I was in my prison they mercifully left me a window looking outward toward the stars. Nightly I gazed into the aetherial void. I said in my heart, 'What if I should be held in this captivity through all my little span of mortal life! If never upon this tyrant-ridden earth I were suffered to clasp my heart's desire! Should I despair? Not so!—Eternity was before us. In some felicitous Eden beyond Sirius and Antares, a just God would suffer us to meet in eternal union, contemplating the beauties of the Cosmos, perfect in our love for one another!' "

The hand within the Chevalier's trembled alike with the mere delight of his voice and with enkindled enthusiasm. "And I, my very dear, while you were from me, thought much the same. To wait through half of eternity would have been short, once I were sure of joining you through all of the other. But what is before us now? Not a dream but a present joy! Favored beyond all other ages, are we not about to witness the regeneration of mankind? Every one about us is saying, 'We are on the verge of a new day.'

[1] Richardson's sentimental novels were at this date almost as popular in France as in England.

Our France which has led the world in war, in letters, in art is about to give the supreme example of human brotherhood. What is our union, but the proof how hoary barriers which have enslaved mankind are crumbling forever?" Then with no perfect logic, she looked into her lover's face. "And are you sure of this, René? Sure you do not begin to regret all that you are casting away?"

"Regret, *ma vie?* Impossible! You may weary of asking this; never will I weary of answering you 'Nay'."

Here by the accepted formula of correct sentiment, René was compelled to kneel and kiss two certain hands, and the owner of those hands had to sigh, turn pale and palpitate out of pure felicity. This proceeding, however, was interrupted by a voice, a kindly gentle voice, which brought both young people suddenly back to hard earth:

"Good evening, my children. Ah—a little engrossed perhaps? No matter. I will look over these books."

The voice came from a man of very modest stature, in clerical black, with an exceedingly benignant face as well as two exceedingly shrewd dark eyes looking out from under his skull cap.

"Father François," cried the two together, springing to their feet. Being both of them "emancipated," they did not ask for his blessing, but he gave them each a hand and next was down on an ottoman close to the sofa, and asking about Virginie's health, while fishing in his pocket for *What is the Third Estate,* "that pamphlet just published by my friend Abbé Sieyès, in which he says some pretty bold things to guide the new States General." And until the other guests came in there were no more "Edens beyond the Stars" nor "Halves of Eternity."

Father François's story was simple. The second son of a very poor noble, he had been forced into the Church, from sheer lack of worldly inheritance. Fortunately he had been of a studious cast; fortunately, too, René's father, the late Chevalier, had needed a family tutor. Father François had spent many years at the old Massac chateau. Denied children himself he had yearned over young René, his pupil, as David over a more dutiful Absalom. Brought by his own poverty into keen sympathy with the poor, he had surrendered himself to the new revolutionary philosophy and inculcated as much thereof as he dared to his charge.

The affection of the latter had been deep and rewarding. Then just as René was about to quit his preceptor for the court, virtue and deep learning for once had had a tolerable reward. Father François had been invited to a lectureship in political science in the Sorbonne. In Paris he had often met Edmond Durand as one savant might cultivate another. If, finally, it was whispered that he had been somewhat instrumental in bringing his late pupil and his colleague's daughter together, assuredly he did not stoop to contradiction.

Father François had never broken with the Church, but he had persistently refused all ecclesiastical preferment. No sinecure·benefice, no "abbey in commendam" had ever been permitted to eke out a very modest stipend. In select circles, however, he passed for an extraordinarily learned and witty man. The best salons were open to him. He could play quadrille when he chose with a President of Parliament's lady. Nobody knew how many of the avalanche of tracts about the coming States General he had actually inspired. One peculiarity he had, indeed, which added somewhat to his reputation. He was one of the few men of learning in Paris who was alleged genuinely to believe in an over-ruling Providence; he was even reported to have said that Christianity was scientifically defensible. We may add that it was largely due to him that René de Massac was not an atheist.

Father François talked; his protégés held hands but listened, and the guests drifted in gradually. A very quiet supper party. Like many a Parisian mansion, the Durand house was open every evening to friends of a certain intimacy. As the salon filled, André would silently count the visitors, then as silently glide to the kitchen to report his "Only seven to-night," or "Cutlets for fourteen."

This evening it was a typical gathering of persons who took their pleasures intelligently and sought the conversation rather than the wine. "A painfully bourgeois gathering!" Laurent would have groaned. This tall raw-boned man of five-and-fifty with a solemn pedantic manner was M. Roland, a prosperous silk merchant of Lyons visiting in Paris, and beside him, young, vivacious, not strikingly handsome but with a countenance of contagious enthusiasm, was "Manon Jeanne" his wife, and Virginie's fast friend.

Close at hand, too, was a young man a little shabbily clad, M. Camille Desmoulins, his face blotched with bilious humors, but his eyes flashing like darts. A poor journalist barely scraping a living as yet, but already he was feared for his mordant wit and merciless pen. With her hand upon his sleeve stood a girl of soft, pleasing features and very gentle manner. Of course she was his betrothed, Mlle. Lucile Duplessis, happy to wait until Camille could win enough by his writing to warrant their marriage.

When, however, Lucile was not stealing upward glances toward her lover, she was casting other glances, more hesitant, toward the man who had entered alone behind her. This newcomer was tall, muscular, with a big head graced by a strikingly ugly face, pitted with small-pox. His dress was less shabby than negligent. He seldom spoke, but then it was in a voice that boomed through the chamber. Enormous power pulsed through his huge hands and masterful stride. The candle-glasses actually began to tingle as he stalked across the room to meet Virginie. Here, in other words, was that prosperous avocat, Georges Jacques Danton.

The other guests concern us not. The dining-room doors flung open. Virginie made excuse for her father's absence at a learned society; everyone dropped into his accustomed chair; everyone except quiet little Lucile talked admirably. There was just enough good Medoc to loosen the tongue. Admirable witticisms were exchanged. The new fire balloons were eagerly discussed. They had been tried with animals. Would it be possible, now, for men to ascend in them? Would the Montgolfier brothers actually hazard their lives (as per rumor) and try to outdo Icarus on the strength of a great bag filled merely with hot air? Manon Roland became especially animated.

"What an age we live in, my friends. Two surpassing wonders together."

"*Two* wonders; explain yourself, Manon"; this from several.

"Of course. The conquest of the air and the States General. How fast the world is being made over!"

"And what a rapture now to live in it!" spoke Virginie all aglow herself.

"Especially in view of what René has just told me," announced Camille. "He assures me that Virginie has promised to make the day when the Three Estates convene her own wedding day. Wonderful celebration; the felicity of France and that of our beloved friends together!"

"To France and to our friends together!" cried many, and all the goblets clicked.

René rose and thanked the company. "It is true. Of course I have pleaded with Virginie 'Make haste.' Of course she being a woman has found all manner of excuses for saying 'Tarry.' At last I said to her 'The royal proclamation sets May Day for the assembling of the States General. What more fitting than that the rebuilding of France should commence with the consummation of our own happiness.' She blushed charmingly and consented. M. Durand consented. My friends—you are all invited——"

After that there were plenty more of joyous toasts and Father François was duly summoned to tell about the Abbé Sieyès pamphlet, and when he had read the three famous questions, "What is the Third Estate?—*Everything*. What has it been hitherto? *Nothing*. What does it desire? *To be something!*" the approving shouts and slapping on the table made all the dishes to dance.

Next the talk shifted to the ultimate models on which they should remold France. There could be only two— Republican Rome and Sparta. Camille delivered himself energetically in favor of Rome. "Where will you find such examples, where such austere virtues? The elder Brutus, Decius, Camillus, Fabricius. Perhaps the cause of French liberty will even produce a new Scaevola."

"Hold, Camille," interposed René, "have we not agreed that, thanks to our reason and philosophy, our victory is to be bloodless? We will not even require the blood of martyrs. Take my own case. I am imprisoned. Reason is brought to bear upon the government. I am released. Reason and enlightenment will even conquer at Versailles.—I am convinced of it.—Rome is not our best model. What has Mme. Roland to say for Sparta?"

The lady's face had kindled with her subject. "You summon an advocate and not a judge, M. de Massac. I was just telling Virginie how in my youth I knew Plutarch better than I did my missal. I have wept at night from the sheer desire to be a Spartan girl. What an incomparable lawgiver was Lycurgus! His country was without commerce, without coined money, without corrupting luxuries. His young men were trained to be strong and manly;

his maidens to be equal sisters and consorts of the men. Sparta before all other lands lived according to the commands of nature. She waged war but in defence only. She fought against luxury as her worst enemy. Sparta is the example for France! Let us rename the Seine the Eurotas!"

"Sparta! Sparta is the model!" shouted several guests.

"A model," dryly observed Father François, "to be imitated by first blotting out two thousand years of history."

"A history that can teach us nothing," protested Mme. Roland, more enthusiastic than ever. "It is only a record of the discords and oppressions of tyrants or what is the same thing—kings."

"Oh! Manon," rejoiced Virginie, clasping her arms upon her breast, "what a rapture to be such a thorough Republican!"

Father François's smile became slightly enigmatic. "Your enthusiasm is contagious, dear Madame; but there is one thing I do not quite understand. I may be very dense. It is agreed that our goal is a Republic founded upon the laws of Nature. It is agreed that we are to achieve our end bloodlessly with little or no appeal to the sword. Permit me to observe, however, that there are still a king and a queen at Versailles. How do you expect to get rid of them?"

"I have sometimes thought of that," admitted Mme Roland unabashed, "yet it seems only a very silly difficulty. Kings and queens are rational beings like ourselves Reason and philosophy will, of course, conquer them also It will all be very simple—they will peacefully abdicate.'

M. Danton for long had sat silent, his large head apparently dropped in a brown study; now he suddenly raised his broad, gnarled face, and his great harsh voice startled the table.

"Peacefully abdicate?—*Huh!*"

CHAPTER IV

ABBÉ VERNET'S DISCRETION IS TRUSTED

ANOTHER antechamber, glass door and lordly Swiss. More gilt furniture, allegorical paintings, magnificent functionaries and guardsmen. The Oeil-de-Boeuf was only one corridor away, and this was the antechamber of the Queen.

It being now late in the morning of the third day after Virginie's supper party, no crinoline cohort of princesses, duchesses and countesses were still waiting their turn to assist Her Most Christian Majesty get out of bed. Instead, various personages were sitting uncomfortably on the gilt chairs waiting to be summoned in for his or her audience. Only one of these patient watchers concerns us—the Abbé Vernet.

The Abbé's hair was smooth, his face was smooth; voice, ineradicable smile, everything else about him was smooth. He might have been of an old thirty-five or just as well a young five-and-fifty. His short black coat had brass buttons, and the lace at his neck almost hid an apology for clerical bands. His sleek little round wig nearly concealed his tonsure. His perfumery, rings and watch fob were perfect. Manifestly, then, he was a social ornament to the Church.

Vernet would have been sadly perplexed if asked to say mass. Like Father François he was the younger son of a poor noble. Family influence failed to get him into Brienne military school but just elbowed an entrance for him at St. Sulpice. At the seminary he was the despair of his pre-

ceptors, but the tolerant bishop presently admitted him to
Holy Orders. He next gained a small benefice in Touraine,
sublet the parish to a miserably paid curate and hovered
hopefully around Paris and Versailles as one of the noble
army, not of martyrs but of "commendatory abbots."

First he was house chaplain to a rich bourgeois, ran on
Madame's social errands and arranged her dinners; also
counseled Monsieur about transactions at the Bourse. Next,
by great luck, he taught Princesse de Guemenée, the erst-
while friend of the Queen (whose salon Emperor Joseph II
once impolitely called "a regular gambling hell"), greatly
to improve her card game. After her historic bankruptcy
and exit from Versailles, he had, however, found other
exalted patrons. He acquired fame as an agent in "delicate
enterprises." He never made premature demands. Some
people said he dreamed of becoming a bishop, but the better
informed thought his hopes were fixed on a lax and affluent
Knighthood of Malta, or more likely on the fifth almoner-
ship to the King. The present incumbent had certainly a
very bad cough.

But Abbé Vernet's thoughts in the Queen's anteroom
were not quite contented. He had lately been involved in
the Abbé d'Espangnac's notorious East Indian speculation.
An unpleasant amount of his own accumulations had vanished. His name had been publicly mentioned at the Court
of the Châtelet. Even worse, his prestige around Versailles
had been shaken. He had not received a coveted benefice.
"Monsieur" the King's eldest brother had deliberately
ignored his bow. Lesser luminaries had shone upon him
coldly. Yet now had come a direct summons to the Queen.
The Abbé was on pins and needles for a chance to
rehabilitate himself in her good graces.

"The Abbé Vernet!" from the glass door, and the Churchman soon made his best congé in the presence of royalty.

Marie Antoinette was in plain white with a few ribbons of black (the special "queen's color") at her wrists and throat. The cabinet of course was magnificent. The regal lady sat at a table which was scattered with black-bound books stamped with crosses, but Vernet wisely judged the volumes were not prayer-books but very free novels whereof Her Majesty was devotedly fond. At either hand of the Queen, upon modest taborets were the Duchesse de Polignac and the old Comtesse de Massac. In the rear Vernet recognized a tall and gracious woman, Mme. de Campan, first lady of the bedchamber; Marie Antoinette, however, made a slight sign and she retired. The Abbé was entranced; the interview, then, was to be somewhat confidential.

The Queen answered his bow with precisely the sufficient nod and drawing back of her faultless hands—nothing haughty, nothing condescending. The Churchman smiled his very best smile, while she, after an affable "Good morning, Monsieur," turned to the Duchess. "You know the business, my dear."

Mme. de Polignac scrutinized the Abbé carefully. "M. Vernet," began she, "the Queen desires me to say something with precision. The matter she would share with you is not merely confidential. It is one in which if her interests are in the least betrayed she will study your eternal disadvantage."

Vernet returned exactly the proper bow. "If Her Majesty and you—most noble Mesdames, find me in the slightest degree to be guilty, I am content to rot in the Toulon galleys. Mme. la Duchesse will be gracious enough to remember how satisfactorily last year I adjusted that affair of the Comte d'Artois and the little opera singer."

"Your success then was undoubted"; La Polignac glanced toward the Queen who signalled to proceed. "I will tell you therefore, M. l'Abbé, that Her Majesty has considered com-

manding your services in this pitiful business of the
Chevalier de Massac."

"Ah!" There was more understanding in that "ah!" than
if Vernet had burst into eloquence.

"In the presence of the unfortunate young gentleman's
aunt, who is here to give you certain information, I will not
dwell on many desolating aspects of the affair. I take it,
Monsieur, you have heard the common talk about Versailles; the Chevalier's infatuation, the merciful interposition of the King in ordering his confinement and then the
astonishing decision of His Majesty to consent to his release
before the least sign of penitence——"

"Of course this is common talk in every boudoir and
cabinet. Such a fine young man. Every heart is bleeding——" Vernet's concluding gesture was worthy of a
Talma.

"To turn him loose!" burst from the Queen's fine lips.
"What was the poor man thinking of? René is released
from Vincennes before I had caught a whisper and then
'Impossible, Madame, to arrest him again.' Oh! the vexation."

The Abbé's countenance was that of a person resolutely
determined to be deaf. "Poor man," he and everybody else
around the palace knew perfectly well was the Queen's
standing title for His Most Christian Majesty. He waited
patiently for the Duchess to proceed.

"You understand, Monsieur, that when my gracious mistress first condescended to desire the unfortunate Chevalier's
arrest from the King, she did so only out of sheer kindness
and compassion. The insane youth had been attached to
her person. His grace, his charm, his thousand amiable
ways (which render his conduct all the more pitiful) had
won her friendship. She had exhausted her arts to per-
suade him.—In vain. He was arrested. The Queen looked

forward, of course, to his tardy repentance and reinstatement. Suddenly he is unconditionally at liberty.—The result is maddening. Not merely is the Chevalier free to throw himself away; the Queen herself is compromised. Her part in the *lettre de cachet* is well known. In every hotel and salon she is being laughed at."

La Polignac as climax to her own emotions began to wipe her eyes. Vernet thought it best to sniffle slightly.

"When will that abominable marriage be perpetrated? If right away, I fear——"

"Not right away; ah! there is our hope, Monsieur," the Duchess reassured. "Mme. de Massac will now explain to you."

The old Countess cleared her throat. "M. l'Abbé will understand this subject is infinitely distasteful to me. But we cannot invoke his aid without speaking clearly. My depraved nephew, upon his release, refuses all intercourse with us. However, we have not sat helpless. The Chevalier maintains in Paris a very small and meagerly furnished apartment (considering his rank) upon the Rue Vendôme. His servants are few and I regret to say incorruptible. Nevertheless his boorish body-servant, Arnaud (once sergeant-orderly to my deplorable brother-in-law, the late Chevalier) the other day was inveigled into a drinking house by an agent of my husband, and when suitably plied gave out a fact that fills us with new hope."

"What is it? Madame puts me in an agony." Vernet's eyes were beginning to widen.

"That adventuress calling herself Virginie Durand will not wed my nephew until May Day—the time set for the convening of the States General."

"Not till May Day!" interjected the Queen, "do you know, my friends, I will believe it no longer if you say 'That Durand woman is diabolically clever.' She ought to have dragged him to the altar immediately. 'Till May Day!' *Ma foi!* that sounds as if she were giving herself the airs and privileges of an honest coquette."

The Queen paused and smiled as if she had made a great point; the other three all smiled also, and Vernet put his hand gracefully in his bosom.

"The insult to Her Majesty," he observed, "of course becomes more intolerable, since it shows such self-will and presumption. Naturally such mad confidence hastens its own punishment.—So we have until May Day—about three months. But Mme. de Massac was about to add something?"

"We also discovered," pursued the Countess, "that my wretched nephew has determined very shortly to visit his estates near Ard, and his old chateau at Massac. God knows what foolish indulgence he may offer his peasants, or what seditious notions he may teach them. Laurent, my son, who disobediently refuses to break with him, goes as his companion. With two such mad firebrands together we dread the worst."

The thought that Laurent might also be infected with vile opinions here overcame the old lady; she also took refuge in her handkerchief.

"Explain the rest to M. l'Abbé," commanded the Queen, and La Polignac resumed.

"M. Vernet is doubtless now aware for what purpose he was taken into Her Majesty's confidence. It is my mistress' pleasure that this abominable marriage be at all hazards prevented. Can you undertake this?"

The Abbé's posture became easy, his voice indescribably bland. "I am overwhelmed by my unworthiness for the trust reposed in me. I cast myself with my thanks at Her Majesty's feet."

"If successful," added the Duchess, "the Queen permits

me to say that she will remember your fitness for an appointment near to the King."

"Your Majesty, I am beside myself with joy!"

"*If successful*," spoke the Queen a little dryly, then added directly, "You have heard these ladies? You will undertake the mission? You understand its delicacy?—What do you propose to do first?"

"If the Queen condescends to trust my discretion, I assume that the ways and means will be left to me also. The expenses, I do not conceal, must, of course, be heavy."

Marie Antoinette flung open the drawer of the inlaid table at her elbow and drew forth a rouleau. "Here are a hundred louis, my month's pin-money. See!" she added with a laugh toward her companions, "for four weeks no more of faro or ombre.—I am penniless!"

Vernet let the money sink silently into a well-concealed pocket.

"The Queen's confidence transports me. But now may I ask Mme. de Massac certain questions, not, I trust, too painful?"

"Anything, anything," wailed the old Countess, "to avert our disgrace!"

"Then," persisted Vernet, "may I inquire, is it indeed true, that the grandfather of this brazen Durand damsel was an innkeeper on the Massac estates?"

"Disastrously true, M. l'Abbé. I've heard he was a mere clodhopper. As a boy he slept with the pigs on the dung-hill, served as ostler and turnspit. Then—the upstart—he must needs learn to read, rose to be innkeeper; then went to Lyons, and Massac was well rid of him."

"Forgive another question. His family of course were peasants. Perhaps some still live on the old estate."

"Oh, yes, Monsieur. They blame him for his upstart airs."

The Abbé stood apparently in deep thought, then expressed himself with precision. "In view of the mutability of the King's policies I regret that this Chevalier was imprisoned. The young man is proud and stubborn. Only a long confinement could have worn him down. Now valuable time has been lost. Still before May Day something may be possible. With the Queen's consent we approach the case from another angle. We ignore the Chevalier; we attack his designing mistress."

"Who should be in La Salpêtrière!"[1] vowed the Countess.

"I am helpless," protested the Queen. "Another *lettre de cachet* is impossible."

"The gentlest measures can well be the best," reassured Vernet. "The case is new to me, but one thing I will probe immediately. The Durand family lives near Ard. To Ard I will at once go. I will make intimate inquiries. It would be a most remarkable mischance if we did not come upon some odd story, incident or scandal which will be useful in dealing with this Virginie Durand or at least with her father."

"I understand," assented the Queen.

"The trip to Ard I must somewhat leave to the guidance of my poor wits. However, in one matter perhaps the Queen will graciously assist me."

"More money?" asked Marie Antoinette anxiously.

"Not at all, Your Majesty. But I shall later, at least, need as a proper helper, an adroit gentleman just now under the frowns of justice. No serious crime—merely an unlucky duel——"

The Queen frowned. "I must avoid scandal, Monsieur."

"We must trust the Abbé's discretion," reassured La Polignac.

"I thank Mme. la Duchesse," bowed Vernet. "There can

[1] The prison for depraved women.

be no scandal. I will not even name the unfortunate gentle-man. He is, however, a nobleman of resources, courage and honor.—M. de Crosne, the Lieutenant of Police is, I believe, devoted to Your Majesty's service."

"Only the King can pardon," objected Marie Antoinette.

"This gentlemen is not a prisoner. Let him merely be permitted to emerge from concealment without fear of the archers and the provosts. Later I may need M. de Crosne's help in a few other matters."

The Queen spread a silver-bound writing desk in her lap and looked upward.

"Well, I can write to M. de Crosne. What shall I say?"

"If the Queen is graciously pleased, simply this: *'M. de Crosne will be good enough not to arrest the gentleman the Abbé Vernet may name to him, and presently to give M. l'Abbé certain lawful assistance in a matter wherein I am deeply concerned.'*"

The Queen dipped her quill, hesitated, glanced at La Polignac, who nodded; thereupon she wrote out the note in a not very literate hand, and signed boldly "*Marie Antoinette, R.*"

Vernet buried the paper in his bosom, bowed profoundly, then stood again at polite attention.

"Anything else?" questioned the Duchess.

"A request which I lay at Her Majesty's own feet. The Chevalier de Massac is naturally angry at his imprison-ment."

"Of course," assented Marie Antoinette. "What of it?"

"He must be disarmed. Both he and his mistress must be lulled into complete security. Nothing must be done to make them take fright and hasten their marriage, lest it should be thwarted. If Massac can be convinced that he has been almost if not quite forgiven—very good."

"Forgiven!" burst from the old Countess, but the Queen gave an almost rippling assent. "'Almost forgiven.' That can be my care.—Of course he won't stay long at his old chateau. He can hardly have forgotten us all so quickly. It will soon be spring at the Trianons, and René——"

The glass door had swung open. The porter interrupted Marie Antoinette herself, as if to announce a super-royal visitor. "Monsieur Frappard, costumer-in-chief to Her Majesty, to consult upon the dresses to be worn in the coming presentation of *Figaro.*"

Vernet glided backward through the door, bowing to the Queen until he was out of sight. The royal lady laughed in an admirable humor. "What an ingenious and resourceful man! I am sure he will win René back. Cheer up, dear Mme. de Massac. We'll all keep in fine hopes about your nephew. And I'm sure the new States General will soon fill up the treasury to the very brim, and pay all the King's debts, and my debts, and leave us plenty wherewith to reward our friends. You, my dear Duchess, and you, my dear Countess—pensions and nice appointments for everybody! Six months from now we'll laugh at all troubles!— And now to see what M. Frappard has to offer us. What —will you costume Susanne in brown?"

Even at that moment Vernet was descending by veritable leaps and bounds the long flights of marble stairs, which led from the Queen's apartments to the great Royal Court before the center of the chateau. Guardsmen and courtiers stared at him. "Has the Abbé seen the devil?" queried a captain of the Swiss from a royal equerry. Vernet heeded not. Already he saw himself King's Almoner and reciting the prayer when His Majesty was dressed. Before the palace a number of very fast hackney coaches known as *enragés* were always in waiting.

"Paris; full speed!" ordered the Abbé, flinging himself into the nearest.

"Ten livres?" queried the coachman.

"Fifteen if you take less than an hour." And as the vehicle flew down the straight Avenue de Paris, Vernet's head went round and round in joyous confusion. "Linio?— Yes, he's my man. An innkeeper's grandchild to deal with! Of course I'll find some key to bring out a family skeleton. —The gratitude of the Shepherdess herself.—Oh! what a beginning. Almoner? Better to begin to dream about the red hat."

CHAPTER V

THE AVOCAT FROM ARRAS

STILL winter, but the roads were beginning to soften, the trees to give their first hintings of bud. It was seventy miles northward from Paris, near the small Picard city of Ard, with its greater neighbor Arras, forty miles farther still. The country sometimes level, sometimes rolling and the leafless forests interspersed with long intervals of hedge-land, meadowland and meandering rivers. The straight high road lined with long regiments of slim poplars would run through solitude for a league, next come upon a semi-starving village clustered around a splendid Gothic church, then run on for another league.

Sometimes from this high road there would wander unpaved tracks impassable during half the year for carts and almost for footmen. Along the horizon from these tracks you might see the pinnacles and battlements of manor houses of crumbling bulk, venerable reminders of the good old days before Henry IV and Richelieu. Few peasants, just now, were on these roads, for the fields were still unworkable, and the season did not encourage harmless strolling, although famine was the standing excuse for the swarms of vagabonds who found thieving pleasanter than labor. The gendarmes and gamekeepers scoured incessantly. The King's judges were always busy. For all their zeal, last week the Arras diligence had been stopped and each of the ten travelers relieved of purse, watch and snuff-box.

In the village of Massac (a very average community) the peasants, just now, were cooking their mid-day dinners on fires of twigs or peat, shivering and grumbling exactly as usual. The bread was very black, the wine sour and watered, the beer pale and thin. If anyone had a bit of meat in the soup, a cheese, or actually a boiled fowl he concealed it carefully; the tax assessors might swoop down and woe then to the simpleton who betrayed prosperity! The talk over all the kettles was the same; the coming harvest, the rapacity of the King's collector, of the bishop's tithe-gatherer and of the seigneur's bailli. Would the grain lands be hunted over this year (as they had been last) just before harvest? How much labor was demanded on the public works? Could certain likely lads bribe off the harsh and hated militia service?

At a few hearths, indeed, people repeated vague stories that "something would be done." The King and the great people would hold a great meeting to promote the welfare of France. "Welfare of France?" Cunning listeners shook their heads. "That doubtless means an excuse for more taxes. We can all be dining on hay next year, just as they are now over at Avremont!"

One place in Massac seemed, nevertheless, to be more cheerful. The inn of the *Silver Swan* spread out its court yards, stables and outbuildings close by the ice-bound current of the Luchy. Dirty and commonplace as the hostlery might be, it was the finest edifice in the village, barring always thirteenth century St. Didier, with its memorable tracery and sculptures looking down upon the muddy marketplace. At Massac, when the river was open, ponderous barges and "water-coaches" (bearing passengers) changed horses for the tow path, and let the watermen break their fasts and wet their whistles. Even in winter-time the rare diligences would stop, and more frequently the mail carts. The *Silver Swan*, therefore, was the village center.

On this present afternoon a cheerful fire of logs glowed in the dingy public room, while a savory roasting smell drifted in from the kitchen. A frowzy-headed boy was laying the cloth for three guests. Two had come earlier but the post-cart had just rattled up, bearing beside the postman a single passenger, a gentleman apparently bound from Paris toward Arras.

The two earlier guests, conversing on the big settle by the fire, gave him a hard stare as he threw off his great coat and muffler. There seemed nothing very remarkable about him as he emerged from his winter wrappings. He was a short, palish, fair-haired man of about thirty; features not quite regular, dull complexioned and slightly pitted by the smallpox. The eyes were a neutral grayish green. The one noticeable fact about him was that his blue clothes were of fashionable cut, and very carefully pressed and brushed, and that his hair was still craped and powdered as if he had risen early to visit the *friseur*. Carefully he was flecking the mud from coat and shoes, while setting down a fat little brief case.

"An up-country *avocat* or *procureur*," [1] whispered one denizen of the settle to the other. Then he addressed the stranger. "Perhaps you come from Paris, Monsieur?"

"Yes, I come from Paris," the tone was a trifle weak and high, and not without a certain timid, nervous manner.

The first stranger rose and lifted a decanter. He was a large, raw-boned man with an over-red nose and a cunning jaw. His dress betrayed much of tarnished gold lace, white cuffs sewed upon spotted sleeves, long hair falling unpow-

[1] The *avocats* corresponded to the English barristers; the *procureurs*, lawyers of a lower grade, to solicitors.

dered in a tangle below his thick neck, and he wore a big sword fit for a dragoon.

"You have ridden hard, Monsieur"; the tone was intended to be hearty. "This eau-de-vie is passable. I am Linio—Baron de Linio.—I drink to your very good health."

The other did not accept the proffered glass. "I thank you, Monsieur. I am not chilled. I drink only milk."

"Milk—devil!" vowed the Baron, "what a choice! I tell you Monsieur Lawyer, that I pity your clients."

"Milk agrees with me better," rejoined the stranger quietly.

" 'Every man to his taste,' said the bumpkin when he kissed the cow! Well—at least tell us the news from Paris. Four days here in this stinking hole with only a greasy pack of cards for company, and not a gazette! More bread riots?"

"No more riots, Monsieur. The Queen is less popular than ever, but the King's promise of the States General somewhat contents the people."

Linio slapped his thigh in disgust. "If the King's councilors had not long ears, those who bawl 'States General' would be cramming the Bastille. 'The King needs money?' Why, then, don't he just take it outright from all those fat bourgeois and doltish tradesmen? The Comte d'Artois hit it squarely, 'The King's expenses should not depend on his income, but his income on his expenses.' Proper principles, eh?"

"Very illiberal principles, Monsieur," said the lawyer nervously but decidedly, while his eyelids and forehead began to tremble up and down with some strong emotion.

" 'Illiberal,' say you!" Linio let his scabbard bang against the table; but his companion, still seated in the shadow, checked a fiercer explosion with a prompt "hist," and before the stranger could reply, a confused brawling noise outside interrupted all of them.

The main door of the inn was forced open abruptly, and in a turbulent mass some twenty persons swarmed into the public room. Peasants, men and women, in various degrees of filth and unkemptness they seemed; then out of the whirl of threadbare blouses, baggy trousers, hoods, ragged shawls and torn aprons there emerged two men in blue semi-military coats, with sabers slapping at their sides and in their clutches a peculiarly miserable peasant struggling in handcuffs.

The fellow looked to be sixty with his scarred face and bent back (thanks to a life of grubbing toil), but forty would have been the wiser estimate. The women screamed; the men vociferated; a dozen pairs of scrawny arms tossed at once in the air. The noise was stupefying. Presently from behind this bedlam there advanced two more men in blue with sabers, forcing a passage for a portly individual in a long black coat, and wearing an extremely large hat adorned with tall raking feathers.

"Way; way for his Lordship, the Chevalier de Massac's high judge, the worshipful bailli Dupré!" somebody began shouting.

"I have it," muttered Linio to his companion, who still kept in the recesses of the fireplace. "An inn serves as the regular courthouse for these scarecrow seigneuries. Now for a bit of sport. That lout will have straps cut out of him."

M. le bailli, with hardly a glance at the guests who promptly retreated before him, cast himself into the arm-chair before the table and pounded with a heavy cane for silence. The men in blue forced back the peasants into an unruly semi-circle and the women partially ceased their shrieking. The host of the inn, with scared obsequiousness, set a fat bottle before the official, smirked and retired, whereupon a lank and oily clerk appeared with his pen and record book.

"*Oyez, oyez, oyez,*" he piped, "the high seigneurial court of our Lord the Chevalier de Massac stands convened!"

"Produce the prisoner," ordered Dupré, curtly.

The fettered peasant was dragged nearer the table. At his side stood forth one of the men in blue—the head game-keeper for the seigneury. The case, he explained in brief gutturals, was a very plain one. Nicolas, the defendant, was a woodcutter in the Massac forests. Already the game-keeper had had difficulties with the fellow. He had gathered an unlicensed number of fallen sticks. He had been so disloyal as to fling stones at deer that had exercised their lawful prerogative of nibbling at the villain's garden. Last year (recited the prosecutor) Nicolas had actually been defiant of the King. The royal salt-inspectors had caught him in the very act of boiling some pickled pork to get the salt out of it, in order to avoid paying lawful tax on what was needed for his table. For that offense he and his wife had been fined fifty livres. Now the cup of iniquity was full. Nicolas had been detected in a great crime.

"Proceed," ordered the judge.

Amid renewed wailings by the women, the gamekeeper recited how that morning he had by artful measures cap-tured the defendant (*flagrante delicto*) conveying a bag toward his cottage. In the bag were eight dead rabbits. M. le bailli would know what the majesty of the outraged law required.

The eight rabbits, mute accusers of felony, were spread upon the table. The women wailed louder than ever. The judge took a pull at the bottle and beetled his eyes upon the prisoner.

"What have you to say, scoundrel?"

There came back a jumble of protests of innocent intent, of "broth for a sick wife" and of "very hard times—how else can one live?" winding up with a prolonged, sniffling— "Mercy! Mercy!"

"How can one live? It is not necessary to live, Sirrah," announced Dupré. "Well, your life ought to be forfeit, only I am naturally tender-hearted; you must pay a thousand livres."

"Oh, your worship, your worship—there is not so much money in all the village."

"You lie—six hundred then."

"I have never touched such a sum in all my life. The salt-tax fine took my last sou."

"You have relatives who will aid you."

"Woe is me, I am an orphan with no brothers or sisters. I appeal to all here to prove this."

Dupré smote the table in anger. "Swine, do you think that I, the clerk and the gamekeeper all come here for nothing—not (as a marked afterthought) to name the rights of our high Seigneur le Chevalier?"

"He's got a heavy stocking. All the seigneury knows it," thrust in the gamekeeper.

"We'll soon learn what's in that stocking," observed the bailli. "Martin—truss him up!"

An awful howl burst from the prisoner; all the women broke out again; from the men present there was coming an inarticulate growling of helpless sympathy and rage. The gendarmes imperturbably, however, dragged their victim to a stout post near the fireplace, and roped him with his face to the pillar. Martin, their leader, deliberately stripped away the wretch's shirt, took off his own heavy belt and stepped back, making the leather swish and snap horribly.

"Now, gallows bird," resumed Dupré, "I am growing too

merciful. Five hundred livres or Martin flogs till his arm drops off."

"I cannot! I cannot!" came back in agony, and the gendarme was just measuring his distance for the first stroke when his hand was stayed most astonishingly. The stranger from the post-cart had sprung between the tormentor and his victim. Short as was his form, and thin his voice, there now was power and passion in them.

"You cannot do this. Wholly illegal. I speak as a man of law, at times even a judge myself. The ordinances of Nature forbid this brutality. Are eight hares to justify gross extortion or what may well prove to be murder?"

"*Mon dieu!*" swore the bailli, "what have we here? Do you teach *me* the law, Monsieur? I'm the law here."

"Beware what you do," warned the stranger. "Dread the vengeance alike of humane men and of the Supreme Being."

"*Sacré!*" broke from the bailli again, as in sheer amazement the gendarme let his lash fall. While, however, this minion of justice hesitated, the heavy paw of the watching Linio swept down upon the little lawyer and almost plucked him off his feet.

"Ah, ha! My fine minder-of-other-people's-business, I took no fancy to you from the minute you rejected good brandy. Your mixing-in here was never invited. Now I've a good mind to teach you some sound 'illiberal principles' before this Nicolas gets what's coming to him."

Linio had clattered out his saber and waved its long blade flat-wise, while he and Dupré exchanged the winks of kindred spirits who understood one another instantly. At a nod from the bailli, two of the gendarmes ran from the wretch at the pillar and seized the little attorney at either side. He turned deathly pale as the sense of his own peril dawned on him, but his dignity did not entirely desert him.

"Oh! Messieurs, you are not serious. You will not assault me thus brutally!"

"Contempt of court, just punishment," came from Dupré, reaching again for the bottle.

"I protested against an act of infamy"; the thin voice now was shrill and filling the large room. "Behold all of you! For that humane act I am at once put in grievous bodily peril. Is this France or Turkey? Do I live in the Eighteenth Century? Does the Author of Good desire——"

"The Author of Good desires you to submit your soul to Heaven and your body to a most salutary chastening!" The words were spoken by Linio's companion, hitherto quite silent. Now he was seen to be a clerically dressed gentleman who was holding his sides with overpowering laughter.

"Say your prayers, pettifogger," ordered Linio, lashing the flat of the saber round his head. "No, I won't kill you—quite. Bah! What is that——"

"That" was another uproar at the entrance to the inn. Amid the excitement inside a ponderous coach had creaked up; travelers now were dismounting, and a powerful military voice was summoning, "Where is my Lord's welcome in his own seigneury!" Then a new scream from one of the hysterical, agonizing women. "Saints and angels, our Chevalier himself!"

A meteorite descending into a crowded church could have produced no greater consternation. Before Linio, Dupré or the gendarmes could shift their postures, much less release their prisoners, Arnaud's ponderous arms had swept back the peasants to right and left, making a clear path for two gentlemen who were advancing straight up to the table of judgment. The bailli's countenance became that of a ghost. As René, with Laurent at his elbow, strode nearer, the peasants were all falling on their knees; then they began bleating together, "Oh, Lord, Lord, have pity upon us! Listen to us. Don't let them kill Nicolas. Don't let them punish that brave gentleman——"

"Oh, ho! Monsieur Linio," recognized Laurent, his eyes dancing in his head. "How did *you* slip yourself away from Paris?"

Arnaud's martial strides took him up to the bailli before that deputy could recover wits enough to uncover before his liege lord, and the ex-sergeant with one sweep smote the big plumed hat from the myrmidon's head.

"Do I come on a puppet show or enter a court of justice?" René's tones went into every mouse hole around the great room. "Is the King of Massac served here no better by *his* officials than is the King of France by his?"—"Equality" had gone out the window; the great seigneur, righteously angry, was present with all his mastery.

"A flagrant offender; a clear case of poaching—Monseigneur," the clerk found breath enough to gasp. "We did not know that you were coming——"

"And so act in my name like brutish bandits. I have heard of some of your doings, Dupré. I purposely sent ahead no messenger." The Chevalier's eye burned through the trembling bailli and his satellites till they seemed ready to shrivel through the cracks in the floor.

"Untie that wretch (with lordly gesture toward Nicolas). Now, has any one here sense enough to give a plain account of this vile melodrama?"

The peasants began pleading and jabbering together, but before they could become intelligible, the stranger from the post-cart stepped forth, nervously readjusted his cravat, disordered by Linio, and clearly, emphatically and not without a certain touching eloquence, recited all that had happened. Linio, during this declaration, had glided toward the door, only to be halted by a thunderous "Let no one quit this room!" from the Chevalier, and a restraining hand from Arnaud.

The little lawyer ended. René glared about him in disgust. *"Ma foi!* I pose as the apostle of enlightenment and here my scarecrow lieutenants make me a Nero or a Bejazet! I can be the laughingstock of Versailles. When will this harlequin of 'seigneural justice' on the estates of France have an end?" Then the politeness of his caste returned to him. He made a bow of faultless suavity to the attorney. "You, Monsieur, who have shown yourself a gentleman of courage and humanity, deserve a better atonement than my bare thanks; and as for you"—his eyes again shot lightnings upon his confounded deputies—"out of my sight and off my lands, or as I am the son of my fathers you shall all freeze in the old stocks before the chateau."

"Off of your lands, Monseigneur?" Dupré plucked courage enough to falter.

"Off of my lands! I dismiss you, and you—and you— village tyrants who abuse my trust, as I discharge thieving lackeys. My procureurs shall trace every sou in your accounts." Bailli, clerk, chief gamekeeper shuffled through the door with a fierce growl following them. Outside they would have to run very fast, lest the peasants dip them in the icy horse pond.

As they disappeared Laurent, whose risibles were always uppermost, began chuckling again. "He! he! Another courtly traveler is with us, Abbé Vernet, the antechamber's darling, and most marvelously in company with our dear friend Linio!"

"Merest accident," asserted the churchman, with unwonted asperity. "Barely thrown together this morning. I was only a chance spectator of this distressing happening."

"Chance spectator? Then you'll be 'chance spectator' of something else. Anselme, Arnaud, you others with us, M.

Linio seems to admire floggings. Take him out, hold him tightly, break my toughest cane over him."

Linio turned livid. "Break a cane? You shall ʀwallow these words, M. le Vicomte. Swallow them or give me satisfaction, me, a baron——"

"A denier for your forged papers," shouted Laurent joyously. "Our valets are almost too honest fellows to thrash you. Out with him——"

"Oh, M. l'Abbé, M. l'Abbé!" appealed Linio, now white as a sheet.

Vernet deliberately turned his back upon him, and took a pinch of snuff. "The Author of Good," he observed ironically, "evidently desires you to submit your soul to Heaven and your body to a profitable chastening."

During these amenities, René, with more decorum, had turned again to the little attorney.

"Monsieur, I regret that I have not yet visited my chateau. It is doubtless disordered and very cold; but to-morrow if you are still in Massac for dinner, I will offer my best amends——"

The man of law bent his short body gracefully. "Alas! M. le Chevalier, I travel on in an hour by the post-cart. Permit me to say, however, that you have just shown yourself a man of humanity, liberality and virtue. You have saved me from great bodily harm. My gratitude will prove enduring.—Ah! Something I have forgotten. Allow me— my card."

René took the card and read:

MAXIMILIEN FRANÇOIS MARIE ISADORE DE ROBESPIERRE,

AVOCAT,

ARRAS.

CHAPTER VI

ABBÉ VERNET BURROWING

COLD and formidable as a palace of ice had risen Massac chateau before its lawful owner. The Chevaliers de Massac had not deserted their ancestral castles for Paris or Versailles more completely than other nobles of pretentious lineage. Once per year the cobwebs had been routed from the cavernous chambers, and next the horses and hounds of the giddy hunting parties had dashed off with gay "Tarata," very likely over the peasants' grain. Then, with the hunting season over, the vast old edifice had been surrendered back to the idling caretakers and to the owls and the bats.

Now the Chevalier's heavy coach creaked over the last mile of melting snow, down a meandering avenue through the oaks and beeches, until it reached that majestic donjon seen above the sky line from afar: the enormous cylindrical keep wherein twenty men once had stood off the King. The donjon had been old on the day of Agincourt. Later owners had added certain less martial and more luxurious outbuildings. Still the military circuit was nearly intact. The coach rumbled across a half-rotten drawbridge over a dry moat. A rusted portcullis showed its unused fangs above them, and René and Laurent at length descended in a courtyard behind walls eight feet thick, and there received the greetings of the sorely astonished old steward.

René knew the great hall well. Much of his boyhood had been spent there under the happy tutelage of Father

François. The stone paved floors, the walls hung with rusty armor, the moldering banners from Ivry, the dusky portraits in Valois ruffs—all were old friends. Known, too, was the great state chamber with its musty tapestries, monumental bedstead, and coverlets of delicate embroidery from the needles of many a noble ancestress. Beyond the narrow windows in the hall waved now the bare twigs of the terraced garden behind the chateau. By the enormous fireplace was the high armchair before its ponderous footstool, the seat of René's puissant grandmother, "the great Madame." It was like entering an atrium of historic ghosts.

Omit the scurrying of the caretakers, the apologies, the elaborate courtesies, the penetrating cold of the great hall; the enormous log fire was at last roaring in the chimney place, the retainers bustled furiously and a tolerable supper was laid. René rummaged that evening among the dusty quartos of the library. Laurent rummaged more gleefully among the old arquebuses and musketoons of the armory. Then a sleep of exhausted youth followed under mountainous feather-beds. After that, the next morning the high seigneur of Massac thought himself ready to begin the reorganization of his dominions, according to the best sentiments of the Physiocrats, Encyclopaedists and of the Sages of Geneva and Ferney.

Alas, for innocent optimism! Alas, for a sublime willingness to immolate personal interests. When René informed the steward that he intended to abolish the burdens upon his peasants, that grave functionary explained to his lord (who, like every Massac, had ordinarily treated business affairs as above his high consideration) that the right to collect many of the severest imposts had been alienated years ago to a fat brewer in Amiens. The right to keep pigeons (who devoured the peasants' grain) had gone to a

Lille stock-jobber. The right to hunt deer for half the year was assigned to a parvenu Councillor at Abbeville. The Chevalier, indeed, had kept his chateau, his pew in the church, with the right to be prayed for first after the King, and the dubious glories of "administering justice." What else? Not enough to keep the head of the House of Massac in shabby gentility, if René's Provençal mother had not left him a snug little portion.

"Better back to Paris," grinned Laurent, as the case unfolded. "Hunt your moonbeams on Rue St. Leonard. Pleasanter and much warmer!"

But his cousin was less daunted; not though the uncapped, grovelling peasants soon revealed themselves into as lousy, superstitious, ignorant a parcel of bipeds as ever exemplified the "Natural Man." Not though the country nobles of the neighborhood, who came to pay awkward respects to Le Grand Chevalier, proved to be mere cider-drinking clowns who screwed their peasants because they needed the last denier themselves, who hunted furiously because they needed hares to eke out their dinners, and whose "chateaux" were famous chiefly for the vast dung-heaps before the doors and the hens and pigs swarming upon them.

Laurent inevitably made mock of peasant and noble sieur alike, and solaced himself with some tolerable winter shooting, and (be it admitted) a somewhat tender affair with the daughter of mine host of the *Silver Swan*. René, however, his philosophy being made of fairly solid stuff, stomached the first disillusionments and did what was possible. A few of the multifarious petty imposts upon the peasants he could remit. Two peculiarly necessitous widows could be made comfortable. Father Benoit, the toiling, ill-fed curé, not merely could be honored by a good dinner at the chateau, but made happy by the promise of a fine new surplice. Finally Nicolas, the wood cutter, could be solaced by two whole louis for the lashing which he had not received, ("The first time a red-handed poacher was ever paid for his rabbits!" Laurent made merry) and a new bailli set upon the vacated judgment seat of Dupré, who, it was hoped, would prove a little less rapacious and more sober than his predecessor.

Two weeks thus, and René had a slight reward in the apparent good will, as well as respect, of the bowing peasants and courtesy-bobbing women. Then, too, every other day, the post-cart for Ard trundled past the chateau, and always it brought a letter, sentimental, tender, romantic, from Virginie Durand, painting the glowing future of their lives in the re-born France.

René, therefore, watched the winter wane with a tolerable satisfaction. If he had not accomplished much, he had at least accomplished a little. "After all," he told Laurent, "the artificialities and chains wrought through two thousand years were not to be abolished in an instant. Allowances must be made—patience, patience." In any case they must stay near Massac until March for the elections to the States General. So the days lengthened with the northerning sun, and neither of the Massacs gave another serious thought to that collision at the inn with Linio and his reverend companion, Vernet.

Linio, in fact, had disappeared from the neighborhood almost as soon as a very sore carcass would permit travel. Vernet showed him little pity. "You threw away all discretion. You could have helped me, but now your usefulness here is ruined. Go back to Paris. Perhaps I shall need you later." Vernet himself also quitted the Massac region speedily, but not before an important interview with Father Benoit, the curé at St. Didier.

Father Benoit was rheumatic and old. He was the son

of a peasant, and "the great Madame" at the chateau had thought him a clever lad and sent him to the cheapest course at the seminary. When the local manse fell vacant, his patroness had "presented" him to it. Here he was fixed for life. Humble, poor, obscure, he had stagnated upon the level of the lower clergy. Commendams and sinecures were not for him. He saw his flock groaning under the tithes wrung out "for service of God," by the officials of the bishop of Ard, and yet he was forced to content himself on a miserable stipend.

His manse had half of its windows broken. He could not afford a housekeeper. In summer his small garden eked out a very meager table. In winter he became almost as lean as his parish, he gave so much food to the children. Yet, with it all, he was a power in the village; besides exercising the mysterious prerogatives of religion, he was the only man in the community, barring the bailli, his clerk and the chateau steward, who could read and write freely, and who actually had a few moldering books upon his shelf.

These facts made Father Benoit almost beside himself with pleasurable astonishment when a splendid personage, calling himself the Abbé Vernet, actually called at the parsonage. Father Benoit was indeed a little perplexed at a churchman who wore a blue coat and flesh-colored knee-breeches, swathed his neck in fine lawn and leaned on a cane, but, of course, high ecclesiastics had their privileges. Father Benoit made a very deep reverence, and wondered whether he ought to kiss his visitor's ring, as he had heard they did a cardinal's. As it was, he dusted his one good chair, put more twigs upon the fire, produced a flask of cherished Côté d'Or, and awaited his visitor's pleasure.

Abbé Vernet proved a delightfully easy guest. He listened with pleased attention to all the good man's woes; assured him that "he had it from a Minister" that the projected reforms certainly included an increase in the emoluments of the country clergy, gave Benoit two crowns for his poor, and finally came around to his own errand. "A confidential matter—high personages, perhaps—in fact, the Abbé could not explain all his reasons—but he must appeal to M. le Curé, as the best informed man in the village, for certain information."

M. le Curé was happy to be commanded. "Good, then; the information was this—had there not once been a certain Durand employed around the *Silver Swan?* Yes—many years ago, but it was necessary to inquire."

Father Benoit could indeed remember. Quite a story. The curé had just left the seminary, but recalled everything. Henri Durand, son of very ordinary peasants, had somehow become discontented with his station, and had actually learned to read. At first he had been horse-boy; then tapster; then innkeeper himself. But his ambition went higher still, although he did not become lawyer's clerk.

"So he left Massac?"

"Very true. A family misfortune probably hastened his act. He lost his wife."

"Here? I learned that he married prosperously at Lyons."

Father Benoit smiled. "I have heard about that. She was his second wife. His first wife lies in our Massac churchyard."

Vernet hitched his chair closer. "So he was married twice? This earlier marriage concerns me a trifle. You are sure it was a lawful union? Village customs can be very lax."

"It was in Father Jean's, my predecessor's, curateship. Perhaps Monsieur would like to see the record?"

Monsieur would decidedly like to see the record. Father Benoit produced the old dog-eared parish register.

There, after much fumbling, he found the brown entry:
*"April 14, 1739. Married this day Henri Durand and
Therese Jogot, daughter of Jacques and Therese Jogot."*
Next followed the "X" marks of several witnesses, evidently
too illiterate to sign their names.

"Other records?" inquired Vernet. Father Benoit turned
a couple of leaves and read again:

*"June 7, 1740, born, to Henri Durand and Therese
Durand—a son."*

Then, tragically following, still another entry:

*"June 9, 1740, died, Therese Durand, wife of Henri
Durand and daughter of Jacques and Therese Jogot."*

There was also a record of the baptism of the babe under
the name of Thibaud, a few days after the death of his
mother.

"The child then was clearly legitimate?" asked the Abbé.

"Oh, yes, Monsieur. The Durands and Jogots were
counted very honest people."

"One thing further. Did the boy grow up? I do not
think his father took him to Lyons."

"Not at all, Monsieur. After his wife's death, poor
Henri fell into a state of extreme affliction. He was able to
sell the inn to advantage and departed for Lyons. The boy
was left with his grandparents. Years slipped by; the
Jogots heard nothing of Henri. Then, at last, came a
letter. I read it aloud to old Jogot. Henri had married
again in Lyons, and seemed to be becoming rich. He had a
son by his new marriage. He did not send for young
Thibaud, for he said he feared his new wife would not make
the boy welcome; nevertheless, he forwarded money."

"Then the boy was well provided for?"

"Alas! no," sighed Father Benoit, "Thibaud from the
first was lazy and incorrigible. He was sent to my school.
I could not even teach him the alphabet. As he grew older

he was often before the bailli, and his father's remittances hardly covered the fines. At last came word that his father was dead. I saw the letter from a Lyons notary to the grandparent, and remember the words, '*M. Durand hearing very evil reports of his son Thibaud, and fearing he can only be a disgrace to his half-brother Edmond, leaves to his son Thibaud one thousand livres, but only on condition that he will never importune or molest his half-brother.*'"

"A clear enough case," remarked Vernet, "still a thousand livres is a tidy sum for a peasant. What became of it?"

"Mostly drunk or gambled away at the *Silver Swan*. The grandparents at length died. All the village was glad when Thibaud departed for Ard."

"Is he still there?" The Abbé tried not to have his tone become too eager.

"Still there. I saw him in the market last year when I went up to a synod. How he lives, God knows. Probably his wife supports him, but I was told he had even sunk to helping out the public executioner when there are brigands to be attended to."

"Give me an authentic copy of those records," requested Vernet, "and here are two more crowns—for your own trouble this time. This has all been in strict confidence, you understand, my dear Father; great interests; high personages."

"I am honored by your confidence, Monseigneur," assured the good old priest, rummaging out some very dirty paper and a half-dried inkstand.

Vernet seized the sheets, made for the inn with most unclerical strides, paid his scot, and was just in time to find a seat in the diligence that was changing horses for Ard.

Ard was one of that hundred of north French cities

which had found due growth during the Feudal Ages, fallen
asleep and never truly awakened. Most of the old walls
had been demolished and replaced by faint imitations of
Paris boulevards. A few straight avenues had been cut.
For the rest, the streets were narrow, crooked, dirty, and
overhung by solemn half-timbered houses. At the Grande
Place the majestic, gray cathedral looked across at the
venerable red bricks of the Hôtel de Ville. Nearby was the
bishop's palace, the intendant's residence, the Palais de
Justice and other indispensables of provincial authority, all
within range of a placidly gurgling old fountain, where
Baldwin of Flanders might have watered his horse before
he rode off to the Crusade.

Nobody was in a hurry in Ard. You never had to dodge
the rushing of cabs and whiskis as in Paris. The greatest
activity along a "Rue" often came from a large, solemn
donkey slowly stepping along the cobbles, his sides bulging
with two great paniers of straw-wrapped wine jars. Abbé
Vernet sighed as he threaded these silent streets. "What a
place to dwell in!" Then he repeated the familiar saying,
"In Paris one lives; elsewhere one only vegetates."

He prospered reasonably in his mission, however. His
first visit was to the office of a well-commended procureur.
"He had been compelled," he told the lawyer, "to make
certain inquiries as to the legal status of orphan girls and
the rights of guardianship." Satisfied with the answer, he
represented that a disagreeable duty forced him to seek the
whereabouts of one Thibaud Durand, occasionally employed
around the Palais de Justice.

The courteous procureur could barely conceal his astonishment to find a fashionable abbé inquiring the whereabouts of such a nice expert at breaking-on-the-wheel, but
he gave Vernet the information. The visitor's walk, there-

fore, next took him down a steep, slippery way, between unusually weather-beaten and tottering houses and penetrated by dark cat-alleys, until at last he found himself close to the swollen, muddy current of the Luchy, where the chilly water was floating along the dead leaves washed down by the recent freshets.

Vernet was prepared for ungenteel scenes and he was not disappointed. An old hag, turpentining a bedstead of debatable history, gave him the final direction. The Abbé knocked, accordingly, at the door of a filthy cabin, so close to the river that a powerful gust might almost have blown the rotting structure into it.

Vernet was not disappointed again when he met a loutish reception and, to his first queries, unveiled hostility. Thibaud Durand had exhausted about every convenient form of degradation. He had become executioner's assistant, partly as alternative to a term for himself in the chaingang, working on the roads. He could have played the brigand at any theater without one touch of make-up. His form, however, was still supple, and his sharp, suspicious eyes glanced from a countenance which reminded the Abbé instantly of a person he had taken pains to scrutinize ere quitting Paris—Edmond Durand. "Relations, undoubtedly," was the inward comment, and Vernet pushed the interview.

He had more satisfaction presently in dealing with "Madame." Thibaud's consort and ostensibly his lawful spouse, was a woman of some five and thirty, of Amazonian physique, an exceedingly firm jaw, and yet with features which, with other costume and surroundings, might have been called comely. It was Olympie Durand, sooner than her companion, who began to comprehend that their remarkable visitor had coins in his pocket, and might actually become inclined to leave certain effigies of the King behind him. Olympie it was who told Thibaud "to stop gawping like a zany and to ask Monseigneur in," and Olympie who admitted first that her husband was a Durand from Massac, and then that he had a "very rich brother—curse the upstart!—once in Lyons, but now in Paris.—And much good do his fine louis do us!"—with a furious gesture toward the unswept stone floor and the broken chairs.

After that, Vernet's path became easier. He talked—and laid a louis on the table; talked still more—and laid down a second louis; still more—and a third louis rested shining beside its two fellows. Olympie and Thibaud both sat listening and eying that gold like two people entering Aladdin's palaces of dreams. All that the Abbé said, all that the Abbé left unsaid, but suggested, can be far better explained later. Suffice it now that his tone became more and more complacent, and Thibaud and Olympie correspondingly cordial. Thibaud even proffered (although the Abbé, with unoffending grace, declined) to let his guest sample a little black bottle "with something very good just slipped across from Holland."

At last, when Vernet took his leave, he made a decidedly pointed remark about, "Your places in the Paris stage tomorrow," and then let his pocket jingle as if he had not completed his liberality.

The moment that he was fairly gone, Olympie and Thibaud rushed for the three gold pieces together. The woman got her claws upon two; her spouse secured the third, then they began laughing like folk bereft of their wits and staring at one another.

"The sky has opened!" cried Olympie.

"We are bewitched," cried her spouse.

"But the gold is gold. It is hard. It is real. It is no dream. Three louis—and soon more, more, more."

"We must pack," commanded her husband, clutching his head; "hurry, hurry."

. . . A little later Vernet at his inn was writing a lengthy letter, to be hastened off by special courier to Linio in Paris.

CHAPTER VII

THE DEPUTY FROM ARD

From a letter of René de Massac to Virginie Durand, Ard, March, 1789:

". . . Oh, my Beloved, my Beloved! An honor has overtaken me which will lift you to the heavens, yet which almost overwhelms me with the awfulness now of my responsibility to the great cause of Humanity.

"You have written me of the excitement in Paris over the elections to the States General, the incessant discussions, the stir in every salon and café, the joyous confusion when, for the first time since 1614, the unprivileged folk of France were summoned to that sublime act of *voting* for electors, who were to choose, in a smaller assembly, the actual deputies for the Third Estate to our glorious States General, which is to transform the face of France.

"Imagine, even in our humble village of Massac, the greatest stir in centuries, when our peasants—soon, I trust, enlightened citizens of a liberated Commonwealth—met at the church and, amid a touching bewilderment, chose two of their number to go up as electors to Ard, at the same time preparing (as they were directed) their bill of complaints against the oppressive taxes and the thousand crushing absurdities of perishing feudalism. Poor fellows, they could not realize that very soon their chains were to fall away; that Freedom, the glorious gift of Philosophy and Enlightenment, was about to become peacefully and painfully the birthright of all Frenchmen.

"But you become impatient at my rhapsodies. Understand, then, that with Laurent I went up to Ard, being still (I loathe to confess it) a 'Noble' and obliged to vote for deputy in the 'Noble' electoral assembly. To Ard we came despite hideous roads, which our postilions only con-

quered with the aid of eight horses and much swearing.
How the little city was alive! What prodigal hospitality;
what health drinking; what good fellowship; what abundance of generous sentiments, even upon hitherto supercili-
ous lips! I repelled with anger Laurent's insinuation that
the Royal Intendant and Monseigneur the Bishop were all
condescension to very humble procureurs and curés, largely
because they had hopes of being chosen deputies themselves.
Perhaps he was partly right. No matter. Our most purblind oligarchs will soon learn the chaste happiness of
democracy.

"At Ard I met that estimable patriot and philanthropist,
of whom I have written, M. de Robespierre. Already chosen
deputy by his native Arras, he said that he was in Ard to
advise his fellow patriots as to certain matters. I found,
also, to my great joy, Father François, who, of course, was
still legally a priest in the diocese and entitled to vote in
the Clerical Assembly.

"Let me hasten to my climax. The Noble Assembly, I
grieve to say, rejected with a deplorable abruptness my
proposal to notify the King that we freely waived all our
old iniquitous perquisites and privileges. The deputy they
chose is an elderly sieur, who I fear will prove no friend
to Liberty. 'A crabbed old fool,' Laurent uncharitably
called him.

"But the Clergy, ah! the Clergy. Passing over the smooth
candidacy of Monseigneur the Bishop, whom did they choose
but our dearest Father François himself. And the Third
Estate—(read, read, my Beloved) after naming the avocat
M. Lieutard as first deputy, being then divided equally
between two other ambitious lawyers, the electors discovered even in a 'Noble' an unfeigned love of mankind. As
a compromise (and I find M. de Robespierre's hand in this)
they actually chose René de Massac as their second deputy.[1]

"What shall I write, O my Soul, except this?—My own
class rejects me. The virtuous People receive me. Back
then to Paris, to duty, to happiness. Henceforth I belong
to the People, to you and to France."

[1] Of course, the great Marquis de Mirabeau, and other noblemen
and clergymen in the States General, were elected as deputies for the
Third Estate.

CHAPTER VIII

THE PALAIS ROYAL

Virginie was ecstatically happy. Spring was at hand. Her marriage day was appointed. Her destined husband had been chosen one of the twelve hundred who were to regenerate France. When René returned to Paris, she drove out with a party of friends, met him at St. Denis and re-entered in radiance at his side. All the vast city seemed joyous to her, from the dingy faubourgs where tradesmen's signs creaked and peddlers and ballad singers raised their bedlam, to the galaxies of great hotels where beyond the opened curtains could be glimpsed the gilt chandeliers, the blazing fireplaces, the powder and the rouge of the well-born guests. Never had Paris appeared so fair and friendly.

Virginie was already the queen of a devoted circle. "We shall have one of the most popular salons in Paris," René boasted to himself. She had all the arts of a supreme hostess; to say just enough; to listen admiringly; to draw out her guests' best witticisms; to put every one at ease. Among the young men and women gathered at the Durand house to congratulate René, he now found his old fellow prisoner, St. Just.

That astonishing youth had redeemed his promise made when he was released; he had called on René just before the latter set out for Ard. René, of course, had taken him to the Durands, and St. Just had at once impressed the entire parlor by his Hellenic beauty and his surprising mannerisms. He had stood stiffly before Virginie, when they were introduced, without a bow.

"You are my friend because you are René's friend," said Virginie, extending her hand.

"I dislike you," spoke St. Just abruptly. "You happen to be a woman, and I always dislike things that I cannot understand."

"But at least I happen to be a person. Can you not find a few things understandable and praiseworthy about me?"

"I will pretend that you are René's brother," and the youth held out his own hand. After that St. Just, who was supposed to be studying law, but who, more obviously, was studying Paris, was nightly at the Durand table. Without the least affectation, he and Virginie would discuss all the riddles of the universe. The youth's admiration for her intelligence and judgment seemed boundless, but it was the admiration for a male comrade, absolutely untinged by sentiment or romance. "A strange creation," Father François once observed. "God has made St. Just without consciousness that there is such a thing as sex in the world. Woe unto him; woe unto some woman if that consciousness should awaken!"

Very gay was the supper at the Durand's that night of the Chevalier's return. René's honor seemed reflected upon all his friends. They rallied him upon the Constitution of France, which he, like every other deputy-elect, was assumed to carry ready-made in his pocket. Once more, also, he had to tell the story of his own election; how two rival attorneys of Ard, each with a notable following, had been brought by Father François and M. de Robespierre to realize that it was better to throw their strength to a nobleman who would prove a true tribune of the people than risk the election of a long-standing enemy.

Finally, St. Just, after decorous urgings, read from his

Republican Institutions, a pamphlet upon which he was
expanding no little juvenile ink. Everybody clapped his
hands at such opinions as, "We must have neither rich nor
poor. . . . I defy you to do away with poverty until every
man owns his own land. . . . Opulence is a crime." There
was, however, polite dissent from the ladies at the propo-
sition that at the age of five all children should be taken
from their mothers and reared in vast public asylums!

Good or bad, in any case, it was all delightfully "liberal."
Of course, one must be very fearless in arranging the ideal
Republic soon to be. The guests at length summoned hackney coaches or started home with their lantern boys on
foot. Only René had remained for an unusually prolonged
farewell, when André, with some air of importance, beckoned him into a corner.

"There's a matter I have not felt it quite right to lay
before M. Durand, but perhaps you, M. le Chevalier——"

"What is it?"

"I grow convinced that M. Durand and Mademoiselle
are being spied upon."

"Spied upon? They have not an enemy in the world."

"Nevertheless, Monsieur, all yesterday I observed a man
with his hat over his eyes, standing near the house opposite
and watching this house as a cat watches a mouse hole.
To-day a woman, offering oranges amazingly cheap, thrust
into the kitchen. A handsome tonguy woman, who brought
the talk with our pliable Bernard at once around to M.
Durand and the places he frequented. Chance took me to
the kitchen. I packed her off and rated Bernard. Still
I am left wondering."

René shrugged his shoulders and laughed. "Not M.
Durand, but M. Durand's intended son-in-law she was
doubtless concerned with. Probably my noble uncle and
aunt have set a watch upon my doings. Now that I'm to

be deputy I need fear no new *lettre de cachet;* nevertheless, I'll be cautious and set Arnaud on the watch."

"Very likely as you say, Monsieur," assented André, not quite convinced; but René was already far up beyond the Milky Way, saying "au revoir" (God knows how many times!) to André's mistress.

The heart of Paris was beating all through that momentous spring, not in the murky faubourgs, not in the chilly recesses of the deserted Tuileries, not even in the wealthy salons of St. Honoré or St. Germain—the heart of Paris beat at the Palais Royal.

The Palais Royal was more than a great complex of buildings and arcades surrounding a pleasant garden. Being the property of the great Duc d'Orleans, the police hesitated to assert their jurisdiction. You could say things in the Palais Royal that meant the Bastille or Vincennes if uttered elsewhere. Just now the cafés and garden were the focus for every chatterbox in Paris. Lanky lawyers' clerks would mount tables and harangue a do-nothing crowd about "The Deficit," peasants' burdens and (ever a greater commonplace) "The Rights of Man." In this place you could buy books, smuggled in from London or Leyden printers, dealing with every delightfully forbidden subject from "Was the Cardinal de Rohan the Queen's Lover?" to "Had ex-minister Calonne embezzled ten million livres?" The Palais Royal was, in short, the paradise for "the emancipated," for philosophers, even for downright Republicans.

Restaurants abounded, ten sous eating places and lordly establishments, where you dined in state for a louis. Most arrogant of them all was Saroni's—if you possessed the touch-stone for admission. Its unwritten law ran that no party not introduced by someone presentable at court could sit reflected in its long mirrors and sample its Italian wines and cookery. The establishment, therefore, was not merely respectable, it was aristocratic—and the magnificent waiters had been schooled to tell a countess from a poor "sieur's" lady even before she took off her gloves.

Evening had advanced. The playhouses around the Palais Royal were emptying and Saroni's had begun to fill especially after the licentious little comedy, "Le Mariage sans Curé," running in the adjacent Theater Beaujolais, rang down its curtain. Parties came drifting in. Intoxicating music was beginning. Saroni's, in short, was about to enjoy a normal evening.

In the rear of the flashing restaurant a number of cozy little stalls were closed off by curtains. Most of these alcoves were occupied by gentlemen of undoubted nobility and young ladies of less nobility but undoubted attraction, all intent on charming little suppers; but one of these well-guarded retreats merely contained two male personages, not indifferent to an exquisite pigeon pie. The twain were obviously the Abbé Vernet and his one-time companion, Linio, and the former was speaking.

"And so we come back to the issue, my dear——"

"Baron," completed the other.

"Well, 'Baron,' if so you prefer. Though I've never seen that patent of nobility which you avow the Duke of Hesse-Zwergdorf bestowed upon you shortly before the police found your gaming transactions so successful that they requested you to leave Vienna.—So we come back to the original issue.—The cast is one to make your fortune if there is only delicacy, delicacy."

"Have no distrust. Everything shall be attended to."

"You understand. This business must absolutely slip from my hands. I lead you thus far. Not merely now do I fail to inquire, I forbid you to communicate further details."

"But one point I'll raise again. You wish to succeed in a certain matter. Very good. But why has the girl got to live?"

"My good Linio," Vernet's hands made his fine rings flash gracefully, "you suggest a horrible thing, utterly repugnant to me alike as a gentleman of the court and a man of the Church. I therefore refuse to listen to you. But more practically, I will add that if anything mortal should happen to the girl—at least, at present, there would be a tempest raised likely to prove very unwelcome to your noble self. Consider. Healthy young women of seventeen seldom die suddenly. Her lover would fill Paris with his uproar. My principals, who are in an agony to have his marriage broken off, would draw the line at *that*. Nothing could avert suspicions. The marriage would indeed be at an end; but perhaps at a very heavy price to our dearest interests——"

Linio's reply was halted by a rattle of cutlery and scraping of chairs, indicating that a new party had taken possession of one of the tables just outside the curtain. Pleasant young voices sounded. Linio pushed back the drapery. "*Ma foi!* I like that ankle and waist!" he confided in so pleased a tone, Vernet was making bold to lift his curtain from the other end, when another voice, as from a nearby table, made him pause abruptly.

"Waiter, how came those people to be admitted? I know every face at court."

"The Comtesse de Massac herself," cautioned the Abbé; "we're best unseen."

The Countess' voice undoubtedly had carried to the table of the intruders; someone thrust back his chair abruptly. Also a signal from the waiter must have brought the proprietor upon a silent run.

"Signor Saroni," spoke the Countess, "we came to your

restaurant because your patrons are persons of rank. How did these young men and women get by your doorkeeper?"

The proprietor had begun general apologies in Italian-French, when one of the members of the offending party broke in loudly, "If you blush for your guests, sirrah, let us begone, but not before I ask this gentleman in the Body Guards' coat whether he sustains this woman's insult?"

"Don't quarrel, St. Just," besought some young woman. "René will come back here immediately. He will explain everything."

"Explain?" cried her companion. "What is there to explain save that he brought us here among a parcel of boors whose courtesy is less than that of fish-wives?"

"Rid us of this *canaille*, or see us depart," rose the old Countess' tones shrilly.

"Messieurs, Mesdames," Saroni began expostulating. "A regrettable mischance—the old custom of the house—I am desolated that my porter——"

Linio had pushed back the curtain again. "Now they will brawl outright," he informed Vernet gleefully.

"Holla! my friends," the voice of René de Massac broke in enthusiastically. "I have the pamphlets. Just off the press.—What is this?—My aunt, my uncle, and even you, Laurent?"

A volume of relief spoke through Saroni's accents. "Ah! Madame, it is as I imagined. These guests were introduced by your nephew, M. le Chevalier himself, who went over to the bookstore before taking his seat. All is explained."

Vernet could not reject the chance to peer out also at the tableau. The Comte and Comtesse de Massac and their son were standing at one table in very stiff attitudes. At the other, the Abbé recognized as seated, Virginie Durand,

Camille Desmoulins, Lucile Duplessis, Danton, and a middle-aged lady, presumably Mme. Danton. Standing between the groups with a very forced smile, was René de Massac. St. Just also was on his feet, gazing as if frozen with anger; his beauty had actually become terrible. René, however, summoned all his resources to control a desperate situation. The Oeil-de-Boeuf had never witnessed a better self-command.

"Madame, my aunt; Monsieur, my uncle, our political differences need not make us uncivil. You will not question the right of any Massac to introduce his friends to Saroni's. Permit me to present them"—and he named over his companions. The eyes of the old Count and Countess sought only Virginie. She had turned pale as alabaster, but arose, and with easier grace than Vernet had thought possible, made her betrothed's aunt an irreproachable courtesy. The Count seemed to be muttering through his teeth. Laurent, for once, gazed silently, evidently somewhat amazed by the grace of Virginie, but the Countess bowed her white-powdered head with well-bred condescension, smiled, and held out her hand.

"So this is the Mlle. Durand who has bewitched our dear Chevalier?" By this time there was perfect silence in the restaurant; even the music had ceased and Mme. de Massac's words went to the remotest table.

"I care much for your nephew, Madame," spoke Virginie slowly and clearly, watching the older woman with dilated eyes.

Mme. de Massac's laugh was gentle and patrician. "I am glad indeed to see you, *chère*. Do you know that at Versailles you have been somewhat talked about? No lies were told about your beauty. It is easy now to see how this little affair all happened." Then to René, "Well, naughty boy, I ought to forgive you for getting caught. But another time choose a less public table; too many eyes should not gaze upon one's kept mistress."

The blow was direct, palpable. Virginie's color came back in one crimson surge. René's other guests leaped to their feet, but all sounds were drowned by the voice of St. Just.

"The swine of the pen have more right to the air they breathe than have you."

The older woman gathered her draperies, motioned airily to husband and son, and swept out with an ostentatious flutter before all the tables. "The carriage, the Hotel de Sully.—Very good taste, my nephew."

"Madame"; the tones of Virginie were now like a lash of cold steel. "God Himself has not the power to teach you the injustice you have wrought."

The Count with an eagle-like glare stalked silently behind his consort, but Laurent lingered as his cousin stood with one arm of protection about his betrothed.

"Dearest fellow," protested the Viscount, "I'd cut off one hand to blot out all this."

The answer came in a murderous dart by St. Just, barely restrained by Danton, and the passionate plea by René:

"In Heaven's name, say nothing more."

Then the thunderous voice of Danton crashed through the craning, excited dining room.

"Messieurs les aristocrats, take pride in your nobility! There dawns a different day."

The others had to lead out René. Virginie was stunned beyond tears, but her lover was raging violently, bitterly. "Both hands of mine I'd cut off, never to have led you into this accursed place!"

With that the second party swept away, despite the desperate gesturing of Signor Saroni. "Bah," observed a

Knight of St. Michel, looking up from his ragout; "this is what comes of giving those vile bourgeois the slightest tether."

Vernet, for his part, had, to Linio's open merriment, abandoned himself to a perfect torrent of unclerical swearing.

At last he subsided enough for connected words. "Damnation upon all women! That bat-blind Countess can well ruin everything—after I implored restraint and silence. There's only one now to help us. How soon can I reach Versailles?"

René exhausted himself with apologies when at length they got him calm. Saroni's had been a familiar haunt of his; that guests under his personal introduction should have been met with insult had been the last thought in his still very trustful head. At his vehement request, St. Just did not send his challenge to Laurent, as the former frantically desired. As for Virginie, who carried herself dry-eyed and proud all the way to Rue St. Leonard, when she was at last alone with her intended, her anguish could have melted a Gorgon.

"Oh! my beloved; we have been too blissful. We have been too confident that God smiles upon us. Even when they put you in prison I could not dream of the depths of your kinsmen's hate. Is there no hideous catastrophe hanging over us? Ought we—ought we even now to go through with our marriage? What can I bring to you saving always more humiliations like this?"

Whereat, of course, René swore a great oath by every power, Christian, pagan and philosophical, that never should aught come between them, winding up with a fervent request:

"How can we end such scenes and silence every tongue

forever? By giving me the blissful right to call you Madame de Massac. Why wait until May before beginning our great happiness? Let me speak to your father."

But Virginie had at last recovered her self-control and her pride: "No, dear heart, you ask the impossible. Yesterday perhaps I would have yielded. To-night I will never give that pitiless woman the cause to say 'She had so little confidence in holding my nephew, that I made her hasten her wedding.' No, I am only a bourgeoise, but I have my pride. Our wedding is fixed for May Day."

René nevertheless pleaded. The next afternoon his pleadings were renewed. He believed that he saw signs of yielding. Another assault might have succeeded, but when he sought his lodgings upon the Rue Vendôme, his valet handed him a letter. The paper was pink and perfumed, but for all that the writing was Laurent's:

"Dearest Cousin: If you are a Christian the Holy Commandments forbid you to revile your parents. If you are a pagan, good breeding prohibits exactly the same thing. I say nothing therefore of the taste and discretion lately displayed by my estimable mother. To me at least, Mlle. Durand appeared to be a lady likely to reward devoted acquaintance.

"But there is a further purpose in these my crow-tracks. Our good Dreux-Brézé has just left me. Evidently the poor opinion entertained of your worthy self by my father and mother has begun to wear away with a certain lady of sufficiently exalted rank. Whatever your Republican notions, I imagine that your career as a deputy, as well as the reception awarded by the world to your intended, will hardly be injured by accepting the olive-branch if it is extended from a very distinguished quarter. I know you will obey the command which Dreux-Brézé transmits. Your old comrades are eager to greet you, and Louise de Broglie (whom I am glad to say you can soon call 'Cousin') adds her petition to mine.

"Laurent."

Along with this letter was another upon white calendared paper and stamped with the crown:

"It is the pleasure of their Majesties to command you to attend the Grand Couvert at the Chateau, Thursday, March the twenty-first.

"Placing myself at your service,

"DREUX-BRÉZÉ."

CHAPTER IX

THE GRAND COUVERT

EARLY spring at Versailles. It was one of those deceptive days which makes the optimist say "The summer is at hand." Buds were starting, throstles singing, the first green peeping out under the golden sunlight. Never had René de Massac seen the residence city more alluring than when he stepped from his curricle in the Cour Royale before the vast chateau.

Not being an introspective mortal he had never bothered his young head about any inconsistency in applauding the most rash republicanism, and immediately after that dressing himself in the mauve silk-ratteen and gold lace becoming a man whom the King again would honor. After all, the Utopia of his dreams ought surely to be a Utopia compatible with the very best of breeding.

René was expected. The splendid fusileers of the Scotch regiment on duty saluted; an old comrade of the Body Guard came out to embrace him. Other old social equals soon hurried up. There was much scraping and "proffering of one's service." Favor or disfavor at Versailles was a game in which there was no disgrace in an occasional setback, and a few weeks in Vincennes never harmed a true gentleman. Besides Massac had not yet consummated his mad-cap marriage. It would be impolite (especially as Majesty seemed to be forgiving) to ask now whether he really intended to go through with it. René in short had been a general favorite, and his wide acquaintance welcomed him back gladly.

The ladies welcomed even more heartily than the men. M. le Chevalier had in fact been such a center of scandal as to become a bit of a hero. Such constancy, such sentiment, such tenderness! So different from merely a liaison with a lady-in-waiting or an Opéra Comique singer! If Virginie had herself appeared, she might actually have been received with considerable courtesy merely out of a curious desire to see her.

So for a couple of hours René's time went pleasantly enough. All the instincts of a youth spent at the court reasserted themselves. It was perfectly natural to convey to the old maréchale that her six face-patches had been arranged extraordinarily gracefully, and tell a younger countess that her headdress and puffs *à la zéphire* were vastly becoming. Then Laurent sauntered up in his best uniform, and upon his arm Louise de Broglie, niece of the great and gouty old Maréchal de Broglie himself.

Louise was a small, dark-eyed, comfortably clinging type of girl, an old flame of René's, and his final romance with Virginie had silenced many court rumors that he and Laurent might end up as deadly rivals. Now all was smiles and friendship, and Laurent turned her over for the nonce to his kinsman with a beaming, "Pity that you and Louise cannot be married. Then she and I could always be together without scandal. Husbands and wives see each other so seldom at Versailles, you know!"

Louise doubtless was not Virginie, but she was very pretty, her hand was dainty, her chatter delightful. It was small hardship to wander with such a companion through the enormous parterres and the parks. The gardeners had just uncovered the protected shrubs, and set out long rows of tubs containing orange trees. Everything was decorous, orderly, a drawing-room in the open air. Everybody knew everybody else; a perfect graciousness prevailed. Etiquette taught precisely when to bow, when to await a bow, and what was the proper thing to say on greeting. To state that René de Massac did not find these once familiar scenes somewhat congenial would be to state a sad untruth.

Thus he and Mlle. de Broglie strolled, saluted, chatted. At length, along the esplanade of the Grand Canal in which a couple of gondolas were idling, they saw the moving hedge of silk, satin, gold lace, silver lace, ivory walking sticks and plumes which told where the human center of all this elaborate pageantry was promenading. For an instant René's step halted, a certain memory of Vincennes hospitalities being still too keen; when out in advance of the shimmering cortège advanced Dreux-Brézé in person, his cheeks as bleached and rouged as ever, his coat a walking fashion-plate, his white wand twirling in one hand, but the other extended with undeniable cordiality.

"Welcome, Massac the Prodigal Son returns! All seems to be forgiven. Sample the fatted calf. In other words—meet the King."

Louis XVI had a great jeweled star on his breast, but nothing could make him a figure of royal dignity when René swept off his hat. The advancing platoon of white, gold and crimson, all fell back as the King nodded with a plain attempt to be affable. The inclination of the thick neck was ungainly, the large limbs were stiff, but the smile at least was honest.

"We rejoice to see you, Chevalier." The manner was almost shy, although the tones were kindly. "Perhaps we have been ill-advised. At least you will not be molested again."

"You are very gracious, Sire."

"I hear you've been elected deputy?"

"Your Majesty's subjects at Ard saw fit so to honor me."

"Tell them wherever you go (the King seemed to be delivering a formula) that we earnestly desire the welfare of our people."

The King nodded again. The phalanx of plumes went bobbing onward, but Dreux-Brézé lingered for another word before he followed the cortège: "A hint, my friend. The Queen is walking by the Basin of Neptune."

The great fountains were spouting in their magnificence when the Chevalier and his companion saw gliding above the shrubbery this time a mass of tall ostrich feathers—the favorite headdress of the Queen. Instantly she was in sight, once more in airy white cambric, her long train managed by a negro lad in gaudy livery and equally brilliant turban. At her side, however, there leaned a weak, pale-faced little boy, who, young as he was, had his hair powdered and curled, and wore a miniature sword. René knew that he was the sickly Dauphin.[1] Behind their mistress walked half a dozen ladies and as many gentlemen in costumes brilliant as the coat of Joseph. Massac failed not with the congé which his enemies envied, whereupon a very shapely hand was proffered him to kiss.

"Well, Chevalier; I find that your republican principles still suffer you to obey your sovereign's commands—sometimes."

"Your Majesty has always found me casting myself at your feet save in one matter where I cannot command my own heart."

"We must not press too many questions. What, Mlle. de Broglie, has that faithless Laurent deserted you already?"

"On the contrary, Madame," answered René, "he and

---

[1] The young prince who died soon after this date, and was succeeded in his title by his younger brother, the ill-starred "Louis XVII."

Mlle. Louise are so devoted that with full assurance he permits me to remain her very good friend."

"Happy Viscount, may this confidence endure after marriage! But really, René, by your getting yourself so astonishingly imprisoned, you played us a very shabby trick. Your part in the last theatricals was execrably taken. I almost wept."

"I am sure, Madame, I never betook myself to Vincennes merely to displeasure you."

Marie Antoinette laughed, a pleasant laugh aimed at herself: "We must really talk of something else. Has not the King said 'All is forgotten'? To-night I shall need your opinion on a certain matter. Do you remember the masked *bal de l'Opéra* last year, and how we all went—Artois, La Polignac and I, and half a dozen of the rest of us? And how we mixed with the crowd, and you danced with me, and we two were taken for an infantry lieutenant and a smart grisette, and how a half-drunk marine officer clutched my arm, and you had almost to fight him?"

"A mad adventure, Madame; lucky that we kept our disguises!"

"So we all said, yet what an adorable time! Now they tell such stories about 'the state of Paris' that Artois quite refuses to take me. Well, you are from Paris now, pray speak the truth, would such a pleasure be unsafe?"

"I dare not deny, Madame, that recent happenings would make the discovery of such a lark unusually awkward."

The Queen flirted her handkerchief: "Mademoiselle can spare you; walk beside me, René! I've missed your droll talk. Of course your remarkable new friends talk terribly about the King, and of course (as I sadly learned after the Necklace affair) still more dreadfully about me. But tell me, please, some of the horrid things they really say."

"Madame," returned the Chevalier, falling into step oppo-

site the Dauphin, "my political opinions still leave me a
gentleman. I will not repeat the slanders of ignorance."

"A Republican should not talk like a courtier. At least,
then, tell why so many hopes are fixed on the States General? M. Necker has explained, but he is only a prosy
banker, one bag of dull figures. Of course the King needs
money (I can't rebuild the model farm at Rambouillet—
isn't it ghastly!) and money, I suppose, means taxes. But
why not just a new edict flatly imposing them? 'Impossible, Your Majesty,' from all the ministers, 'the state of
France forbids.' 'Why forbids? What forbids a king?'
Then another buzz of big words. I have to forget them
all, and to plan a new fête at the Trianons. Now you are
clever, René, and are not like M. Necker. Explain to me
this 'state of France.'"

No greater pleasure could have been proffered René de
Massac; to explain the needs of France to the Queen herself! At once he became eloquent. Being a very winsome
person indeed, Marie Antoinette at least gained a more lucid
idea of taxation, forced labor and the public debt than any
King's Counsellor had hitherto afforded. She listened atten-
tively, and the walking ladies and gentlemen wisely left
them alone together until they neared the imposing western
façade of the palace and the Queen had to go in to dress.

"Thanks, René; I feel myself, oh so much wiser!" Again
she proffered her hand to kiss; then in an undertone, "After
supper and the little play we must walk and talk again."

            .   .   .   .

A thousand candles. An enormous room alive with color.
The capitals, bases and volutes of the Corinthian pilasters
were of gilded bronze. Behind gorgeous screens in one of
the four overhanging balconies, a band discoursed soft music.
The multitudinous mirrors framed with gold reflected the
living forms of the seated women, their wavy coiffures, the

alabaster of their powdered necks, the pink of their cheeks. The gentlemen beside them with their brocade, laces and jewels blended in perfectly with their companions' finery. The service was of gold or of exquisite porcelain.

Noiselessly, tirelessly in and out of the gilded doors glided the blue or crimson velvet of the regiment of waiters. Sword at side, diamond on finger, point lace at wrist, each lackey of grandeur seemed himself a companion to the King. The Second Dish-Remover showed all the dexterity of a great surgeon determining life and death; so it was with the Overseer-of-the-Roast, and the Director-of-the-Pastry. For any but the Captain of the Guard to have announced to the King "Supper is served" would have implied a palace revolution; another revolution, if Majesty had been notified of dinner by any save the First Lord of the Bedchamber.

About twenty sat at the royal board. From time to time the King and the Queen, from their dais under the fleur de lys canopy, would raise their voices and address some polite remark to their nearest guests. Quite as often they would turn toward the fifty-odd ladies and gentlemen who stood watching at a respectful distance just outside the gangway for the servitors, and mention some name. Immediately the favored person would step near the dais, bow, exchange a few sentences with the liege lord or mistress, bow again and fall back into the gazing company.

Louis XVI did nothing to lighten the heavy pageantry. He had no small task. His dull eyes only kindled when tactful mention was made of hunting or of his favorite hobby—lock-making. But the Queen (though she notoriously hated the Grand Couvert) atoned for him by incessant, although often pointless chatter. When the King finished a course the plates were instantly changed, irrespective of the progress of his guests, but this was no hardship. His appetite was prodigious; he was gnawing another chicken wing like a schoolboy, while the others sat toying with their forks.

Vast joints, pyramids of poultry, a wild boar, veal garnished with pigeons, a lordly sturgeon flanked with red mullets—even the King could not do justice to every course whisked in and out. The waste was enormous. To-morrow the restaurants at Versailles would be retailing the dishes out of which Majesty had taken two bites.

"And is it true, Chevalier," asked the melancholy-faced Princesse de Lamballe, the Queen's particular friend, "that they are still very short of food in Paris?"

"You can see the long queues waiting before the bakeries," answered Massac. "Many feel themselves lucky if they get a small loaf after standing for hours."

"How distressing!" commented the Princess, nibbling at a large bonbon.

Finished at last. The Second Almoner had murmured his hasty "Thanks." The little clink, clink of the silvered swords of the whisking lackeys ceased. The King took the Queen upon his arm, and led his guests into an over-ornate anteroom where all the guests formed an uneven circle and stood at a kind of attention, while their sovereigns passed before them addressing a conventional remark to each.

"The Grand Couvert is completed," at last sounded the majestic voice of Dreux-Brézé, to most general relief.

. . . After the formality, the most charming informality. The guests of the evening mingle with the guests of other evenings who that night have stood as decorous watchers. The King and Queen disappear, reappear in new costumes and jewels. The talk becomes sparkling. What delightful *mots;* what convulsive "indiscretions"! In the numerous half-lighted corners little groups are seated near together. The connoisseur can delight himself in the small spirituel heads, the slender hands, the inimitable gestures and demeanor, the pouting lips, the mutinously turned faces, the plump little wrists peering from their nests of lace, the rapid rustle of the opening fans.

Music once more, and the polite whisper "To the theater." The doors of the royal play-house are open. Everyone finds his own seat. No disagreeable friction as to rank, although by a natural law of gravitation the princesses and duchesses somehow find themselves nearest to the royal box. The theater, from the sculptured ceiling peopled with sporting cupids to the floor with its diamonds, its pearls, and its tier upon tier of gorgeous costumes, seems a gigantic animated bouquet, whereof the eye can scarce support the brilliancy. The Queen does not appear that night on the stage in one of her favorite shepherdess parts, nor the King as the "Village Miller" (his great strength makes him able to carry about heavy meal sacks). However, some of the younger sprigs of the court put on "The Hunter and the Milk-maid," and every one thinks that M. de Miromesnil, the Keeper of the Seals, presents a very smart and finished "rascal lawyer."

The play is not over-long nor taken over-seriously. When amid polite clapping the curtain goes down, the company as politely melts away. It is still only eleven in the evening and mankind (at Versailles at least) lives chiefly to be amused. Etiquette now relaxes completely. You can pass the King or Queen without salutations, while those personages wander about at will. In one apartment there are billiards, in another cards, from a third gay voices summon "violins" and soon wide skirts and walking swords are flitting about in gavottes, the brisk *chaconne,* or the Queen's importation from her Austrian homelands—the Hungarian waltz.

. . . René had just quitted one friendly group to join another, when a hand touched his arm. "Come, my friend." It was the Queen herself and she led him away.

"It seems summer already," she remarked; "we will go out upon the terrace. I think there will be fireworks."

In the coming and going of lights no one remarked them. The Queen's costume again was pure white. Soon they were away from the heated air of the chateau and were moving down the ample staircase which descended from the terrace of the Parterre of the South toward the dark watery sheen of the Pool of the Swiss. Behind them there glittered all the high windows of the vast illuminated chateau. Before them more lights gleamed here and there from the arcades of the splendid Orangery. Constantly they passed other strollers, vivacious chatter, veiled allusions, coquettish glances. From under many of the marble statues which rose white and ghostly along the pathways, came now pretty rustlings, musical voices.

Once or twice the two were recognized, but it was a standing prerogative of the Queen's to take an evening stroll with some congenial young cavalier, while the King (with his correct bourgeois habits) was already being put to bed with all the ritual of the morning *lever* now reversed.

"We have missed you, René," spoke the Queen, as they swung down a bosky avenue with the Orangery now behind them and the faint steely twinkle of the Basin of the Mirror beginning to gleam ahead. "Tell me truly; has your life in Paris and Ard, your friends made there, the strange notions that have turned your head, left you no regrets for leaving *this*—where the world at least would have said 'You have every right to be happy'?"

"A certain regret, yes, Your Majesty. I have been indeed happy in many friendships here. But I have persuaded myself that when my friends at Versailles see humanity as I now see it, the old companionships will become dearer than ever."

"Majesty?" questioned his companion softly. "Why when we are alone must you keep reminding one of your well-wishers that she is also a queen? Remember how we used to pretend that I was your elder sister. Call me again 'Antoinette.'"

"Yes, if so it pleasures you, Sister Antoinette," said the young man smiling.

"That is better. Now we will become a trifle personal. You still persist in your project for marriage? You are deeply in love? Well meant interference has merely hardened your resolution?"

"Yes, Sister Antoinette."

The statue of a Diana with her stag reared its white sculptures in the soft darkness. The seat, barely visible beneath the image, was empty and the Queen led on to it.

"Is it true that your marriage with all it implies is set for the first of May? I have not brought you here to chide you. Merely to ask whether in making an alliance such as none of your race have contracted, you wish to proclaim openly your contempt for your old friends, for those who despite all your freaks and follies have cared for you— who—who care for you still."

"Not in the least, Madame—I mean Sister Antoinette."

"After all," pursued the Queen in a reminiscent vein, "those of us who are said to possess 'rank' and 'family' must pay the forfeit if we would enjoy our glitter. Often, often we must marry as others bid us, and say farewell to a tender passion." The Queen sighed palpably; René knew that she referred to the Swedish Count Fersen, who had been everything to her but her lover.[1]

"Sister Antoinette," answered the young man, avoiding

her glance while his cane stirred lightly in the gravel, "I will be plain with you. My rank is not royal. My hand is my own to give. If I find my happiness in Paris and not in Versailles my philosophy forbids me to say to my happiness, 'Nay.'"

A long moment passed in silence, then the Queen resumed: "You are not angry with me, René, about Vincennes? Of course you have heard everything, and it seemed all for your good. You are not still angry?"

"I am human, therefore I was indeed angry. But the fire has burned away. My happiness with Virginie is so intense that I forgive all but my implacable aunt who has cast shame upon her."

"Give real proof then that you have forgiven." The Queen's tones had become insinuating and tender. "Give proof that your new passion has not poisoned your heart against your elder sister."

"Anything, Sister Antoinette, anything you may ask save a promise not to wed Virginie Durand on May Day."

"I do not ask it. I only ask you to show yourself a true Massac in the service of your King."

"We Massacs are a fighting race, who prove their loyalty by proffering their blood. Europe, unfortunately for that, is at peace."

"For which thank God," spoke the Queen; "and the sacrifice I ask is only trifling. Your marriage is set for May Day. This is March the twenty-first. In two days set forth for the Hague."

"For the Hague, Sister Antoinette? Why would you banish me?"

"Listen, René, a serious question has arisen touching the reinstatement of the Prince of Orange by the Prussian army. A special messenger is needed, one who can take to the ambassador oral as well as written directions. Not a person known as one of the diplomatic staff, but some young private gentleman traveling for pleasure, who can slip across the Austrian Netherlands unrecognized in his mission by my brother Emperor Joseph's police. M. de Montmorin, the foreign minister, requires such a man. I said to him 'To-night I will provide one.' You will go, René?"

"Alas, how can I exist so far from Virginie? When can I return?"

"The business ends a week before May Day, I promise you. Believe me, you will sacrifice very little; from now on you will see less and less of your intended. The last person a bride-to-be can have time for is her betrothed.—I have your promise? I can tell M. de Montmorin?"

"Ah! Sister Antoinette, I am in distress; let me answer to-morrow."

"Then," spoke the Queen in a disappointed accent, "I see I am not truly forgiven. No Massac of the older days would have hesitated before such a mission from his sovereign."

René seized her hand and kissed it: "Say not so, Sister Antoinette. You shall not impugn my sincerity.—Tell M. de Montmorin that I will go."

Marie Antoinette's eyes flashed even amid the darkness: "There spoke our true Chevalier de Massac! I knew his mad philosophy had not lost him. You have my thanks, René, and when you return, if you still *must* push through your amazing marriage I will see what it may be possible to do for—your wife."

. . . Fireworks sprang up that instant by the Cross of the Great Canal. All the retreats among the promenades were penetrated by the long, wavering shadows of the ruddy light. Rockets hissed; blazing balls flew upward; a peacock of colored flames spread his glittering tail above the water. "We may be missed," said the Queen, arising and leading again toward the chateau; and her farewell later with René upon the great parterre again was more than friendly.

The young man sought a bed at his cousin's apartments with his head in a confused whirl of republican protests, and of very human delight at the Queen's astonishing graciousness. We repeat that he was still very young, very human, very little inclined to study strict consistency, or to penetrate motives deeply.

Under the window, as he fell asleep, two young officers of the Body Guard were placing their sentries. Muttered the first: "What made the Queen so devilishly gracious to that lunatic Massac to-night?"

"Damned if I know," rejoined his comrade. "It was for some fine end of course! But this I'm certain of—never bother about *lettres de cachet* when a few nice words from the Shepherdess can work so much better."

CHAPTER X

WHAT ANDRÉ TOLD

THE French embassy at the Hague occupied a tall, majestic brick mansion on one of the quiet, spotlessly clean and eminently burgherly streets near the Binnenhof, the seat of their High Mightinesses the States General. René had found his travel to Holland not too uncomfortable for healthy youth, with an admixture of just enough secrecy in passing through the disturbed Austrian Netherlands to give zest to his mission. The reception at the embassy had been cordial, the business on which Massac had been dispatched of quite sufficient importance to justify a confidential messenger, and the manner in which he discharged a delicate errand proved most satisfactory.

All this did not make the journey to Holland disagreeable, even if René surrendered himself constantly to a delicious melancholy over what he had left in Paris. Virginie herself had professed great pleasure at his accepting the Queen's command. It was a high honor; better still, it was a proof he had been forgiven for throwing up his post at the court and defying the laws of his caste; better still, he would be in a stronger position to invoke powerful patronage after the States General had assembled, in case the much discussed reforms did not go through quite smoothly.

"I shall be waiting for you, my beloved," she had assured, as he for one of the last times, embraced, "you will return long before the first of May. I promise that my preparations then will be complete. We can belong entirely to each other."

René in fact suspected that she was slightly relieved to have him go, and not to press her again to hurry the marriage. His aunt and uncle, he understood, had returned to Versailles, and another encounter with Virginie was hardly to be apprehended. St. Just, Desmoulins, Danton, and all the other friends had promised every attention. With tears and with intense but not too poignant emotions he had set out upon his way.

The mission at the Hague seemed finished. Massac talked of an immediate return, but the ambassador raised difficulties. A few days more and his guest could take back a portfolio of papers not to be entrusted to the ordinary courier. The Chevalier therefore found what amusement he could about the Hague, stared at the Prince of Orange's picture gallery, traveled with a young attaché out to Leiden; diverted himself with the canal life, the round Dutch boats and the equally round Dutch women. One thing only perplexed him. "No letters from Paris": although not merely Virginie but M. Durand and several younger friends had promised to be good correspondents. Vexatious this, but not alarming. Belgium was in increasingly violent insurrection against its Austrian over-lords. Probably all the mail bags, even to the embassies, were being stopped at the frontier. It would be better, no doubt, for him to return the longer way via Cologne and the Rhine-lands.

It was a pleasant April afternoon, with all the spring sunshine and young greenery glowing, when René reëntered the embassy after a stroll by the placid canals. In the vestibule the porter accosted him:

"A man awaits you, M. le Chevalier. From Paris, he says, on urgent business."

"From Paris; urgent; where is he?"

Before the porter could speak twice, René was turning hot and cold. A splashed and disheveled figure was before him, André, major-domo of the Durands.

The face of the good servant was stamped with unspeakable grief. He had evidently traveled to the limit of his strength. When he saw Massac his hands shook and his voice seemed sticking in his throat. The mere sight of this functionary, of wont the most calm and immaculate of mortals, was itself enough to terrify.

"Monsieur; Monsieur, why did you not answer? Why did you not come?"

"Answer? Come? What mean you? I've heard nothing."

"Many letters; piteous, imploring."

"I've had none. For God's sake, André, tell what has happened. How is Virginie?"

"Gone, Monsieur, torn away; oh! horrible."

"Torn away—but her father, M. Durand?"

"Dead, Monsieur, nearly three weeks dead."

The bewildered porter caught the Chevalier while he reeled as if a ball had struck him. As for André, his long tension at an end, he broke into passionate tears. Then the manhood of the nobleman asserted itself. He was deathly pale, but at least his words came firmly:

"This way, my friend. What ever has happened? Tell me at once, spare me nothing."

. . . The story of André (oft interrupted by his own piteous ejaculations) in sum was this. From time to time he had believed that the espionage upon the Durand home had continued, albeit not in a seriously offensive manner. The day after René set forth for Holland a message had come to Mme. Frimont, Virginie's aunt on her mother's side, that her own sister-in-law was seriously ill in Limoges, and thither she had departed immediately. Two days after

that M. Durand had left his house on an evening to attend
a supper given by some savants across the river near the
Sorbonne. In his thrifty bourgeois fashion he had walked
attended by a single linkboy. There had been unpleasant
happenings lately in the darkened streets, still nobody considered such a promenade to be dangerous.

The supper party had ended somewhat late; M. Durand
quitted his friends, set forth homeward with his escort, and
what next befell depended largely on the testimony of the
terrified linkboy. Apparently the unfortunate gentleman
had taken one of the tortuous streets leading to the Pont
Royal when he was suddenly waylaid by two footpads.
The terrified boy dropped the lantern and ran bawling for
his life. M. Durand then may have tried to defend his
purse; in any case two or three gentlemen on the streets,
alarmed by the boy, rushed to the scene, and found M.
Durand stabbed and dying and his assailants making off.
One of the gentlemen, however, was an active fencer. He
ran one of the villains through the body, the wretch dying
instantly, before he could name his companion who escaped.
M. Durand was hastened in a carriage to his home and the
best medical aid in Paris summoned, but he expired in the
arms of his daughter half an hour after they laid him on
his bed.

"That was the first calamity," said André huskily.

"Tell now what befell your mistress," ordered René with
an awful calmness.

The second part of the story was so inexplicable that
Massac wondered whether much suffering had not warped
the loyal messenger's recollection.

"The next day *He* appeared."

"He" was a flashily dressed elderly man of horrid appearance yet with features caricaturing André's dead master.
With him was a woman younger, but hardly less repulsive.

They had flatly announced themselves to be the late M.
Durand's brother and sister-in-law, and demanded the
right to "see and console their niece." André had immediately shown them the door; he took the couple to be stark
mad. Virginie had not been disturbed in her anguish.

The next morning nevertheless (the very day of the
funeral) the couple had appeared again. This time they
were accompanied by an oily procureur flourishing papers
with seals. The lawyer had warned André and the other
servants of the dire penalties for preventing "her lawful
guardians" from having access to Mlle. Durand. André,
in the interval, had recollected certain things his late master had once dropped about his own family history. He
had to admit that "M. and Mme. Thibaud Durand" might
not be complete impostors. However, he stood his ground,
he referred the couple to M. Edmond's family procureur,
M. Gresset, and then excluded them from the house. Virginie during the funeral had borne up heroically. A competent messenger was already dispatched after René, who
had probably just reached the Hague. "A few days must
bring him back!" Meantime, Virginie, refusing to go to
the homes of friends, had remained at the Rue St. Leonard,
comforted by a widowed cousin of her mother.

The next day the Thibaud Durands appeared again.
With them now was M. Gresset himself. The credentials
of the alleged uncle appeared to be flawless. Beyond a
doubt he was Virginie's oldest and nearest male relative
on her father's side. "She was only seventeen, a minor,
and M. Thibaud was her lawful guardian." With great
reluctance the procureur therefore forced André to summon
Virginie to a distressing interview. The utterly boorish
character of this "uncle and aunt" could not be concealed
despite a very thin show of bonhommie and "family affection." Virginie presently had rushed from the salon, double-

bolted herself in her room and abandoned herself to a paroxysm of grief.

The Thibaud Durands became at length more threatening, demanding the immediate custody of their niece. This André and M. Gresset vigorously denied, and the lawyer cautioned them that their brother's estate was absolutely beyond their reach. Virginie was M. Edmond's sole heir. If she died without issue her entire property passed by will to her mother's relatives. The Thibaud Durands could never touch a livre. Still he could not deny that Virginie as an unwedded minor was technically their ward. He could only advise temporizing until Mme. Frimont and other maternal kinsfolk could intervene, and the Chevalier could return. The new uncle and aunt seemed exactly the kind of persons whose claims to guardianship could be readily bought off.

Another day and another. On each the intruders appeared with their procureur, formally demanded their niece, and were unflinchingly repelled by André. The daughter of the great savant, Edmond Durand, could have commanded distinguished protection and service, but Virginie protested passionately against being put to the mortification of having respectable Paris know that her father had possessed such a half-brother. "Besides René would now be back immediately." The matter therefore was kept as quiet as possible, although "the other Durands" were apparently setting nondescript watchers around the house to keep their niece from slipping away.

Still, however, René did not come, and André in desperation went privately to several friends of his late master. They were sympathetic enough but treated the matter as simply a clumsy raid on Virginie's fortune; that she was in any personal peril no one really imagined. Finally, when not the slightest word came from the Chevalier, André betook himself to M. Danton as a more aggressive man-of-the-law than mild M. Gresset. M. Danton unfortunately, however, was in Arcis-sur-Aube on one of his periodic visits to his mother.

One more anxious morning. No word from the Chevalier, none even from Mme. Frimont. Then the blow fell stunningly. The Thibaud Durands appeared on Rue St. Leonard, this time with a coach and three plumed and sabered sergeants of police. They waved under the nose of André a document signed by the Lieutenant of Police himself. "Warrant for a stubborn girl," announced the leader, thrusting back first the helpless major-domo and footman, and then the wildly protesting cousin-companion herself. The house was entered, Virginie dragged forth in an agony. André's last glimpse of her had been of her struggling form being thrust into a great berlin. He had seen it lumber into Rue Honoré, then found legs to take himself to M. Gresset. That gentleman hurried to the office of the Lieutenant of Police, and the deputy Lieutenant had curtly told him that the recovery of disobedient wards or children for parents or guardians was a common official duty, and that the Thibaud Durands' papers had been unassailable.

"After that, M. le Chevalier," concluded André simply, "seeing you still did not come, I asked myself 'Did he receive the message?' I set forth myself for the Hague, and I went by the Rhine-lands."

One hour later René de Massac went through the southern gate of the Hague toward Delft as fast as gold, prime horse flesh and frantic youth could carry him.

Rotterdam, Antwerp, Brussels, Valenciennes, Compiègne; the rider passed them in a flame. Questioning Belgian officials had been bullied and swept aside. Sleep and rest were things forgotten. Arnaud, René's sole companion, who had

followed "the Old Chevalier" to the wars, galloped with
him as the veteran never had galloped before. Eight-and-
forty hours saw them pounding down the Rue St. Denis
with a terrible light blazing still in Massac's eyes.

The afternoon was waning but the tired horses were
flogged straight on to M. Gresset's office on the Place de
Grève. René found the mild-mannered procureur within,
and in the briefest possible time secured confirmation of
André's story. "Where now is Virginie?" he demanded at
the end.

The kindly lawyer threw up his hands. "Have I the
power to trace her?—The berlin that carried the Durands
was noticed upon the Rue St. Honoré; after that Paris
swallowed it.—But I assure you, Monsieur, I have seen to
it that these scoundrels have not touched as yet one farth-
ing of the property."

"The property!" With an ungracious curse bursting from
his throat, Massac flung himself out to seek a more redoubt-
able helper—Georges Danton.

The avocat's office, in an old building upon the Rue
Tixandrie, was now closed, but soon René discovered him
at his comfortable flat on the first floor of a house at the
corner of the Rue des Cordeliers and the Cour du Commerce. Compassion as well as power vibrated through the
voice of the big man when his hand gripped that of his
visitor:

"Yes, I have heard. Back from Arcis only four hours
ago. Camille was here to tell me. He and all your other
friends are beside themselves. Why did not Virginie appeal
to them instead of shutting herself away? If I had only
been in Paris! If that Gresset had not been such a pedantic ass!"

"Do you question this abominable claim to kinship? Is
there legal color behind the kidnaping?"

" 'Kinship'? Very likely. 'Legal color'? Very possibly too. But if Gresset had seen in these hideous doings anything but a clumsy attempt at blackmail, we might have explored the rat-holes of the law, won long delays, got at the inwardness of this plot, blasted it. Now the deed is done; the scent is very cold. Still I am your friend at service. Clear your memory and answer questions. What sent you to the Hague?"

Even in his grief René was fain to admire the calm legal mind with which the avocat probed into everything. At last Danton paused:

"Do you still believe, my dear friend, that Virginie was carried off solely because this gallows-bird of an uncle hoped to rifle an heiress? Could he get all the letters sent to you stopped?"

"What else, the wretch? She was innocent as an angel. Not an enemy in the universe. Her father died suddenly: then this Thibaud Durand marked her instantly for his prey."

"Good fellow," affirmed Danton, "you grow to man's estate and still you walk in virgin guilelessness. You need a guardian yourself. Virginie was about to be married. Who opposed that marriage?"

René's hands swung in vehement denial: "My aunt and uncle are implacable, but after all they are Massacs. To some things a Massac cannot stoop. This is one of them. Besides, they did not send me to the Hague."

"Who did then? Of course you have just told me."

"No, no," protested the Chevalier even fiercely, "there are ugly things I grant, but *she* is incapable of such a villainy. M. Durand was alive and well when she asked me to accept the mission.—Some hellish coincidence."

"Say rather," corrected the avocat with a low voice but a very hard eye, "there is a certain impulsive and willful lady of great power who, when she desires a thing, in sheer ignorance is capable of using smooth agents who blindfold her as to their necessary course of action when they promise her success.—Yet how does this aid Virginie? Go to your apartment, sleep, steel yourself for the worst; come to me in the morning and I will bring you all the tidings possible."

Morning, after a sleepless night despite unspeakable weariness, brought news if not consolation. Danton had put forth a devouring energy. Though the evening had commenced he had flown straight to the Châtelet, the vast, grim prison and police office near the Tower of St. Jacques. "I must see M. the Lieutenant General of Police." His Excellency the Lieutenant General, of course had left his bureau. Danton, who had observed a well-known carriage waiting its master near the entrance, merely extended a half-louis to the doorkeeper, and Danton soon saw His Excellency the Lieutenant of Police.

M. de Crosné, master of a veritable army of "archers," "sergeants" and "mouchards" (secret agents), became a most uncomfortable great man when Danton pressed him. The avocat already had fame as a very successful and aggressive pleader before the High Court of Appeal. He asked blunt questions and looked straight into the Lieutenant's eyes. M. de Crosné was speedily wishing he had not acceded quite so promptly to the bland suggestions of an unnamed personage. Before long M. de Crosné was inwardly praying heaven that he might not be caught as the chief victim of a public scandal. Candor becoming somewhat the best policy, Danton therefore gained if not all the facts, at least very many of them.

First of all as to the bandit who killed M. Edmond Durand? His body had been identified as that of one Vadier, professionally "The Lizard," late of the galleys and undoubtedly willing to use a dagger for pay. He himself had been killed in his tracks by a M. de Linio. "Not that 'Baron' de Linio, the notorious card expert?" "The same," Crosné confessed reluctantly. "Was it not amazing then that Vadier had perished so very suddenly, before he could be seized and interrogated?"—Perhaps so. "And had Linio been examined as to how he came so opportunely on the assassin?"—A regrettable oversight: he had been questioned only perfunctorily. "And yet was not the 'Baron' himself wanted earnestly by the police?" Another regrettable mistake: by this time M. de Crosné was fidgeting nervously.

Pass now to Thibaud Durand. The Lieutenant of Police had of course the clear duty of assisting parents and guardians in recovering stubborn girls, but this was a most amazing case:—Mlle. Durand, a most respectable young woman, friends, wealth, betrothed to a nobleman. What pains had been taken to test this upstart uncle's fitness to have her custody?—M. de Crosné by this time was growing somewhat red.

"The Lieutenant would be good enough to recall that there were decisions of Parliament that infamous persons forfeited all rights of guardianship." The "Yes" was extremely uneasy, but "a deputy had handled the case"; very possibly, nevertheless, there had been a little precipitation, although Thibaud's demand for police assistance had seemed absolutely legal.

Still the avocat continued to search his memory, and to compare descriptions of "Mme. Thibaud Durand" with those of a certain Olympie Buchez, who had been an accomplice in a notorious shoplifting case a few years back, and who had served her term in the St. Pelagie bridewell. "His Excellency would recall?" His Excellency did recall— "doubtless a mere coincidence."

"A mere coincidence!" Danton's tone became steely.

He began to talk about the Chevalier's projected marriage and cast hints of deep intrigues and high personages. The Lieutenant of Police at this point cut him short, confessed that "possibly a slight mistake had been made," and heartily promised that all the machinery of his office should be invoked to find Thibaud Durand and get the case reopened. M. de Crosné was sincere enough now: inwardly he was in fact wishing he had a certain Court Abbé in a snug cell in the Châtelet with permission to use torture. What had presented itself as a safe and not unusual shutting of one's eyes to formal duty suddenly had become a very different business. Danton left the Châtelet satisfied he had done all that was then possible.

For the next three days René existed on hopes. The "outward police" and the far more efficient "secret police" bestirred themselves. Haunts of evil were explored. Reports soon came in of Thibaud Durand's sojourn in Paris. He and Olympie had lodged for a few weeks in a cheap tenement across the Seine near the Church of St. Geneviève. It was established that Linio had undoubtedly been among their few visitors. On the day that Virginie was carried off, Thibaud had hired a closed coach, and after the three police agents had seized her and placed her in the vehicle, had thrust two crowns upon each with "Your work's ended." Then he had ordered the coach driven to an inn outside the barriers and near the Bois de Boulogne.

The two hired postilions were soon brought in to testify that they had heard cries and struggling inside the coach, although Virginie had been helpless as a kitten. The resistance, however, soon ceased. At the inn a strange, closed cabriolet with a heavily muffled driver had met them. Thibaud had hastily given the postilions a liberal pourboire, then lifted out his niece. By this time Mlle. Durand was hanging in his arms in a kind of stupor. Thibaud and his wife had thrust her in the cabriolet, entered themselves, and immediately the whip cracked and off the unknown vehicle tore northward possibly toward Neuilly. The honest postilions were somewhat distressed: the thing seemed brutal and unusual. But the proceedings had police countenance, and they had their money. Therefore they drove the coach back to Paris.

"Had not Mlle. Durand been drugged in the berlin?" demanded Danton at the hearing.

"Why, so it might seem, Monsieur."

With that the discoveries ended. The police had run upon a blank wall. The strange cabriolet apparently had emerged from nowhere: into nowhere it had vanished. Linio had disappeared as completely. Urgent appeals to the authorities in districts as remote as Orleans, Rouen and Reims produced nothing, although backed by great offers of reward. Inquiries could be made near Ard about Thibaud Durand, but they would take much time. From Limoges, however, came a distressed letter from Mme. Frimont. Her sister-in-law there was perfectly well, and the summons for Mme. Frimont to come to her had been forged. She was returning immediately in great anguish to Paris. Finally the messenger sent after René reappeared. He had been halted at the frontier as an Austrian secret agent, held long in custody, then suddenly released. "Mistaken identity and abject apologies." *Cui bono?* Another "coincidence"!

The friends of René shuddered when they saw his face aging from day to day with ever strengthening despair. In his anguish he took himself to Versailles to demand an audience with the Queen. What violent scene might have ensued history records not, for upon arrival he was told that the King, Queen and immediate court had just set forth for St. Germain. The Dauphin was worse, perhaps the change of air would better him; in any case the Queen was refusing all audiences in order to discharge her duties as a mother.

Back then again to Paris and overpowering discouragement. René ceased at length to haunt the Châtelet, and hang on the idle conjectures of police sergeants who took his money. Virginie, he averred, had been murdered; he could only avenge her, although Danton vowed quite otherwise: "Not murdered; that could have been compassed with ease without all this rotten comedy. She lives; we shall hear something." But more days glided, and "something" was not heard. The ocean might have closed over Virginie Durand and her unlovely kinsfolk. Concerning De Massac's inward thoughts we say nothing. The faintest clue he would have followed to Otaheite, yet he seemed doomed to linger and brood in Paris.

St. Just's consolations to him became terrible: "After all this hideous plot why have you not taken Hannibal's oath —not of eternal warfare against Rome, but of eternal warfare against kings? *Now* do you believe that the Utopia will come painlessly; that men will not be tried with fire and made to drink of the cup of fury and the dregs of the cup of trembling?"

"I begin to agree with you," came the hopeless answer.

The next time René saw Father François, he said to him, "My Father, this calamity has destroyed my faith in God."

"Say rather, my son, faith in God is the one thing which makes such calamities supportable."

"I have lost Virginie; what in life have I left?"

"You are a man, a Frenchman, a deputy. You have France left. You owe it to France to hasten the day when crimes like this will become forever impossible. A good soldier does not desert his colors because of private grief. Do your duty. The battle is just before us."

Father François was right. While Massac had been agonizing, April had almost waned. From east, west, north, south the twelve hundred chosen by the Three Estates were converging upon Versailles.

BOOK II
LIBERTY"

CHAPTER XI

A CHAPTER OF HISTORY

Deputy René de Massac writing to the Avocat, M. Paul Colet in Ard, May, 1789.

". . . Inasmuch, Monsieur, as you are one of my most friendly and influential constituents, I report as follows to you confidentially:

"Once more we are in Versailles, where in the inimitable phrase of Voltaire, *'Kings are condemned to magnificence.'* Alas! my friend, that magnificence has not provided a proper insight into a Great People's needs. I am overwhelmed with apprehensions. This briefly is what has happened:

"On May the first, the King-at-arms and his fellow heralds proclaimed with great solemnity the convoking of the States General.

"On May the second the twelve hundred deputies were received at the Palace. The curés came in their cassocks, the bishops in their purple, the nobles in the superb costumes of the old days of Henry IV., but we the six hundred spokesmen for the Third Estate were strictly commanded to appear only in the soberest black. Less flattering still we were only admitted by narrow side entrances into the Royal Cabinet, after the Clergy and Nobles had been given a far more honorable reception. The King, the Queen and the royal brothers [1] received our bows with the most chilly courtesy, the King sitting as impassive as the bronze Buddha I have seen at Leiden. Dreux-Brézé, the Master of Ceremonies, addressed us as 'Good People' as he might so many peasants. Clearly the Court was determined to teach

[1] The Counts of Provence ("Monsieur"—Louis XVIII) and Artois (Charles X).

127

us deputies of the Commons our humble place. We left the Royal Reception perplexed and even angry.

"On May the fourth took place a splendid procession of the Holy Sacrament. The pageant devoured all thoughts of religion. The display of copes, canopies, gold lace and plumes was superb. But I observed that few people cheered the Queen, concerning whom the most unfriendly rumors were current.

"May the fifth was the actual day for convening. We met in the *Salle des Menus Plaisirs*, the 'Hall of the King's Small Diversions.' A glittering spectacle it was of the Princes of the Blood, and the Court officers and ministers surrounding the King and the Queen, but we 'Men in Black' again, by our insulting treatment, were made to feel ourselves an inferior order of beings.

"The King's speech was short and inconclusive. The speech of M. Necker, the Finance Minister, whom all expected to present a wise programme for the rehabilitation of France, droned through two mortal hours and left us wondering. He talked simply as might a bank manager facing his directors: endless figures and 'deficit, deficit,' but nothing about civil reforms. Were we to meet as three separate bodies, so that the Court could drive its wedges between the Nobles, Clergy and Commons, or as one body where the liberal Clergy uniting surely with the Third Estate would give a majority for sweeping reforms? *That* was, and is, the colossal question: and King and Minister have given it not the slightest answer. Yet upon that answer we all dread may now hang the actual fate of France.

"Nevertheless I maintain hope. We have two notable leaders, the Abbé Sieyès sitting for the Paris Commons, and above all the dauntless Marquis de Mirabeau, who already stands shoulders above us all, thanks to his courage, eloquence and sage liberality. Our mutual friend from Arras, M. de Robespierre, is confident that we may still accomplish great things. I hear indeed an incredible rumor —that the old Maréchal de Broglie, at the behest of the Court, is bringing up numerous regiments to overawe the deputies if we fail to cringe to royal dictation. This outrageous tale I refuse to believe; but true or false, my constituents in Ard will find their representative a soldier at his post. Accept, Monsieur, my highest considerations, etc., etc., . . ."

. . . .

While these words were being penned, M. l'Abbé Vernet, in an unusually secular dress, was leaning across the table in an obscure Versailles inn, facing a person who, despite a muffler and wig, might possibly have been taken by the curious for M. le Baron de Linio. Vernet certainly was in better humor than his companion.

"May the fifth," went his remark, "and the world must observe that the noble Chevalier de Massac still perforce clings to celibacy."

Linio comforted himself with an oath: "Much good have *I* gained by it! As nice a bit of work as was ever brought off—and what so far to show beyond a few louis and the private thanks of your reverend self? At least I thought that I might walk around Paris again without disguise."

"Softly, my dear Baron, softly," enjoined the Abbé. "I regret exceedingly that the Lieutenant of Police has somehow resumed his anxiety to renew your distinguished acquaintance. It seems to be beyond my power to dissuade him. You recall that I refuse to press you for details about your doings, but again you have my thanks."

"Thanks don't clink like a money bag. I tell you I'm getting peevish. Thibaud and that termagant of his grow importunate. We have the girl—what use is she? Where is her fortune?"

"Softly again, my friend. I regret to criticize; but that sudden departure from this life of M. Durand at the hands of the Lizard, that was a little *too* providential. Of course we must take every advantage of the sudden dispensations of God; and again I firmly decline to ask questions, yet let me add this, I have had to smooth and even (considering my cloth) to prevaricate to my noble principals in order to explain certain happenings in a way to quiet delicate consciences. Since you compel me to say it—some things might have been managed a little better."

"In any case the trull is far from Paris. That's what was bargained. You forbade us to kill her. She is alive.—I do not exert my talents solely for my health.—Well now?——"

Vernet laid down his fork and his manner became more ingratiating: "My dear Baron, I need not commend to you the Christian virtue of patience. I need not remark that recompense can come in several ways.—Virginie Durand is an heiress."

"You needn't remind me. Much of her property we've handled so far!"

"Of course, of course. All things come to those who wait."

"*Peste*, speak plainly even if you are a court abbé."

"Well then, she can be worth infinitely more to you, my friend, if she's living, than if she's dead. That high-born lover of hers——"

"Has set the police again after me."

Vernet dropped his voice to a cautious whisper: "That high-born lover of hers may soon have more troubles than the loss of a mistress. Listen. This grand spectacle to-day can turn most readily into an abominable farce. Perhaps the States General will prove docile, will do the will of the King—of the Queen, of course I mean, and of Artois and of the high Noblesse. More probably it will prove as obstinate as twelve hundred asses. In that case when there are still more regiments in Versailles—prut! Our Chevalier and his friends then had better to flee France or they will go to Vincennes or the Bastille for a pretty long sojourn. My authority is the best——"

"Then the girl," Linio's tones suddenly became excited, "stays completely in our hands, and she is an heiress?"

"And you are unmarried, my Baron," completed Vernet.

Linio leaped to his feet with sheer joy as he comprehended. *"Bon dieu!* What a prospect you open. My head whirls. I cannot take in my good fortune. You will be the author of my happiness."

The Abbé folded his napkin complacently: "At length then you see my wisdom when I said 'Do not let the girl by some misfortune die.' Only two months now to wait, my dear friend."

CHAPTER XII

THE VOICE OF MIRABEAU

FIVE weeks while the green of May changed into the deeper green of June, and while Versailles seethed with intrigue and with rumor. The States General had obstinately refused to proceed to business. In their own hall, despite protests by Lafayette and other liberals, met the Noblesse. In their own hall, despite protests of a strong minority of the curés, met the Clergy. But in the Hall of the Small Diversions the six hundred in black stubbornly refused to organize until the other two orders joined them.

All France knew what that would mean. The Third Estate would vote as a unit, and aided by a sprinkling of liberal nobles and churchmen it would dominate the assemblage; then farewell to discriminating taxes, *lettres de cachet*, sinecures, unearned pensions. Let the deputies meet separately as three jangling orders, and the court could block everything. The fate of the realm hung on this one issue.

"Bide your time," Father François observed knowingly to René, "we are coming over."

Finally on June the tenth the Third Estate, having for the last time summoned the other orders to "join us," declared itself competent to speak for all France. Two days later it named the great astronomer Bailly as its president. On the thirteenth it cheered three curés who seceded to it; and on the fourteenth it threw down the gauntlet, voting itself the *National Assembly of France*, and declared all taxation "illegal" save after receiving its own high consent.

Prodigious talking around all the restaurant tables that night; a still mightier talking in the gilded corridors which led to the Oeil-de-Boeuf.

. . . .

"We are summoned to give a fresh start to history," announced a deputy on the fifteenth of June; but how now would history be newly started? Great nobles shook their canes on the street at the Third Estate deputies. The display of soldiers grew ever more menacing. "We shall soon be back in our provinces," wrote one member to his family, hoping earnestly that it would be really "home" and not a cell in a royal fortress. The chamber of nobles was faction rent and almost brawling. At length on the nineteenth Massac, with every other Commoner in the hall, started to his feet. The thing longed for had happened.

A noise like thunder was rising in the streets. A priest in a cassock thrust himself into the hall, a noisy throng was behind. "Won! Won! Won!" rose the shout. Behind the priest was a purple surplice, another, another, and a lord abbot. After these cheering, weeping for very joy, were a hundred and forty-three priests and prelates. The Six Hundred stood, cheered, shouted "Long live the good bishops"; then almost smothered with their embraces Father François and the other champions of the fusion.

Not less the cheering because of the report that the defeated anti-liberal prelates were already storming the King's cabinet "to save his clergy from rebellion and infidelity."

"The first move on the chessboard is ours," remarked Father François, while René rejoiced, "but await to-morrow."

. . . June the twentieth. A rainy Saturday morning.

The palace had kept ominously quiet. By twos and threes the deputies came plodding down the narrow Rue St. Martin to enter the Hall of the Small Diversions. Umbrellas were dripping, mud was splashing on the black stockings and knee breeches. Before the entrance pressed already a wetted, steaming mass of heads and umbrellas, but the door was fast closed. Massac forced his way through the ever denser crowd and read for himself the words upon a small scrap of paper nailed upon the door *"Closed by Royal Order";* while from within came the noise of hammering as from many carpenters. No ceremonious warning; no advance notice whatever. The door was bolted fast. Shouts and much pounding returned only echoes.

Who spoke it first? Or did twenty call it together? Did the thought flash at the outset from kindling eye to kindling eye, "To the Tennis Court"?—A great shoving to get inside the great bare area; murmurs, louder voices, conflicting counsels, then above the milling, jostling throng rose the commanding form of Bailly the president, standing upon a table and beckoning for some kind of order.

"We are barred from our place. No notice was sent me. It is rumored that our hall is closed to make ready for a royal session. What is your will? Shall we wait for another speech by the King, a speech perhaps not truly his own, or shall we take firm action for the welfare of France?"

"Action! Action!" all in one roar.

"Good then, Messieurs. What action is proposed?"

"Let us go to Paris. Paris will protect us," came the high voice of Abbé Sieyès.

"Flight is cowardly," flung back several.

Then on a chair leaped Mounier of Grenoble, his tones commanding first silence, then evoking a thunderous cheer:

"Let us take an oath, let every deputy take an oath,

never to separate until a Constitution has been established for France!"

"Constitution! Constitution! We swear it! We swear it!"

Grave men suddenly were in a kind of frenzy. Out of somewhere there came ink, pens, a long sheet for inscribing names. Every deputy present, barring a single weak-kneed doubter, crowded to sign. Indescribable emotion surged over the members. They were no longer a programless mass awaiting the promptings of the King. They were a sovereign assembly present to execute the passionate desire of France. René de Massac, young and possessed by an intense ecstasy, embraced, or was embraced, by half a dozen utter strangers. Iron cheeks were wet. "CONSTITUTION! CONSTITUTION!" All the resentments for a thousand years of feudal wrongs were bursting up behind that word.

Bailly shouted off the oath once more. Once more the upturned faces thundered "We swear it!"—Then out into the streets again; the rain was still falling, but the deputies were laughing, gesticulating, cheering like men turned mad. No chessboard move now, but an ultimatum to the palace. "Treason," no doubt, so busy tongues would soon be volleying to the King. But the oath-takers were indescribably happy; the long tension was over; they were bidding the Oeil-de-Boeuf and all the regiments in Versailles to dare their worst; while unseen voices, stronger than all the cheering, were saying in each heart, "Fear not; behind you is France!"

• • • • • • •

June the twenty-third. Another rainy, sultry morning. The court at length was showing its teeth. The soldiery had been at the background in that great pageant on May the fourth. They were brutally conspicuous now. Along the half mile from the Palace to the Hall of the Small

Diversions four thousand men with bayonets fixed stood to their arms. Amid the park groves and shrubbery, and even more openly before the wide barrack parades were the great masses of infantry waiting the call to action. As René de Massac took his way to the National Assembly ("States General" no longer) fate again sent him upon Laurent, this time hasting across the plaza before the chateau in his best gala uniform. The lieutenant of the Body Guard greeted affably, then took his cousin by the arm. "Best-loved simpleton, you know that I abominate your principles but that I would shed my blood for you. Don't carry your heroics too far."

"We may differ as to what is 'too far,'" smiled René.

"Well, 'too far' is another trip to a royal fortress and much more than six weeks of the Fat Boy's hospitality. To-day the court is going to show its teeth. Caution your friends."

"I pray you to speak plainer."

"*Parbleu*, cousin! I always have to pinch myself as reminder that you've joined the enemy. There are now some things that I've no right to tell, but this fox at least may slip from the net: Your 'assemblies' and 'oaths' have put a certain high lady into a most majestic temper. She'll stick at nothing to be rid of you. Only the Fat Boy's good nature stands as yet between you and some very firm orders to Broglie, the commandant.—Don't fail to heed to-day what the Fat Boy has to say."

"I know the King, Laurent. We can scoff at him, but his heart is honest. In a few things at least he must stand fast."

"Do not trust to him. Fear the Shepherdess; fear Artois."

A trumpet summoned from the Marble Court of the palace, and Laurent departed on the run.

. . . One more great spectacle. Between the streets

lined by the bayonets swung the long cortège of the gilded carriages, outriders and plumes. The populace of Versailles crowded up behind the soldiers, but there was no cheering, not even at the passage of the King. Louis looked fat and unhappy under his billow of silken robes. The Queen held her head erect, but the women in the crowd whispered, "She's well rouged" (the invalid Dauphin had in fact died scarcely two weeks before). Artois alone was laughing, bowing to every one. Had he not all but drafted the speech which his brother was to deliver?

Once more the Commons were "taught their place." The Clergy and Nobles had all been admitted before the Third Estate could enter the hall by a narrow side door, and fill the least honorable benches. There were defiant scowls and audible asides; many of the deputies, in fact, had firmly seated themselves before some resplendent functionary had proclaimed his "Gentlemen, the King gives you leave to sit down."

At last the King was on the throne, but at his left Marie Antoinette (a sheen of silk and a blaze of jewels) stood upright. Louis turned to her with all the grace possible, and motioned her to her own throne. She courtesied but still continued standing, as if determined to focus all scrutiny upon herself and show to every dissident that if the voice which he heard was the King's, the will which spoke behind it was another's.

Louis rose with a twitching, bustling manner, and read forth his own speech. His accents were loud, clear, and this day certainly his meaning was unmistakable. Soon the reactionary nobles and prelates were applauding. There were plenty of gracious sentiments, promises of good things for all Frenchmen, but there was to be no "division of authority." The "States General" were to meet separately in their three old orders. They were to pass no legislation

touching the rights of the Clergy or Nobility, or of seigneurial property. They were not to decide when or how
the later States General were to be held. Above all the
deputies were to remember that nothing must shake the
ancient power of the King. "Remember, gentlemen, none
of your plans can become law save as *I* approve." And
the final words rang out harshly: "I command you therefore to disperse at once. To-morrow let each one of you
go to the hall assigned to his order. *Such is my will.*"

Naked despotism had spoken; the old despotism of Louis
XIV. Amid dead silence the King resumed his seat, then
rose almost instantly and turned to depart; the Queen was
immediately beside him and took his hand with a sweeping
glance of unmistakable triumph over the twelve hundred
tense faces before her. Out went the royal pair amid a
loud rustle of silk. Out went all their colorful escort after
them. The "Royal Session" had passed into eternity.

Silence prolonged; and then, not without victorious smiles
from dukes and marquises, the entire body of the Noblesse
rose and marched with dignity out of the hall, even the
liberal members, even Lafayette going with them; for had
not the King spoken? A motion next among the purple
robes, the bishops were rising. Many of the curés among
the Clergy stirred, hesitated, and part at least followed the
prelates, part sank back in their seats. But the six hundred
Men in Black stirred not, solid and stiff they sat with
unmoved faces, every man of them listening to the beating
of his own heart.

This the end of the regeneration of France? This the
end of countless hopes? This the vindication of the Oath
of the Tennis Court?—To hear the snap of the whip from
the chateau!

Still they sat, waiting, wondering, hardly whispering. A
noise at length, workmen entering, the lowering of the great

canopy above the throne; the banging removal of the vacant
thrones and the stools of the princes; the rolling up of car-
pets. But the Men in Black stirred not.

And now outside the open portal there gleamed bright
steel, swords, bayonets; the blue uniforms of the French
Guard, the red of the Swiss Guard; finally came the rattle
of musket-butts as they grounded on the pavements. The
soldiers did not enter, but directly through the door and
out before the silent deputies, with a squeak of crimson
morocco shoes, strode the figure of Dreux-Brézé.

The Master of Ceremonies had rouged more than ordinarily. His wig was craped to the last hair. His dress
was a marvel of red, violet and gold lace. The gems flashed
from the white hands that held the white staff of office.
Straight before Bailly the President he walked, bowed not
at all, but spoke a few words in tones so low that few could
catch them. For the first time voices came from the
benches, "Louder!" Bailly, deathly pale, was answering
"The Assembly must consider the question," when Dreux-
Brézé, tapping his wand loudly on the planking, flung out
his command with accents hard as iron. "Messieurs; you
have heard the King's orders. His Majesty bids you retire."

Then even while the uniforms shone by the door a great
voice broke from the front benches, the voice of Mirabeau:

"We have heard the words put in the mouth of the King;
but you, sir, who have neither place here nor right of
speech, go tell those who sent you, *that we are here by the
will of the People, and that only bayonets will drive us
out!*"

Then a thinner voice, but calm and resolute, the voice of
Sieyès: "We are to-day what we were yesterday; let us
deliberate."

Dreux-Brézé's jaw fell slightly. Apparently he tried to
speak but the retort failed him, yet lifelong etiquette did

not forsake. With silent gravity he backed out of the hall, this time with an ironic congé toward Bailly. At the entrance he was seen speaking with an officer and the officer was shaking his head. "No orders," heard the deputies nearest the door. Then, wonder of wonders, the muskets of the platoons snapped up to shoulder, the soldiers were heard tramping away, followed by a deep, low cheer from within the hall.

The debate was vigorous, but counsels were undivided. *Voted*, that all the earlier enactments should stand. *Voted*, that the Third Estate should still demand the attendance of the other orders. *Voted* (chief item of all, that the person of each deputy should be sacred, whoever arresting one becoming an enemy of the Nation.

Adjournment at last. The commands of the King had been defied as royal commands had not been defied across the centuries. *"The Will of the People!"*—when before had such a sovereignty been proclaimed in France?

.   .   .   .

Dreux-Brézé himself brought to the palace that answer which smelt of gunpowder. The swords of the Body Guard rattled in their scabbards. The Queen herself (deathly pale now and trembling with anger), with "Monsieur," Artois, Condé and others of the Blood made haste to seek out the heir of St. Louis and Charlemagne.

"His Majesty is not in the Oeil-de-Boeuf." Where then? "His Majesty is at his diversion of lock-making."

No ceremony: "The case is urgent." At length they found the Very Christian King in a remote workroom in a wing of the palace. The place was cluttered with tools and benches. Two men stripped to their shirts were busy over a vise. One was obviously a hired mechanic, the other (hair disheveled, neck bare, hands dirty) was Louis, busily shaping a key with a file. His looks gave the intruders no welcome; his smile was weary; his whole air bespoke, "I have done just as you asked me; why disturb me again?"

"What now, Madame? What now, Messieurs?" was his greeting with strained civility, laying down the file.

"What now, Sire?" Marie Antoinette's words came in a torrent. "Must the King of France be the last to know what his entire court knows already? The Third Estate has defied you!"

"Well?" The King's tone had become still more weary.

"The deputies stubbornly refuse to disperse. When Dreux-Brézé reminded them of their duty, they drove him from the hall with insults."

"Well?"

"They have defied you; do you hear me, Sire! They continue their sitting, vote their pretended decrees, adjourn at pleasure. They persist that the other two orders must join them."

"Well?"

"Holy Virgin!" moaned the Queen, her eyes darting fury; "do I talk to the King or an impostor; to the heir of Francis I, Henry IV, Louis XIV or——"

"Calm yourself, Madame," interposed Monsieur with studied deliberation. "Permit me to talk to my brother." —Then he continued, "I cannot conceive, Sire, that you will fail to do instantly what alike your royal honor and the safety of your realm demands."

"Do what?" Louis' large eyes were blank and inquiring.

"Bid your junior colonel to take three companies. Clear the hall where these rebels meet; clap all their leaders in black dungeons; bid the heralds proclaim that the States General be dissolved."

"Dissolved?" The King's face began to comprehend, but his uneasy smile had changed into a heavy frown. "Dissolved? You would actually have me break up the States General with soldiers, brother?"

"What else? Was that not as good as resolved upon yesterday in the Council, if the fools ventured to defy you?"

"But France, its hopes, the deficit, the taxes! No, no, it would be too harsh. I dare not do it. Such disappointment among my people, my *good* people."

"*Scélérat!*" burst from the Queen, turning from white to red; "am I Maria Theresa's child and yet wedded to a bourgeois tinker?"

"Does not the blood of Henry of Navarre run in our veins, Sire?" observed Artois loftily. "Shall we hesitate to draw his sword at the summons of honor?"

Louis shook his head vehemently: "Honor to draw it against Frenchmen? No, no!"

"Where is Maréchal de Broglie?" demanded the Queen. "Let us have end to this. He shall get his orders."

"The Marshal is at hand, Madame," informed Condé, as into the workroom walked the veteran general. Artois turned to him instantly.

"M. the Marshal, your coming is timely. The King is about to impose upon you certain commands."

"And I, Monseigneur, have even now hastened to the King, to beseech him to hear me, before issuing what I fear those commands will be."

"What have you to say then?" demanded the Queen unceremoniously.

"Simply this, Madame; my officers have just told me 'None of the French regiments will fire on the deputies.' "

A bursting hand-grenade might have caused less consternation. Marie Antoinette's hands flew to her throat. Monsieur, underbreath, murmured, "Jesu!" Artois and Condé crossed themselves.

"Are you sure, Marshal?" whispered Monsieur at last.

"Sure, upon my father's soul. The men are bewitched. I dare risk nothing and the King must wait."

The King's face shone with a marked relief. "Well then, confound it—let the deputies stay."

His eyes went back longingly to the file and the key. The Queen threw up her hands in a kind of horror, then turned almost fiercely upon Broglie. "So we are driven to the last resort—to the Swiss and the German mercenaries."

The Marshal nodded. "Your Majesty speaks well—they can be relied upon."

"Will they be summoned to Versailles?" cried Artois.

"They will be summoned to Versailles."

"And how long then before——"

"Two weeks, Monseigneur."

The Queen, who had turned her back upon her husband, clinched her fists, unclinched them, then laughed shrilly, hysterically. "Two weeks! Good—we will bide our time; and by then that man, I say *that* man will learn that he happens to be a King and will learn how to give his orders."

The company quitted the workroom with the slightest possible adieus. The last they heard was the rasping of the file as Louis bent over the workbench.

CHAPTER XIII

THE FOREST LEAVES HAVE EARS

NICOLAS was a peasant, ignorant and poor. The winter had been hard in Massac village, but the Chevalier's steward at the chateau had distributed a little black and moldy bread. Nicolas, therefore, had not been driven to live on boiled stalks and dried grass, as had the peasants in some neighboring villages.

Nicolas had married young, because married men were not subject to harsh militia duty. He and Brigitte had atoned for their lack of lands and livres by having fourteen, or, some people said, fifteen children. No matter if the count was mixed, all but six of the babies had died soon after birth. Brigitte was now only thirty-five, but she was as withered, wrinkled and gray as an old woman. Nicolas, we have already said, looked sixty and was actually only forty. Their two eldest daughters were married, and Nicolas was long since a grandfather.

He was regularly a woodcutter in the seigneurial forest, but he also tilled a little strip of land which he had ploughed this spring with Brigitte tagging at the wooden plough,. along with Ninon, their thin, old dun cow. Manure lacked and even seed grain was scanty, so the yield might be deplorable. Still Nicolas' spirits were reviving with the spring. They had not starved, the smallpox had not ravaged the village, and in the stocking were two bright louis, the Chevalier's gift. They were saving this treasure to buy a hand cart with iron tires, invaluable for dragging wood.

The spring had been quiet, but as June advanced most remarkable things began to be told in the village. Nicolas could hardly believe his ears when one afternoon he squandered two sous over a pot at the *Silver Swan*. Long Aubri, a well-to-do peasant, had just sold his pigs in Ard. He was displaying, per custom, the fine olive coat with brass buttons, he had brought back, and the ear-rings for "his old woman," when a most usual question was asked, "Did you hear whether taxes were to be higher this year?"

Aubri at once held up a finger. "I heard a wonderful thing. A carter straight from Paris told it. There are to be *no taxes* this year."

"No taxes!" The tap-room gave one great echo of incredulity.

"Listen, neighbors. They say that the great men who went to Versailles to talk with the King, our Chevalier and the others—'deputies' they call 'em—have issued a kind of decree that all the old taxes are 'illegal'—yes, that's the word, 'illegal.' And now it's wrong to collect 'em until the deputies have made some kind of a better law for France, which they call by a queer name—ah! I recall it—Constitution."

An old peasant shook his head. "Too much brandy, Aubri. Taxes and winter come from the Good God—not to be avoided!"

"I'm very sober. The carter said the deputies wanted to have some new taxes equal on everybody alike, from marquises down to lads with just their ten nails. That seems incredible, but of this thing I'm sure. If taxes now are 'illegal,' I'll save up no good silver this year to pay them."

"And forced labor on the roads? And the bishop's tithes? And the seigneurial dues?" came from many.

"Why," admitted Aubri, "if one thing goes, I'm sure they

all must. You can't swing a scythe for mullen stalks, and miss hitting the thistles."

Nicolas went home whistling; all his friends seemed to be whistling. Every man was calculating, "What can I do with sous and livres saved up for the collector?" The heavens, in fact, seemed to have rained money. Many a fellow forgot his work and ordered an extra pot just to celebrate.

Of course, Nicolas told Brigitte, and Brigitte promptly ordered, "Not to believe that fool Aubri, but to go out with his axe." Her spouse meekly obeyed and went through the forest looking for the dying trees that he was permitted to take, but the golden vision kept dancing in his head. "No more taxes, no more tithes, no more insolent gendarmes." He was in no mood for chopping. "I am bewitched," at last he said to himself, and he knocked off work altogether.

In this absent fit he ranged deeply into the forest. Soon he was beyond the limits where he was allowed to take timber. If he met a seigneurial officer he also would meet trouble. No matter. He felt positively reckless. He wandered down a piny trail which he had not trodden for years, startled a red deer, and plunged still deeper. Presently, however, he stood stock still. Before him was a tiny clearing, containing a small cabin. The woodcutter knew that this had been deserted for years and yet—blessed saints!—a gray column was rising from the smoke hole.

Nicolas slipped his axe through his belt, and began edging on all fours through the shrubbery like a fox stalking a hen-roost. Infinite curiosity had mastered him. The cabin might be held by seigneurial rangers—yet this was unlikely. More probably the denizens were salt smugglers or professional poachers—but this was not quite the right spot for them. Nicolas plucked up courage and crept closer still. The cabin was moss-roofed and weather-beaten. The crazy shutters and the door had been drawn, but one of the shutters appeared to be partly open, and at length the woodcutter began to hear voices. A woman seemed to be speaking. His ears now pricked like a rabbit's. What business had a woman in a place like this?

The woodcutter surveyed the spot carefully. The path to the cabin was trodden hard; chips and refuse lay by the door and plentiful hens' feathers were sprinkled about. "They've been here some time and had plenty of chickens," muttered he, licking his lips. Then he saw bushes and a small tree giving covert to the very spot where the shutter swung open. Nicolas made sure his axe was handy, then crept on. His woodcraft made him agile and noiseless. Soon he was directly under the casement.

A man and a woman were arguing within; the man's voice was strident, the woman's shrill. Nicolas instantly suspected that somewhere, years earlier, he had heard the man's voice.

"So you gave her the drops again?" spoke the man.

"I did, poor thing," spoke the woman.

"Poor——" swore the man. "Don't *you* begin to pity her! Tell me this, my noble Madame, just now what good is she?"

"Ask yourself, my high-born Monsieur."

The scuffle and clatter within made Nicolas surmise that the gentleman had perhaps flung a wooden trencher at the lady, and that she had dodged it dexterously. Then the conversation resumed more placidly.

"The devil eat you!"

"After he has eaten you, my dear."

"How long will she sleep now?" pursued the man.

"All day and all night last time; perhaps as much this time. But I had hard work giving her the drops. She's knowing——"

"That's because she's of my blood. Well, M. le Baron or M. de Lucifer has come and gone again. Why, instead of saying 'kill her,' did he suddenly grow so devilish kind to her?"

"He'd better. No killing of her while *I* boil your soup."

"You've boiled too much soup in this vile, lurking place, and I've split too much wood while we've waited. 'Your fortunes are soon made,' so he told us. Are they? Are they?"

"Yes, it was nice in Paris, but once here—ugh!"

Nicolas by this time had grown very brave. He swung himself up the tree, caught a limb, gained a glimpse into the cabin. He saw a squalid room, but on the table was a roast fowl and a tall bottle, with the man and woman now seated opposite each other. The woman was tall, muscular and with such a jaw that Nicolas thanked the saints Brigitte did not have quite her physique; he would fear being throttled. The man was broad, powerful and black, but his face was still turned from the woodcutter. In the corner there rested significantly two guns. Peasants were not allowed to have guns, and since the pair certainly were not officers, of course their business was lawless. Nicolas' determination to see the man's face intensified. He clung to his tree and waited.

The woman crushed a chicken bone in strong, white teeth and resumed: "Two months here now, and only 'Wait, wait' for our orders. I tell you the girl is drooping. Every time we give her that sleeping stuff she gets worse. She's got wonderful spirit, but her body's slowly breaking. Why not bargain with the Chevalier?"

"And how do it, pray? Can you write a letter? Can I? 'Most noble M. le Chevalier, how many livres for returning your betrothed?'—Oh! Linio's got us bound hand and foot. This seemed a nice, safe hiding place at first. Good fare.

I knew the spot. But how get away? If Linio should split on us, we're broken on the wheel."

"You saw how he simpered and smirked," pursued the woman, "when he saw her last; how he tried to look the fine gentleman. Soon he'll be talking about a priest."

"A thousand devils you say!" burst from the man, and at the curse he leaped from the stool, forthwith turning his head. Nicolas barely checked his own outcry as he dropped from the tree: "Thibaud Durand—I knew him after twenty years."

. . . Nicolas swung down to the ground, glided noiselessly back into the trees, then (safely hidden) stood for a long time clutching his head.—Thibaud Durand, the black sheep of the village, suspected but not proved to have fired Nicolas' father's hay-rick after an altercation at the tavern. Thibaud Durand who, more certainly, later had assisted the public hangman of Ard to turn off Nicolas' own brother, convicted of salt smuggling. Also that name which the pair exchanged—"Linio;" the very same as that of the bully at the *Silver Swan*, who had threatened the humane M. de Robespierre, and then was himself so righteously caned by the Massac valets.

Likewise, it was clear that Thibaud and his companion were detaining some girl; that their actions called for concealment, and that the pair named "The Chevalier"—the liberal Chevalier, who had given the two louis, as interested in the girl and concerned for her release. To the woodcutter there was only one "Chevalier" in all the world, his lord and benefactor.

After another clear glimpse around the cabin, and making sure of certain landmarks, Nicolas plunged into the green wood upon a run. When he emerged at his cottage, his face was torn with brambles, his blouse was half off his back. Brigitte first stared at him, then scolded furiously;

then listened with bewildered eyes. Neither he nor she could sleep a wink all that night.

. . . The next afternoon Nicolas was afield again with a prodigious hunting instinct possessing him. This time he made straight for the closed woods and the cabin. The locality was on the Massac lands, but very near the edge of the seigneury, and he rightly concluded that all communications passed now through a path which led to the next village of Garnes, where alike Thibaud and Linio would hardly be identified. There was little intercourse between the peasants of Massac and Garnes; an old neighborhood feud had kept them rather at arm's length. The cabin, therefore, was a very safe lurking place.

While Nicolas was working his way through the underbrush, with the thatched roof now clearly in view, a sound sent his heart up into his throat—hoof beats! But it was not a mounted forester. A horseman in a gray coat swung down the path, dismounted at the cabin door and began to unload well-filled saddle-bags. Thibaud came out to greet him, and the rider clearly enough was Linio, who swaggered cheerfully inside and could be heard greeting Thibaud's companion. The same casement that had been opened before was opened now, but Nicolas dared not approach it. On the contrary, his eyes were glued on the rear of the cabin. He had imagined that the latter contained only one room. Now he was certain there was some kind of an inner chamber, whereof the window shutter was open, but across which there were set solid wooden bars. The shrubbery did not come as close as he might desire, but a stump and a sapling made it possible to get fairly near without quite exposing himself.

Nicolas felt that any instant Thibaud and Linio might pop in sight with the guns. He was naturally, too, a somewhat cowardly man, but devouring curiosity again was eking out his courage; therefore he dared greatly. Even while the three voices jangled from the front of the cabin, he made a dart for the barred window, caught the timbers with both hands and swung himself high enough to look within. Outside it was hot summer sunlight, and the interior of the cabin was so black and dark that for a moment he only blinked and murmured, "The room is empty." Then his eyes saw clearer, and upon a rude straw bed he beheld a young woman.

The young woman was sitting with her head resting on one hand, with the other she was stroking her brow, as if shaking off some kind of stupor. She was only partly clad, but Nicolas had wits enough to know that her garments, if now somewhat torn and worn, were of fine materials, such as boasted by no peasant. Her hands looked very soft and white—hands that had never known hard toil. Her face was almost concealed by a great tangled mass of light brown hair, out of the midst of which were visible her lips —moving in a kind of helpless murmuring. Then she partly brushed back her hair.—Nicolas had never seen such a face before; so like that of the statue of Our Lady of Sorrows in the parish church, except so pale, so deathly pale. The very sight of her terrified him; he almost let go of the bars and dropped to the ground.

Suddenly the woman lifted her eyes. She looked straight at the window, next her pupils dilated, her mouth opened as if to scream. Probably Nicolas' dishevelled head was a horrid enough apparition, and the peasant was half out of his wits himself, but now his patron saint sent him three most timely words:

"I hate Thibaud."

The woman did not scream. With a spasmodic start from the bed, she darted to the window, then spoke in a kind of ghastly whisper, "Who are you?"

The woodcutter wanted to cross himself when that amazing white face came up so close to his own, but he could not let go of the bars. He could only stammer out "Nicolas." Then his good angel assisted him again: "The Chevalier saved me."

The woman turned her head as might a trapped animal toward the door. Voices, grating and dissonant still proceeded thence, and the tones of Thibaud emerged clearly: "I tell you, Monsieur Fine-Clothes, she's my niece, not yours. She's to be disposed of according to *my* own notions."

The woman, Nicolas knew now that she was quite a young woman, spoke again, so low he barely heard her.

"Is this place on the Massac lands?"

"Yes, Madame, yes." (Nicolas was sure she ought to be called "Madame"). "The chateau is within two leagues."

"I thought so, though they would not tell me. Now why did the Chevalier save you?"

Nicolas' answer about the trial at the *Silver Swan* was not very coherent, but the woman seemed to understand immediately. "René told me about it. You ought to be grateful. Would you win his gratitude now a thousand fold in return; would you be rewarded richly, richly?"

"Yes, Madame, yes." Nicolas thought the cabin and the trees were spinning around, the adventure was so amazing.

"I am your Chevalier's betrothed. We were to have been married—ah! long ago. Thibaud Durand has stolen me away, he and Olympie, his wife, and that Linio, whose voice you hear and who calls himself 'Baron.' Thibaud calls himself my uncle, and so, perhaps, he is, but I think he would kill me if Olympie would let him. Sometimes she seems to become a little kind.—Now you will bring help; bring the chateau steward, bring the gendarmes. I am Virginie Durand. Be quick. They will force the drops

on me again. I am just emerging from a hideous stupor.
They give me the drops whenever I resist, and they think
that I may break away——"

"The drops, Madame? I do not understand."

"A medicine called opium. It makes you sleep even
though you struggle to keep awake. Now run—bring help."

"Alas! Madame. I am only a poor woodcutter. None
will believe me. If I make an uproar will not Linio and
Thibaud kill you first and me the next?"

The woman was pressing her hands to her forehead to
clear her senses. "Write then; write all that you know to
the Chevalier de Massac. Write immediately. If I still
live he will make your fortune."

"Write?" Nicolas' query implied he might as well have
been urged, "Climb up to the sun."

"Alas, poor man, of course you cannot write; and I—
have I seen paper, ink or pencil for three months?"

The voices in the cabin were breaking off; the door of
Virginie's prison might open instantly, or one of her jailors
go round the building and discover Nicolas.

"You must go now," continued the prisoner. "If they
find you they will shoot you like a rabbit. But come back
just when the moon rises. I will discover a way to write
something. Probably they will let me take supper with
them if I am quiet and patient. I will be quiet and patient.
Swear that you will not fail me."

"I swear I will not fail you, Madame. I swear it by St.
Anne, by St. Gervais and by the Holy Mother herself."

"Off," ordered the prisoner, barely in time, for Nicolas
heard the bolt of the door rattling. The peasant dropped
to the ground, just as Olympie's deep voice sounded over
his head, "So you are awaking from another restful sleep,
my dear."

. . . Nicolas broke his fast upon a hard hunk of bread

as he sat in the coppice until the moon rose. He knew those woods as a priest ought to know his book; still that night his knees were unsteady.—After the darkness came, he might have abandoned the whole adventure and hastened home with some faltering lie to Brigitte, except for the oath which he had taken. Two mighty saints and the Blessed Virgin would surely conspire his ruin if he failed to keep tryst.

At last he set off again for the cabin. The woods were terribly black. Despite a life spent in them, he almost lost his way, and he was all a-tremble lest every bush conceal a horde of pixies and "little people." At last, to his unspeakable relief, a solitary taper gleamed through the tree trunks, and almost simultaneously the first beams of white moonlight fell across the roof of the old cabin.

Linio's horse was rattling his tether near the entrance. The night was warm, the cabin door now was open, and by the rush candle Nicolas could see the trio around the table —Linio gesticulating, and sometimes giving a bang with his scabbard against the table legs to emphasize his argument. Thibaud, with his elbows on the table, was following him with dark, suspicious eyes. Olympie, her strong arms folded, and a red handkerchief wound around her head, sat a little distance back in a kind of majestic silence. Nicolas wasted no time, after making sure that the prisoner was not with her jailors. He glided to the rear of the cabin and swung himself up to the barred window, coughed very softly, and was rewarded by the extension of an arm that gleamed like snow in the moonlight.

"Have you written, Madame?"

"Yes, good Nicolas. Take this quickly." A piece of leather was thrust in his hand. "I found an old moldy knapsack. Olympie had let me have a needle to mend my skirt. I have pricked out a message. You cannot understand, but any one who can read can follow it.—Oh! It was terrible to-night. Linio thinks to marry me; he urges my uncle, 'It will give us a hold upon her money.' Thibaud is keeping him off, 'Why divide? If the girl dies am I not her heir?' Olympie shakes her head, 'Take care, both of you. The Châtelet won't help us again. One slip and we get just three ropes between us.'—Olympie is beginning to soften toward me, but she cannot keep the others back forever. Thibaud will get his price and in one week, two or three, I see Linio having his way. They will give me drops, have in a strange priest, then pretend that I say anything."

"Our Blessed Lady preserve you, Madame!" vowed Nicolas, deeply moved.

"Our Blessed Lady preserves those who have friends to preserve them. If I am not rescued soon, tell the Chevalier this, 'He need not fear that I have truly become Linio's bride.'"

"But I swear by St. Anne, by St. Gervais, and by the Holy Mother herself," repeated the peasant doggedly, "that the Chevalier shall read what you have put on the leather!"

Noises again from the cabin—Linio was going forth to look to the tether of his horse. Nicolas, in a kind of enchantment, kissed the long white hand. He never thought of pixies as he made his long way through the green wood. Once home, however, Brigitte stared at the pricks on the leather with a kind of incredulity. Was her man's story believable? Had he not been bewitched in the forest? Was not the devil behind the whole business, and should not the one thing for a Christian to do be simply to thrust the moldy stuff in the fireplace? "Make their fortune?— Cause their damnation rather!" Nicolas nevertheless was mindful of his oath. He resolutely prevented her.

However, there was only one man in Massac whom he dared to trust with such a secret. The next morning, cap in hand, he was bowing and scraping at the door of the manse. He gave the pricked leather to Father Benoit.

CHAPTER XIV

THE LONGEST ROAD TO PARIS

"NATIONAL Assembly!" Rejoined almost immediately by all of the Clergy after the Men in Black had defied the voice of the King. Joined, amid great cheering, by forty-seven liberal Nobles the day following. Joined, amid greater cheering, by all the remaining Nobles (some oh! how reluctantly) the day after that "at the express wish of the King."

The great legislature for the regenerating of France was therefore constituted, organized, was preparing for action. Speeches and committees, speeches and committees—did life for Massac contain anything else? And the Chevalier became very accustomed now to certain voices, often from the tribune:—Mirabeau, Sieyès, Barnave and the accurate, thin, but carrying accents of Robespierre. Leaders were emerging; parties were forming; but all were passionately devoted to redeeming that great oath to give an abiding law to France.

Had the King capitulated? Had he actually swallowed a defiance such as no earlier monarch since Hugh Capet had endured at the hands of his subjects? It was true, in any case, that Artois was observed to be smiling a little more complacently than ever, and that his sister-in-law appeared to assume a complete gaiety. Massac heard that they had put on *The Marriage of Figaro* again at their private theater. As for His Majesty, he was reported to be interested only in shooting partridges on the enormous game preserves, and perfecting a very complicated lock for coffers.

Had the King capitulated? Why, if he had, were so many regiments still entering Versailles? What was old de Broglie doing, inspecting, reviewing, button-holing noble officers incessantly? Along all the roads now were rising the incoming clouds of dust. Citizens were wakened before dawn by the tramp of the entering battalions, by foreign battalions. No more native French troops were arriving at Versailles, that was certain, but seemingly all the King's mercenaries—the thousands of Germans and Swiss, tall, blonde moustached, swinging along under their forests of nodding shakos. Orders in German were shouted along the streets; German gutturals almost drowned out the French in the cafés frequented by the military.—And wherefore?

Frequently Massac drove into Paris "to see my friends," and to press with vain questioning and sinking hope at the Châtelet. Always the same: "Alas, M. le député, we are desolated. Still no trace of her." Then he would betake himself to the Café Procope, to try to cover his heart before Danton, Desmoulins and the others, under a brave show of enthusiasm over the great triumphs at Versailles.

Certainly there was plenty of stir now in Paris. The Palais Royal could not accommodate all the orators. Clubs were being organized everywhere—apparently just to provide congenial spirits with a constant excuse for talking. All the essay-mongers were busy, and René was handed six full-dressed and wholly irreconcilable constitutions for France all in one day, and almost threatened with mobbing if he did not have each one enacted immediately.

Hopeful enough it was that every printing press was clanging, that new journals seemed to be multiplying like rabbits, and that Camille Desmoulins was being stormed now by publishers for his mordant articles. But other things sent Massac back to Versailles very thoughtful. Men of property were growing perplexed. Serious robberies were increasing. Shopkeepers were installing very solid shutters. The French Guard had defied their officers and rescued eleven mutineers right out of L'Abbaye prison itself. The bread lines were still lengthening, and in the hungry faubourgs, if there was a certain willingness to excuse "the good King," there kept increasing a fearful tendency to say that it was "The Austrian" and the other rich folk at Versailles who made the black bread full of chopped straw and the children so pale and puny.

Desmoulins walked with René one night from the Café Procope to the latter's lodgings. The journalist was truly serious: "We hold a charged Leiden jar here in Paris. One touch can discharge it. If the deputies can't relieve the people—*pouf!*"

"We will not fail them," assured the Chevalier.

"Have you the decision? Why so many foreign regiments in Versailles? Why is the Royal Allemand here in Paris? Look out."

. . . Thoughtful still was Massac while he sat on his bench the next day in the Hall of the Small Diversions. Gone already in those ten weeks was that juvenile confidence that mankind could be made virtuous and happy by invoking high-sounding, noble sentiments. In its place had come some faint understanding of the immensity of the task of remolding for a nobler life a nation of five-and-twenty millions; and with this consciousness, as never before, there was mingled the iron determination to give a new law of justice and righteousness to France. Woe unto him who thwarted!

After the adjournment from the long debates on "one chamber or two" in the new parliament, which was about to be ordained, René had set out for the *Fox*, where he was quartered along with Robespierre, when Arnaud fell in one step behind him. A few coughs by the old orderly explained that he wished to communicate.

"Well, what is it?" at length came from the master.

"More foreign regiments to-day, Monsieur."

"I have two eyes; I can see that, sirrah."

"Perhaps the English or Spaniards are threatening Versailles."

René beckoned his Achates up beside him. "Stop chasing the fox about the barn. Say what you have to say."

Arnaud's tone became slightly confidential. "M. le Chevalier is aware I have—ah! certain friends still at the chateau. These friends hear many things. If Monsieur will spare my services this evening perhaps some advantage——"

René laughed. "Ah! sly dog. Which one of the Polignac maids is it *this* time?"

Arnaud's voice became aggrieved. "It is for France, Monsieur.—But I have permission?——"

René nodded. Arnaud disappeared down the Avenue de St. Cloud and his master spent the evening puzzling over the project for abolishing the old provinces of the realm and substituting "departments." When somewhat late Arnaud again presented himself, René knew instantly an event had happened. All the old scars on the veteran's cheeks stood out and his voice shook.

"News, Monsieur, news."

"I never welcome servants' hall gossip."

"News for all France, Monsieur. Necker is dismissed."

"Ma foi!" The papers slipped from the deputy's hand.

"Broglie is made Commander-in-chief. Foullon, who said the people could eat grass, is set in Necker's place. The Swiss and Germans will hold the roads to Paris, stop all news and at the first word will break up the Assembly."

"Fellow, you rave," from Massac at last.

"If I rave, grill me eternally in Hell.—Listen. Nanette and Clementine told me. They dress Mme. de Polignac. She had come straight from the Queen and was so full of triumph that she burst out at once to the Princesse de Conti, 'The King fought hard, but the Queen and Artois overpowered him. Necker is chased from office and ordered to quit the Kingdom. The foreign regiments will quickly do the rest.'"

"Arnaud," spoke his master with unnatural gentleness, "either you are the greatest of unhanged villains or you are the benefactor of France. Come with me to Father François."

. . . The lecturer had a quiet room at the *Star and Crescent*, half a square away. He was just returning for the night when the others broke in upon him. He received Arnaud's story (details now added) calmly and without incredulity. "As I expected. What else were the foreign regiments for? Why did the King return such a vague answer to our deputation of deputies to-day when we besought the withdrawal of the soldiers? Well—so our dream of regenerating France is snuffed out——"

"Oh! my Father," burst from René.

"Unless," pursued the priest, still calmly, "the goodness of God shall make the wrath of man to praise him; unless Paris bestirs herself mightily in our aid."

He paused, as under their window there clattered a strong patrol of cavalry. An officer bawled something in German. Arnaud leaned from the casement and followed the troop with his eye. "They are taking the Paris road, Monsieur," he reported. "It is as Clementine told me, all the exits from Versailles are to be blocked."

Father François sighed heavily. "So it goes then—vanishes like many another dream, our vision of France remolded without violence, without hatreds, in a spirit of love. How truly once more it is spoken, 'I came not to send peace but a sword.'" Next to Arnaud, "Do you know the roads from Versailles?"

"Every one of them, Father."

The lecturer's fine white hands fell on his pupil's shoulders. "Then you see the task; one for a fighting Massac and not for a man of books and peace such as I. Get you this night to Paris, and God give you power to make men hear you. It is the only way. I go now to Mirabeau to strengthen our hands for to-morrow."

The Churchman added grave words of worldly advice and sound wisdom, after which the Chevalier buttoned his coat. "I am ready. I beseech you to bless me, Father." He had not done this for years, but now he knelt and Father François made over him the sign of the cross, then bent and kissed his forehead. Without another word, Massac rose and followed his servant out into the shadow-wrapped street.

*   *   *   *   *   *

"Horses?" But Arnaud miraculously discovered a patriotic groom at the Noailles stables, who had just shaken his fist at the German patrols and who scrupled not in such a cause to lead out two mounts that could have swept the purse at Longchamp. Arnaud piloted his master down dark meandering alleys, each conducting his horse by the bridle. The hoofs fell silently on the dust; there were no patrols as yet at the crossing of the lesser streets, but in the Boulevard de la Reine several mounted men were already riding slowly back and forth where the faint moonlight was striking gleams from their lance tips.

To pass unchallenged was impossible, but René knew the uniform and led his horse boldly up to the nearest trooper. "Here, Royal Hesse—where is your commanding officer?"

The soldier leaned from his saddle, and saw a gentleman followed by a servant, both in the act of mounting. He had been ordered to halt any riders toward Paris, but these strangers did not seem headed toward Paris, and besides the question was disarming.

"He is stationing the patrols along the Boulevard du Roi, *Mein Herr,*" came in very halting French.

"I must find him immediately; new orders from the Marshal."

The gentleman and the servant leaped into their saddles. The trooper hesitated an instant; neither of the strange riders was in uniform, but French officers sometimes went about in mufti, and these had apparently come directly from the palace. Undoubtedly they had business with his captain. While he thus deliberated, the two were pounding boldly up the Boulevard du Roi. Suddenly he saw them swerve to the left and disappear down the narrow way beyond the palace theater. "Suspicious certainly, but best to say nothing about it," reflected the trooper; they were well mounted and if he reported, he would only get himself reprimanded now for letting them pass.

René and his companion pricked side by side through the winding bridle paths of the enormous park. No fireworks to-night; the fountains were at rest; the gay crowds from the palace had forgotten the kiosks and delicious seats under the shrubbery. Once or twice they thought they scented patrols, but Arnaud, whose eyes were like a bat's in the dark, always found a saving twist in the heavily shaded avenues. At last the foliage became irregular; they passed some kind of a hedge-row, the western confines probably of the royal compound. Then something white shone vaguely before them, the walls, no doubt, of a farm house. A drowsing cock awakened at the hoof-beats, crowed once, went to sleep again.—The Chevalier and his servant were beyond Versailles, but on the side remotest from Paris.

. . . Years afterward, René de Massac recalled that ride as men recall memorable dreams. It was the eleventh of July, or had been before midnight. The night was heavy and hazy, few stars, little moonlight, and there was the threat of thunder in the air. The fleet horses, hardly winded as yet, carried them northward steadily. They would make a wide circuit, enter Paris from the north, give the laugh to all Broglie's Germans. Through sleeping Rocquencourt they flew unchallenged and were skirting the hill near Marly, confident of being now beyond hindrance, when, at a sudden turn in the road, there was a rattle and a challenge. *"Wer da!"* Four figures were in the highway. Through the dark came the bare glint of their gun barrels, but by a godsend none of the patrol were mounted, a weary vigil having caused them to dismount and tether.

René's answer was a shout and a spur, which made his steed crash over one of the Germans before a trigger could draw. The other three muskets blazed out together through the night; the balls sung over the riders as the two horses tore down the dim white road. The soldiers were shouting wildly, dogs were barking, men and women were thrusting night-caps from the village windows.—Then silence again, and the horses still galloping. Was it not all a dream?

But Arnaud had drawn up beside him with words of wisdom. "M. le Chevalier, you received fire like an old soldier, but if the patrols are out so far, know this—the bridge at St. Germain will be guarded."

"What then?"

"We must find a ferry that is not guarded."

"That will be hard."

"On the contrary, M. le Chevalier, I have an old comrade, Claret. Lost a leg at Yorktown, but that did not spoil his arms. He works the ferry boat beyond St. Germain at Carrières. He's a stout fellow and won't refuse a friend."

More white roads while giving St. Germain a wide berth. Trees, farm houses, trees, farm houses, but no more patrols. Broglie's network did not reach so far. Then the broad, steely shimmer of a noble stream, the Seine; the horses clicking over the cobbles of a little street; a halt at the last house by the marge; Arnaud shouting, and a voice from an upper grating.

"What the devil do you want, a dose from my blunder-buss?"

"Holla, Claret, have you forgotten a comrade's voice? I've a noble lord here who wants passage."

"Noble lord to perdition! Let him cool his heels till morning."

"But he rides in the service of France; the Assembly is in danger."

"France? the Assembly?—That's different. Wait a bit."

A faint lantern. A powerful form, half clad, stumping and grumbling down to the ferry, Arnaud explaining every-thing with immense importance. The horses banging onto the clumsy boat. A paddle working powerfully in the violet-black water. Then the eastern landing. The proffer of pay to the ferryman. "Pay? Damnation! It is for France."

Again the white road, the black trees, the ghostly farm houses. Was it not all a dream?

The horses were tiring now; through Sartrouville and on to Argenteuil they had to go less rapidly, but with the roofs of Epinay in sight, the riders again gave the spur. St. Denis, with a hundred kings and queens sleeping under its minster, they avoided, for perhaps Broglie had flung his Germans thither. Then open country once more, the road, the trees, the farm houses. The first touch of dawn now was just lifting the darkness from the east, and the cocks were sounding their clarions. From the barns came the rattle and lowing of waking cattle. At length the farms were closer together; and now the road was edged by high garden walls. They had made a complete circuit and were entering Paris from the north.

The good horses had gained their second wind. René was conscious of no desire for sleep, but as he pounded onward steadily, a kind of pageant of former days seemed to be gliding before his eyes above the rhythm of the saddle. Now he was on the theater boards at the Trianon; now he was in his cell at Vincennes; now walking with the Queen, listening to soft words by the music of the fountains; now (ah! pain) saying that long farewell to Virginie ere setting forth for the Hague.—"What was awaiting in Paris? Could that vast, undisciplined, inchoate city save the deputies, save France?"

Figures again in the highway; a challenge, this time in good French, "*Qui vive?*" Men with bayonets were standing in the road before a tavern. There was just light enough to see the uniform, the blue and white of the French Guard, and Massac drew rein.

"I am a deputy from Versailles. I come with messages of weight. Permit me and my servant to pass."

"From Versailles? And by the St. Denis road? Why is that, Monsieur?" Twenty men with guns were crowding out now beside the horses.

The case demanded boldness and René's voice put on power. "I speak to Frenchmen, to French soldiers, not to mercenaries. Know that all the direct roads to Paris are held by the Swiss and Germans; that the Assembly is threatened; that all the hopes of France are in danger unless

I get through with my message and Paris comes to the Assembly's aid."

"Swiss and Germans? He says the Assembly is in danger."

"That was the rumor when we left the barracks. Now it's confirmed."

"What shall we do, sergeant?"

"Do, comrade; take him into Paris, of course, and then teach the Austrian and the Monseigneurs to fife another tune."

"Ho there! Va-de-bon-coeur," flung in Arnaud, "is it too dark to recognize a comrade? Get Monsieur at once through the barriers if you love France."

The whole platoon, shouting, cheering together, immediately ran on beside the horses. "A deputy! News from Versailles! Down with the Austrian, down with the bloodsuckers!" From the string of houses all the way to the octroi-barrier there rose at once the banging of doors, as men and women, scantily clad, rushed out into the high road. The octroi-gates themselves flew open by some magic, while the increasing crowd behind the horses followed with a kind of ascending roar. Faubourg St. Denis was pouring out its unwashed thousands, as ahead of M. le député already there raced the most improbable rumors.

Broad daylight now. The long shadows and fierce lights of early morning were pencilling all the tall gabled houses and stately pinnacles. In the streets the crowd grew incessantly, and Arnaud could only implore, "Make way, make way, good people," and let the throngs swirl them onward. Then, at last out of the human sea, there emerged a familiar face; some one was standing beside René's horse, and assisting him to dismount. It was Camille Desmoulins, of wont afoot very early.

"What has happened, my friend?"

Briefly as he might, the Chevalier told him.

"We must unmuzzle the tigress called Paris," spoke the journalist.

"Will she not devour us?"

"Very likely, but first she will save France."

CHAPTER XV

NEARING THUNDER

SUNDAY, July the twelfth, 1789, and when before such a Sunday in Paris? Few of the pious that morning were hearing mass. Black-frocked priests, brown-gowned and gray-gowned friars, nuns in their flapping habits could be seen mingling with the clerks, the poor journeymen, the solid bourgeois as well as the muscular market dames and pert grisettes, who were all idling or promenading near the Palais Royal.

"Necker is dismissed." No messengers from Versailles seemed to be coming through, and yet the rumor appeared to be confirmed. The Genevese banker had his critics, "just a man of money bags." No matter; he had demanded the States General and defied the Austrian and Artois. What foul thing did his dismissal mean?

Why were the foreign troops converging on Paris? German hussars on the Champ de Mars, Swiss infantry beyond the Tuileries, more Germans controlling the roads to the south and east. The food supply of Paris seemed to be in their clutch. One order from Versailles and seven hundred thousand persons might starve; starve because Paris stood by the Assembly.

Where were leaders? What were the Electors who had named the deputies doing, while they mustered at the Hôtel de Ville and shook their fists at the demoralized syndics of the old city government? Where were weapons to hold off the alien mercenaries? Why were so many dark, criminal

faces on the streets amid the break-down of the police?—
By noon the Palais Royal had almost become one seething
mass of bodies and heads. The café waiters had long since
given up serving their coffee and sugar-and-water. A
dozen orators vociferated, but no one heeded their wordy
theorizing.

Then across that tumult passed a universal "Hist!" Two
young men were seen springing upon a table before a café.
One figure was hardly known, although a few spectators
whispered, "Le Chevalier de Massac," but the other was
familiar now to every Palais Royal assemblage, "The journalist, Camille Desmoulins." Necks were craning, thousands were edging nearer; the whole garden seemed now
"as full as an egg" when Desmoulins began gesturing for
attention. Yells answered him at first, then came the required silence, whereat his voice went out like a clarion
through the orange tubs and chestnut trees, and men who
heard tossed on his words to the eddying throng outside,
clear across to the steps of the Louvre.

"*Citizens* (not "Subjects of the King"), there is no time
to lose! The story is true; Necker is dismissed, the Assembly is in danger."

A second of silence, then a low swelling growl like nearing
thunder.

"Citizens, the deputy de Massac, friend of our rights,
comes straight from Versailles through the bullets of the
German patrols. He confirms it—that in Necker's place
they set Foullon."

"Who said the people could eat grass!" René had never
heard the howl of wolves; he almost heard it now.

"The other ministers are like him. Broglie is over the
army. He has ordered up the foreign mercenaries."

More howling.

"The Assembly is in danger. The King refused it an

answer when it protested against the alien regiments. Soon the Assembly will be dispersed, its leaders in dungeons, France betrayed."

Fiercer howling.

"Citizens, we are all in danger, our wives, little ones, everybody who loves France. The dismissal of Necker sounds the knell of a St. Bartholomew for patriots. This night the Swiss and Germans can begin their massacre. We are men. We are strong. One resource is left. *To arms, Citizens!*" Above his head shot his hands, waving two pistols.

"Arms! Arms! Arms!" The yell made all the tiles to quake from the Tuileries to gray old Notre Dame.

Once more Desmoulins beckoned. "Citizens, we need a sign and a color to distinguish patriots. Shall it be red, the color of the free order of Cincinnatus, or green, the color of hope?"

"Green! Green!" from hundreds.

"Good then, green is before you. Let us show our color, fellow patriots, and then to action."

Desmoulins leaped from the table, sprang to the nearest chestnut and thrust a sprig in his hat. In a twinkling this tree was stripped, then many others, and the thousands shouting, struggling, eddying, were thrusting out into Rue St. Honoré, next drifting in great bands, some toward the Tuileries, some toward the Seine, but the most of them eastward toward the Hôtel de Ville, while with the incessant cry for "Arms!" blended now a mighty shout as from a storm-whipped sea, *"Long Live the Nation!"*

. . . A day for the best and a day for the worst. A day for intoxicating visions of a world set free, of humanity virtuous and rejoicing, advancing toward the long ages' goal. A day for every thief to creep from his den, for brigands from the country to hasten through the unguarded barriers, for pickpockets to reap full harvest, for frightened women to scurry home from insults on the streets, for anxious shopkeepers to barricade their store fronts.

From the Palais Royal a crowd rushed to Curtius' Wax Works on the Boulevard du Temple. The proprietor hastily surrendered the bust of the idolized Necker, and that of the liberal Duc d'Orleans. Upbearing these trophies, the thousands surged back toward the Place Louis XV,[1] when drawn up against them appeared the horses of the Royal Allemand in military array "to protect the statue of Louis XV from insult." Jeers, a few stones, a saber flourished by the colonel, Prince de Lambesc, a loud command, and the cavalry were charging out upon the populace.

It seemed over in a twinkling. The cavalry chased the paraders into the Tuileries gardens, where placid bourgeois were still promenading and children scampering on the gravel. The Germans lashed the crowds with the flats of their sabers. The waxen busts were smashed to fragments. An old man fell bleeding under a sword cut. "*Allons!* Chase the canaille down!*" Lambesc was ordering, then jerked his own horse upon its haunches. For right before the troopers was forming a solid platoon of blue and white, the French Guard, with their fixed bayonets, and a firm voice was ordering, "Form to repel cavalry!"

The Germans and French Guards gazed in one another's eyes. The infantry, cocked and primed, stirred not and presented their muzzles. Lambesc looked at his lieutenants and they at him. Certain orders had come from Versailles, but none about beginning a civil war. Very sheepishly the Germans turned, and amid a perfect whirlwind of taunts and curses, rode back across the bridge to their camp at the Champ de Mars.

And now the flames were leaping. From St. Antoine to

[1] The later Place de la Concorde.

the Bois de Boulogne, the most precious thing seemed to be
a good musket, the next a rusty pistol. Every gun shop
was being plundered. Crowds ran about hunting for gunpowder as for hidden gold. "Arms! Arms!" The bells
all together were saying it. St. Roch on the north was
answering St. Jacques on the south, and deepest of all,
Notre Dame's mighty carillon was flinging its summons
from La Cité. "Arms! Arms!" Butchers' cleavers were
caught up. Great knives bound to poles provided pikes.
Bakeries were emptied by hungry patriots who forgot to
pay. Other patriots sought liquid valor at the taverns.
Darkness at last, but not for sleep, what with the incessant
bells, outcries and trampling. The wooden octroi-barriers
had been flung down and fired, and a fearsome red glare
ringed the horizon. At intervals musket shots from uneasy
German sentinels sounded from the Champ de Mars. What
a night for the women and children!

Amazed, terrified, fascinated, René de Massac, after Desmoulins' summons, ranged for a while the less perilous
streets. The fearfulness of the unpent forces overwhelmed
him. A sense of Mohammedan fatalism, of being the plaything of a blind, insensate power, almost deprived him of
initiative and clear thought. In his rooms on the Rue Vendôme he sought a few hours of the sleep of exhaustion, but
excitement at length drove him from his pillow. Well after
midnight, with saber and pistols, and guarded by Arnaud,
he set out to cross the river for the Café Procope, near the
Luxembourg, where he felt sure of meeting his friends, but
near the Pont Neuf he ran suddenly upon a great press of
men, some with old muskets, some with improvised pikes,
some with merely clubs, all marching behind a drum. Yesterday morning they had been harmless lawyers' clerks,
carpenters, shopkeepers, barge men. Now, under half a
dozen torches, their faces shone red and demoniacal. Many

were singing, but none the same song. Then an eye lit on René, known by his appearance at the Palais Royal.

"Deputy de Massac! The pure patriot. He's been a soldier. We were looking for a leader. Here he is!"

"What is your wish, Citizens?" The word came as naturally to René's lips as if he had used it all his life.

"We're from the Cordeliers district," spoke a bookbinder, apparently clothed with a little authority. "We're trying to form a battalion, a *National Guard,* to stop the brigands, to protect the Assembly. We all want to help, but none of us know how to command. Now you can be our major."

Shades of loyal Massac ancestors, "direct vassals of the King!" Their scion accepting the leadership of an insurgent mob!

Still ruled by fate unseen, René answered without hesitation, and without consciously willing his words or action:

"Very well, Citizens; but naming a commander means yielding obedience. Do you swear to obey my orders?"

"Yes, yes, so we swear," from many together.

"I accept then for the present. Where were you going now?"

"To the Hôtel de Ville—for better weapons; to learn what we can do for France."

"Fall in then, Citizens. Let us all go to the Hôtel de Ville."

René drew his sword and marched beside the drum, which went thundering along the Quai de la Grève. Above them, to the left, lowered the dark outline of Notre Dame, its belfry still clamorous. Soon they were approaching the Hôtel de Ville, the vast building now one galaxy of lights.

The plaza before the city hall was packed. Members of the French Guard were moving hither and thither, waving their guns and shouting wildly. Equally wild was the horde of country folk, armed with iron-shod staves, who all that afternoon had been flocking into Paris "to save the city from the bandits." A number of huge cressets and bonfires here and there flung out an unearthly radiance over the jostling thousands. Any man who failed to have a green ribbon, or at least a green leaf in his hat, was liable, on discovery, to be knocked down and have his clothing torn to shreds. A very large woman, with hair streaming about her face, was elevated upon a high horse-block. She was screaming "Long live the Nation!" every time the civic tocsin up against the stars tumbled and clanged in its belfry.

Every conceivable report was flying. "The Assembly is dissolved at Versailles!" "No, the King as yet did not dare." "The French Guard were attacked by the dragoons again." "Yes, and drove them back with musket shots." "Bezenval has five thousand Germans at the Champ de Mars—ready to massacre us." "He is terrified. The people will tear his men in pieces."—All this at intervals blending into one rending shout, "Arms, citizens! Arms!"

The Cordeliers "company" kept step sorrily enough, but at least they moved in a solid column behind their strangely acquired major and the drum. The one thing apparent to René was that if method did not soon emerge from this madness, all Paris might dissolve in pandemonium. The city must find leaders speedily, or Antoinette and Artois could do their worst.

"Follow me, Citizens," commanded Massac, and the Cordeliers forced themselves in a human wedge up to the main steps of the Hôtel de Ville. A frightened municipal sergeant greeted the Chevalier with a kind of relief. "Oh! Monsieur, you seem to be a man of honor and influence. Make your followers hold back these crowds. They are about to rush the building."

René mounted the uppermost step, and beckoned to the Cordeliers to clear a ring before him.

"Give ear, Citizens!" He strained his lungs to the uttermost and a fair number heard him. "Only the enemies of the people can profit by tumult and disorder. Wait patiently. I will go in for you and demand of the magistrates the arms which you seek. We cannot all enter. I swear to return speedily."

"The good deputy de Massac. The friend of the Nation!" bawled many voices. "He's the right stuff."

Bidding the Cordeliers men to defend the steps, René entered the corridors of the enormous building. Candles everywhere, with demoralized clerks, civil sergeants and beadles scurrying about, but nobody to give orders or even to answer questions. The Chevalier at last found a doorkeeper who seemed to be keeping half of his wits. "Where is M. de Flesselles, your chief magistrate?" he demanded.

"In the great hall parleying with the Electors; at least there he was, Monsieur, before the last uproar began."

A great staircase, a high majestic hall revealed itself, imperfectly lighted, with the shadows going up among the Gothic arches and tracery of the ceiling. Underneath extended a long table behind which a white-faced elderly man in a red robe of office was confronting a large, irregular group of respectable bourgeois, white-faced themselves. One of the group was standing before the rest and gesturing earnestly. René caught part of his words between the beats of the tocsin.

"The people are determined, M. de Flesselles. They demand arms to protect them from their enemies and the enemies of the Assembly. We—the Electors of Paris—entreat you to order their issuance, otherwise nothing can avert a fearful outbreak."

"I have no power, Monsieur. Muskets are the King's, not mine to distribute. I have sent to Versailles.—As soon as word comes——"

The provost of the Merchants, first official of Paris, found his words dying out amid the indescribable yell that was coming in from the windows. There was a significant stir among the Electors, and with the next silence René cast himself in boldly.

"I am without authority in Paris. I am only a deputy of the Assembly. But I tell you that waiting word from Versailles is waiting the hurricane. I come from the streets, the square. Unless measures this instant are taken to organize the people, to arm them properly, to give them leadership, by to-morrow no man's life, no woman's honor is safe through the length and breadth of Paris."

"Messieurs, Messieurs, five minutes more and the mob will enter," cried an agonized civil sergeant, rushing in. "It breaks loose again and the Cordeliers men are weakening."

Flesselles collapsed into his chair, his head went down on his hands as they rested on the table. "Tell them, tell them anything——" was all that the others heard.

One of the leaders of the Electors nodded. René took two stairs at a stride and gained the entrance just as the Cordeliers men were almost breaking apart from sheer pressure by the numbers before them. The Chevalier leaped upon the granite block which upheld a cresset, beckoned frantically for silence, and got it in the nick of time.

"Citizens, the Provost and the Electors are determined that you shall be contented, but muskets and ammunition are not here at the City Hall. The arsenals shall be opened and weapons distributed; but first we must form into companies. Without discipline we are helpless against the mercenaries."

"That's true!" trumpeted some old soldiers far out in the press.

"Go at once to your proper districts. Elect captains, lieutenants. Join the new National Guard. Then you can fight for your liberties. Any delay will only please the enemies of France."

"Long live the patriot Chevalier!" roared many of the Cordeliers men. "There's sense," a dozen others added.

And so, by that hair's breadth which can settle the whim of multitudes, the crisis for the moment passed. The Hôtel de Ville was not stormed and the tired crowd began to dissolve. The lawless element, seeing the joys of sacking a public building vanish, melted off, each man to his private plundering, while little by little even the bells grew calm.

René wiped the sweat from his brow, and turned back to the great hall; under his red sleeves Flesselles was still trembling in his armchair, while the Electors looked at the deputy as do men who would learn their fate. "Messieurs," Massac assured them, "the Hôtel will not be rushed. But as you love your homes and the safety of Paris—waste not this respite."

. . . .

A night of fury followed by a day of calm. The frenzy of humanity had for a moment exhausted itself. The crowds ceased to range the streets.

Messengers began drifting from Versailles. Broglie had not troopers enough to stop all of them. The Assembly had not been dissolved. First the Court had waited after its first stroke to ask, "Are not the deputies intimidated?" and then when the couriers pricked in from Paris, there had been anxious scurryings around the Oeil-de-Boeuf.—Like Dr. Faustus of the legend, the Queen and the Monseigneurs with infinite pains had called up the Devil, like Faustus, now they found the Fiend unexpectedly ferocious and hideous. More anxiety descended on them with the reports from the colonels in Paris. "Even the Swiss and Germans dislike their business. We dare not order them to clear the streets."

No one at the Hôtel de Ville or at all the innumerable section meetings knew this, but every one knew that the threatened bolt from the military was withheld. And while Versailles hesitated, Paris girded for action. The fourteenth would not find the city helpless.

Sixty districts in Paris; two hundred men to be enrolled in each; these to elect their officers; six hundred men then to be added to each two hundred; forty-eight thousand men ready, therefore, to patrol the streets, to stop looting, to fling defiance at the mercenaries, at Broglie, at the Monseigneurs behind them. Such was the National Guard which sprang into being in that night and that day—almost as Pallas leaped full armed from the head of Jove. No one could name the author of the plan, no one arranged its details. It was born spontaneously, irresistibly out of the fears, hopes, passions of the mighty city.

The Electors sat at the Hôtel de Ville, Flesselles and his associates having almost abdicated. The shops were still shut; in the areas behind them proprietors and clerks were struggling with "drill," pretending that broomsticks were muskets. Real muskets were still in passionate demand, but how they seemed to be multiplying! Who could have dreamed that so many lethal weapons had been concealed in Paris. Every smithy was hammering out pike-heads. Nevertheless, the cry was still "Arms! More arms!"— Thousands more of firelocks or the city, the Assembly, France were not safe.

The night of the thirteenth was quiet, preternaturally quiet. From the pillaged bakeries and burned octroi-barriers you might have said Paris was just recovering from capture after a siege, but save for the constant patrols and the perpetual countersigns, the city seemed silent as the grave.

As for René de Massac, he spent most of the day and the

evening in a wine shop which he had never seen before, giving orders to men whom he had never seen before. The two hundreds of the Cordeliers had confirmed him in command by acclamation; the six hundred who joined them had saluted him as "major," proud as they were to be led by an actual member of that Assembly which was the hope of France. He had told five or six of the oldest, steadiest men that they were to be his "captains." The captains had instantly created their lieutenants and sergeants. There had been infinite discipline and just as infinite good will. The Chevalier, like many Frenchmen of his class and age, had read his Shakespeare, and with a grimace he could now recall the line concerning those "who have greatness thrust upon them." But all that hectic interval he could never truly emerge from his dream. Was his commanding destiny bearing him onward to the traitor's quartering block or to the hero's pantheon? What matter? He had no moments for anything save the furious task in hand.

Nothing more from Versailles. Massac surmised that once again it was the old story—the King hesitating, then refusing to sign the order to Bezenval, his general in Paris: "Risk everything and crush the mob." The one thing certain, however, was that clubs, brickbats and improvised pikes could never stop troops-of-the-line. Firearms in great supply must be had, or swelling hopes would end in wholesale tragedy. As the evening advanced, René bade his captains report on how their companies were armed, and the returns were brief and significant. "Eight hundred zealous patriots, one hundred assorted muskets, fifty pistols, very little powder, but perhaps three hundred pikes."

That seemed to be the best. The plight of the other battalions could well be more serious. Then, even as Massac strove to put on a brave countenance to cover a vision of the lancers spearing the helpless bourgeois flying down Rue

St. Honoré, Arnaud jogged his elbow. *"Mon* Major," Arnaud revelled in military titles, "this just now comes from M. Desmoulins."

The scrap of paper was unfolded.

"I have just learned it. Thirty-two thousand muskets in the Hôtel des Invalides. Camille."

CHAPTER XVI

THE LIGHTNING

THIRTY-TWO thousand muskets, twenty-seven cannon, guarded only by a few old "invalids." Of all the suicidal blunders of the dying old Régime, what surpassed this—to leave the life blood of insurrection within the very limits of Paris?

. . . Tuesday, July the fourteenth. Again the tocsin, Notre Dame's deepest voice, with all the sister belfries answering. In the Hôtel de Ville the old magistrates and the Electors were alike quavering prisoners of another utterly suspicious mob. The real government of Paris was elsewhere and it was in action. Two cries, nevertheless, were dividing the city, "To the Bastille!" "To the Invalides!" Some of the new companies went one way, some the other. As for René de Massac, on Desmoulins' prompting, he had induced (he could not say "ordered") his battalion to head east toward the Invalides.

Another message, this time slipped through from Versailles, had just reached him.

"The Assembly holds firm and the Court hesitates. At last, so I hear, they have driven the King to agree to tell us to-morrow either to accept the mandate of the Royal Session or to stand dissolved. Forty thousand copies of the proclamation dissolving the Assembly are being printed, and a hundred millions of paper money to pay the cost of crushing the people. Soon I fear it must be 'Your lives or ours.' We trust the patriotism of Paris. Receive now the prayers of your FATHER FRANÇOIS."

. . . A stately Mansard building, vast, rambling, impotent for defence, such was the royal Arsenal in Paris. A garrison actually of a few score retired footmen of the nobility, with the Comte de St. Germain, their gouty old commander. A sea of heads before the Invalides, waving banners and plenty of cudgels, if very few muskets. Blood-curdling yells which stirred the pigeons on the cornices, and the thunderous summons, "Bring out the arms!" That was the scene when Massac stood face to face with the hopelessly courageous governor.

"The weapons are the King's," words not without sideward glances toward the barracks on the Champ de Mars. "On his command only I surrender them."

But Bezenval and his mercenaries came with no rescue. And wherefore? Because that general doubted just now whether his junior officers and even the Swiss and Germans themselves would obey any order to fire on the people. Then, while Massac hoped against hope it would not be needful to dash that brave blockhead St. Germain down, one of the Cordeliers captains twitched his major's sleeve. "See—that side door to the Hotel is open. Why talk longer?"

"This way, Citizens," ordered Massac, and in most unmilitary haste, a score of Cordeliers men rushed the unguarded portal. Other doors flew open in a twinkling. Glass smashed incessantly. Through twenty windows, in poured the thousands. The helpless governor did not even have to surrender; he was merely bundled aside.

"Muskets!" "Swords!" "Pistols!" "Cartridge-boxes!" "Powder!" The rush into the building resembled that of a robber horde into a cavern of gold. Since there was no bloodshed, there was infinite good nature. Men staggered out with all the muskets which they could seize from the racks, then divided with their whooping, cheering comrades.

Many a patriot stood struggling with the strange intricacies of flint-hammer and priming pan. René knocked the tinder box from the hands of one bewildered fellow just in time as he stopped to light a pipe while smashing open powder boxes.

But amid all the jostling, snatching, squabbling, there was a certain intelligence. Muskets at last found their way into reasonably proper hands. The Cordeliers captains having obtained swords, flourished them to purpose. The battalion drummer resumed, and the energetic "Fall in, patriots!" at last began to be obeyed, while Arnaud and a few more veterans went down the files, filling up the cartridge boxes. "Now the tigress gets her claws and teeth," spoke Massac in his heart, as he saw those long, ill-poised lines of gun-barrels.

Claws and teeth—but where to use them? The Swiss and Germans stood passively on the defensive on the Champ de Mars, but while the Chevalier and a few others who knew the difference between a mob and a regiment, trembled lest some fool raise the cry "attack them!", a new rumor came flying down the hot July wind. "The cannon of the Bastille have been trained upon the people. Our brothers are about to be mowed down. We have arms now. Across Paris instantly—aid the patriots!"

No chieftain gave any order. An electric impulse had simply possessed one of the bands. It began edging away toward the Seine bridges. The Cordeliers men followed en masse, carrying their "commander" with them. Making the best of necessity, Massac drew his sword and marched beside the drummer, and the battalion advanced with tolerable order, the men proud to display their new array of muskets to all the windows now lined with white-faced, wildly excited women. Immediately it was evident that all Paris, armed and unarmed, was marching eastward, down

Rue St. Honoré, along the Quays or around the ring of the Boulevards, but all toward one focus: "To the Bastille! To the Bastille!"

The King's gray fortress rose at the eastern extremity of Paris. For half a millennium it had stood, the granite sentinel of royal power, and often enough had its portcullis lifted to pour forth men-at-arms, ready to teach the city folk their place. Since the battles of the Fronde, the Bastille had indeed degenerated into merely a prison. Louis XIV and Louis XV had found constant use for its dungeons, which, at one time or another, had pent up nearly every prominent author of France. Of late, it is true that its hospitalities had been somewhat supplanted by Vincennes and remoter strongholds of Majesty, and in 1789 it contained only seven prisoners, mostly common counterfeiters. No matter. The Bastille was the symbol of harsh despotism, menacing Paris with its cannon, and now, as the public skies grew black, every peace-loving householder within range of those cannon was a-tremble.

The fourteenth had opened warm, overcast, sultry, with hot dust blowing about the street. Since dawn an unsteady multitude had been packing into the Place St. Antoine, just beyond the lowering northern bastion of the Bastille and the moat. It was being said (not untruly) that the Governor de Launay had loaded his cannon, sent to Bezenval for reënforcements and had received back the order, "Hold out at all costs." The crowds had been shouting and flinging stones, which hit the walls and plashed harmlessly into the moat. Above the ramparts there whipped in proud defiance the white flag with the golden lilies—the standard of the King. Launay apparently needed no cannon. The mob would be as impotent against the Bastille as against the Matterhorn!

But were not those guns peering from port-hole and battlement ready to fling death into the square and all the surrounding houses? Why were not the cannon withdrawn if the Governor meant no ill? The good folk with shops and homes within range were anxious, and a deputation of the Electors had gone to Launay, begging him "Take the guns away."—Smooth words met them, and several cannon were actually dragged back into their recesses, but in position they were still, and outside the angry uproar became deafening. It was approaching eleven o'clock. The yells were growing even fiercer when into the square came the pounding of drums and the glint of gun-barrels, the van of the marchers from the Invalides.

The newcomers wedged in behind the earlier manifestants, at first a bit tired by their long tramp across Paris. The white-and-gold flag was still whipping the clouds; upon the battlements a few uniforms in red were moving about, otherwise the fortress seemed lifeless as an enormous tomb. The calm, however, was ominous. Thousands, all now with muskets, were pouring down every side street and up from the near-by Seine. The white-and-gold flag excited their fury like the red coat of a matador. Either, reasoned Massac, as he studied the scene, the mob must be quieted speedily, or it would not be quieted at all.

The Cordeliers men, proud of their "major," forced a way for him close to the outer gate, where a little delegation was parleying with a red-faced and uneasy lieutenant. "We must see the Governor," went the demand; and René saw that the group was headed by a sober and competent colleague of his own, M. Thuriot, a deputy from Paris.

"I can admit only two," the officer was saying, and as Thuriot cast about him, he accosted Massac with obvious relief. "We are the only deputies present," he announced. "Accompany me, Monsieur."

. . . They passed inside. The first drawbridge, the "Governor's Court," the second drawbridge, and then the "Great Court," all hemmed in by the granite. Outside, barely audible, sounded the growling of the mob. Launay emerged from within the great mass of narrow-windowed buildings. He was a white-headed old soldier, who evidently was sparring for time by a great show of civility. "Would Messieurs les députés honor him by taking a glass of wine?" "M. Thuriot and M. de Massac needed no refreshment and would rather converse on serious business." "Good then; the Governor of the Bastille awaited their requests."

The requests were that, inasmuch as the cannon of the fortress were terrifying the inhabitants who lived within their range, the guns be not merely drawn back, but forthwith dismounted.

Launay smiled, then shook his head. "Of course, Messieurs les députés knew they were asking the impossible. The castle belonged to the King. To dismount the guns required a royal command."

A long argument, politely conducted at first, then with sharper glances and rising voices. "The Governor had only eighty-four invalids and a detachment of thirty-two Swiss; how could the city fear him?"—"Good then, if his force was so small, why did he refuse, for mere form's sake, to content the people?"—"But the deputies were not aware he was under orders—M. de Flesselles, the provost himself, had written him, 'Temporize until reënforcements.'" The deputies, with some heat and curling lips, assured M. de Launay that "M. de Flesselles had practically abdicated as a magistrate. The Electors of Paris were in control.— 'Reënforcements' would not be permitted."

. . . By this time the noise without was making the flag pole quiver, and an old sergeant saluted with: "Excel-

lency, either we must fire or satisfy the people very soon."
Whereat Launay made grudging concession. "Go then to
the Electors, gentlemen; get them to pledge responsibility
and I will dismount the guns."

The parting bows were correctly civil. The deputies
crossed the inner drawbridge, held by a few very nervous
artillerymen, one of whom was flourishing a lighted lin-
stock. An instant more and the great sea of faces in the
area before the gateways opened before the pair. The multitudes were denser, more ugly than earlier; every sinister
rumor had spread, even one that Launay was holding the
deputies as hostages. As they emerged, a great cheer went
up, followed instantly by shouts. "Will he take the guns
away?" The deputies were crossing the outer drawbridge,
with Thuriot holding up his hands and striving to make
himself heard: "Be calm," when there was a rush, a scuffle
and past them into the Governor's Court thrust a few
weaponless lads, bawling what all Paris had been calling
for three days, "Arms—give us arms!"

And then—not till God's Judgment Day will sinful man
know how it happened—there was a flash of fire, a thunderous report and a cannon ball tore its way from the
fortress into the living wall outside. The drawbridge rose
even as Massac leaped from it, while from all the battlements belched the powder smoke.[1]

A heap of dead in the Governor's Court and all around
the fortress, the crowds giving back in terror. The royal
lion was roaring and scattering the currish pack.—But only
so for an instant. The shrieks of the dying, the whistling
of the balls, if they sent much of the seething mob to the
rear, brought to the front other thousands with muskets in

---

[1] Probably the attack on the Bastille was precipitated by sheer
nervousness among the defenders, but sane and sober men of the
time were ready to cry out, "Treachery!"

their hands and the will to use them. From the areas below speedily there came back a steady fire of small arms, searching the port-holes and checking the reloading of the cannon

Half of the Cordeliers battalion suddenly evaporated, but the remainder stood their ground, formed into a kind of line, and looked to their major for guidance. Never before had Massac fired a shot in anger; his lieutenancy in the Body Guard had been only a glorified toy-soldiering, but every fibre in his body now tingled with the consciousness that came of fighting ancestors. He gave his orders clearly and the men took courage from his courage, and by his direction sought refuge from the grape-shot behind the stone enclosures around the gate, watched the port-holes and fired steadily wherever they saw powder-ladle or rammer working. Though here and there an attacker fell, yet there was no flinching. The castle thundered, the area spat back its fire—and so for sulphurous hours.

The castle thundered, and by that very thunder drew to itself all Paris. The people were advancing by thousands with every conceivable weapon; lawyers from the Palais de Justice, students from the Sorbonne, little shopkeepers, ample merchants, starving clerks and portly brewers, all the worthy, all the refuse of an enormous city. A priest marched up with half his parish behind him. Those who had only fists, brandished them; those who had pikes, waved them; those who had muskets, blazed incessantly against the enormous barriers of rock still frowning down on them. And louder than all of Launay's guns, rose the incessant cheer, *"Long live the Nation!"*

The first discharges of the fortress had been deadly; not so after the people by the gates had scattered. The cannon balls bounded over the paving stones, crashed through house walls or tiled roofs, sent women screaming into the streets, but only seldom found a human victim. Most of the attackers had withdrawn at too great a range for effective grape-shot. Their own feeble musket balls flattened upon the granite and dropped into the moat, but their hail was unceasing. When one band of attackers had exhausted its zeal or its cartridges, it fell back, making room for another. And at last came the first reward for the mob. The outer drawbridge had been lifted, but a single plank across the moat remained. A dash through the smoke, and two headlong fellows crossed the plank and hewed through the ropes. The drawbridge fell with a crash, and immediately fifty axes were beating on the outer door.

The lull next of an instant. Upon the roof of a house, in plain view, again stood forth Thuriot; he had a message from the Electors to the governor, and waved a white flag: "I would negotiate." But the blood of Launay was up—three shots from the battlements answered him, while all the areas yelled back with returning fury.

Axe-work well done. The outer gate had been beaten from its hinges. Despite all the thunders from the towers, the throngs were now in the Governor's Court with the inner drawbridge and the inner gate still before them. The cannon on the battlements could not be depressed enough to fire into the courtyard, but now the musketry volleys of the defenders were devastating. Soon upon those slain at the first onslaught was added a hideous mass of the dead and dying.—But still the leaden sky, the white flag with the lilies whipping against it, still the spitting musketry from the areas, with the ever-increasing "Long live the Nation!"

Massac had led the Cordeliers men over the drawbridge and into the Governor's Court. Before this assault, he had already missed Arnaud amid the smoke and welter, and gloomily imagined that the veteran had fallen. What event more natural in such an hour?—His own mood had become desperate. The inner fortress seemed still as impervious to musketry as to the beating of naked fists, and if the Bastille held fast, the King kept his stronghold within Paris itself, whence to crush down the rebellion.

The Cordeliers men were brave, sending their pellets against every porthole, but the thing had gone on for hours now, and flesh and blood must begin to weaken. The Chevalier exposed himself recklessly. "Better (he told himself) to go off with some cannon ball, than to live to await the crucifixion of France and his own doom as a rebel. Many a Massac slept his long sleep upon the bed of honor."

Hark! Just as certain of the most daring men in the Governor's Court were casting fitful looks behind them, a strange grinding and roaring, ever nearer in the streets. More grinding, and renewed cheering. Up from the quays long lines of men in blue and white—the insurgent French Guards. They were tugging at ropes with a prodigious crowd adding a helping hand, market women, boys, bourgeois in black, journeymen in rusty blue, a big priest even, and at the end of the ropes cannon, ah! cannon—the guns from the Invalides! Astride of the foremost eight-pounder sat a powerful figure, lifting his body and swinging a sword, Arnaud himself.

Despite a frantic volley from the towers, this gun was forced over the quaking drawbridge and into the Governor's Court. Arnaud leaped down in ecstasy beside his master. "I knew that pea-shooters were getting worthless. I found my old Yorktown comrades. Now let us talk to those dog-brothers within."

The cannon's muzzle was trained on the inner portcullis. In the areas and in the Place St. Antoine the other guns stood in long batteries. Then the thunders from above were answered by the thunders from below. Half-naked men plied their rammers like demons. Through the smoke great chips of masonry could be seen flying. The iron bars of the porthole gratings were dashed asunder. Over a parapet hung the body of a Swiss. And all of a sudden the fire of the fortress seemed stricken with a wondrous quieting.

"Again!" Once more the battery. More shivered parapets and shattered gratings, and hardly a shot in reply. Something within had happened. The blackened gunners reloaded and stood upholding their linstocks, waiting for the smoke to clear from the battlements. Presently the cloud lifted enough to show a corporal in a pensioner's coat standing in an embrasure beside a silent gun. He was waving a piece of white paper in lieu of a white flag, and beckoning for a hearing.

"Do you surrender?" came from hundreds below.

"We would retire with the honors of war," called the corporal.

"Honors? To the devil with honors!" roared the scornful answer. And others shouted, "Where's Launay?"

"We have defied him. He wished to blow up the fortress rather than yield. We told him that we could not resist all Paris. We will fight no more, if you give us our lives."

"Yes, yes. We pledge you your lives. Only cheer for the Nation and not for the King."

"Long live the Nation!" sounded from the battlement, and almost immediately with whir and rattle the inner drawbridge fell. Being near to the front, Massac had not the slightest choice save to be carried over the bridge by an irresistible rush of men—bloody, powder-grimed, laughing, howling, exulting, cursing, calling here, "String up the cutthroats!", there, "No vengeance!"

Inside the massive inner court he felt none of the curiosity of the swirling throng around him to explore the guard room, the turrets, the dungeons, even the torture chambers. He saw (too far off for him to raise voice or hand to save) old Launay, "the traitor," beaten to his knees and slaughtered with a butcher's cleaver. He saw a pack of lads scampering up to the highest tower to next tear down the white-and-gold flag of the King from its halyards and rend it into bits. He saw brutal wharfingers from the river chasing a group of terrified pensioners, with "Kill! Cut their hearts out!" But his own Cordeliers men interposed nobly with, "No blood upon our laurels! What have *you* done to storm the Bastille?"—and if there were deeds of shame, there was no general massacre. Most of the garrison was spared.

Still moving in a kind of dream, wherein he kept demanding of himself, "Awaken!" René watched the crowning scene of all. "The prisoners! Bring out the prisoners!"—and forth the seven wretches were dragged, terrified beyond their wits and expecting instant death, only to be smothered with kisses, lifted high in chairs, borne about the streets in one orgy of triumph.

A deep voice at Massac's shoulder. "I always thought that Paris was a tigress." He turned and saw the large face of Danton, seemingly the only collected mortal in all those transported thousands. The dream broke. The younger man knew that he grasped reality, the reality of an eternally altered world.

"Happy are you," spoke Danton again. "You have stood beneath the lightning bolt. The lightning has left you unscathed. Now take your story to Versailles."

.   .   .   .   .   .

Arnaud in some manner recovered the horses. They rode through Paris by the most tortuous of the back streets, all the main thoroughfares being blocked by the surging mobs. The shop fronts were still battened tight, and every householder who had good shutters blessed his fortune. Still, except near the City Hall, the crowds were more raucous than lawless, and there was little looting or common crime, and being far from the Hôtel de Ville, the Chevalier saw not that indescribable scene when Flesselles, "traitor to the people" for having encouraged de Launay to resist, paid for his blunder by being torn in pieces.

At the barriers leading to Versailles a very self-sufficient "Captain" of the National Guards was stopping all exits; deputy or no deputy, he seemed loath to let de Massac pass until a "Lieutenant" fortunately recollected seeing the Chevalier at the Hôtel des Invalides and a grudging egress was granted. The road to Versailles, however, was like traversing a region of the dead, the long highway deserted by cabs and riders, the villages all barred fast, with here and there frightened women peeping between closed shutters to see two riders sweep past. Sèvres and Chaville, silent as if by pestilence, then the struggling villas and closer roofs of Versailles, and finally a picket of Germans, who, however, crowded up beside the riders, hungry themselves for news, and, truth to tell, with the air of men concerned for their own safety. Arnaud gave them a few words and Massac left them "ohing" and "ahing."

The Avenue de Paris at last, the great reaches of the chateau, an officer running with undignified haste from the guard room. Doubtless the Chevalier was one tatter of blood and dirt, but the immaculate Brézé had never a reproof when, with a dozen more as noble as himself, he got the news from the messenger's own lips. Silk and crinoline were hanging over each of the balustrades. There were shrill cries of high-born dismay echoing down the upper corridors all the way to the cabinet of the Queen. Versailles had been charged with rumors for two days. All that day not one reliable courier had got through from Paris. And now this! This!

"Where was the King?"

His Majesty, despite anxious rumor and uncertainty, had elected to go hunting. The Duc de Rochefoucauld-Liancourt, the one sure friend of liberalism at the court, accepted the ungracious task of seeking now the King of France. With René at his side, they rode out to the great game preserves beyond the chateau. The shadows of the long summer day were falling across the trees, the hunt was gradually returning. They heard shots in the distance, met keepers bringing in the slaughtered deer, heard now the horns and the "Taiaut! Taiaut!" summoning home the dogs.

A lordly master-huntsman condescended to inform the Duke that the King was approaching, and Louis rode up, gun in hand and a flush on his heavy cheeks from brisk galloping. When he saw the Duke, he reined and his smile became puzzled; when he saw Massac, the smile became more puzzled still. Rochefoucauld almost forgot his salutation as he beckoned to his companion. "Tell the King, Chevalier."

In the fewest possible words, the messenger told the story of the day. The King's heavy jaw fell slowly, as his bewilderment increased, then at last he found speech. "Why, this is a revolt!"

The Duke bent low in his own saddle. *No, Sire, this is a revolution.*

CHAPTER XVII

CRUMBLING SPLENDOR

On the eleventh of July, Necker had been dismissed and the foreign troops ordered to draw their coil around Versailles and Paris. On the fifteenth of July, Louis XVI was writing with his own hand to the deposed finance minister, begging that he resume his portfolio, and one of the deputies was adding to a letter, "Yes, truly we shall be free. Our hands will never wear shackles again!"

The Assembly had stood fast, had voted its confidence in Necker, had sat *en permanence* ready for any issue. And now the troops had failed the Monarchy, and Paris had become one armed camp. If the Oeil-de-Boeuf had not yet been stormed, Broglie at least had no power to prevent it. There were white faces in the great galleries, the parterres, the Orangerie, the enormous park. When Majesty arose on the morning of the sixteenth, this prince had been conspicuous by his absence, and that duke had sent excuses. Majesty had to receive his shirt from merely a baron. Dreux-Brézé mournfully assured his intimates that here was proof positive that the dissolution of society was at hand.

Faces were certainly pale enough a little later when the King, having partaken of his chocolate with admirable appetite, saw his cabinet invaded by the Queen, by his two brothers, by Condé and others of the high and hitherto mighty. The Queen's toilet appeared hasty. Artois vainly fumbled in a pocket for a forgotten snuff-box; Monsieur

196

quoted Horace incessantly, a well-known habit of his when he was very nervous.

Louis received them, however, quietly, sitting and stirring his last cup of chocolate, and beckoned for his company to be seated. Marie Antoinette declined the proffered chair with a toss, thereby condemning all the others to remain standing; then with excited faces they crowded around the King.

"Have you heard?" demanded his consort.

"Heard what, Madame?" asked Louis with heavy courtesy.

"The Assembly has last night voted to ask you to visit Paris. To put yourself into the wolves' den; to condone the rebellion; to put the seal of royal approval upon the violation of your fortresses, the slaughter of your officers."

Louis continued to stir his chocolate. "What would you have me do? What does Broglie say?"

"What does Broglie say?" groaned Monsieur. "Oh, Sire, my brother; where were your ears? Broglie has fled."

"Broglie fled!" The royal spoon clattered down upon the carpet.

"It is true, Monsieur, shamefully true," hissed the Queen. "The Marshal, who was so confident in his Swiss and his Germans, started last night for Sedan. He said that he believed the frontier garrisons were still very loyal, that he could raise them and come back to our rescue. Who knows? He has deserted us. We must save ourselves."

"Save ourselves?" echoed the King, reaching for the spoon, which all the company were too excited to retrieve for him.

"Save ourselves, Sire," cried the Queen, eyes enkindled, cheeks now surging with color. "We have laid away one son. We still have another. For his inheritance if not for ourselves we must play the part of the sovereigns of

France. See——" And she held out a tightly corded
packet.

"What is this, Madame?" asked Louis with a certain
curiosity.

"My jewels, Sire. Packed already."

"Where shall we go, Madame?" resumed the King.

"To Metz. The garrison is strong and surely is loyal.
Those troops are far from Paris. They will not be wrought
upon by the republican canaille. We will come back with
them and conquer France."

"Conquer France, Madame?" Louis' eyes at length
dilated; being very large eyes the effect was almost startling.
"Do you know what you are saying?"

Marie Antoinette's hands tightened, her foot tapped the
floor. "Would to God that I were a man!" rang her answer.

"I entreat you, Sire, my brother," put in Artois, who
had been gnawing his lip, "to heed the counsels of the
Queen. You owe it to your rank, to your house, to your
kingdom to teach these rebels the lesson earned by their
crimes. Our great ancestor Louis XIV——"

The King rose from his seat not without a certain dignity: "I am not Louis XIV, brother. If I were, there
would have been no States General. You say 'Fly to Metz.'
What proof that the troops there are more loyal? Why
was I lied to about the Swiss and the Germans? Why
were my wishes overborne about the Royal Session—about
keeping Necker?" The King reached for his hat, thrust it
beneath his arm and beckoned to the gentleman-in-waiting
near the door: "Tell M. Bailly, the President of the Assembly, that to-morrow, acceding to his wishes, I shall accompany a delegation of the deputies to Paris."

The princes bowed with studied if ironical ceremony, and
the Queen's congé was equally elaborate. The King simply nodded to them stiffly, the uncertain smile still upon

his face, but the instant the glass door had clicked Artois exploded into all the oaths in the arsenal of his princely rank; Monsieur shrugged, muttered and frowned sardonically; the Queen cast the jewel packet upon the floor and wrung her hands passionately. "If—if——" was all she could say for the moment.

"'If' what, sister?" suggested Monsieur, the calmest of the group.

"If worst comes to worst, I at least was not born in France. When my child's throne seems in jeopardy, I can recall that I have an imperial brother in Vienna. *His* troops will not mutiny."

Monsieur shrugged a second time. "Parbleu, sister. I hope it won't come to that!" And then half reflectively: "You are right—I wish that you were a man."

His spirit had continued willing, but René de Massac's flesh at length had proved itself weak. After his interview with the King he told his tale to Father François, then weariness and emotion conquered. For four-and-twenty hours he lay dead to the world in his Versailles chamber. For two days more he rested there literally waiting for his head to clear. Thus it was he escaped being asked to join the group of deputies who on the seventeenth accompanied the King to Paris.

Coming without the Queen and his unpopular brothers, the Parisians welcomed Louis gladly. He was still "the good King," victim like themselves of the overweening court. "Welcome!" and *"Vive le Roi!"* blended joyously with *"Vive la Nation!"* True, certain moments might have made the old Valois and Bourbon monarchs rise out of their graves, as when Louis was told to his face that "once a King had conquered Paris, but now Paris had conquered her king." But Louis had known how to keep his phlegmatic smile and to pin the tricolor cockade [1] upon his own hat. He had confirmed Bailly as the new Mayor and Lafayette as chief of the National Guard. Therefore he returned to Versailles amid long cheers; and the "Revolt" had indeed been sanctioned as the "Revolution," and Louis Capet seemed to be one of the very few men in France who did not take in what had actually happened.

The King smiled, but the palace groaned, and groaned still more as tidings multiplied. Not merely had Foulon, venerable sinner, who had bidden the people to eat hay, been torn in pieces, but mobs had violated the aristocratic avenues of St. Germain itself. Sedate old noblemen had been dashed in the mire, sedan chairs upset, stately footmen thrashed, high-born ladies pelted with mud and ribaldry. Saroni's restaurant had been sacked from end to end, then suddenly reopened with the significant sign, "Café du Peuple." A shabby coat and a tricolor cockade formed the only safe walking costume. Carriages with armorial bearings had their windows broken. As for the Bastille it was already being demolished stone by stone, not a few of its blocks being cut up to make souvenirs. With reason the palace groaned.

But the high-born mourners around the Oeil-de-Boeuf were a dwindling coterie. Broglie had already taken the road toward the Rhine. The smiling, sensual Artois, who had talked so glibly of "the sword of Henry IV," had fled in the night, with his servant lashing the coach horses. Condé fled. The Duchesse de Polignac, the Queen's evil genius, fled, poorly consoled by a tear-blotted letter from Marie Antoinette herself. Many another fled. And after that, although M. Hübli still opened and shut the glass

[1] Camille Desmoulins' green cockade had been abandoned as being the color of the hated Artois. The precise origin of the famous *tricolor* adopted immediately to replace it is somewhat uncertain.

door, although the royal shirt and the Grand Couvert still required their solemn liturgies, Dreux-Brézé and his fellow courtiers could only moan their Ichabod, "the glory is departed from the palace."

The palace mourned, its adversaries of course triumphed. All of Massac's friends came to congratulate him. M. de Robespierre sat stiffly by his couch and spoke of "honorable scars" (where a grape-shot had scratched him) and carefully likened the uprising of Paris to the expulsion of the Tarquins. All the Chevalier's circle agreed that the recent uproar would have no successor. "The Revolution is achieved!" Henceforth, amid only the peaceful arguments of virtuous patriots, there would be established the reign of philosophy and enlightenment!

The speeches in the Assembly were of the rhapsodic order. Resistance to the Revolution had vanished in thin air. Tricolor banners now flew before the most aristocratic hotels and the palace itself. The German and Swiss mercenaries disappeared suddenly. In the court milliner's and dressmaker's windows as suddenly there appeared caps with "Equality puffs" and gowns with "Liberty flounces"! René was delightfully sure that everybody now was expectant, contented, happy. Had not the last bulwark of tyranny crumbled, as France advanced rejoicing to her Utopia?

Save for the one thing gnawing at his inner heart, Massac for a few ecstatic days moved amid perfect contentment. The Revolution was no dream and he himself had helped to make it a reality. His conduct since that exciting night he had flung up his commission in the Body Guard seemed completely justified. Only Father François ventured to put a little curb upon his satisfaction. "We are starting on a long road; we have crossed the first barriers, but there remain many toll-bridges."

"Toll-bridges? But the King has accepted the Revolution, the army has accepted it; the Queen is helpless; Artois and Condé have quitted France. What is there to fear?"

"Many things, and most of all ourselves."

"Why are you always a questioner, Father?"

"Because it is always best to question everything, except the eternal goodness of God."

Then suddenly came a more serious blow to the Chevalier's complacency in the form of a visit from Laurent.

His cousin had not visited his room at the *Fox* since René had appeared as deputy at Versailles. The latter was just now returned from a session which thrilled with the glowing liberalism of Barnave. To his surprise he saw Laurent not in his uniform of the Body Guard, but in simple gray and black.

"Jolly times you and your friends provide us, cousin," was the visitor's greeting.

"But not jolly coats and stockings, it would seem. What would you?"

"Well, most beloved donkey, your high-born and superlatively elegant associates have made it eminently wise for me to take a trip to Brussels."

"To Brussels? *Peste*—you are not Artois, Laurent!"

"No, my dear general of carters and bargees, I am not Artois, but I am favored with a father who is accounted Monseigneur's peculiar friend. I have also a mother who is more than the bosom intimate of La Polignac. Yesterday as we were driving near Meudon our coach was accosted by—well, let me say some of your elegant comrades of the fourteenth, acting of course in the name of your new and equally genteel principles, 'Liberty, Equality, Fraternity.' In behalf of Liberty we were loudly cursed, of Equality our carriage was stoned, the true meaning of Fraternity I regret to say we did not stop to test. An exalted patriot—ten days ago I might have preferred to say 'brigand'—had hold of the horses' heads. I was unpatriotic enough to flog him off, and by putting the horses at speed we avoided—fraternizing. In slightly different words we had a narrow escape. —Pardon therefore the weakness of my mother. You know her nerves. She feels now that the air of Belgium is at present more healthful than that of France."

"Your mother and I have hardly been dear relations of late," admitted the Chevalier, "yet this accident I sorely regret. Of course there will be (he spoke confidently) deplorable ebullitions among the masses. The populace has not yet learned how to use its new freedom."

"It is learning; never fear that," spoke the Viscount with a grimace.

"Your parents' actions," completed René, "are their own. But you? Does the Queen spare you so readily in times like these from the Body Guard?"

Laurent drew his chair closer and looked about him like a man deliberating about risking a confidence: "Listen, cousin. You and I (worse luck!) are on opposite sides of this tennis court, but I can trust you with my honor as I trust myself.—The Queen wishes me to go with them."

"Wishes? You are in no danger. Why should she send *you* away?"

Laurent's lips opened uneasily as if he had possibly said a word too much: "Why, but simply to guard my parents, to be sure."

René thrust back the mass of papers upon his table: "Dearest cousin. You have said that your honor is safe with me.—Safe it is. And because I would have it equally safe with the world let me speak as one comrade to another.—Has the Shepherdess been bewitching you as— ah! one night, she was once bewitching someone else?"

The Viscount's discomfort visibly increased: "You knew that she was friendly to all of us who had the entrée."

"I know it. And you know what the people call her everywhere."

"The Austrian?"

"Of course; and if princes must mate with princesses Maria Theresa's daughter is worthy to be Queen of France. But France is not her fatherland, it is only the kingdom of her husband, the heritage of her children. Do you begin to understand?"

"She is a beautiful woman, foully maligned. Whoever has gentle blood and a heart of chivalry——"

"Laurent," spoke the Chevalier, "beware of such a summons. It has brought noble heads to the block and sprinkled blood on provinces. The Queen looks on France as if all the realm lay as a fair estate beneath her windows. It is such a thought that forced the Royal Session; that brought up the mercenaries; that now sends Artois, Polignac, your parents flying from the realm. There is something better worth risking life and honor for than even the behests of the Queen—it is France herself."

Laurent had recovered his equanimity: "Plague on you, cousin. I say a few simple words and you fly off into heroics fit for the *Hermiade*. Faith, I think that serving the Queen and serving France are much the same thing."

"Take care, dear fellow. We must differ, but take care that you differ with wide-open eyes. We are Massacs, and plenty of Massacs in the old days may have conspired or fought against their king of the hour, but never against the safety of France."

"Conspired? Fought? *Parbleu*, René, it's only to be a harmless little trip to Vienna after landing my parents safe in Brussels."

The Chevalier clapped his hand on the other's shoulder: "Your honor is indeed safe with me. But for your own sake I entreat this—think for yourself, and do not become the tool of others.—When do you set forth?"

"To-morrow, René, and"—with a sheepish look upon the carpet—"I have something else to add. Beside my mother a certain lady goes with me."

"A certain lady?"

"Confusion upon it! Why was it so hard to say in the first place—the women are wringing their hands over such a wedding. I am to be married this afternoon at St. Louis' to Louise de Broglie——"

At which the Chevalier's shout made the panes of the window to rattle, despite any wistful twinges.

. . . Laurent was married and he, his wife and his parents were gone, after friendly greetings between the Chevalier and the bride, very cold nods between the Chevalier and his aunt and uncle, and an almost passionate farewell between the cousins. Both, under a mighty show of handclasping and embracing, were registering what each keenly felt, that the true days of separation were at hand, when each Frenchman of honor must choose solemnly his own path and follow devotedly to whatever its end.—For weal or for woe he must accept the Revolution or must strive against it, henceforth there could be no safe inglorious neutrals.

Laurent was not unmindful of the wistfulness and melancholy upon his cousin's face as he swung his bride up the high steps of the berlin. "Keep a brave heart," he encouraged, "I give you the Spanish proverb, 'To-day for me but to-morrow for thee.'"

"Farewell, nephew," waved the old Comte de Massac grimly. "I say again what Artois said when he left, 'Back in three months.' Prepare then for your lesson."

The coach rumbled off into the dust of the St. Germain road. René stifled the reflection, 'Another chapter of my

life is closed,' and for four days gained a relief from private
sorrows by renewed faithfulness at the Hall of the Small
Diversions. The new constitution was being vigorously
debated—one chamber or two? And ought the King to
possess a veto?—Then all unwarned, as the Chevalier
quitted the Hall one torrid afternoon, a man accosted him
at the entrance. It was André, the old servant of the
Durands, whom Massac had left in charge of his Paris
apartment.

"M. le Chevalier, this letter is from Picardy. The disorder of the country must have made it very slow in the
mails."

The cheap paper was addressed with many flourishes:

*"To the exalted, high-born and very noble René, Cheva-
lier, Seigneur and Député de Massac."*

"A petition, doubtless," sighed the recipient. "When will
the Assembly cease to be pestered?" Then he broke the
wafer, and ten seconds later André saw his master change
color. The letter was signed, *"Benoit, Curé de Massac."*

CHAPTER XVIII

THE GREAT FEAR

Good Father Benoit had been sorely perplexed over Nicolas' pricked leather. If the peasant had not been as illiterate as the priest's gray cat, Benoit would have doubted the entire business. As it was the curé did not discard Virginie's appeal, although being alike cowardly and irenic he had not dared to organize a searching party to visit the cabin. He simply wrote to the Chevalier, using as grand a style of composition as possible (the Chevalier being very near to the King), reciting the woodcutter's story and copying the few sentences marked upon the leather. After that Benoit left the epistle at the *Silver Swan*. Here it remained four days, then by a customary mistake the post cart took it to Ard, and then slowly (the country having become direfully unsettled) it crept back toward Paris. Late in July neither Benoit nor Nicolas had heard a word more about it.

Nicolas in fact had had his own problems. First his eldest married daughter had twins—what a neighborhood flurry! Then three men in blue coats appeared as usual to collect the salt tax. Nicolas knew their methods and waited trembling, but they visited Long Aubri the first. Lo! to official horror Aubri's salt box contained *clean* salt, not admixed with sand and refuse, proof positive therefore that the commodity had not been bought from the King but lawlessly smuggled.

"Aha!" spoke the corporal of the blue coats. "You know

what that means. Get your cap. You'll come with us to Ard."

Thereupon Aubri's Angeline ran into the village square throwing her apron over her head and shrieking, bringing all the neighbors out before the smithy. Then happened something unprecedented since the founding of Massac. Denys, the smith—Aubri's nephew—swung around with his largest hammer, and half a dozen of the stoutest peasants seized pitchforks. "Leave my uncle alone!" ordered Denys. The three men in blue muttered something about "Cowardly dogs bark the loudest," and looked for their guns; next they cursed, for Angeline had knocked all the flints out.

The three collectors took no one with them to Ard. They were glad to make off themselves, leaving behind them guns, cartridge boxes, hats and coats. "The dragoons will burn your haystacks to-morrow!" shouted the white-faced corporal as the pursuit ceased on the brow of the hill.

When the trio were gone, the peasants all blinked stupidly. Heroes were they or suicidal fools? The women got their movables ready to flee into the woods while Denys, Aubri and Nicolas took the captured guns, paraded around and tried to look fierce. A day and a night and no dragoons, then in rattled the mail cart; André edged up by the driver as he tried to wet his whistle at the inn:

"Know what happened at Soissons?" Of course nobody knew, and the fellow winked and continued: "Well, there was old Benet, the grain speculator. He had crammed his warehouse waiting for famine prices. A big crowd waited on him with 'Open, open, we want bread!' He seemed a trifle slow. 'To the lamp-post!' shouted somebody. 'That's what they're doing in Paris,' bawled another. I saw them burst in his doors, put on the rope and swing him off on

the lamp bracket. The minute he was up a woman began
a kind of litany to the lamp-posts:

> 'Scare-crow of rascals, avenge us!
> Terror of aristocrats, avenge us!'

When I left Soissons boys were tossing about the flour
like so much snow."

"Where were the constables?" asked a peasant.

"Helping the boys," laughed the driver.

"Where were the sheriffs?"

"Barricaded in the Hôtel de Ville, and happy they weren't
up on the lamp-posts themselves."

"And the dragoons?" This was followed by explanations
as to what had happened in the village.

"*Citizens!*" condescended the driver. "Fellow Citizens—
can it really be you haven't heard about the Revolution?"

"Revolution? What's that," whistled a very old peasant,
"a new game that they're playing in Paris?"

The self-important driver thereupon delivered almost an
oration. Its purport made Nicolas' brain to spin. He later
told Brigitte that the world must have been turned upside
down, for the King could not give orders any more, neither
could that heartless Austrian woman, his wife. His great
castle at Paris was being demolished; private soldiers were
as good now as their officers and poor workingmen as fat
bourgeois. No more imposts, no more salt tax, and of
course no more men in blue coats nor dragoons. That was
the Revolution. It had happened almost over one night.—
Hurrah!

"And we peasants?" demanded the skeptical Brigitte.

"Don't say 'peasants' any more. We're all 'Citizens,'
just as good as the seigneurs. We can cut wood and shoot
deer wherever and whenever we want to."

"Holy St. Anne," vowed Brigitte at last, "what a blessed day!"

But Brigitte was less happy when that night Nicolas reeled homeward. He and forty others had asserted their new citizenship by sacking the house of the most hated man near Massac, the agent for the Amiens brewer who had bought up most of the seigneurial taxes. The agent had very wisely decamped, but not with his well-stocked cellar. Nicolas was full of eau-de-vie and bit Brigitte's ear when she thrust him into bed. The next day all of the forty lay like logs, and their wives found the Revolution rather perplexing.

No work in Massac all that week. After mass on Sunday Father Benoit read off queer proclamations from some great man at Ard. The big words implied that something wonderful had happened at Paris, that France was sure soon to be prosperous but that in the meantime "all good citizens and patriots" (how Nicolas loved to hear those words!) must work as usual and pay the old taxes. Clearly here was some error. The Revolution, of course, meant that the old taxes were gone like last year's grass. Had Father Benoit read the long papers aright?

Monday, however, there was fearful panic. Two farmers had started for Ard to do some trading. In a lonely spot they had been set upon by five tall, black fellows with guns. One traveler who resisted had been shot like a rabbit. The other barely escaped after being stripped to his blouse. That night every woman went to bed shivering, "The brigands! The brigands!" The next morning no mail cart came from Ard, but only terrible rumors. "The city was in the grip of rioters. Shops were being plundered and women insulted on the streets." Travel on the high road had almost ceased. Only a big berlin once clattered up to the *Silver Swan*. The curtains had been drawn, but while the postilions cursed the ostlers for not changing the horses quicker, a white and frightened but very aristocratic old face had peeped out of the door, then banged it shut. Clearly something strange was happening!

Most certainly too every tax collector, gamekeeper, provost, and every other official whom the peasants had dreaded more than they did the devil, all had miraculously disappeared; that is, all but Voullard, the lanky tithe collector, who was caught slinking across the bridge toward dusk. Not a farmer but had seen him claim the fattest fowl, the fullest sheaf for the bishop. Voullard was promptly dropped in the current as naked as God made him. Could he swim? At all events he vanished forever from Massac.

One emblem of the old still remained. Hedged above its trees rose the donjon of the Chevalier's chateau, with the steward's and caretakers' families inhabiting it. Very soon a band of peasants roistering through the park shouted, "Let's go through the castle!" However, they quickly discovered that the drawbridge was up, while a man with a gun visible upon the turret over the gate-house discouraged close acquaintance. The Revolution therefore did not quite extend to the chateau—as yet.

The chateau's master furthermore was personally popular. He was not the bishop nor the tax-farmer, and Long Aubri said plainly that if the Chevalier was down at Paris making the Revolution for them, it was rather a shabby requittal to raid his property. The others all seemed to agree, except lame Silvain (the glibbest talker in the village), who said "Yes, if the chateau was his property. But didn't it rather belong to that great thing Le Peuple which so many now seemed to be praising?" Silvain's argument was not pursued. The drawbridge seemed undebatable. Nevertheless, was the Revolution complete while the chateau still was standing? Little groups debated it through one summer gloaming after another. Then followed fearful stories about "the brigands." Nobody knew exactly who they were. In fact, barring the small bands of lawless wanderers, none were visible. "Ard had been burned flat," went one story. The next day the city was reputed safe and tolerably law-abiding, thanks to the new National Guard. Then suddenly one afternoon the parish bell set up a clamor. A terror-stricken lad ran in blubbering that Garnes (the next village) was being sacked, he had heard an awful shrieking, and the ruffian horde was surely headed for Massac. Garnes was certainly in flames.—At this all the women and children started, squalling, for the woods. The men, with every weapon available, formed on the road, to do battle for their hearthstones.

They did not have to do battle. Just at dusk a Garnes peasant wandered in. Everything, he vowed, was quiet. The shrieking had come from a farm where they were killing pigs. The "flames" had been only the afternoon sun on some red house roofs.—It was pitch-dark, however, before they got the women back from the woods.[1]

* * * * * * * *

After Nicolas' visits to the cabin, for a few days life had worn a brighter aspect for Virginie Durand. Crushed and beaten as it was, her hope was a tenacious plant. The least nurturing revived it. At first she had imagined (having had nothing to do with peasants outside of romances and Watteau pictures) that despite the woodcutter's protests of helplessness he would promptly bring a relief party. Then as a couple of days slipped on, she began reckoning on the time of the posts to Paris. Someone had surely written to the Chevalier immediately and the post cart

[1] The good villagers at Massac had an alarm which seems to have been precisely like that of several larger French towns during this summer of confusion.

would take one day to Soissons, another to Paris. As for
René she told herself four-and-twenty hours of furious
riding could bring him to the chateau—and after that?—
Why he ought to be thundering in with his rescue already!

Four days, five, six, a week. All was as before. Nearly
another week. Not the least change in her monotonous
captivity. Had René even been in Paris to receive a message? What had befallen him in Holland? Not the least
sign of Nicolas. Had not his visits been only a part of her
fearful dreams engendered by the opium?—The one evidence she possessed that the episode had been real was that
the old leathern knapsack, once lying in a corner of her
prison, had certainly disappeared. It was too insignificant
an object, however, for any of her jailers to notice.

Virginie manifestly was drooping. She had ceased to
rage and struggle, and Olympie in turn ceased to force on
her the drops. Her appetite flagged. Whenever the others
saw her, she was either sitting or lying listlessly on the
pallet in the inner cabin. Olympie began to grow alarmed.

"The girl is pining away," she announced one afternoon
to Thibaud. "All the spirit is gone out of her. She needs
medicine, a physician."

"A grave digger would help us more," returned her consort concisely.

"Would help us less, you hulking fool. Do you think
the lawyers who've gripped onto her property will simply
let go of it and smile when you say, 'My niece died on my
hands. I am her lawful heir?'—Oh! there would be a lovely
process and plenty of questions.—But, after all, there can
be deaths that hurt one more than that from a slip noose."

"Silence, woman; you turn my stomach!" ordered Thibaud, seizing his hatchet and quitting the cabin to kill a
fowl.

Olympie, however, was sincerely troubled. Without probing all of her history, it can be said that she was a child of a Paris small grocer. Evil circumstance had started her downward, ending in that arrest as an accomplice of shoplifters. Fortune then had smiled to the extent that she was only sent to Ste. Pelagie while her more guilty companions mounted the gallows, but when she was released her reputation was gone. She had fled to Ard and had become contracted to Thibaud. Were they married? Olympie affirmed that they were. Thibaud (in less affectionate moments) swore that they were not, and Olympie sometimes confessed to herself that Thibaud was probably right. They had been on the point of separating when Vernet had opened the grand speculation as to Virginie Durand. Until that venture was ended, perforce the pair stuck together.

Olympie had boasted she had drowned all scruples and remorse "like kittens in the river." She had entered upon Linio's and Thibaud's project with entire willingness to cut a throat at the proper instant. But Olympie had failed to understand a very intimate companion—her own self. It was impossible day after day to have the custody of Virginie Durand, and not to be subjected to a powerful influence. Desperately as the prisoner had resisted, she had never put off the dignity, modesty, noble self-control which became her father and her lover. In her bitterest moments the contrast between her inborn delicacy and the sordid creatures who ranged around the Bridewell had not been lost upon Olympie. Little by little the attitude of Virginie's custodian altered. She had actually tried to seem conciliatory; had administered the stupefying drops as infrequently as Thibaud would suffer her; had permitted trifling indulgences; and had finally gone to the uttermost (which was not very far) that the others would permit her toward making captivity tolerable.

They had come to the cabin between Garnes and Massac as a refuge for a few weeks. "The great Abbé whom I serve," Linio had boasted, "will soon arrange everything." The weeks, nevertheless, had lengthened into months, summer was more than half over and the "great Abbé" had apparently arranged nothing. Olympie began to nurture the vehement suspicion that the reverend gentleman, having broken up the Chevalier's marriage and satisfied his unknown principals, cared not two straws more about the affair, but had simply urged Linio to "marry the girl" as the easiest manner of dismissing the subject.

Linio came and went. Sometimes when he discussed marrying the prisoner and Thibaud made difficulties, he was conciliatory, sometimes very ugly. It was easy enough to agree that after marriage the property should be divided equally, half to the husband, half to the uncle. Easy enough for the Baron to say, "Leave me alone with her in the cabin overnight—she'll be clamoring to have in the priest in the morning."—Unfortunately, however, Thibaud's polite attendance upon the courts had taught him a little of the law. The husband's control of a wife's property was nearly absolute; and where was the procureur whom the Durands could rely upon to draw up a pre-nuptial contract that could get through the Palais de Justice if Linio repudiated it? The arrangements always broke down upon that, Olympie artfully stimulating Thibaud's distrust.

Then Linio's attitude gradually changed. He rode in with amazing news. The world upset; strange things at Versailles; stranger things at Paris. Queer doings even at Ard and among the peasantry. One evening the Baron tore back with his horse in a foam and a bullet hole through one coat-tail. He had been beset by robbers in the forest. "A close shave." After that he and Thibaud took turns watching almost all night, and Olympie grew more uneasy than ever.

Linio seemed possessed of a new idea. He stopped hectoring and would sit watching his companions out of the corners of his eyes like a man planning something. If Olympie seemed to notice, he would pull out the paper he obtained in Ard, and pretend to read, then mount his horse and disappear in the forest. Olympie's distrust mounted unceasingly. She could barely spell, and Thibaud of course could not do even that, but the long black lines on the Baron's paper troubled her. At last in the middle of one afternoon Linio rose with an extraordinarily pronounced smile, and bowed very ceremoniously first to Thibaud and then to Olympie.

"So, my friends, you still refuse to say 'Marry and divide,' eh?—Well, this evening we will resume the argument. Perhaps I can find a better way to plead my cause. Perhaps I may even say 'Marry without dividing at all.'" He clapped on his hat and swung into his saddle. As he did so the paper which he had thrust into a pocket rolled out upon the ground, but the horse was prancing and he did not notice. The instant he was gone Olympie was upon the sheet as a cat upon the mouse, and carried the printing straight in to her prisoner.

Virginie read the journal to her; read things which sent the color momentarily back into her own cheeks, and which almost set Olympie to gasping.—France was being reborn. The King was a despot no more. The palace was helpless. The Assembly was drafting a constitution.

All this Virginie devoured with raptures, but her custodian barely comprehended; Olympie understood better what was on the back pages. The enthusiastic editor of the "Voice of the People" (a new venture in Ard) was fain to admit that there had been certain ebullitions attending this emancipation of France; in fact there had been "regrettable disorders." Corn-factors and unpopular royal officials had developed a habit of dying very suddenly. Travelers' coaches were being everywhere stopped. The mail carts hardly ran at all. "More regrettable still," the Ard prison had been broken open by a mob, thereby releasing many "doubtful citizens." The woods furthermore swarmed with blackguards, and bands of peasants were raiding and burning isolated chateaux as the best means of abolishing seigneurial dues forever.

Olympie left her prisoner in her transports and ran back to Thibaud.

"Lump," she announced, "do you smell the broth Linio is brewing? Do you know what he means by 'argument to-night'?" Then she rehearsed what Virginie had just read.

Thibaud's oaths were quite worthy of an executioner's helper.

"If the woods are full of escaped jailbirds, Linio's game is certain. There are only the two of us, but——" He grasped his gun, snapped back the pan, and renewed the priming.

"Of course he is off in the woods now, compounding with some gang to slit our wind-pipes and carry her off. I've already suspected as much," completed Olympie.

"Devils of hell," swore her companion, "I wish I were back in Ard. I wish that smooth Abbé was in torment. It was you that backed him up and persuaded me, woman——"

Olympie prudently laid hands on the second gun: "Bray sense, even if you must have long ears. You were the keenest of us after this thing once opened. Rage and curses won't stop Linio. I at least want to be alive to-morrow."

"So do I. He may be back in an hour with a dozen jailbirds."

"I think not. Such brisk fellows won't do his work on first promises. It'll take a lot of talking; besides he's got to make sure they won't take the girl away from him.— We've got at least until dark."

Thibaud threw down his gun, and collapsed upon a stool, clutching his head. *"Bon dieu!"* he vowed. "Again I see nothing to do but to kill her."

"A fine way to smooth down Linio! Then if we made off he could set the law on us to track us."

"There's little enough law in France now," urged Thibaud.

"Plenty enough still for our undoing if Linio cares to steer it."

Thibaud continued to clutch his head and to curse. "We'll have to kill her!" he reiterated.

"Think of one thing, blockhead. Think of the Chevalier. Compound with him. He's as good as King now."

"How get her away?" groaned the man; next he beckoned toward the shelf. "My head isn't right. Pour me a stiff dram, you trollop."

Olympie went over to take the bottle. Then her gaze went from Thibaud on his stool to the door of the prison chamber and back again. "He'll do her presently," she whispered to herself. "The spirits'll heat up his courage. If not that, Linio gets her—unless——" No one saw her eyes, although sparks were coming from them. Her hand was closing over a small vial. "Now or never," she completed.

"What's keeping you? My head spins," bawled Thibaud.

"The cork sticks," responded his consort, at length extending a small pannikin.

The man took the contents at one swig. "That's queer,"

he remarked; only to be assured that it was "The Dutch-man's best."

Thibaud continued to sit clutching his head and cursing to himself; presently, however, his mutterings abated and his head and shoulders actually slid forward upon the table. There was still an hour of daylight, but for all that the fellow was breathing heavily. Olympie dashed a billet of wood across the cabin; despite the clatter he did not stir. Whereupon with a lightning dart she flung open Virginie's prison: "Quick, my bird, quick."

Virginie emerged, white and trembling. She held her hands to her breast: "I could hear everything. He is going to kill me. Oh! let him be swift. I've long prepared for it. Better that than Linio."

"He shall never touch you. See, he lies like a clod. I have given him your drops, poured half the vial into the eau-de-vie. But if you have heard, why then you know already.—We must hasten." And Olympie spurned her unresisting consort with her heel.

"We hasten? Whither?" Virginie reeled unsteadily; and her jailoress refilled a second pannikin, reassuring with, "Only good liquor. I've forgot you haven't walked for months. No matter, Olympie is strong. Lean now on me, for we must get deep into the woods by dark."

"Into the woods," still wondered the girl, "and where then?"

"To the chateau. It belongs to your Chevalier. Some of his people are there, a steward, a caretaker. You will talk to them. They will keep us safe."

Olympie had flung a coarse cloak over her prisoner's shoulders, seized a like garment herself, then thrust in her belt a wallet of bread and cheese and a stout knife.

"Take your chance, lout!" was her farewell to the stertorous Thibaud. "I at least have kept my senses."

Despite her weakness when once on the threshold Virginie burst from the cabin like a swallow from a broken cage. "Not that way, poor fool," Olympie had to command, chasing her down the path. "That's how Linio will come. Here—on my arm. And now it's into the greenwood for us!"

. . . The ferns and brakes closed over them. The shadows were growing long among the trees, and Virginie was panting as they went up the dry bed of a spring-time brook, but Olympie's strength failed not. They had advanced a good two miles by the time it was pitch-dark in the dingle.

Well that they had done so. Just as the last shadows merged into blackness Linio arrived at the cabin with five low-browed fellows carrying guns and swords. Thibaud was now lying face upward upon the floor. He barely groaned when they prodded him with their sword points.

CHAPTER XIX

THE CHATEAU DREADS THE HOVEL

If the will could have ordered the deed, René de Massac's ride after opening Father Benoit's missive would have surpassed any courier's feat in the annals of France. Benoit had written ramblingly and hesitatingly; he had entreated the mighty Seigneur and Chevalier to "condescend to pardon his presumption" because the matter was so improbable; but he had made it clear that apparently a young woman calling herself Virginie Durand was confined by one Thibaud Durand and others in the woods near Massac village.

The "Declaration of the Rights of Man," the bill of liberties for delivered France was just coming before the Assembly for first debate. To one deputy at least this charter of freedom suddenly became the least important item in the world. Nevertheless the madness of surging hope did not wholly destroy the Chevalier's method. Enough of the unsettled state of the land already had come through to Versailles to dictate certain precautions; money and credentials, and Arnaud again had to secure horses, this time one also for André, for it would have been sheer cruelty to leave the devoted major-domo to eat out his heart pacing the streets of Paris.

Once more René knelt before Father François for his blessing: "Before I rode for France, now I ride for Virginie —if God can save the first He can save the second!" After his benediction, Father François raised and kissed him—his

own tears falling fast. Then the little cavalcade of three
pounded northward on the straight road for Picardy.

They had not gone five leagues before René had cause
to thank his friendly saints that he was a deputy. At the
bridge across the Seine at Conflans they were halted in the
twilight by a whole company of armed men, some with
muskets, some with pitchforks, declaring themselves to be
the local National Guard, on the lookout for "foes of the
Nation." Ordinary passports were waste paper. "No
thoroughfare until morning." And one burly fellow suggested that the whole party had better be searched for
"letters to Artois." René had need to put on his boldest
front, while Arnaud rattled his scabbard and looked significantly at his pistols. At last by compromise the three
riders, escorted by at least two score of excited and suspicious patriots, had been taken up the steep streets of
the town to the little Hôtel de Ville, where an uncertain
and demoralized mayor looked over their passports.

Fortunately his courage sufficed enough to tell the escort
(whom he justly feared) that "The gentleman's papers
were all right. In fact he was the great Député de Massac
who had had such a part at the Bastille." Whereupon,
disappointed of a lynching, the leader of the "guard" did
the next pleasantest thing—called for rousing cheers for
"The patriot deputy," and, dragging René with him, insisted
on having "such a national hero" drink "confusion to all
tyrants" and other "national toasts" at the *Crown and Bell*.
If after this the National Hero somewhat scanted the hospitality, Arnaud made tolerable amends. At last amid
bravos and handclapping they were suffered to depart, but
three mortal hours had been lost. Instead of resting their
weary horses at Beaumont they were fain to do so at Pontoise—with Paris only well behind them.

The next day was much the same. Work seemed to

have stopped in all the villages. Peasants with old guns and pitchforks were patrolling the roads. "France is infected with *patrolism*," punned a disgusted traveler at the inn at L'Isle-Adam. The formula "Show your papers" came almost hourly. If the patrol leader could not read (and he seldom could) a stranger had then to be detained until the coming of some patriot a trifle initiated into the mystery. Suspicion breathed in the air. Nobody could explain what really was suspected. No matter; everyone must be questioned or even searched as if "Revolution," like the Palladium of Troy, was a kind of holy image likely to be smuggled out to the ruin of France, by some anti-patriot Monseigneur while he fled to the country.

The second night found Massac only at Compiègne. After the weary and harassed syndic had certified his papers he added a friendly query:

"You surely will not ride northward to-morrow, M. le député?"

"Why not, M. le syndic?"

"Because the peasants are now beyond restraint. All the jails are emptied, and the roads beset. The Beauvais diligence has just been halted, the travelers stripped to their bones, a respectable young woman carried into the woods."

"Then can I hire an escort of gendarmes?"

"Alas! Half of our gendarmes have run off with the jailbirds; the other half barely suffice to keep our shops and homes from instant pillage."

René and his servants rode on the next morning with pistols loose in the holsters. The high road was absolutely solitary; no riders, not a woman working in the fields. Then after leagues there rose a great column of smoke soaring above a wooded eminence, which presently began to flame like a volcano. Next they met two peasants in the middle of the road, gazing and gesturing in a kind of ecstasy.

"Where's the fire?" demanded Arnaud.

The younger fellow began turning uncouth handsprings, and then danced up and down, snapping his fingers. "They've lighted it! Burning! Burning! Long live the Nation!"

"What mean you?"

The older peasant at last recollected enough to pull off his cap. "Ah! Messieurs, he's cheering because of the bonfire at Aignan chateau. The old seigneur has starved us since we were brats. His lady made us beat the moat all night to keep the frogs from croaking. Now we are free. Plenty of bread, no more taxes." And he swung his cap and bawled to the naked countryside, "Long live the Revolution! Long live the Nation!"

The Chevalier rode on with the smoke spreading out like a vast canopy in the heavens, visible for many miles. At length André pricked up alongside:

"Monsieur, forgive a question. How long ago was it when that priest put his letter in the post at Massac?"

"Nearly three weeks now, my good fellow."

"Much can happen in three weeks, Monsieur."

"I know that, André." Massac's face was like a thunder cloud.

Nevertheless they dared not force their horses. Getting relays was out of the question. At last a hamlet and the creaking sign of an inn, but no signs of life save a few frightened cats. Much pounding by André at last produced the peeping glance of an old woman through a barely opened shutter.

"Within there," rang the summons, "fodder and something out of your pot for three!"

"Oh, misery! Are you real travelers? How did you get

through? All the rest here have fled to the woods. I was left—too weak and lame. Holy Mother of God, but I were better off in a purgatory!"

The shutter closed with a bang. The riders found water in a trough, tore hay out of the stack, devoured bread and cheese from their own wallets. Then they resumed. Still the straight, dusty, solitary road, but at last a turn covered by a thicket and willows. Arnaud gestured warningly:

"Something is moving behind there, Monsieur."

René glanced about. Nothing but bare, rolling country behind, no side path, no habitation. "Something has got to be dared, Arnaud," he observed, never reining.

"Ah! Your father would have said that!" snorted the old soldier, drawing his pistol, as did André.

The three swept forward, and there by the turn in the willows stood out six or seven men across the road. They had blouses and tattered jackets. A couple leveled fowling pieces, the rest brandished pitchforks or pikes.

"Halt!" they shouted in chorus. The Chevalier whipped out his sword and rode straight at them. "Oh! Lord," rang his warning, as the steel flashed on high, "grant pardon for the blood I am *about* to shed."

One gun missed fire. The saber caught the barrel of the other and set its discharge whirling through the air. The peasants broke like water, tumbling over their pikes as the three horsemen slashed through them. Arnaud let off a pistol to make them run the faster.

"I could make a better brigand myself," was his disgusted comment. Nevertheless the encounter nearly knocked up the horses; it was needful to walk them two miles. Night was falling again and before them was only Roye. The lights of the thrifty old town gleamed a welcome, but at the gate the unusually friendly captain of the National

Guard (in other days a coach-builder) after scrutinizing the passports, spoke out his surprise: "Have you really just come from Compiègne?"

"Even so, M. le capitaine."

"Thank the *bon Dieu* you are alive then, M. le député. Here in Roye we keep order, but the peasants have turned wild.—Look!" There was indeed a red light on the horizon to the east. "It is Mahieu chateau. Acheres chateau has barely ceased its glowing."

"Why burn them? Were their owners so oppressive?"

"At Acheres, yes; but at Mahieu the sieur was a very father to his people. I hear that they killed him. 'Revolution' has gone to the peasants' heads like strong waters."

René led the captain aside from his nudging, wondering guards: "Monsieur, you are a rare thing these days, a man of sense and courage. For pressing reasons I go on to my own chateau of Massac, six leagues further toward Ard. Is it burned yet?"

"Not to my knowledge—but of course to-night—who knows?"—with an eloquent shrug.

"I understand. My need is very great. I will pay well for ten stout men who will obey my orders."

"Impossible, M. le député. No man would quit Roye to-night. Our women are in agony, fearing an attack any instant."

Massac snapped his teeth. "Then I and my servants ride forward alone. At least get us three fresh horses."

"They can be had, Monsieur. But the risk—you can well be murdered ere you have gone a mile."

René's voice grew deeper: "*Mon capitaine,* my betrothed is near Massac and her risk is greater still."

"I comprehend." The captain (really a very intelligent fellow) made his eyes twinkle. Orders were given. At the

inn the travelers snatched an irregular meal, and three good
horses were led up. Sundry women indeed appeared out
of nowhere, sobbed over René, "Oh! he's so handsome,"
and vainly besought, "Do not fling your lives away," but
at last they were disengaged. The friendly captain escorted
them through the northern gate where his lieutenant
(otherwise a stationer) and twenty more National Guards
were staring out fearsomely into the gloom. The last "good
luck" was tossed after the riders and again the road
stretched away before them long and dim in the starlight.
The lamps of the town faded one by one behind them as
René pricked home with the spur. "Six leagues, six leagues
to Massac and then?—then?"

"Monsieur, Monsieur," pleaded Arnaud behind, "not so
fast! You have the best mount. You abandon us."

The day that the Chevalier received Father Benoit's letter, his kinsfolk had journeyed as far as Ard. Their troubles
on the way had already made the old Countess frantic to
be safe outside of France. All the restraints which, ever
since Cæsar's legions had brought their law to the Belgæ,
had made the Have Nots tremble before the Haves seemed
vanished. Age-long bitternesses, envyings, hates were
unreined. Suddenly it seemed a crime to belong to the
most arrogant and self-sufficient aristocracy in Europe.

Before the unwieldy berlin trundled into Pontoise, its
inmates learned to take it as a matter of course that bands
of half-naked urchins should greet them with stones and
a kind of chorus, "Aristocrats to the lamp-post!" At Pontoise itself the hulking brewer, now mayor of the National
Guard, after scowling at their papers, impudently demanded
of the Count and Countess, "Why are you leaving France?
Don't you love the Revolution?"

Even at the inn they were greeted by sadly distracted

publicans, who had been enjoying little rich custom ever since "the glorious July fourteenth," but who barely concealed their fears lest harboring "unpatriotic emigrés" might lead to having their establishments sacked from garret to cellar. The waiters and horse-boys had actually become insolent and extortionate overnight. At Creil a hostler boldly demanded a double fee from the Count, and Laurent barely held back his father from bestowing a caning, a proceeding (hitherto the prescriptive right of every nobleman) certain to end the whole journey at the local jail.

Long before the berlin reached Ard, the roads were deserted, the villages nigh empty, and bands of vagabonds were met who counted the Massac party, then muttered "too strong" and shook their fists, while here and there could be seen the columns of smoke now rising.

The Count and Viscount were well known in Ard. Nevertheless, even the President of the tribunal on whom they called seemed none too anxious to welcome old acquaintance. "He regretted that his house was full of kinsmen who had moved in from the country. There had been riots, and—popular extravagances. It was hoped the worst now was over."

But although in Ard itself returning sanity and the compelling fears of everybody with ten crowns to lose had restored tolerable order, advance toward the frontier seemed blocked. The bridges on to Arras were down. Post horses were not to be had for love or money. Worse still, by this time the brigands were out in reality, not mere gangs of lawless peasants, nor packs of wandering robbers, but great bands, well armed, desperate as devils, and made up largely of the liberated jailbirds. They were plundering whole villages and carrying off girls by dozens. They had raided the isolated convent at Matre; God alone knew the fate of the poor nuns. Besides this fact, the feeling against emigrés in Arras and farther north was so strong that, until passions abated, it would be impossible for the Massac party to travel on—brigands or no brigands.

At these reports the Countess grew whiter and bit her lips, the old Count swore his "Ten million fiends," and Laurent, whose jovial humor and devil-may-care courage had alone made the journey thus far possible, was momentarily at his wit's end. The inn at Ard was uncomfortable, crowded and costly. The riots might resume in the city. The old nobleman vowed that he would never call twice on chilly and cowardly acquaintance. As the delay now promised to be serious Laurent risked a suggestion.—Massac chateau was in easy reach. M. Viaud, the steward, would welcome them. The brigands were all beyond Ard. What better refuge therefore? Besides the new Vicomtesse Louise had never seen the family castle.

His father and mother alike puckered and coughed at intruding upon the possessions of their unloved nephew, but Laurent and Louise were urgent, and the inn, after a couple of days, seemed intolerable. So the berlin again was harnessed and the horses swung toward Massac. That the uproar and insurrection could actually penetrate to that seat of dozing peace entered none of their heads. Laurent's chief anxiety was how he should keep his parents and bride amused sufficiently at this most uncourtly refuge until the public breeze had veered and they could continue to Brussels.

The half day's journey was accomplished with no more perils than the customary revilings and a few stones. Massac chateau lay apart from its village, which they did not enter, and at length with deep satisfaction the Viscount saw the great cylinder of the donjon rising out of the embowering oaks and beeches. Not a soul accosted them

as the coach plodded down the grassy drive and reached
the clearing before the castle.

A century of public quiet had permitted the erection of
various stables, sties and other homely outbuildings
beyond the drawbridge, while retaining space for the
ancient seigneurial stocks and gallows. Suddenly, however, the horses were pulled in short and the berlin abruptly
halted. All the outbuildings had vanished into a heap of
ashes that was still smoldering. The drawbridge was
raised. The gallows, still in place, displayed an object
swinging sinisterly. It was the body of a man in a blue
coat, and already the crows were busy about it. Upon the
foot of the gallows was pinned a bit of paper rudely
scrawled: *"Here shall be hung the peasant who pays any
dues and the lord who receives any."*

. . . M. Viaud, the steward, received his guests with
trembling courtesy. "Heaven forbid" (he vowed) "that a
Massac should fail to be welcomed at Massac chateau, and
yet it was only yesterday that the outbuildings had been
fired."

The victim on the gallows was in fact the agent for the
stock jobber who had bought the right to keep pigeons;
the peasants had caught him somewhere and brought him
up from the village that morning. Merciful God, how he
had struggled and pleaded!—Had the chateau been attacked
directly? No, although last night several musket balls had
entered the lighted loopholes. How many men had M.
Viaud? His son, his son-in-law, himself and two others.
They were not afraid of anything—not yet.

Laurent gave his accustomed whistle. His own party
included, besides his father and mother, his wife and two
maids, the Count's and his own valets, two grooms and a
coachman. Seven men therefore to eke out the five caretakers. But the Count and the steward were old and rheu-

matic; the Count's "gentleman" was a simpering fop who knew nothing but hair dressing, and one of the grooms had already shown himself cowardly before the hootings.

Nevertheless the donjon, seemingly at least, could be defended by two girls able to drop the inner portcullis. Unfortunately, however, as the Viscount well realized, the donjon had its Achilles' heel. Back in the days of Mazarin, that sagacious minister had insisted that the feudal chateaux should be effectively disarmed. A great section of the stone cylinder had therefore been blasted away near the base; against this, and communicating with the lower rooms of the keep there had been later erected a rectangular building of more elegant apartments, in the ornate taste of the day.

This new structure had indeed its bars and shutters over the many windows. It could defy a pack of ordinary robbers, but into its fabric there had entered many timbers and the slating on the roof was old and one end had been eked out with shingles. The surrounding moat too was shallow, dry and little more than a sunken garden. In short this new wing of the chateau constituted anything but a fortress. One rush of a determined body of men could master it, and the wing once on fire the communicating flames would soon render the whole interior of the donjon a single glowing furnace.

The Viscount whistled a second time as he reviewed the situation. Gladly now would he have had his family back in the inn at Ard. The afternoon however had waned even while the steward marvelled that the noble lords had come through without an attack on the roads. "It had been only by the Providence of God!"

Certainly any return by night might be suicidal. There was nothing for it, therefore, but to abide until morning and then to search the fates. Laurent accordingly put on the boldest face possible. His wife and mother removed their riding masks, and the musty security of the familiar apartments comforted the older woman's nerves despite all recent happenings. The maids unpacked the coffers, the party spread itself in the ample chambers and the caretakers' wives bustled about with a sufficient supper. The evening was pleasant and the Countess at length fell to fanning herself. "I congratulate ourselves, my dear," she presently informed the Viscountess, "we have escaped those desolating quarters in Ard. Here we can abide until the country is safe for travelling."

"Perhaps, Madame," suggested Louise, sighing with relief, "we can even stay until France has recovered its wits. Such insanity cannot last forever. It will spend itself like fire. Then we can all ride back to Versailles."

"Three months," spoke the old Count oracularly, snapping and unsnapping his snuff-box, "three months was what Artois said. *Peste*—if there is still justice in God or man, it should take three weeks! We nobles will all rally; ten of us can scatter five hundred of those roaring Jacques.— We must organize our own battalions, all of nobles, all. We alone know how to fight. We have been merciful and forbearing.—That's been all the harm. No more magnanimity; no more leniency! Mercy becomes a crime. We'll teach those wolves and those fat bourgeois sheep who are again their masters. A rope over every tree, I say."——

Laurent, listening with mixed feelings to this flow of wisdom, was aware that Viaud had entered the great hall where his guests were supping.

"M. le Vicomte," he announced, "perhaps I should inform you. A young woman has just asked admission to the chateau. My son on guard received her. She seems to bring certain information."

The old Countess started up instantly, delighted at the chance to give orders.

"Information? A young woman? Who is she—a peasant?"

"Her dress is perhaps a peasant's, but her speech is that of a Paris bourgeoise. I will forthwith question her."

"Bring her in, steward," commanded the Countess, anticipating her son and husband. "A peasant who speaks like a Parisienne! *I* will question her."

Viaud bowed and presently the mothy arras parted, and he reappeared escorting a slender figure in a very tattered cloak. Under the light of the few candles, which sent long black shadows flickering around the great hall, nothing momentarily could be seen of the stranger's features, save that they were ghastly white. Mme. de Massac stirred in her heavy armchair.

"Well, my good damsel," she commenced, "what brings you here?"

As her voice sounded clearly, the newcomer was seen to sway backward and make a clutch at the tapestry.

"I—I," she began thickly, and then in a kind of terror, "who are you, Madame? How came you?"

Laurent took a step nearer. Courtesy to the fair sex was his second nature. "You seem unwell, Mademoiselle. This is my mother, the Comtesse de Massac.—Drink this wine."

The girl pushed back the hood that shrouded her face. It shone forth pale as a ghost's, while her hair fell in a tangled mass over her shoulders. "Not here, do not make me talk here. Oh! if I had known *that* woman had come, I would never have sought the chateau."

"The creature is mad," vowed the Countess.

"Perhaps I am. The opium must have done it. Saroni's! Ah, that day at Saroni's! The insult. Again my head swims."

"Your name, girl?" demanded the Count, springing to his feet, then gazing transfixed.

"Virginie Durand!" shrieked the stranger, bursting into hysterical laughter. "Oh! let them burn us all. No matter."

"*Ciel!*" cried the Countess, leaping up in turn, "you—of all the wretches in the world, to be here. What are you doing, coarse hoiden, in this my nephew's chateau?—The artful boy——"

But here, in mercy to all, Laurent recovered his faculties. With a presence of mind worthy of the antechamber, he placed himself between his mother, who was starting forward in menace, and Virginie, who clung to the arras, shaking with sobs.

"Madame mother, forbear, I implore you. This mystery we must unravel. If this person speaks truth, she is the betrothed of my cousin the Chevalier. If she's that, damme if I care whether she's princess or beggar; let's have fair play. Assist me, Louise."

The Viscountess, who lacked not sympathy and intelligence, followed her husband. Together they conducted the newcomer into a quiet apartment, where Virginie at length became partially quieted. The sudden collision with the old Countess had unstrung her utterly, but at last her story began coming out. If Laurent and his wife hardly understood it entirely, yet they could at least get the gist.

After fleeing from the cabin with Olympie, Virginie and her companion had spent the night in safety in the woods and at first dawn had pushed on toward the village. Virginie imparted to Olympie her interview with Nicolas, and Olympie agreed it were better first to reveal themselves to the woodcutter and get him to sound the situation at the chateau in order to make sure of their welcome. Nicolas' cottage on the edge of the village was found, and he and the far more suspicious Brigitte, mollified by Virginie's pleadings, not unaided by a couple of crowns of which Olympie had thoughtfully relieved Thibaud before quitting the cabin.

At this point, however, their good fortune slackened. Virginie had collapsed utterly, thanks to the nervous tension, the effects of the drug, and the strain of the flight through the forest. Nicolas and Brigitte harbored her with apparent fidelity for several days, and with them, she and Olympie had seemed quite safe, safer than in the menaced chateau. Then suddenly, after Virginie had somewhat recovered and could walk a little, Olympie came to her with a very troubled face.

Linio (as they knew already) had collected a small band and tracked them vainly in the forest; after that he had disappeared. Now he was returning with a whole pack of outlaws—thirty, forty, the pick of the jail delivery at Ard, men hardening for the galleys. They had approached the village with none other than Thibaud. Somehow he and Linio, each thwarted in their hopes, made up another pact of convenience. Linio distributed smuggled Dutch schnapps to the peasants and got them as excited as Iroquois.— "While the chateau stood (ran his tongue) they could not be free from rents, tithes and taxes. Other manors were burning. Had now the Massac peasants less fidelity to the Revolution than those at Thorel and Demours? If the Chevalier was actually a deputy, all the more shame upon him for 'oppressing the people.' "

The first result of this gospel was the firing of the outbuildings and the hanging of the agent. But the assault on the chateau had delayed. The peasants had stood in decided awe of the great donjon and the caretakers' guns; whereupon Linio made a promise. "The next morning all the peasants from Garnes would join them." Numbers would be irresistible, M. Viaud would open peaceably, or he and his be torn in pieces.

This had been Olympie's first news budget, and her second was more personal.—Linio and Thibaud keenly suspected that the runaway women were hidden in the village. After the sack of the chateau there was to be a search of every cottage and hovel, and Olympie had already heard Brigitte telling the doubting Nicolas, "We can't ruin ourselves. We must give them up."

The fugitives were thus driven to a second flight. But by this time Linio's men were prying into every corner of the greenwood, and even if undiscovered, the women would have starved there in a couple of days. To crown their perplexity, Virginie was still so weak that she could never walk to Ard. One desperate hope alone seemed to be open. The chateau still held out, and Linio's plans might fail. At least M. Viaud would have a better chance if he were warned. Taking advantage, therefore, of the sultry gloaming, when Nicolas and Brigitte were occupied and the village seemed very still, the two women wormed their way through the park, up to the entrance of the chateau. There Olympie, after kissing Virginie many times and calling heaven's punishment on herself for "the wrong I have done my White Bird," quitted her tearfully. "Never fear for me. I have good legs. To-morrow morning I am with friends in Ard." Thus left alone, Virginie called to the younger Viaud, and was hesitantly admitted.—And that was the whole of the story.

. . . Laurent de Massac possessed all the courage of his line, but he left Louise (not unmoved) to comfort and restore their visitor, and with a very troubled face sought out the steward. "My mother, my wife, my cousin's betrothed are in this chateau—what now is best?"

Worthy M. Viaud's face was equally troubled. "Voices

are sounding in the park, as if from many men. From the top of the donjon we can see a great bonfire in the village; a hundred peasants seem to be dancing around it. All our windows must be darkened. Again they are being shot at."

The Viscount reckoned his numbers; twelve men including his father and Viaud, who could at least pull triggers; but the coachman had found a large bottle and was hopelessly drunk and the Count's valet was already gibbering white, thanks to the stories he had been hearing. The donjon might laugh at any direct attack, but Laurent could imagine the fate of the exposed wing. Let a body of men pile combustibles into the dry moat and fling in a torch, the whole structure would soon be flaming, and after that the inmates could only pray for merciful deaths. The proper defense was obvious; a heavy musketry discharge to keep the incendiaries at distance. Forty guns could give this, but how could only ten or at best twelve, with the peasants excited to recklessness——? "Pah!" the Viscount laughed to himself, "the age of miracles has passed!"

Nevertheless, what Laurent could, he performed. The windows were barricaded tightly, the old musketoons and blunderbusses in the armory were dragged from their dusty racks, cleaned, primed and loaded. Barrels of water were brought to desirable spots. The grooms and under caretakers were exhorted to quit themselves bravely.

Any better hopes?—The steward thought there was a chance. At Cridon, half way to Ard, there was a small garrison. The commandant was a brave and competent man; his dragoons were reputed to be more loyal than many troopers during the uproars. In so desperate a case, to save a countess and viscountess from death or worse he would probably send aid. One of the caretakers, a bold and active fellow, against large promises, said that he knew of a wood road and would undertake to get through. With a suitably urgent letter from Laurent, they let him out through the old sally-port, and he vanished into the gloom, leading his horse until clear of the park. It was then ten in the evening. If the messenger prospered, aid might be expected by dawn; until then there was nothing but to wander through the vast cavernous rooms, to stand guard and to wait.

Virginie Durand had lain in silent exhaustion after discharging her message. The Viscountess, who, if a Broglie, possessed a woman's heart, found relief from her own terrors by ministering to her. The old Countess simply glared with dumb rage, when her son passed on Virginie's story, but the Count was more vocal.

"Is there no chance that we could buy off this Linio by turning out this adventuress to him?"

"You forget, my father," observed his son tartly, "that I at least have the misfortune to be a man of honor."

They took their turns watching from the crest of the donjon. Increasingly they were conscious that the woods about the chateau were becoming scattered with men. Distant voices, the crackling of boughs, the gleam of camp fires between the black tree trunks all betrayed this. Owls scared from their haunts took their flight screaming. At intervals guns flashed out of the void and their bullets spadded harmlessly upon the walls of the chateau. Once or twice ribald shouts or viler threats were tossed up from behind the trees nearest to the drawbridge. From the village the glow of the great bonfire was gradually sinking to a dim redness, but the bursts of drunken revelry were increasing. Presently, out of the dark of the trees, there came a shriek, piercing, terrible, and then a second. After that a tense silence, followed, after much waiting, by a scampering of feet and a call at the very foot of the donjon.

"Here's the rental for your Lordships!"

Some object hurtled upward and fell on the roof of the new wing of the chateau. Laurent himself (the rest all shrunk from the risk) went out upon the tiles and retrieved the missile. He brought in a blood-soaked handkerchief, closely wrapped, and opened it in the presence of the others in the dimness of the great hall. The cloth contained two human ears, newly severed, and a piece of paper marked in blood:

"No soldiers will come from Cridon."

The old Countess crossed herself in silence, then held up her white head proudly. "After all, my friends, there can be worse places to die in than here in Massac chateau, yet it's a pity they don't send us a priest. Nevertheless" (her smile would have honored the Grand Couvert) "there will be certain compensations. At least we can depart without witnessing the marriage alliance of our amiable nephew.— The lady must condescend to depart with us."

CHAPTER XX

THE TRICOLOR

THE night advanced, cloudy and with little moonlight. There was nothing, apparently, for the Viscount to do but to pace the battlemented crest of the donjon and to listen. There was a serious possibility that the peasants would not wait until dawn should give heavy advantage to the defenders' muskets, and try to fire the vulnerable wing of the chateau in the gloom; but Laurent surmised wisely that the Garnes men had not arrived, and that too many of the Massac peasants were reeling drunk for Linio or any other leader to bring them as yet into action. At last, while it was still very dark, the thrushes began calling out of the beech boughs, and then appeared that first barely perceptible graying in the east which told how the night was waning. For the twentieth time the Viscount had stepped below to reëxamine the priming of his gun, and exchange with the younger Viaud their "Nothing more yet," and he had remounted the giddy staircase when his weapon almost clapped itself to his shoulder. A strange figure was leaning from the parapet.

"Ho there!" he summoned, then dropped his butt. Against the violet gray of the sky line was traced the slim figure of a young woman. "Virginie Durand, as I am a sinner." She was in very truth bending from the battlement, a target clearly outlined for any lurking villain below.

Laurent's hand fell on her shoulder. "Back, Mademoiselle. You expose yourself rashly.—I thought you were asleep."

"*He* is coming," said Virginie confidently, leaning out into the void.

"He? Her mind wanders," Laurent cursed underbreath. "Malediction! Must I have this new trouble added?"

"He is coming," repeated Virginie, resisting all effort to draw her back. "I have felt him ever since I came to the chateau, nearer, nearer, nearer." She spoke in a kind of transport.

"He? Mademoiselle. What do you mean?"

"René! All through the months I have been calling for him, calling for him. Now, at last, something is answering me. 'He approaches, he is at hand.' The voice has strengthened hour by hour all through the night."

"Clearly, Mademoiselle," spoke the Viscount, not without tenderness, "you are ill." And he called down the staircase, "Louise, Louise!"

Virginie began beckoning out into gloom. "I vowed that God was not good. I cried out to Him, 'Oh, but to die!'—Now there is answer.—René is nearer still. He has been speeding through the night.—There! Look."

She pressed her hands tightly to her breast, then pointed from the parapet. Perplexed as he was, Laurent could not refuse to follow the white outline of her fingers. His wife was now beside him, gently striving to take Virginie away, but she clung with one arm to the masonry. "Look!" she summoned again.

Laurent once more elevated his gun. Undeniably three figures were gliding from the barely traced shrubbery, and were approaching, not the drawbridge gate, but the sally-port on the opposite side of the donjon, where a few planks made an unsteady bridge over the dry moat.

"Holla!" sounded a hearty voice. "If you've still your

roof over you inside, don't keep the Chevalier de Massac waiting before his own chateau."

"Arnaud!" shrieked Virginie, releasing the stones from her strengthless fingers, "I knew it. God has answered me."

Laurent descended three steps at a bound. The watchers below had already unbarred the sally-port. Marvelling and suspicious, they nevertheless let three figures cross the planking in the face of their levelled gun barrels. By the glint of a single lantern, the Viscount saw René de Massac, followed by Arnaud and André, flinging back his cloak. Often had the cousins clasped hands and embraced heartily; never so heartily as now. With all their heads in a whirl they found themselves up in the great hall, barely illumined now by the faint gray bars of the dawning.

The Count and Countess had heard the challenges, and for once they greeted their nephew with a certain rejoicing. "We claimed your hospitality, nephew," spoke the old nobleman with his stateliest bow, "and your amiable peasants welcome us with their genteel Republican eccentricities. Nevertheless——"

René heard not. Louise's voice remonstrating on the stairs, then a cry, a flutter; the Chevalier had flown toward it like an arrow from the bow. Laurent promptly turned upon his parents.

"Madame mother, my father; damned if I'll pretend to be sorry! Leave them alone."

The old Countess gave an aristocratic toss. "You are right, my son. We have done our full duty."

. . . When René and Virginie were conscious of anything more in this world, they saw that the great hall was empty, and that in the strengthening light only the Valois ruffs and the Louis XV wigs of the dark array of family portraits were scowling down on them.

"All night I knew you were summoning me," at last René found the words. "Every pace from Roye I heard your voice along the road and through the woods—calling, calling. Oh! my beloved, God is with us this night and day!"

"God may be about to take us unto Himself; the peril is great."

"God has not brought me fifty leagues through peril and wrack even for the bliss of dying at your side. We are to live—live for the new, the delivered France."

Virginie still clung to him. "That were too great a joy. I had given up hope. I had said, 'Some things are too good to be.'"

"Oh, my beloved!" he cried again.

. . . A musket shot recalled them promptly from heaven to earth. One of the watchers had seen a dark figure prowling near in the woods. Steadily the light was strengthening, an hour might bring the chateau anything. With Virginie upon his arm, the Chevalier ascended to the crest of the donjon, where nearly all of the others were gathered. If glances had been swords, the eyes of the Count and Countess would have been murderous, but with supreme wisdom, that noble couple held their peace.

Arnaud had already detailed how his master's party had reached the chateau. The three had ridden until about a league of Massac when, taught caution by abundant warnings, they had turned loose their horses and advanced on foot. Soon they had detected a couple of sentinels, but had evaded them, thanks to the darkness; next they had stumbled on a sorely befuddled peasant and had caught and throttled him before he could cry out, after which a knife held to the fellow's throat had produced a fairly lucid story. The chateau was beset; Linio with his jail-birds was raising all the village; the Garnes men were expected in the morning. It was said, furthermore, that a party of great folk in a big coach had driven to the chateau that self-same afternoon. Linio had said, "Let them all pass in; the more mice for our mouse-trap."—After that Arnaud and André had gagged the peasant and bound him to a tree. No doubt he would be found at daylight.

Never for months had René de Massac so commended himself in his kinsfolk's eyes as when he took command of the scanty band of defenders, whilst that twilight strengthened into morning. He surveyed all his cousin's dispositions, praised them, improved them. The drunken coachman suddenly seemed to become quite sober and pushed and tugged heartily. The count's valet ceased whimpering and demanded to be taught how to load a musket. The castle women stopped praying to the saints and began placing the tubs of water. Laurent, as suddenly, felt a crushing load lifted from his shoulders. The Viscount called René's attention to three powder barrels. "Left for the fall shooting—I have placed them (with bated whisper) to blow up the donjon if worst should come to worst."

"It will not come to worst," returned his cousin quietly.

Marvel then it was for those who had known him all his days, and had smiled or mocked at his boyish enthusiasms, his naïve humors, to see how the call to action had brought out the resourceful, collected soldier.

"It is the *old* Chevalier again," whispered the rejoicing Viaud. "It is the son of his father."

René surveyed the powder barrels, then beckoned to Arnaud. "You were an artilleryman at Yorktown and before the Bastille."

"At command," quoth the delighted veteran.

"Take Anselme and two others. The old culverins must be still in the crypt of the donjon. I saw them three years ago. Bring up the two soundest. We can lash them to timbers for carriages. You understand."

"Yes, yes, oh! what a thought!" The old soldier almost dragged his helpers after him. Forth from the dusk and rubbish of the crypt emerged two small cannon, half buried no doubt since they had fired their salutes to Richelieu, but solid still in brass and trunnion, and around them the artilleryman labored with the energy of an enormous bee. On the Viaud women René laid certain other commands, which made them most busy with their needles.

The Chevalier's army was very small, but of a sudden the chateau seemed teeming with energy. It was René's gift to be able to encourage with a word, with a second word to summon all the resources of a subordinate into action. At midnight the people of the chateau had been nerved to sell their lives desperately; at dawn they were ready for victorious defence.

The three women, the old Countess, Louise and Virginie, forgot all else as they looked on the Chevalier with ever-swelling hearts. His aunt even ceased to glare upon Virginie. His· uncle obeyed his orders as meekly as the grooms. When René stood by an open porthole, the old Countess implored piteously, "Do not throw your life away"; to which the Chevalier merely answered politely, "Madame, my aunt, I have no time at present for dying," and continued his survey.

At length, all that twelve pairs of manly hands, not un-aided by the women, could do had been done. The chateau stood on its defiance. Full morning now. The sun was sending dazzling bars among the trees. The air was warm-ing, with full promise of summer heat. Presently, through the grove, pealed the clangor of the church bell from the village, and after that came a great whooping and shouting, as of many voices.

"They have come from Garnes," muttered Viaud at the Chevalier's side; "not long to wait now." Nor was the surmise a wrong one. Among the trees there was a scurrying of feet, with forms here and there in the underbrush approaching the chateau on every side. Presently from the nearest coppice a horn sounded, then a voice: "We would parley."

"What have you to say, gallows meat!" roared Arnaud.

"You have back your messenger's ears. From him we have learned all about your weakness. All the countryside has risen against you. The chateau will become your gridiron. Hear our terms then—we promise that most of you can go."

"Oh! generosity; your conditions?"

"The clothes on your backs, and safe departure for all but three."

"Which three?"

"The fugitive Comte and Comtesse de Massac, enemies of the people; ('We'll fry and eat their hearts!' interposed a villainous voice) also that vixen who escaped to you last night, the niece of our good patriot, Thibaut Durand."

"What of her?"

"She's pretty. Never mind the rest."

A broadside of oaths exploded from the veteran, but above them clear and stern, rang the tones of René:

"Who speaks thus? No man of Massac makes this vile demand for the affianced wife of his deputy to the Assembly."

No answer for an instant, then a jangle of contending voices from the coppice. "Why, it's our Chevalier's voice, I recognize it." "It's the devil's voice, don't be fooled."

René pursued the advantage instantly. "Listen, patriots and citizens; what are your wishes? It is your own friend and neighbor that speaks to you. Why do you threaten the chateau? If you have proper demands, have I ever refused to listen? Have you been told yet that I have journeyed directly from the Assembly in order to redress just grievances? Stand forth, some of you. We are old friends, let us reason together."

"Saints and angels!" swore some one from the thickets, "it is the kind seigneur. We've been deceived."

More mutterings and contention, then a voice, which Virginie, standing by, murmured "Linio's," answered, rasping as glass: "We're not put off. March out, all of you; hand over the two aristos and that hoiden, or take the worst. We give you three minutes." But other voices called from amid the trees: "No, no. We don't want blood, we don't want the chateau, only no more forced labor, no more imposts, no more hunting."

Despite the shudders of the women behind him, René leaped upon the parapet, and stood forth straight and tall, facing the park, which was now swarming with faces.

"Here stand I, René de Massac. If you wish my life, take it. If you are patriots, citizens of the new France, assert your new rights by resisting traitors. France is in peril; the Revolution is in peril by those who seek to bring back the tyrants by first plunging the land into anarchy. Where are Long Aubri, Denys the smith, Nicolas the wood-cutter and Father Benoit? I trust them and I know that they trust me. Send them into the chateau. I swear as a citizen and a deputy of the Nation that either I will content their demands or send them back unharmed."

More confused growlings, gesticulations, angry appeals and angry refusals all through the oaks and beeches.

"Fling out the banner," commanded Massac.

Whereupon, up the staff above the donjon there climbed a broad flag, red, white and blue, wafting out upon the puffing breeze. "The colors of arisen France; the colors which float to-day from every house in Paris, as token of loyalty to the Revolution. I call on all patriots to defend it from insult. Never, henceforth, shall other flag float above Massac chateau."

René swept off his hat, and waved it, saluting the banner, while very confused now grew all the voices beneath the donjon. Men were shouting, "The citizen seigneur, the honest deputy. He'll do the right thing. Send the four in to him." But above all rose the tones of Linio. "Asses! Sheep! Fine lies won't abolish the imposts.—Ready now. Form for the rush."

"Form yourself, master," called back others, "put your own men first."

The Chevalier answered shout with shout. "Citizens of Massac, I trust to your patriotism, but not to that of the anti-patriots I see moving among you. Separate yourselves quickly or take great harm. You honest men from Garnes also stand back. The Nation commands me to repress disorder, to punish crime. Whence come these strangers in your company, these anti-patriots inciting you to defile the Revolution?"

"From the jails!" bawled some candid peasant.

"Silence this babble," roared Linio. A musket cracked. The ball sang above René's head and tore a gash in the blue stripe of the spreading banner.

A kind of horrified gasp seemed answering from many among the trees: "The new flag of the Nation; they've defiled it."

But Massac saw now the compact body of men, wolfish, haggard, with white teeth and long matted hair, forming under the command of some leader, then gliding rapidly toward the moat. In front of their coarse jerkins they held thick bundles of faggots to protect themselves from musketry. They advanced with fierce yells toward the point where the dry moat was shallowest and the timber work of the wing most exposed. One or two bore torches.

The move was plain. In a twinkling a vast bonfire would be crackling against the chateau; after that the inmates could only make their choice of deaths.

The Chevalier's voice rang above all the babel and clamor around the donjon:

"In the name of the sovereign People, halt!" His hand caught and stretched wide the folds of the insulted banner.

A volley of unspeakable abuse answered him, a pistol ball clipped the corner of his hat, while the attack swept roaring onward, full forty men nearing the moat, but with the donjon silent and to all seeming helpless.

The band was on the verge of the moat. They were lifting their faggots to cast them, when Massac's shout rose yet again in clarion menace: "Long live the Nation!"

A clatter from on high. The uppermost porthole of the donjon had sprung open. Involuntarily the assault paused. From the trees the gaping peasants saw the muzzle of a cannon bearing straight along the verge of the moat.—A lightning flash; a deafening report; the donjon hidden in smoke—then silence while men counted twenty. Next moaning and screaming indescribable from the long, struggling windrow, where Arnaud's charge of scrap iron and broken chains had raked the whole line of the attack.

The survivors were running back for their lives, howling.

"Ready the second cannon!" René pealed above the din.

It was never fired. The single blast had dashed the last indecision from the wavering peasants. Linio's outlaws (those that escaped the discharge) in a moment were racing pell-mell among the trees, casting away guns, axes, coats, everything that might hinder flight from the raging country folk that pursued them. "Death to the anti-patriots! Death to the polluters of the Tricolor." Never had public wind veered more quickly. A hundred peasants had remembered all in a twinkling that their Chevalier was the most liberal and patriotic of men; that they had always known that Linio was lying; that they had come themselves to the chateau merely to protect it from outrage.

While the younger, more active fellows chased the remnants of the escaped prisoners, other peasants speedily rushed toward the moat, swinging pitchforks and axes to complete the destruction of the wounded. "Hew in pieces! Get ropes!"

They were met by Massac emerging alone from the sallyport, his hands empty, but a red-white-and-blue cockade conspicuous upon his bosom. "Do not disgrace our victory, my friends." They all paused in a respectful circle before him; most of the peasants pulled off their caps; some of the oldest fell on their knees, the traditional reverence due the lord of the soil returning in all its power. "The blow of the Nation is terrible, but when resistance ends, its mercy is that of a pitying father. If these unfortunate men are already criminals, the new France will provide just tribunals.—Secure the prisoners, bind up their wounds; send them in safe convoy to Ard."

Prompt obedience answered him. Things had instantaneously resumed their wonted order at Massac, with the lawful seigneur giving his proper commands, and the loyal peasantry obeying. The wounded convicts were dragged away. Linio was searched for in vain, he was not among the six corpses that they buried, and some Garnes men recalled seeing him running like a hare, swiftest of all who fled. Thibaud was missing, too, but he had always been a fellow to hang in the rear. At length, the Chevalier ceased issuing orders to the scraping and cringing scores of men who, an hour before, had been breathing forth threatenings and slaughter. Right and left the young landlord bowed and smiled.

"And now, my good fellow citizens of Massac," spoke he,

"we have dealt justice to the anti-patriots. Let us deal justice to patriots also. If I mistake not, there were certain friendly requests which you wished to proffer the owner of this estate. It is my pleasure to hear them."

There was a general turning of heads with an exchange of sheepish glances; at length, Long Aubri found an awkward tongue, after again pulling off his hat.

"It is true, Monseigneur, I mean M. le député, that there were a few of us who expressed some hope, I mean were so bold as most respectfully to imagine that perhaps there would be less hunting over the standing grain; that perhaps we would be permitted to shoot pigeons if they settled on seeded fields; that possibly——"

Aubri's voice trailed away and he scratched his poll, but René in answer smiled and beckoned to the entire knot of shifting, sidling rustics. "We understand one another entirely, my friends. We folk of Massac need no long speeches between neighbor and neighbor. Follow me, pray, to the garden."

About thirty shuffled after him as he led down the old gravelly walks, grass grown and barely tended now, to where, under the very shadow of the donjon, a venerable stone bench, fragrant with moss, rested upon a pair of equally moss-bearded dragons. Viaud, the steward, already there, had planted on this bench a brass-bound casket and a lighted brazier. While the peasants nudged and wondered, René opened the casket and took forth a yellowed parchment with dangling seals.

"Who of you can read?" The ensuing silence grew lengthy until Denys, the smith, acknowledged some license to the mystery; yes—and here was Maître Lacaille, the innkeeper, and Father Benoit himself, still shivering at the violence and uproar, but plucking up courage and curiosity now that the peril was abating.

"Draw near, you three," the Chevalier commanded. "Look on this scroll (they could at least see the big red seals); it is the grant by Philip the Fair to the Seigneurs of Massac of the right to take toll on the crops of their peasants—*Voilà!*"

The parchment dropped upon the brazier, smoked, went up in flames. From the casket René drew another scroll: "The right to take levy upon the price whenever a peasant would sell his lands—St. Louis himself gave it!" Fire and ashes also. The right of the dovecote, of the tax for the mill, of stocks and gallows, of the control of game, of the levy on wine, finally of the seigneurial land tax itself—all lay a crumbling heap upon the broad stone.

The Chevalier held open the empty casket. "My fellow citizens, the ancient rights of my fathers I resign to the sovereign People. I and my heirs trust to the generosity and wisdom of France to indemnify us. We claim no rights now in Massac beyond the rights of every lawful land-owner.—Can I do anything more to content you?"

"Long live the Nation!" quavered old Viaud, still trembling for his own safety.

"Long live our Seigneur de Massac!" bellowed the thirty voices. And then ("Citizens or no Citizens"—as Nicolas later told Brigitte) there was one rush to kiss the young man's hand, while one or two were fain even to kiss his feet.

René saved himself from being crushed or smothered, and next he put his own strong hand upon the cassock of Father Benoit.

"Come into the chateau with me—instantly."

"And wherefore, dear son?" The Chevalier's haste was so mastering that the good old priest was immediately out of breath.

"To marry me, forsooth!" flashed back the words, while

the peasants still cheered and wondered in the garden, and the sally-port door clicked behind them.

In the great hall all the women were still gathered, very white and with the caretakers' wives all telling their beads. Virginie stood arm in arm with Louise, the Count and Countess were silently facing them, while Laurent, with grinning countenance, was keeping a kind of truce between. The old Countess gave one glance at her nephew, a second at the curé, then demanded abruptly, "Why this priest?"

René de Massac's face was grimed with sweat, dust and powder-smoke. His hair flew scattered upon his shoulders. The lace at his wrists was in tatters, his coat and stockings were caked with mud, but Laurent forever insisted that Dreux-Brézé himself would have envied the bow which he then vouchsafed the Countess.

"Madame, my aunt, Father Benoit is here that you may do me the honor of signing as the first witness at my marriage with Mademoiselle Virginie Durand."

The lady drew her cloak about her delicately and shivered as became a *grande dame* of sixteen quarterings. "You could have spared me this, nephew," she observed quietly, "but what God ordains to be, must be."

. . . . . .

Four days afterward René and his wife said farewell to their kinsfolk, the Count and Countess having insisted on resuming their travel to the frontier. Reassuring tidings had come in; the new National Guards were everywhere restoring a degree of order; but the Count had looked up at the Tricolor above the donjon and observed with his most aristocratic shrug, "I grow old. France is no place for me while that strange flag floats above Massac chateau, and its owner is ashamed of his ancestors."

"I atone for their sins," pungently retorted his nephew.

Louise, however, wept in Virginie's arms, and Laurent

embraced his cousin, not once, but many times. "Dearest, bravest fellow in all the world, how I wish that I could look with your generous eyes upon this your topsy-turvical Revolution."

"Would to God that you could, Laurent," was the earnest answer.

"Parbleu! We must each see the world through our own eyes, not through our friends'. At least we can still love each other, though I must cry *'Vive le Roi'* and you your outlandish *'Vive la Nation.'*" Then he kissed both of Virginie's hands. "Before God, mother or no mother, I'm glad that you are now a Massac—Madame, my cousin." And his last shout was a challenging yet good-natured, "Back in three months," as the coach rolled away north-ward.

. . . René and Virginie remained at Massac chateau in great peace for another ten days. Wondrous news presently spread to them from Paris. On the night of August the fourth, caught in a generous ecstasy in which marquises and archbishops had vied in a frenzy of sacrifice, the Assembly had decreed the abolition of all the age-long imposts and burdens which had weighed upon the peasantry of France. The enthusiasm had been contagious. The Te Deum had been sung in the Palace chapel; the Assembly had actually proclaimed Louis XVI "the Restorer of French Liberty."

In the woods about Massac, René and Virginie wandered during these days in a kind of golden dream, all dangers vanished, the peasants almost ready to kiss their feet. When the time came for the ride back to Versailles, the story of the scene at the donjon had gone before them. Bevies of girls brought to the wife of "the Patriot Deputy" their rose garlands. The married pair had even to slip away from the banquets and civic celebrations proffered them by zealous magistrates in every market town. Versailles at

last, with friends, congratulations and a delirium of welcome which nearly overwhelmed the still exhausted bride.

At length René and Virginie found themselves sufficiently
alone with Father François to be able to kneel for his blessing. After he had laid his hand upon them, he raised up
Virginie and upon both cheeks he kissed her.

"Dearest Father," said she, "if it were not for leaving
René, I could die of sheer joy. My love is complete and
the Revolution is finished."

"Dearest daughter," said the lecturer with his profound-
est smile, "it were best to live. Your love may be complete,
but the Revolution is only just begun."

BOOK III
"EQUALITY"

CHAPTER XXI

Entry in the diary of René Massac, September, 1791:

. . . "This day the harness slips from my back. Thanks be to Heaven I am no longer a deputy. We have redeemed the Oath of the Tennis Court. We have given a Constitution to France. A just God and a liberated Nation must now do the rest.

"Two years have produced changes often crammed into two centuries. New laws, new viewpoints, new philosophies! Gone are the old provinces, old magistrates, old taxes, old feudal abuses. The King is only the first official of a democratically governed people. Gone are half of the court nobility into exile, following the first emigrés after the fall of the Bastille. Gone are all titles of nobility. Henceforth I am simply René Massac, the proud member of a free citizenry.

Even outwardly Paris shows the change. The streets are no longer named after 'Saints'; it is only 'Rue Honoré' or 'Rue Leonard.' Everybody must wear the Tricolor cockade or risk being mobbed. The stones of the Bastille have been made up into tobacco jars or cameos. The Nation rejoices in profound peace. After the tumults of 1789 has come the healing quiet of 1790. True, our new paper money, the assignats, based on the sequestered church lands, seem sinking to a discount, but that is the merest trifle. The Revolution has triumphed. 'Citizen' is even replacing 'Monsieur.' Can I not felicitate myself upon living in such an age!

"Heaven has been even more kind to me personally. Virginie, more beautiful than ever, presides over the most joyous little salon in all Paris. Henriette is the most adorable of infant daughters. In our parlors there gather daily Camille Desmoulins and Lucile (married now over a year), Danton and that other rising patriot, already idolized by the Paris populace as 'The Incorruptible,' I mean, of course, Robespierre. True, he is a little over-fond of reading off to us his long speeches intended for the great Jacobin Club, but then do we not hear words which in a few days will pass as oracles through half of France? That remarkable youth, St. Just, still dances in harmless attendance upon Virginie. He also is a rising sun in politics, and a passionate admirer and supporter of Robespierre.

"But we do not encourage political discussions. Books, tric trac and Virginie's harpsichord make our parlor a happy refuge from public turmoils. Then, too, behind our Rue Leonard house is part of the garden of an abandoned convent. Fine old chestnuts, a bit of greensward and a grotesque little fountain make it a delightful place on fine days wherein to pour chocolate. Here is our paradise. The rest of the world is forbidden to matter.

". . . To-day the King has accepted the Constitution. We forget his wavering, the flight to Varennes, the deplorable stories about the Queen. Paris is en fête. The Tricolor waves everywhere. Everyone sings the joyous *"Ça ira!"* 'That will go!' meaning our glorious Revolution. The King, with the Queen upon his arm, walks out beyond the Tuileries (where he now resides) across the Gardens, without guards and surrounded by the acclamations of an enfranchised people. Wonderful fireworks. Boundless enthusiasm. Never is Virginie more enchantingly happy, yet she must have her question:

" 'Why, René, does Father François smile still again in his queer little way, when I say "Nothing *now* can possibly undo our Revolution?"'

" 'Because (I answer) Sorbonne lecturers are professionally obligated to smile whenever a pretty woman says anything they have not first read in Latin.'

"Only St. Just—who walks out with us—scowls because so many people to-night shout, *'Vive la Reine!'* Virginie reproaches him: 'The Queen has accepted the Constitution, too. All the past is forgiven.'

"I return home to-night in great content. One thing only

perplexes me. In a small café to-day I saw the Abbé
Vernet, remarkable now for his anti-monarchist principles,
deep in conference with a man who, despite a heavy beard
and an upturned military collar, I could have sworn was
Laurent. But he and Louise are safe in Coblenz; we passed
letters only last month. Were he in Paris, whose door
would he darken sooner than mine?—Clearly my eyes are
tricking me . . ."

CHAPTER XXII

THE PRISONERS IN THE TUILERIES

VERSAILLES was becoming a city of echoes, a memorial to departed grandeur. It was otherwise in Paris. Looking down the avenues of the Champs Elysées, between the magnificent avenues of chestnuts, and across the glowing flower beds and quaint glory of the gardens, beyond the sparkling glory of the fountains, there rose in 1791 the majestic façade of a palace, infinitely harmonious in color, picturesque and noble in form, to which all surrounding objects led and contributed splendor. This was the Tuileries, the gilded prison now of strengthless royalty.

When, at the mandate of Paris, in October, 1789, the King and Queen had abruptly quitted Versailles forever, the Tuileries had not been used as a royal residence for nearly half a century. Its vast tiers of apartments were the respectable refuges of aristocratic families in straitened circumstances. The palace had almost, in fact, become an enormous residential hotel, with partitions running across the abandoned halls of state, and private kitchens in royal anterooms. All this suddenly ended. The shabby-genteel guests were hurried to other quarters. The partitions were torn down; the old decorations refurbished; gilded furniture and other paraphernalia of luxury hurried out from deserted Versailles. The Tuileries again appeared as a meet residence for a King and his court.

Around the "King of the French," his consort and those of his family who remained with him, there was still main-

262

tained what, to outward eye, seemed all the pomp and circumstance of the First Gentleman of Europe. Most of the
Princes of the Blood indeed were gone, and with them many
of the Noblesse of oldest lineage, but there had been plenty
of aspiring younger sons and heads of less ancient houses
to fill their places. Dreux-Brézé still flourished his white
wand. Royalty, in short, still appeared to be royalty.

But all Europe knew that Louis XVI was now the prisoner of his apparent greatness. For over a year he had
not ventured to quit Paris, save during that disastrous episode when he was haled back from the flight to Varennes.
The mere appearance of the royal carriage horses ready for
departure would have brought an angry crowd into the
Place du Carrousel before the palace; the actual sight of
the King and the Queen entering the coach would have
meant a mob, a mustering of the civic militia, and the
courteous veto of the drive by that "traitor to his nobility,"
Lafayette, Commandant of the National Guard.

The King had put on weight while he complained of the
surcease of his favorite hunting. The Queen (since the
return from Varennes) hesitated to thrust her head from any
of the palace windows overlooking the public ways, lest
some coarse epithet be flung at her by a loiterer. Fortunately, except on fête days, the ample Tuileries gardens
provided walled-in privacy, and here Marie Antoinette
could stroll in peace with her children, with Princess Lamballe, Mme. de Campan and other loyal friends. But the
life in the great park at Versailles, the Trianons, the shepherdess plays, the palace theater, all those other things
wherein the Queen once "glittered like the morning star,
full of life, splendor and joy," had faded with all the remaining shadows into the gloom of the irrevocable past.
The Old Régime had perished, although the human centers
of the Old Régime might live unhappily on.

The seventeenth of September, nevertheless, witnessed an apparent change. The Constitution had been accepted. The populace seemed resolved to be friendly. The King and the Queen, with that physical courage which neither lacked, deliberately and without guards walked out into the crowded gardens. The result had been reassuring. No insults, but only constant cheers from their "fellow citizens." The royal pair reëntered the palace amid the congratulations of all their anxious friends.

Even in the Tuileries the crisis was assumed to be over. "Thanked be God," said the first valet to the first gentleman-in-waiting that evening, "the Revolution at last is finished; *now* we can all settle down in peace and quiet;" while under the royal windows facing the Carrousel some friendly patriot sang before turning in for the night:

> "Our good King has done the right thing!
> Our good Queen, let 'er have her fling!
> Let troubles cease
> And us all have peace!" [1]

Unfortunately, however, nothing in this evil world remains "finished," and it was only the second morning after the "Fête of the Constitution" that two gentlemen might have been observed entering the Tuileries gardens somewhat stealthily by a small gate, which was seldom opened, and then going into the palace itself by a partially concealed door upon its western and more private side.

The visitors were not impeded by the ordinary phalanx of sentries and gentleman ushers, for the Master of Ceremonies himself had been near this door to receive them, and then to whisk them on rapidly past the scrutinies of a few under-chamberlains, although the latter scowled on identifying one of Dreux-Brézé's charges: "That renegade

[1] Once more the English translation imitates the very dubious "poetry" of the French.

Abbé Vernet. What is *he* doing at the palace? Why do their Majesties now and then have to receive him?"

Dreux-Brézé, while he hurried the visitors up the great staircases, had seized Vernet's companion by the arm. "Alas, my dear—Frenade (that's what I'm told to call you), what a change, what a melancholy change since we parted! The death of all etiquette! The cadets, whom perforce now I have to employ, do nothing aright. Do you know of the latest horror?"

"Something desolating, no doubt."

"Yesterday the King's stockings were passed to him ahead of his shirt. I could have hanged myself with sheer mortification."

"We all have our sorrows these days, my dear Marquis."

"And must try to bear them like philosophers and noblemen of France. I am commanded to bring you in for audience immediately. Of course (with a genuine sigh) you are prepared."

The gilt chairs of the anteroom were reasonably garnished with idling gentlemen. A magnificent porter was still at his station. When Dreux-Brézé whispered to him, he at once threw open the inner door and rolled out his proclamation:

"The Abbé Vernet and Captain Frenade—enter, gentlemen."

Frenade, otherwise Laurent de Massac, passed inside, and instantly cast himself on both knees. Before him, seated in stiff armchairs, were the King and the Queen.

Laurent was measurably "prepared." Louis was sitting before him, stouter than of old, puffier of lips and cheeks, but not more disordered in dress and hair than of wont in the old days at Versailles. But the Queen—ah! the Queen. Laurent saw a middle-aged woman, upon her face written lines wrought by months lived in spiritual torture. All her bright color had fled; her hair was almost white—even as it had turned in a single day and night after the horrible return from Varennes. Her figure (she was then six-and-thirty) had lost all of that girlish suppleness and slim grace which two years earlier made her excel in the young shepherdess parts at the Trianon. Even her voice, when she spoke, had a hard metallic timbre, which went to the newcomer's soul.

He remained kneeling, holding up his hands as if deprecating the devastation, until the King, in a very matter-of-fact, kindly tone, bade him arise.

"You are heartily welcome, Viscount, although in that disguise I should hardly know you."

"Oh! Your Majesties, what shall I say? The shame of this; the miseries of your position; the dishonor of the throne!—every generous heart in Europe cries out against this."

"We still are comforted by our friends—such as you, Laurent," spoke the Queen, extending her hand, which the young man (ignoring the King) made haste to kiss fervently.

"By your command, Madame," bowed Vernet, "I have brought our 'Captain Frenade' hither. My principles being well known, there will be less suspicion if he is seen in the palace in my company. It were wisest, nevertheless, to request M. de Dreux-Brézé to be less cordial in his manner when we go out; and even a few insulting words flung after us both will do no harm."

"Yes, yes," declared Marie Antoinette, "spies are everywhere. Even here, we had better speak in low voices. You understand our condition, Laurent?"

"All is understood, Madame," spoke the Viscount, again standing. "M. Vernet can arrange as he wishes. I am told that he is devoted to your interests, despite his activity among the miscreants."

"M. Vernet," rejoined Louis, "is a trusted friend of the throne. For two years now he has wisely connived with the incendiaries. Since the enactment of that Civil Constitution of the Clergy, which we accepted only with the sword at our throats, he has, despite the groanings of his conscience, affected to embrace the new schismatic order in the church. For this he shall, of course, receive due dispensation from Rome—and reward from his King—as soon as possible."

The Abbé bowed once more, and twisted his long, smooth fingers. Laurent was not wholly happy while he looked on him; certain honest royalists had certain firm opinions, but he could only say, "M. Vernet has been most helpful to me since I reached Paris three days ago."

"We understand," resumed the Queen, "that you come direct from Vienna. Did you see my brother, the Emperor, there?"

Laurent bowed in his turn. "The Emperor Leopold honored me with his confidences, Madame. He had been in conference with the Polignacs and others devoted to you. I need not repeat his sentiments as to the enormities committed by the French people, and the flagitious treatment of Your Majesties." The Viscount paused; truth to tell, he would have been better pleased if the Abbé had not been present, but the Queen only smiled eagerly and the King bluntly ordered:

"Go on."

"His Majesty, the Emperor, repeated to me what he has said more officially in company with the King of Prussia at Pillnitz, that he regards the present situation of Your Majesties 'As a matter of common interest to all the sovereigns of Europe,' that the 'most efficient means must be employed to reëstablish the King of France in a position of power and absolute freedom,' and that orders shall be given to their troops to that end."

"Very good," nodded Louis; but the Queen added a little cynically, "Such words can mean nothing."

Laurent's gesture was deprecatory. "I will not conceal from Your Majesties that the Emperor finds his position difficult. He is anxious to serve you, but not to make your condition worse. He is beset by Monsieur and by Monseigneur d'Artois to declare war, but as a Christian monarch he hesitates to convulse all Europe save for the plainest of reasons. Furthermore, Your Majesties' position may be changed. If you have fully accepted the new Constitution——"

The Viscount here saw the Abbé slowly rubbing his jaw. "Continue," directed Louis.

"The Emperor, in short, affirms that if it is Your Majesties' purpose to forgive past outrages, to accept the Constitution, and discover by experience how far it is compatible with your own honor and the welfare of France, he will do his uttermost to prove a peaceful neighbor and a helpful brother monarch."

The King looked toward the door knob vacantly; the Queen played nervously with the folds of her dress. As the silence became awkward, Laurent yet again dropped on one knee, and drew from his bosom a small packet which he extended to the Queen. The seals with the Austrian double eagle were clearly visible. "From your brother, Madame; it will confirm what I have said."

Marie Antoinette did not open immediately; instead, as the Viscount rose, she said directly:

"You had a level head, Laurent, in the happy old days. You come from the Emperor; you know our emigrés; you have just seen our changed France. 'Accept the Constitution?' Well—what do you say?"

The young man colored. "I am a messenger, and not a councillor, Madame. What ought I to say? In our cafés and pensions in Brussels, Coblenz, Treves, we emigrés feed one another's fury and exaggerate our quite sufficient wrongs. Nevertheless, since recrossing the frontier in this beastly disguise, I have discovered a new France, new laws, new officials, above all a new spirit in the people. The peasants do not cringe and pull off their caps to a good coat as they did three years ago. It's the same with the bourgeois. Before I left Coblenz, I said, 'Ten battalions can march through that canaille to Paris.' I do not say that now. The other night I witnessed the fête. I heard Your Majesties cheered. I said to myself, 'If it is the King's will to bury the past, to seek peace and not a foreign invasion, no loyal subject ought to say him nay.'"

"Bury the past?" echoed the Queen. "*Bon dieu*, how can one shut the door upon memories?"

"I said I was no councillor, Madame," repeated Laurent uneasily.

"We must deliberate," announced Louis, rising with a certain heavy graciousness. "We regret, Viscount, that your long and faithful service in the Rhine-lands has hitherto been paid only with a feeble thanks. Your noble parents are well, I trust, and Mme. la Vicomtesse, your wife——"

"I left them in Coblenz, Sire. They loaded me with messages of devotion. Thousands of emigrés you know are in the Rhine-lands. They eagerly await your summons. Either at the word of their King their swords will all flash out together, or equally, at your behest, they will return to France and cheerfully accept the new laws and make the best thereof."

The King shook his head. "Such is not quite the story that has reached us. Condé and my brothers are said to swear that nothing can reconcile them to returning to France save as conquerors. Is that not so?"

"No doubt, Sire. But they are not all of the emigrés. We grow weary of exile. If it were right, we would return peacefully to France."

"Return peacefully. Ah! I hope it can soon be possible."

"We must deliberate," thrust in the Queen curtly, a certain hard light coming suddenly into her eyes.

"Certainly, Madame," smiled Vernet, "you must deliberate; Captain Frenade returns to Vienna in three days."

"Till to-morrow, then. Next time you must be brought in still more privately by the concealed passage. Farewell for to-day, Laurent"; the Queen seemed anxious to end the interview and held out her hand. The messenger kissed it, then that of the King. Soon he had bowed himself out and was quitting the palace with Vernet. Evidently the Abbé's suggestion had been slipped out of the cabinet, for one or two insulting *"perfides"* and *"scélérats"* were flung after them as they glided down the staircase.

"A thousand congratulations," complimented the Abbé, as they crossed the Seine by the Pont Royal. "You managed admirably. In my character as representative of the new 'Constitutional Church' I have to be received frequently by the King, and yet am desirably unpopular with all at the palace, save with a very few initiated. Now, Monsieur, pray amuse yourself discreetly until Thursday. You can then take your packet directly back to Vienna."

No one was beside them on the bridge. Perhaps Laurent had his opinion of the Abbé, but if the King and Queen reposed such complete trust in him there need be no hesitation about confidences.

"I was 'prepared'; yes, M. Vernet, but not sufficiently prepared. *Ma foi!* the change in the Queen is terrible. What must she not have endured? We exiles learning by hearsay could not realize her misery. 'Tis enough to make even my Jacobin cousin, René, weep for her."

"These times help to make saints or philosophers out of all of us, M. le Vicomte. There's no finer end than martyrdom, at least so the Church says."

"Before heaven, M. Vernet, don't jest. The thing calls for sublime wisdom. She asks *my* opinion! The case makes my head spin. If it were only a private matter, what would I not give for a good talk with René! Of course, he now is hopeless."

"Hopeless," sighed the Abbé deliberately. They had stopped in the middle of the bridge, secure from the least eavesdropping. "He has gone far beyond his first bad principles. Now he is hand in glove with Desmoulins, Danton, Robespierre, who fume with rage because we have not yet the Republic. I understand he is even the confidant of Dr. Marat."

"That squat, scrofulous villain, the author of ' The Peoples' Friend,' the vilest, most abusive, anti-royalist sheet in Paris? Oh, no, M. le Abbé, I know my cousin. You report the impossible."

"It is clear, Monsieur," said Vernet dryly, "you have been long from France. The virus has entered calmer veins than those of our ci-devant Chevalier. His marriage, I grieve to say, has justified all our fears. An enthusiast before, he is a fanatic now. His admiration for Brutus is such that I would hesitate to leave him alone with the King."

Laurent's honest brow was troubled. He had not seen his cousin for over two years, but friendly letters had been exchanged, and René had by no means written as a fanatic. He had, in fact, deplored the calamities of the King and the Queen and his own helplessness to aid them.—And yet the Abbé ought to know.

"I can't follow you, M. Vernet. My cousin was never thus. He was always impersonal in his politics. I pray you to recall the prohibition which you laid on me. Let me visit him. He will never betray."

The Abbé lifted a dead twig that rested on the parapet, slowly broke it in twain, then dropped it in the stream. "I cannot consent to any imprudence, 'Captain.' When you set out from Vienna you recall your orders—to travel strictly incognito in Paris, and to communicate only with persons of approved fidelity. Your cousin has chosen his path, we choose ours. Those paths are separate."

But Laurent snatched the last words. "Separate paths? Are they so forever, Monsieur? You heard what passed between the King and the Queen. The King seemed in no wise averse to making the best of a bad case and accepting the Constitution in good faith. Then we can all return."

"The *King* seemed so." Vernet ceased frowning and passed into the mildest possible laugh.

"Yes, I said the King," rejoined the messenger, now eyeing him sharply.

"My noble friend," spoke the Abbé, still continuing to laugh, "in all the years when you were at Versailles who, pray, did the King's thinking for him?"

"Then," rejoined the Viscount slowly, not without a tinge of regret, "I fear that I cannot say to my parents and my wife at Coblenz, 'Prepare for a speedy return to France.'"

"Except behind Hapsburg and Prussian regiments, my friend," continued Vernet, with just the proper playful melancholy in his tone.

Laurent shook his head in marked dissent and might have delivered himself further, when a woman was seen advancing along the bridge, casting about her shrewd glances to make sure that she was not watched. One might well have noticed her, for she was a striking giantess, meanly dressed and bearing merely the tin cup and copper tankard of a licorice-water vendor, but with a swing and stride about her which made Laurent look twice. At sight of him, indeed, she halted at a discreet distance, but Vernet crooked a finger toward her and she drew near.

"What is it, Madame?"

"I expected you to pass here. *He* wishes to see you," she said directly.

"Very good. Where is the token?"

She produced a broken sou from her pocket and passed it to the Abbé, who, with a little delicate fumbling, opened a purse and produced the missing half of the copper, which fitted its mate completely. Vernet gave her a friendly nod.

"The message is confirmed. Tell him I shall be at the café this evening. Tell him also that the business is going well."

The woman took back the coin, slung around her jug and offered licorice water, whereof both the gentlemen partook in order that passers on the bridge might imagine them her customers. As they did so, the giantess vouchsafed the Abbé a kind of smirk. "M. Sanson gave the appointment yesterday. Ah! Monsieur, to you we are so very grateful."

With that and a kind of grotesque courtesy she was gone. Laurent gazed in a kind of bewilderment, but Vernet only adjusted his black gloves. "A valuable woman; an invaluable woman. Of course, we have to employ all kinds of agents and emissaries. She brings me a message from a devoted servant of the King."

The Viscount, nevertheless, seemed a trifle perplexed.

" 'M. Sanson gave the appointment.' But is not Sanson also 'M. de Paris,' the public executioner?"

"The barest coincidence, *mon* 'Captain.' This M. Sanson chances to be a respected butter-merchant with whom I have a trifling interest. He has merely hired this woman's husband as a drayman."

The Abbé and the Viscount soon bowed and parted, Vernet, so he said, to hasten to the Cordeliers Club, where an important speech was expected upon the new bishoprics; Laurent to proceed to a small, quiet hotel in the Latin Quarter, where the cooking was very tolerable.—No doubt the Abbé was an invaluable agent for the King and the Queen, and yet there were certain wholly indefinable things which the Viscount did not like. Was Vernet precisely the person to be invited to share the innermost hopes of afflicted Majesty?

Laurent had no power, however, to probe the situation. Three days later he was himself riding back toward Vienna, it could not be said with entire satisfaction in his heart; nevertheless, he was resolved to discharge his orders faithfully. He had not seen René. What, in fact, would his cousin have said if informed that Laurent bore in the sole of his boot a paper unsigned but written in a hand that any chancellory in Europe would have recognized as that of Louis the King?

"The bearer of these lines knows my opinions and can express my will."

CHAPTER XXIII

THREE KINDS OF PATRIOTS

VIRGINIE MASSAC, one morning in September, set forth across the river to the Cour de Commerce on one of her periodic visits to Lucile Desmoulins. The day being bright and warm, she had taken the *bonne* to trundle the wagon of small Henriette. Unfortunately Lucile had gone to some family reunion at Charenton, but before returning to Rue Leonard, Virginie was glad enough of an excuse for sauntering across the Luxembourg Gardens.

The Revolution, to be sure, had made the shrubbery and walks over-free to a small army of scampering and very dirty gamins, who even scrambled on the marble statues, many wheezy old men were exchanging their troubles on the benches, and the leaves were falling. For all that, Virginie rejoiced in the wide grass plots, the plane trees, the flower beds, the gravel paths and in the few last venturesome butterflies. She was walking on in a comfortably vacant mood, turning over the project for a winter in England, when a voice directly behind startled her.

"Madame."

A tall woman with a licorice tank slung upon her back was bending over the perambulator and the astonished *bonne*.

"Olympie!" cried Virginie, and instantly the woman had quitted Henriette to seize her mother's hand and cover it with kisses.

"Oh, what a beauty you've grown!" vowed Olympie. "How your color's come back! First I saw you, and then the little one. 'Hers," I vowed at once.—Alas, she seems afraid of me!"

"But I am not afraid, Olympie. Here is a fine bench under this big sycamore.—Where have you kept yourself? How hard René and I have sought you!"

The licorice-water vendor had much to say, but some trouble in saying it. After leaving Virginie, she had reached Ard without difficulty, but had lain very quiet lest, by some bad luck, she might put herself within the reviving power of the law. She had heard of Linio's repulse at the chateau and of Virginie's immediate marriage thereafter. Then Thibaud reappeared. The disaster at Massac and the loss of every hold upon his niece had put Olympie's consort in a very contrite mood. He had pleaded in a maudlin fashion for a resumption of their life on the old terms, and Olympie had forgiven him for reasons as good and as bad as those for which thousands of passable. women have received back thousands of worthless men. They had, therefore, resumed life together.

But to earn a living in Ard seemed nigh impossible. They had drifted again to Paris, where the confused state of the city now left little to be dreaded from the police; but empty hands and hungry mouths were more numerous than ever, and the pair had almost starved. Olympie tried selling flowers at the Halles, then old clothes under the Colonnade of the Louvre; finally she had been driven to tramping the streets with a licorice-water jug. This barely kept them in bread, especially since Thibaud seemed constitutionally unable to turn to any steady work.

"Why had not Olympie sought Virginie with her troubles?"

The giantess tossed the dirty red handkerchief that bound

her scattering locks. "Thank the Good God she still had such a thing as pride—after the way they'd used Virginie!"

"But you do not look so very hungry now?"

"Ah, my White Bird!" A sly glance crept into Olympie's dark eye. "We've had a turn for the better."

"I am so pleased. What was the good fortune?"

Olympie now began to seem somewhat embarrassed. "Well—at last we found a patron.—You—you won't be too angry. The day we met him I'd tasted nothing. Of course you have nothing now to dread."

Virginie's look took on a great intelligence. "You must mean then—Linio?"

Olympie nodded. "My stomach was rattling; don't blame me."

"I don't blame you, Olympie, but I wonder much. Paid by Linio? It can be better even to be hungry than get a cell in La Force."

"Oh, fear nothing, Madame. It's only to carry messages and to collect news."

"Messages? News? What kind of news? Is Linio again at his old haunts, the gamblers' dens by the Palais Royal?"

Olympie was clearly embarrassed. An intense desire to pour out her heart to Virginie struggled with the knowledge that her income depended on discretion. After a little the former motive largely triumphed:

"Oh, no, White Bird. Citizen Linio now seems to be a changed man, careful, law abiding. So devoted to the Revolution! It is his duty to thwart the aristos and the fearful anti-patriots. We collect wine-shop gossip for him, tell him what good and bad patriots are saying, worm ourselves into the friendship of the servants of the old nobles who haven't deserted St. Germain."

"This may be patriotic service, Olympie, yet have a care.

Linio can serve no cause for nothing. He may really be taking the money of Monsieur and the wicked Artois."

Olympie shook her head vigorously. "Oh, no, Madame. Besides he is such a friend of that great patriot, Abbé Vernet, who has just done us such a service."

"I'll ask M. Danton his opinion about Abbé Vernet, but what was that service?"

"The appointment of Thibaud, Madame. The Abbé prevailed on M. Sanson to take him for assistant. True, now that the Constitution is proclaimed, no doubt everything will be lawful and peaceful. Still we trust there will be always a few robbers. Then the new machine adopted by the Assembly—the guillotine, they call it—is so ingenious. Thibaud goes over to-day to M. Sanson's house in Faubourg Denis to practice with it on pigs. They say that it can——"

"Faugh!" groaned Virginie, rising in disgust.

Olympie with wisdom changed the subject; she began playing with little Henriette. Virginie meantime produced an assignat.

"We must return, but listen, Olympie. If Linio is now a true patriot the past must not be raked up against him. New France forgives old injuries. But can such a man really change? How does he get this money which he pays you?"

"That I don't know, Madame. Sometimes I've wondered."

"Perhaps you do right to wonder. Will you make me a promise?" And the assignat was extended.

"Anything possible, Madame."

"Then if you see or hear sign or word which makes you doubt his fidelity to the Revolution come straight to Rue Leonard. I will order André to let you see me."

"I surely promise this, Madame."

Olympie's pride did not forbid her fingers to close firmly

over the paper money. She kissed Virginie's hand devotedly, gave an affectionate peck at Henriette, and was soon stalking away toward the Rue de Vaugiraud, where a number of wine rooms supplied a perfect breeding place for idle talkers.

. . . .

Almost at that same moment and only a few squares from the Gardens, Virginie might have found her husband at Café Procope, opposite the Théâtre Français. The place was crowded, great puffs of tobacco were rising, coffee cups were rattling on the marble-topped tables, journals were crackling, and by the door boys were bawling off, "The Revolutions of Paris," "The Revolutions of France," "The Peoples' Friend," and every other sheet, decent or filthy, with which the city now abounded. Desmoulins, having already written out his morning satire, was peacefully rattling dice for no purpose whatever, St. Just was smoking in silence, Robespierre was calmly penciling notes on the margin of an official report, Massac himself was vaguely wondering who would join him at whist, when, looming through the smoke cloud and elbowing its way, came the huge form of Danton rising like a Goliath above the crowded tables.

Desmoulins laid down his dice box. "Take care, everybody. Danton scowls; that means that Jupiter intends to thunder."

They all moved their chairs to give the big man room. The journalist was right. Danton was frowning portentously.

"What is the matter, Georges?" demanded René.

Danton spread out a paper. "Who of you has heard of a Captain Frenade?" No answer. "Well, then, to the city procureur's office there comes this demand for assistance from the mayor of Chalons-sur-Marne. A Captain Laurent Frenade was halted there four days ago. Claimed to be a Belgian officer with an Austrian commission, traveling of course on 'private business.' Something suspicious about him, searched, a portmanteau full of queer papers. Taken to the Hôtel de Ville for further investigation. Then was carelessly guarded—(the devils take those provincial gendarmes!)—made his escape before they got around to stripping off his clothing. Daring, desperate fellow. Plenty of royalists in Chalons of course to aid him.— Well, the alarm's out, but he's well over the Rhine by this time."

"Deplorable laxity," observed Robespierre, slowly sharpening his pencil with clean precise strokes, "but why does this plague the Substitute Procureur of Paris?"

"Because," answered Danton, slapping the paper on the marble before him, "most luckily he left his portmanteau behind. The contents show that he was a courier for the aristos here in Paris. Ciphers mostly, but we've got a proper man working on them. Many of the open papers are unsigned; still we hope that the authors of some can be smelled out."

"A case then for the new tribunals," suggested St. Just, knocking the ashes from his pipe; "but again we ask, why all this frowning?"

"Because," roared Danton with another fierce slap, and a voice which all the room noticed, "we have a traitor!"

"A traitor?" echoed several.

"A traitor, my friends. The seized documents already deciphered prove this clearly. An initiate into all that passes in the Cordeliers, at the Jacobins, nay at our tables here in Café Procope itself. He is writing directly to Vienna."

"And you suspect?" asked Robespierre calmly.

"Suspect? Perdition, I suspect as yet nobody! If I were suspecting I wouldn't be frowning here, I would be annihilating."

"Really, Danton," continued Robespierre in a slightly peevish manner, carefully closing his penknife, "if I were you I'd not raise my voice so loudly. All the café is listening."

"Let the café listen then. Let the traitor know that his villainy is being uncovered. Let him write to Brussels, to Coblenz, to Treves, to Frankfort, 'I am being unmasked. Expect soon to hear I am in The Conciergerie.' He and his employers will at least act with greater prudence in the future. France will be the gainer by that."

"Listen, Georges," urged Desmoulins, "you are too excited. That does not make a good prosecutor. You take disloyal sentiments too seriously. Of course there are anti-Patriots in Paris. Of course we have betrayers. All that will not injure France. There are five-and-twenty millions of Frenchmen. It will be years before the handful of aristos and the ultra royalists cease to groan and to cavil. They are just one grain in the great wheat sack of the nation. If those papers are treason, let the authors be prosecuted, but do not frown and rage about it."

"I deal with actualities, Camille," retorted the big man; "we have a traitor in our inner circle here in Paris. He can do the Revolution much harm. I would crush him." An empty eggshell lay on the table. Danton's great hand closed over it.

"I too deal with actualities," spoke the precise cold voice of Robespierre. "The sovereign people who have resumed their power in France are intelligent, virtuous, merciful. They will not be destroyed by a few helpless dissidents.

If we can find this traitor as you say, we should render him harmless, but punish him calmly, only as an indication of the Majesty of the Law, not for any harm that he can actually do to the Nation."

"Pah!" cried Danton in disgust. "I'm not fond of Robespierre's subtleties. I say that this Captain Frenade and those who write his infamies deserve death. I'm frowning because I can't rise from the prosecutor's seat and demand it."

"Evidently, my friends," sounded a cheerful, friendly voice, "something is disturbing the Substitute Procureur of Paris. I judge that all the café knows by this time that somebody has been forwarding anti-patriotic sentiments."

It was Father François, who had come over from the Sorbonne to drink his morning coffee and read the journals. Danton suddenly looked somewhat sheepish. "A plague upon my unruly tongue! Of course I nigh deserve death myself for blowing out this warning to the traitors.—But if you could only see the foul stuff deriding the Revolution that's now spread upon my desk, you'd forgive my explosion."

The others edged over their chairs; the lecturer fell into his accustomed station. "My friends," he observed in his ever genial manner, "we can behold this Revolution of ours only through one pair of eyes at a time. My eyes are not Danton's; they are not Robespierre's. If I were a Monseigneur who had been trained to think that God had created France simply to supply me with pensions, palaces and mistresses, my eyes would be different still. Since we claim to be philosophers, vindicators of enlightenment, we must set the example of moderation, calmness, lenity."

"Excellent sentiments," commended Robespierre.

"We must distinguish between the offensive and the dangerous. A railing, furious marquis is nothing. His children will grow up with better opinions. A successful intrigue to bring foreign troops into France is different."

"Different indeed," burst from Danton; "if I could only read you those papers!"

"No doubt we are all to be hanged, or preferably to be drawn and quartered. Monsieur's and Artois' proclamations from beyond the frontier leave us no doubts as to that. But René here can have no fears of leaving Virginie a widow while Austria and Prussia refuse to stir. And Austria and Prussia, my friends, will never stir save on one condition."

"What is that?" from all the table.

Father François carefully put sugar and cream in his cup, next let his voice fall so that only the friends in his circle could hear him: "The one condition is this: that the King of the French himself shall ask the other Kings of Europe to destroy the Revolution. *Then,* my friends, I will learn to scowl like Danton."

.   .   .   .

On the Rue des Cordeliers, a street then tortuous, narrow and fetid as were most of the quarters of Paris, and not far from the Luxembourg was the wine room of "Mucius Scaevola." The name had been the "Maréchal Saxe" until just after the Bastille fell; then the proprietor had felt it commercially incumbent to change his swinging sign very abruptly from a garish portrait of the royal general to a still more garish portrayal of a prim and smiling Roman youth plunging a dagger into a very cross and uncomfortable-looking Etruscan. The wine shop, which was half underground and reached by a few descending steps, was ill-lighted, ill-furnished, ill-swept and ill-smelling—in short, it was extremely like a hundred other Parisian wine shops which ministered to the needs of thirsty patriots.

Nobody in the Mucius Scaevola liked to be saluted as
"Monsieur." "Citizen" here was already the only proper
honorific.

At the very time Father François sipped his coffee in
Café Procope, that other ornament of the Church, Abbé
Vernet, was sitting at a dirty table in a corner of the
Mucius Scaevola. His position indeed was so far to the
back that though the sun was bright outside he was glad
of a candle to make darkness visible. The Abbé had a
pack of greasy cards upon the table, perhaps to give some
excuse for his loitering in the wine shop, but his interest
was in the conversation with two men who had shared a
late breakfast with him.

One of the pair was manifestly enough Linio, flashily
dressed as usual, a little heavier in body and jowl than two
years earlier, and wearing one of those large, curling mustaches which were coming to be an accepted sign of ultra-
Revolutionary principles. The other was a very small man,
barely five feet in height, but strangely built; the neck
short, the face broad and bony, the nose large but curiously
flattened, the mouth large again and with a peculiar con-
traction in one corner. The light was so dim that it was
hard to decide whether his complexion was sallow or
swarthy, but his hair was certainly brown as well as
extremely disorderly, and even through the gloom came
the flashes of a pair of remarkably brilliant eyes.

This personage was on his feet at the moment, gesticulating vigorously, rising on tiptoe to emphasize a word, and
speaking in a strong, sonorous voice, albeit some infirmity
made it impossible for him to enunciate his C's and S's
clearly.

"I tell you, good citizens," spoke the stranger, "we are
deceived. All honest people are deceived. The better
patriots they are the more they are deceived. The more

a man is a patriot the more he becomes foolish. What did I write in 'The Peoples' Friend' yesterday? 'O ye dreaming Parisians, ye Parisians who pride yourselves on your knowledge—yet are as ignorant as asses!'"

"Traitors are assuredly around us, Dr. Marat," assented Vernet.

"Around us? You mean everywhere, Citizen Abbé. The King and Queen are traitors. The retiring Constitutional Assembly—traitors. The new incoming Legislative Assembly—traitors. The avowed defenders of the Constitution, Lafayette, Barnave and the rest, traitors. The smug moderates like the Rolands—traitors. Those smooth-speaking new deputies from the Cironde—traitors. The glibbest talkers at the Jacobin Club—traitors.—All traitors. I distrust everybody. I refuse to be denied the right to distrust everybody. All public life is bad.—What have we accomplished up to date? Nothing but to discover our general rottenness. Cut all the traitors off therefore and begin anew!"

The editor had crossed his arms over his short, thick chest and seemed declaiming toward the Infinite. Vernet (who knew him well) simply waited for the spasm to spend itself, which it did presently; for Marat very suddenly flung himself back into his chair, and without the least apology pulled out a greasy pewter box of some ointment and began smearing its contents upon the livid scrofulous patches upon his neck and wrists. The Abbé drew away his own lace sleeves very gingerly to avoid contact, then resumed a conversation evidently interrupted by the spasm of oratory:

"The Citizen Doctor is correct as usual in his surmises. If the Revolution is to be saved from its enemies it will only be by the zeal and sacrifice of all its champions. We arranged this conference in order to make some suggestions as to coming issues of 'The People's Friend.' Let me sum up therefore: the Citizen Doctor will not fail to continue to speak with his usual boldness against the aristocrats."

"Of course."

"Against all those who under guise of zeal for the new Constitution suggest that enough innovations have been made for the present."

"I will devour them."

"Against misguided persons like that René Massac, who the other night at the Jacobins advocated moderation and forgiveness of past wrongs."

"I'll say 'Artois has paid him.' "

"Against such fanatics as that Father François, who holds that it is possible to remain alike a devout Christian and a good patriot."

"I'll say that he's seeking the Red Hat."

"And above all—on the importance of this we are agreed —you will impeach the sincerity of the King in accepting the Constitution. You will not spare the Queen. You will hold back nothing to undeceive the people concerning them?"

"I'll crucify them both, tear Antoinette's character to shreds, serve up the old Necklace scandal, make her unfit to sit with women of the town."

"Then, Citizen Doctor," assured the Abbé, extending a small roll of notes over which the editor's hand closed like talons, "I trust that you will some day receive the public thanks of the Nation."

As Marat without the scantiest ceremony glided away, Vernet took out an elegantly chased snuff-box, sneezed politely, and carefully cleared his throat. Linio, who had sat in silence through the concluding dialogue, tossed down the last of his cognac-and-water and began fumbling for his gloves, remarking, "A pleasant friend, this Citizen Doctor of yours! I think that I prefer the gallows birds that deserted me in Picardy; they're sweeter company."

"Useful, my dear Baron, useful."

"Don't say 'Baron' here," commanded Linio with anxious glances each way.—"Well, we get deeper and deeper. Wish we could strike bottom! Do you know, Abbé, I give as little as any devil this side of hell for King or for Constitution, but I'm wondering this: wouldn't your turn and my turn be better served now by shouting either *Vive le Roi* or *Vive la Nation* all of the time, than by shouting one thing at the Tuileries and another at the Mucius Scaevola? Which'll it be? This double game can get too dangerous."

"Which fact makes the game so fascinating, my friend."

"Too damned fascinating. You've heard that Laurent de Massac barely slid away at Chalons?"

"And left a portmanteau behind him? Yes."

"Bless my fates that none of *my* writing was in his. bag. I hope none of yours."

"There was none identifiable, my dear—Citizen. I was at least prudent enough to attend to that. And nothing discoverable of the Queen's." Vernet's glance was extraordinarily subtle.

"*Bon dieu*," cried Linio, "I believe you know something of how the Viscount came to be halted!"

"Oh, no, my friend." Vernet's lips were still inscrutable.

"I swear it, you do. I know you're damnably clever. I'll give you odds against Lucifer, but sometimes a notch will slip. We've worked together very well in this last venture—you the head and I the hand, and I like as well as any man to spend what you say is the Queen's money. But I tell you now this double risk's now heightening. The White-and-Lilies or the Tricolor—which flag is it to be?"

"Citizen Linio," said Vernet, drawing on his own slightly

perfumed black gloves, "if you can answer that question you will answer something that is perhaps tormenting wiser persons than even your own very astute self. At present I am only conscious of one great fact, that better than I love either King or Nation I love a certain humble Abbé. And I'm very certain that I'll serve *his* interests the best by working for one very useful end."

"And by that you mean?"

"War."

CHAPTER XXIV

THE DAUPHIN'S SAND PILE

SEPTEMBER sunshine. October rains. November tempests.

René Massac did not visit London that autumn, as he had projected. The King's proclamation indeed had read, "The term of the Revolution has come, let the Nation resume its happy nature." But October had not half spent itself before into Massac's heart as into that of many another thoughtful man was stealing a fateful question: "Would the new Constitution endure?"

France had accepted the Revolution, implicitly, absolutely. By no internal convulsion could the work of the Fourteenth of July be overthrown. But what of despot-ridden Europe? Every monarchy, every aristocracy was horrified and trembling. All the thousands of emigrés were warning passionately, "Your turn the next!"

Could Europe afford to let the Revolution endure? Could Austria, Prussia, Spain, Russia and the rest remain under their despotisms while their most powerful, most cultivated neighbor had become astonishingly liberal? *"Europe?"* an increasingly ugly question mark, stood out before every French patriot's eyes all through that tense winter of 1791-92.

The new "Legislative Assembly" ordained by the Constitution met in October. Since the members of the old "Constitutional Assembly" had disqualified themselves, the new parliamentarians were mostly well-intentioned but pitifully inexperienced men. They quarreled with the King's ministers, quarreled about the doings of the emigrés beyond the frontier, quarreled worst of all about the treatment of that great part of the Clergy which would not swear allegiance to the new "Civil Order" in the Church.

René Massac was no longer tied down to the windy public debates in the old "Riding School," but he was frequent enough at the old Jacobin Convent across the Rue Honoré, from whose tribune Robespierre, Danton, St. Just, or other darlings of the hour such as Brissot, Pétion, or Barbaroux, the "young Antinous" of Marseilles, would thunder against the enemies of the Nation. The Jacobin Club excelled even the Cordeliers Club [1] in its influence across wide France; some even said that applause from its benches was worth more than applause in the new Assembly.

Massac watched the autumn drift by amid increasing perplexity. Somehow the assignats were always dropping lower. The Pope had denounced the Revolution and most of the Clergy were following him. The tasks before the King's ministers were enormous, but they were proving themselves to be simply a cabinet of small, grievously uncertain men. The new deputies delivered windy orations, and seemed only united in suspecting everybody, not merely King and ministers but one another.

And now was rising a murmur, a mutter, at last an angry demand—the call for foreign war.

"War!" cried the nigh helpless Royalists. Out of the great shuffle of an armed conflict could not the King recover his own again?

"War!" cried devoted Constitutionalists like Lafayette. Would not a foreign danger surely consolidate the Nation?

"War!" demanded the eloquent orators in the new Legislative, those charming deputies from the Gironde, Vergni-

[1] Danton was active in both organizations.

aud, Gensonné, Isnard and the others who hovered about
Mme. Roland's most potent salon. A war would be sure
to reveal the weaknesses of the new Constitution and bring
about a more complete liberalization.

Only one faction resisted; the men of the Jacobin
Club, some of whom now were saying "Republic" almost
openly, but who stated even more openly that the sacrifices
of war fell always upon the poor and the innocent.

Being no longer in active politics, Massac shared no state
secrets, but he was miserably conscious of the incessant
intrigues, the wheels within wheels, the tension ever tightening, the perilously increasing suspicion that the Tuileries
was compounding with Austria, a suspicion which well-
informed men began to take for a fearful certainty. Then
came an episode which burned itself into his memory.

. . . It was a very mild afternoon, the grass still tinged
with green and a few bold sparrows chirping over the straw
and litter; Nature apparently was forgetting that it was
mid-December. René had been alone to a lending library
near the Demi Lune, and while strolling homeward noticed
that one of the gates leading into the Tuileries gardens
stood open. The gardens were now ordinarily barred from
the public except on fête days, but in fine weather the sentries seldom questioned a few respectably dressed people
if they wished to promenade inside, and René, with no very
controlling impulse, turned into the gate.

He was sauntering along the broad paths, much lost in
troubled meditation over the latest report that Condé's
emigrés had made a vicious and absolutely futile attempt
to seize Lyons, when a childish voice brought him to a
standstill. Unconsciously he had strolled close to the palace. Under a leafless chestnut there was a sand pile enclosed
in planks. Within a boy of about six, with delicate features and dainty hands, was tossing about the sand with

a little shovel. Close by him a woman, quietly clad, sat upon a stool, while at a little distance two Swiss guardsmen pacing with their muskets watched intently.

Massac's hat swept off. The woman rose and slightly nodded. "I did not see His Highness," said René, instantly recognizing Mme. de Campan. "He is much bigger than —than when I last had the honor of saluting him."

The Dauphin dropped his shovel, leaped out nimbly and seized the visitor by the skirt of his coat.

"Come and play with me, I am lonesome. Where is papa? He said he would come and play while it was so nice and warm."

Mme. de Campan scanned René, evidently striving to recall his face. The ex-deputy bowed to her also, then smiled. "I fear His Highness' mother will hardly reckon me now as a proper playfellow."

Her eyes lighted. "Oh! M. le Chevalier—we keep titles still in the palace—the day was so fine and the gardens so empty!" She was evidently in some quandary how to receive the visitor.

"I also imagined the gardens were empty, Madame. I must be hastening."

But the Dauphin did not release the stranger's coat. "Come and play with me," he repeated in the voice of one already used to being obeyed.

Massac lowered his face beside the gentle, chubby one raised to him. "Well, Your Highness, in one realm at least our Kings keep all their powers. For a moment then——"

He was taking up the small shovel when a voice sounded at his very side: "René!" He was face to face with the Queen herself.

Clinging to Marie Antoinette's hand was a girl of twelve. Mother and daughter were alike dressed very simply in white. They were quite unattended. Neither the Queen

nor Massac lacked social address, but for a lengthening
moment they both gazed almost stupidly. Since that evening in the Versailles gardens René had not exchanged a
word with the Queen; he had seen her nevertheless at public
functions and he was slightly better prepared than Laurent
for the whitened hair and the aging face; for all that this
close view of the woman whom he had loyally served for
years was staggering. For an instant he merely stood hat
in hand, incapable of salutation.

Marie Antoinette recovered the first. Not waiting his
bow, her own head bent with precisely the proper inclination, then her hand was extended as of old, and her voice
came to him penetrating, melodious:

"We shall both be debtors to Louis, René, if he restores
our friendship. See, he forbids us to meet save on the old
cordial terms."

Massac congeed and without hesitation lifted the hand
to his lips with the grace becoming the Galerie des Glaces.

"His Highness, Madame," spoke he, with hat pressed
upon his breast, "knows how to appeal to me now that I
have a little one of my own."

"Your own? Yes, René, I've heard you had a daughter.
What a pity times are changed. I could have stood her
godmother once."

The young man felt his color rise, while the Queen herself perceptibly flushed. To both the episodes preceding
his marriage returned vividly. Marie Antoinette bit her
lip, the other began explaining apologetically how he came
to intrude, but the Queen quickly cut him short:

"Ah! René, why explain? Does your new 'Liberty' forbid belief in good angels? They brought you to the
Dauphin. How often during these fearful months and
years have I fought with my desire, 'Send for René de
Massac.'—Well, here you are. Amnesty is proclaimed.

Have your stern principles no room for reconciliation with your one-time friends who are still called 'King' and 'Queen'?"

"I have always believed Your Majesty acted out of motives of friendship, even though in some manner you suffered yourself to be hoodwinked into aiding half-consciously the abduction of my affianced wife. But I feared, thereafter, that I could render you no kind of service, and accordingly our paths have separated."

"Oh, René!" The Queen's tones were poignant now. "Can you not indeed render us service! You have stripped the Throne of its glory, you have remolded France. We here are only prisoners of state. Have you no magnanimity?"

"For your mortifications and sorrows, Madame, I have always mourned. I have lamented too the insults and molestation of very many of my fellow nobles. It is our misfortune, nobles as well as princes, to atone for the sins of our ancestors."

Marie Antoinette let the young princess steal her arm about her waist, while with her own hand she fondled the curls of the Dauphin. "And must *these* expiate the errors of their unhappy father and mother?"

Massac knew he was being moved with unmanly emotion, but the Queen released the Dauphin and turned with a firmer voice: "See, the King has followed us. He desires to play with his boy. Misfortune has brought us together. We are often with our children now."

Louis XVI approached with crunching strides over the gravel. His red coat was loosely buttoned and he swung a gilt knobbed white cane. Behind him a lieutenant of the Swiss guard followed at respectful distance. Being slightly short-sighted, the King came up close before he stopped with an astonished *"Ma foi!"* on recognizing the visitor.

Marie Antoinette summoned him still nearer with a wave of two fingers:

"What a lucky day, Monsieur! A kind saint sends René de Massac into the garden. Louis detains him. We have conversed, we shall again be friends. Is that not luck, Monsieur?"

The King nodded stiffly but genuinely. His large mouth smiled. "We have over many visitors these days, but a sad lack of real friends.—Glad to see you, Chevalier." He looked about as if groping for the right thing to say next, but his wife immediately continued for him:

"Oh! the fatigue of meeting the persons whom now we must daily receive. No respect. Even compliments are gross and indelicate. Daily the court grows thinner. Every morning I ask, 'Where is this one of my intimates?' 'Alas! Madame, he or she left last night for the frontier. It did not seem safe even to let you know.'—But we, *we*, the King and I, have to remain."

Massac's memories of the abortive flight to Varennes were keen, and of how the King's act then had almost convulsed the Nation. But even as the Queen spoke the grumbling of carts in the Rue Honoré suddenly became almost deafening. He realized, as not before, how the Tuileries gardens were now the only airing spot for the couple who, three years earlier, could at pleasure go on progress through broad France.

"You know well, Madame, that all the more thoughtful friends of the new order deplore those circumstances which prevent your traveling freely. As the Parisians come to behold their King and Queen loyally coöperating with the Constitution, the only check upon your movements will be the constant demonstrations of public affection. I hope that you can soon return to Versailles."

"*Parbleu*, I hope you're right!" burst from the King.

"See how fat I'm getting. Twinges of gout already. All from lack of hunting, Massac. What good wouldn't a brisk gallop in Meudon woods do me! Now it is nothing but papers and delegations, and forever more papers and delegations. My only comfort is with the locks."

"Your Majesty keeps this hobby, then?"

"Yes, I've a work room still in the palace. Ministers and committees can't pursue me there, and my appetite holds good. Damme, if that failed I'd have to abdicate."

"The King of course misses his hunting," observed the Queen with a visible shrug, "and these too (with a glance at her children) would be far better for a scamper in the woods instead of being pent up behind sentries.—And when do you think we can go back to Versailles?"

"Why, Madame," rejoined Massac, "if popular confidence can be increased it might be by spring.—That is unless France labors under the fear of war."

Marie Antoinette's color mounted palpably. "War? Why do you say that, René?"

"Your Majesty knows what is common report, about the appeals of Monsieur, Artois and Condé to the Powers, about the declaration of Pillnitz by Austria and Prussia, and finally—I speak frankly, for the thing is on my heart —the constant rumors that the Tuileries itself flirts with the treasonable voices, 'Restore the royal power by the foreign bayonet.'"

The Queen grew still redder. "Where is your old courtesy, René? The King has sworn to support the Constitution."

"Undoubtedly, Madame, and yet——"

Marie Antoinette interrupted with an unconcealed gust of sudden anger. "Do you impute perjury to him who is still your King?"

The young man held out his hand appealingly. "God

knows, Madame, I have not sought this interview. Yet now I am forced to it I say that only yesterday I encountered a very firm rumor about clandestine correspondence between the Tuileries and Vienna."

The Queen from red was actually turning pale, yet she strove now to control the situation with a very forced laugh. "You were always a pert boy, René. Do you remember that how after that play at the Trianon you told me boldly, 'Your acting to-night, Madame, was execrable'?"

"This is not a matter of private theatricals, but of the safety of France. I entreat you, Madame, as we once were friends and hope once more to understand each other: let this utterly perilous report be instantly denied."

The veins in Marie Antoinette's forehead stood out, her bosom heaved with unrestrained passion as if Massac's words had touched her to the quick. "Denied? What if it were not denied? What if after insults, ignominy, virtual imprisonment, what if the King, what if I too *have* appealed to the crowned heads of Europe and besought them to bring us back to what is rightfully our own!"

"Madame, Madame," pleaded Mme. de Campan, touching the Queen's hand, while the King stood staring in blank dismay, "you forget yourself, you cast away discretion."

The Queen's lips shut tightly. Her color after a moment returned; then her smile became that of a reconciling angel.

"Oh! René, of course I have spoken foolishly, indiscreetly. I only said 'what if.' Of course you did not believe that wicked report. Of course the King and I are loyal to the Constitution."

Massac was sufficiently uncomfortable, but alas! for the Queen's disarming gesture, he had known that smile and supplicating opening of the hands of old; he eyed the King steadily and saw that Louis (the worst of actors) was only growing very red and shifting from foot to foot. At last the King blurted jerkily, "I love the Constitution—I detest Austria and Prussia."

The Queen's lips curled undeniably at the betraying awkwardness of her husband. Out of intense pity for her situation, and yet overwhelmed by the seriousness of the fact just betrayed, Massac strove to ease the situation by a bow and then clapping his hat on his head: "Sire, Madame; the times bewitch us all into a most unwelcome discussion of politics. I have trespassed too long on the time due to the Dauphin."

Marie Antoinette, however, held out not one but both hands and seized those of Massac; her voice took on a strained familiarity. "What, do you have to go, René? Do you remember how happy we all were at Versailles before that fearful winter when you said you must leave the palace? How happy we were then, all one great pleasure-loving family together!—Can we ever be happy again?"

"Yes, Madame." He spoke steadily, but she must have seen the sorrow gleaming through his eyes. "Friends we can be and very happy—when above all other friendship we set our love and our loyalty to the New France."

For almost the first time in their acquaintance she would not meet his gaze, and stood once more dumbly, with her face averted, but still holding his hands. The Dauphin, delighted at his father's presence, had forgotten all about Massac and was dragging the King upon the sand pile and thrusting the little shovel into his grasp.

"We must see you again at the palace, Massac. The next levee is Tuesday," the King threw over his shoulder, carelessly beginning to heap up a sugar-loaf hill of sand.

"Yes, yes," spoke the Queen hurriedly, "we must see you again. We still have a few bright moments. You can divert us.—I am sure you are still my friend."

Massac's answer came very slowly: "For Marie Antoinette the woman, the wife, the mother, I have forever friendship. If for Marie Antoinette the Queen I cannot have the same friendship it is because after what I have glimpsed to-day, I know that she will not let me."

"Before God," she cried, dropping his hands, "you do not take my foolish words in earnest. You will not betray——"

"I betray nothing, Madame. Royalist, Constitutionalist or Republican, a Massac is a man of honor. What has passed in this unsought interview is buried in my breast."

She let him lift her fingers to his lips, while her own lips were trembling. "Yes, René, thus it must be. We are what we are. It is then to be *adieu* and not *au revoir* as for a moment I vainly dreamed.—Well, tell this to Madame your wife, that the woman she doubtless has come to hate has endured such humiliation that the bitterest foe can well pardon what she may do in desperation, can pardon and perhaps can even weep for her."

. . . René walked to the Rue Leonard, threading the crowded streets mechanically. A thousand emotions wrestled within him. The contrast between the gray-haired, sorrowing, almost frantic woman he had quitted, and she who had been the enchanting life of the glittering pageantry of Old Versailles, was painful beyond telling. All the tenderness, all the chivalry of a man of gentle instincts was rising within his breast.

Yet, the absolute betrayal, when he had touched half-wittingly upon the rumored appeal to Austria, had come as a lightning flash to reveal the potence of the coming storm. René Massac had known the perfumed life of Versailles, and too well he had known its passions, its purblind hates, its inveterate prejudices.

"A woman whom all the world would reach out its arms to save," he spoke to his own troubled heart, "but who can save her from herself? I am sorry that I entered the gardens.—Yes, it is indeed *adieu!*"

. . . . When he crossed his own threshold, Virginie met him with an excited face: "To-day Olympie came just as she had promised, and I have detained her to see you."

CHAPTER XXV

THE KING'S STRONG BOX

STORMS and darkness. Wild winds. Rumors unceasing, and ever the terrifying question—"What of Europe?"

In the Legislative Assembly the fiery young "Girondist" orators lashed themselves into a patriotic fury, harkening to their own eloquence. A glittering vision was before them. "Liberty" carried to all Europe by the sword of France.

Across the frontiers, at Coblenz, Treves and other mustering points of the emigrés, war was equally at a premium. The disorganization of the French army was notorious. Half of the officers had emigrated. Half of the privates had mutinied and often calmly gone home. The National Guard seemed a military scarecrow. Let a few brigades of the Hapsburg "White-coats," and of the veterans schooled in Prussia by "Old Fritz," once cross the frontiers and the Revolution ought to tumble like a house of cards. Back to Paris and Versailles then all the seigneurs and the Monseigneurs, and oh! what rejoicing vengeance for the hangman!—Every noble idler playing tric trac at the Three Crowns at Coblenz was devoutly sure of it.

Deeper shadows and fiercer storms. A Constitution so cumberously devised that a government of trustful friends could barely have caused it to operate. And behold!—between the Tuileries and the Riding School there was only

301

friction, backbitings, and soon open distrust, sickening every lover of France.

René Massac kept much apart from his friends during these months. He haunted unfamiliar places. Sometimes he was caught stealthily interviewing a tall, nondescript woman who bore a licorice-water cylinder. Danton once rallied him openly:

"Take care, I hear that you are being bewitched by a strange lady. Remember how Barnave went out to bring back a certain other lady from Varennes in disgrace, took a ride in her carriage, got out of it her devoted slave."

"I am not bewitched," answered Massac without laughing, "and I *am* working to serve France."

"Then you are working for peace," sententiously completed St. Just. "What did Robespierre say yesterday, 'War will ruin the Revolution. We shall be beaten because we shall be betrayed.'"

Nevertheless, even René's best friends were puzzled: he neglected the Jacobin Club, despite an open slur in "The People's Friend" against "a ci-devant Chevalier whose patriotism has cooled." Virginie often had to preside over the supper alone, and even Father François could not draw his one-time pupil out.

"I saw Vernet to-day," once began the lecturer.

"What is he doing now?"

"Why he's actually just been elected 'Constitutional Bishop' from a small department, and is charmed when you address him in private as 'Monseigneur.' He offered me 'his influence' to procure me a similar honor."

"And you told him?" asked Massac.

"That certain recent doings by churchmen did nothing to strengthen my belief in God, but much to strengthen my belief in hell. At which, of course, he only smiled very gently."

"The scoundrel is a power, nevertheless, and not to be quarreled with without reason. Do you rely on his loyalty to the Nation?"

Father François gave his little laugh. "Yes, because I rely upon Vernet's loyalty to himself. But have you had cause to doubt him?"

René only coughed, then held up his hand to check closer queries. "My Father, please don't ask me questions. I'm engaged on a tangled skein and no friend as yet can help me. Yet pretty soon, perhaps, I can ask your discreet aid in something touching the safety of France."

This had been in March. Then on the twentieth of April every bench in the hall of the Legislative was crammed, for on the dais stood the King himself, beside General Dumouriez, his foreign minister. The General read off the latest arrogant and studiously provocative demands of Austria. The deputies hooted and gesticulated. Louis XVI, "in a very ordinary voice, peering short-sightedly at his notes, as if reciting some matter of tedious routine," read off a request for a declaration of war on the Hapsburg Empire.

The deputies raged. The debate was hardly of decent solemnity. "Victory will be faithful to Liberty," shouted Pastoret from the Tribune. "We must declare war against Kings and peace with all peoples," thundered Merlin. The few followers of Robespierre and Danton protested in vain. "War is declared, Messieurs," rolled the President's voice. "Only seven votes against it."

. . . .

The King had returned from the Riding School, enjoyed his luncheon, flung off his heavy, gold-laced mantle, and now sat ruminating soberly in his inner cabinet. The Queen, almost in dishabille, was pacing the rugs with impatience and excitement. The windows of the cabinet commanded a fair view of the verdant gardens, and she leaned forth frequently, as if awaiting some sign below. At length she darted back, all animation, to the King. "Some one comes running. It's been voted."

Louis sighed deeply, but did not go to the window. Now there was coming a distant rumble of cheering and hand-clapping, as if from the Rue Honoré.

"The messenger I had posted," cried the Queen. "Sooner than I expected.—At last! At last we glimpse daylight."

The King sighed more deeply. "Well, you have your wish," he remarked at length. "Once more I've done just as you urged me."

Here the door opened with unmajestic suddenness. Mme. de Campan showed her intelligent face. "Sire, Madame, war is declared!" The lady-in-waiting was close to tears with excitement, but the Queen almost clapped her hands. "So much the better."

"Oh! Madame," protested Mme. de Campan, plainly astonished. "How can war be 'better'?"

The Queen laughed like a schoolgirl. "My dear Jeanne, war has been hanging over us so long that at last it comes as a relief, like parting with an unfriendly tooth."

"Oh! now I understand, Madame. It is good that you are so courageous and can take it that way."

"We have no choice save to be courageous these black days.—Now leave me alone with the King for one hour.— No disturbance, I say."

But before Mme. de Campan could courtesy and retire, Dreux-Brézé—his wig for once in serious disorder, presented himself. His congé, too, was absolutely irregular.

"The Duc de la Rochefoucauld demands private audience and at once. I told him, 'Their Majesties would be alone— impossible.' Yet he makes a scene and will not be denied."

Marie Antoinette shook her head vigorously, but to Dreux-Brézé's mild astonishment, the King spoke firmly. "Admit him." The Master of Ceremonies, therefore, bowed himself backward through the door, and an instant later the Duke was kissing hands with the King and Queen. Mme. de Campan had prudently eliminated herself, and Louis, with his usual ponderous courtesy, beckoned to Rochefoucauld to be seated.

The Duke was a handsome man of five-and-forty, reckoned, indeed, among the ultra-liberal Noblesse, but a staunch personal friend of the King. Now his face was flushed and he labored manifestly under an extreme tension. Etiquette dictated that the King should speak first, but the Duke broke forth without waiting. "It has come!"

"What has come, M. le Duc?" demanded the Queen coldly.

"The war, of course, Madame. I know that Your Majesties have been under diabolical pressure. I know that the last provocations from Austria have been terrible. Yet, as the son of an ancient house, devoted to the service of the throne, I had hoped it would not be needful to give way."

"You are general for Normandy, not minister of foreign affairs," spoke Marie Antoinette ironically; "why then does M. de la Rochefoucauld honor us with his wisdom?"

The Duke's color deepened. "Sire, Madame, you are both suffering under great humiliations and wrongs. So are your kinsfolk and my fellow nobles, and even the most righteous anger can often give bad counsel. I repeat my regret that the insulting threats from Vienna have hurried this action."

"Well," said Louis, stolidly regarding him; "what will you?—War is declared."

"Sire, Madame, my post is no longer at court, but in Normandy. Duty calls me to-night to Rouen. Duty bids me take this last hour and speak a plain word to Your Majesties. It cannot be that you know what in the cafés, theaters, clubs, salons, all now are saying. I were a traitor not to disclose to you the universal rumor, however outrageously false it may be."

"What is this you mean, M. le Duc?" demanded the Queen, her eyes wide and blazing.

"The rumor that now creeps like poison through France is that the war will not be conducted by the palace faithfully, that the public enemy of the Nation will not be the private enemy of the Tuileries."

Louis stirred in his chair heavily, the Queen rose and pointed to the door. "M. de la Rochefoucauld, are you here to insult us? Have we not one left of the old nobility to make himself a bulwark of that throne which his fathers so often defended with their blood?"

The Duke fell on his knees and seized her outstretched hand. "Madame, Your Majesties, never have my fathers defended the throne better than I by my anxious petition would protect it to-day. Drive me from your presence, brand me a disloyal ingrate, but from this moment onward reject as the voice of the devil the suggestion, 'Deal with Austria.' "

"No, no, Rochefoucauld," ordered Louis, standing beside his wife and gazing about distractedly. "You don't have to kneel. I know your loyalty. The Queen knows it. Only you are uselessly distressed. Can't you take my word for it?—Of course, now that war's declared—everything—well, it will have to cease.—I mean, of course, that the story's all a lie, and that I'm sure the army'll fight its best."

"Sire, Madame," the Duke bowed with his hands to his breast, "I have discharged a harsh duty. If my words prove unnecessary, I am the happiest man in France. When next you honor me with an audience, let it be to receive my abject apologies for the words just spoken before my King."

Rochefoucauld went out with the air of a man who had left none of his doubts behind him. The instant he quitted the room, Marie Antoinette glided to the door, slipped the bolt noiselessly, thrust her handkerchief in the keyhole, then, with another lightning movement, seized a blue silk scarf and hung it so that one end dangled in clear sight from the window.

"He suspects," remarked Louis sourly.

"He is an enthusiast—almost as crack-brained as poor René de Massac. He may suspect—let him! He knows nothing."

"Perhaps he is right, Antoinette."

"*Peste!* Right?—What do you mean?"

"We are on the brink. I have said that I would never fight against my people."

"*Your* people!—Traitors to their King, you would say."

"Times change, Antoinette!" Louis' fingers drummed upon the arms of his chair.

"Times change foully. I'm sick of bemoaning our sorrows. Now for the last time, be firm!"

"I would never fight against my people." The King's face was drawn, his fingers continued their drumming.

The Queen's eyes took on a hard glitter, her voice was deep with emotion. "This is the hour for which we have worked every instant since that hideous return from Varennes.—War at last.—The papers are ready prepared for the emergency.—Be firm."

"The hour for which *you* have worked, Antoinette. I, no doubt, have had my wavering moments. It has been hard to know my duty. I always love France."

The Queen seized her husband's wrist; with her other hand she seemed pointing toward the paneled wall.

"Be firm. The messenger will be here in a moment. There is not an instant to lose. In another day the frontiers may be sealed to our most daring couriers; that is why all is now ready."

Louis refused to rise and wearily shook his head. "But these are not private letters to our kinsmen. These now are disclosures to the public enemy. I suppose even a King can commit treason. I have sworn to the Constitution and have just asked for the declaration of war."

Antoinette continued to pluck at his hand. "Be firm! Away with fine words. I am your wife, mortally insulted, threatened, virtually imprisoned. I am the mother of your children. I am your Queen and the child of Maria Theresa. I have the right to speak. It is your weakness that has put us in our plight to-day. Be firm."

The King rose slowly, but did not turn in the direction she pointed; instead he paced the floor, clasping his hands behind his head. "We can make a hideous mistake."

"Be firm. Every act of yours since they whispered those accursed words, 'States General,' has been done too late. It was weakness to say 'Yes' to blundering Necker and convene the deputies. Weakness after the Royal Session, after the fall of the Bastille, a thousand other times. Again and again have you yielded to these men who would abolish the very name of the throne. We have discussed all this. The papers are ready, written by us both and sealed up by myself awaiting this signal.—For the last time, open the strong box."

Still Louis paced and frowned sorrowfully. "Listen, Antoinette. You are an Austrian; it is not unreasonable that you can scarcely understand. After all, a King is still a Frenchman. When we fled to Varennes we planned to come back to Paris behind the army of Bouillé. God ordained otherwise. That would have been civil war, but it is lawful to march against rebels. Next, we have played with Austria and Prussia, hoping that the threats of the Emperor and the King would help to give us right. That too failed. Now we are at open war with Austria. Your Vienna nephew is my official enemy.—The case now is very different.—Do you not see?"

The Queen threw up her hands like a woman beside herself. "*Bon dieu*, what have I done to endure such torment! We princesses are married about by our parents and ministers when we are children, but at least to husbands who should possess some vision of their own dignity. O my Empress Mother, now with the saints, look down upon thy daughter and pity her! The husband to whom thou gavest her is a poltroon!"

"This is distressing, Antoinette," said the King, his heavy features working miserably.

"Life itself has been distressing now for three hideous years; but at least I have dreamed that my husband, after his poor manner, stood by me."

"You always look at these things simply as they touch yourself, Antoinette, yourself and your near friends. I, alas! being the King, have to think also of France."

"France!" The Queen's voice sank to a sobbing whisper. "France? Well, then I will show you France. Come."

She led him, unresisting, through a small door into an inner room, partially darkened. There, on a soft bed, lay a boy, cozily wrapped, and sleeping the deep sleep of peaceful childhood. She made the King bend over him, as she lifted his rich curls one by one, and slowly let them fall back upon the pillow.

"Here, Sire, is France. Your son, mine; the heir of Hugh Capet, Philip Augustus, Henry IV, Louis XIV, the heir to vast dominion builded in blood across the ages; the heir to the proudest throne in Europe now reduced to a mockery. And *this boy's father* hesitates to save his lawful heritage!"

Her voice rose slowly to a wail. "Do not waken him," besought the King.

"No, I will not, Sire"; her tones again were barely audible. "I will not wake the Dauphin of France to discover that his father has forgotten how to be a King."

"Oh, gracious God," groaned Louis hoarsely. "I have not deserved this. I cannot endure it. Why was I ever doomed to reign; why was it not Monsieur or Artois?— Well, you must have your will, Antoinette. Pray heaven it's for the best.—Hark!"

The sound of a light tapping, as from within one of the panels in the cabinet, brought them out of the sleeping chamber immediately. The Queen stepped to the spot whence the sound proceeded, put her lips close to the wood, and asked softly, "Who is there?"

"Your messenger, Madame," in muffled tones from within.

"I know the voice, but give the last password."

"Glory to the Lilies."

"You are very prompt. Wait a few moments and we will admit you." Then she beckoned to the King, gesturing imperiously toward another place in the panelling.

Louis twisted his lip, muttered under breath, "You force my hand," but complied. At a point where the casings seemed firmest, he touched some hidden spring. The panel flew back, disclosing an iron box set within the timbers. The King drew forth an intricate key, clapped it to the lock, and immediately the box swung open and a thin packet, already corded and sealed, could be taken forth. Marie Antoinette darted upon the object before her husband had finished turning the key. The moment the packet was fairly withdrawn, the King closed and relocked the strong box, pressed upon the wood and the panel slid back into place.

Still grasping the packet, the Queen reapproached that other part of the casing, whence had come the muffled voice. A second concealed spring, a second turning of a panel larger than its fellow, and a deep, narrow closet, let into the massive wall, revealed itself; a tiny slit in the masonry made darkness visible and the rear of the closet faded off into a twisting staircase, presumably circling downward in the angle of this wing of the Tuileries. All view within, however, was concealed for the instant by the figure of a man who darkened the aperture, then slid silently into the room. He was cloaked, booted and spurred, and in his hand, while he bowed himself almost double, was a big three-cornered riding hat.

"At command, Madame," was his muttered greeting to the Queen. The latter gave one last glance to make sure he was alone, then approached her visitor almost eagerly.

"You have chosen your time well, Baron Linio," spoke she, in bated whisper. "To have so diligent a servant is consolation in times like these."

"It was arranged that I should be ready, Madame, to receive the packet you told me I was to convey the instant war was actually voted. I was on the watch for the blue scarf which you are accustomed to hang at the window when my poor services are needed."

"And the sentinels at the foot of the tower whence you ascend?"

"Our faithful Vernet's care provides that they shall always be reliable Swiss, who possess neither eyes nor ears."

The Queen lifted her eyes in a kind of thanksgiving. "Tell Abbé Vernet that I thank God daily on my knees for his sagacity and zeal." Then she held out the packet. "See, it is ready. I have sealed it myself. The King's letter is inside."

With a clumsy attempt at devotion, Linio pressed the papers to his lips, and kissed them audibly. "Your Majesties overwhelm me with this confidence. I humbly understood that the packet was to go to the Comte de Mercy, the late Austrian ambassador, who is now in Brussels."

"To him, Baron. He will read the contents and forward them to Vienna."

"Then, Your Majesty, I will convey the packet outside the barriers myself. Lest I be traced, at Sevran I will meet another messenger as loyal and courageous as myself."

"You will both ride fast. Every hour now the lines through the armies will be tightening. That is why the papers must go out to-day."

"The best horses in France will be under us, Madame. The second messenger at Sevran has been waiting these three days to burn up the roads."

Louis had been steadily regarding Linio with the air of a man who desired to say something, but by a manifest effort he held his peace. The Queen, on her part, opened a casket and took thence a purse which gave forth a heavenly clinking sound to the messenger. "This will speed your way. Sevran is not far; say that to-morrow at this time you are again here to report your success with the second messenger."

Again Linio bowed double. "Your Majesty's trust and condescension will lift me to heaven."

Marie Antoinette's response was to draw a topaz of price from her finger. "And this as a foretaste of your sovereign's gratitude. Ah! when a happier day shall dawn, what reward for faithfulness there must be." A certain noise in the antechamber recalled her. "Alas, further privacy will draw suspicions. You must depart."

Linio glanced inquiringly at the King, who still was standing surveying him moodily. "My duty to Your Majesty."

"A safe journey, Monsieur," said Louis very stiffly, but the Queen held out her hand to kiss as she waved graciously toward the concealed staircase. Linio replied with a most uncourtly scrape and flourish, then drew the panel rapidly behind him.

The Queen clapped her hands very softly. "At last!" she cried.

"The plunge is taken," rejoined the King, gazing soberly out of the window.[1]

[1] The existence of the secret strong box of Louis XVI, and the use of private staircases to enable his and Marie Antoinette's agents to pass in and out of the Tuileries are among the commonplaces of history. Equally so among them is the fact that the Austrian armies were invited in, and were informed of French military and diplomatic plans, by the King and the Queen after war had been declared.

CHAPTER XXVI

CITIZEN LINIO (no man had "patriotized" his name more promptly than the ex-Baron) made no great haste in starting for Sevran. The April afternoon was fine, the trees in green feather, the flower markets in the squares one burst of color and fragrance, and now shops and offices were closing and turning dandified clerks and smart grisettes out upon the promenades.

The Constitution certainly had not brought with it Spartan austerity. If many noble folk had lost money in the hubbub, many non-noble folk had made money and rejoiced to spend it. New and gorgeous restaurants were multiplying, there were more gambling hells around the Palais Royal, new theaters were opening, usually to present "plays of occasion," abounding with patriotic sentiments, if sometimes hardly betraying the genius of Corneille. Jewelers' shops were especially brilliant with bargains, so many countesses had had to raise money on their diamonds before leaving abruptly for London or Brussels.

The fine day had brought out all the street orators. Where Rue Denis converged on Rue Honoré, Linio found his way blocked by a crowd listening to a young man of striking appearance standing upon a table, and just now enlivening his declamation about the declaration of war by a recitation from Voltaire's *Brutus*.

"If in all France [1] a traitor linger yet
Who would a master brook, a king regret,
Then let the wretch in death a torment find!
His guilty ashes, cast upon the wind,
Leave but his name here, odious ever more
Than that of tyrant all free men abhor."

A roar answered from the crowd, though the lines had worn long since threadbare.

"That's St. Just, Robespierre's great friend," remarked somebody.

"What a face he has, and what a tongue!"

"And what admirable sentiments. He stands for 'thorough' in case the Tuileries now plays us any disloyal tricks."

Linio wedged his way through and strolled onward thoughtfully. He fully intended going to Sevran. "An avoidable lie," he had once told Vernet, "is the token of an imbecile." And on the whole, he was determined for the present to play true to the Queen. Yet what a wonderful speculation the Revolution was!—More exciting than whist, ombre, faro or all those other games which had won him a name in Milan, Venice, Dresden and Vienna.

After that unlucky failure at Massac, Linio had had his dumps, but he was a sanguine Gascon, had drifted back to Paris and was soon hand-in-glove with Vernet. The latter's cleverness fascinated him, a perfect king of gamesters if he only had not chosen the Church! Yet Linio was wondering a little about his own cards. Taking the Queen's money as her secret messenger, while passing outwardly as the particular friend of Dr. Marat was very delightful, still one presently might have to choose a single side and stick to it. The war would surely involve at least that.

Linio felt of his packet, and made a very shrewd guess

[1] "Rome," of course, in the original version.

of its contents. If only genteel Mme. Roland or Dr. Marat could reward him sufficiently, no doubt it would be a sublimely patriotic act to turn it over to them. Unfortunately, however, the best patriots were usually the worst paymasters. The King and Queen still could pass out the heaviest rouleaus, and on the whole their prospects seemed much the better. The King was still the King and mere froth and fury would not overthrow him. The new French army was now a laughingstock in every officers' club in Europe. Prussia was siding with Austria. England was sure to join them; after that Spain, Sardinia and all the small-fry princes would join in the great hue and cry against the defilers of Monarchy.

By the time the messenger reached the junction of the Boulevard de la Villette with the Rue Martin, the sun was dropping lower. All the little refreshment kiosks were gay with tricolor flags. Solid bourgeois were sitting on hired chairs along the edge of the boulevard and listening to a band crashing out patriotic airs. "War," as yet, was only a matter for animated conversation. Over in a puppet booth a remarkable model was being displayed—the new machine officially adopted for cutting off heads. It was decapitating cheap dolls, and the children all screamed joyfully when the little knife fell and the head and sawdust fell down into the basket.

"If we could only use it on those horrid aristos!" sighed a fat woman with big earrings, fanning herself with a newspaper.

"No chance of it, my dear," rejoined a friend; "the Nation's too merciful. This is only for brigands."

Linio indulged in a superior grin. "Six months," he reflected, "and where will all those tricolor flags be? What a sight if the Magyar and Croat lancers course down these boulevards!"

His mind was made up. The one sensible thing to do was to stick by the King. He stepped up to a hackney coach, bargained with the driver, and soon was rattling off the eleven miles northwest toward Sevran. The delightful approach of evening with the air charged with the fragrance of bursting spring gave Linio a sense of great well-being, not lessened while he kept fingering the large topaz from the Queen.

Possibly, however, he would have been a trifle less contented had he known that from the moment he emerged from the private door at the Tuileries, before which was pacing the resolutely blind Swiss sentry, a tall woman with a licorice-water canteen had watched him, followed him, and never lost sight of him till she saw him drive off on the road to Sevran.

. . . . . .

Sevran, on the highway to Soissons, was an utterly commonplace village, boasting merely a dirty street, dirty stuccoed houses, an ugly parish church and a few straggling villa estates of prosperous Paris tradesmen. The *Three Pigeons* was an equally commonplace inn with a dirty courtyard, dirty wine room and unusually dirty hostlers and tap boys. Sevran, in fact, had been chosen by Linio as his rendezvous because it had absolutely nothing about it to excite suspicions, and because it possessed an innkeeper who sometimes, in private, held up a glass and whispered, "*Vive le Roi!*" although carefully keeping a huge tricolor flag dangling above his doorway.

Linio had been to the *Three Pigeons* several times and was apparently expected, when his carriage rattled over the courtyard cobbles. He paid off the driver liberally, to avoid giving that worthy any cause to linger and complain, and was at once greeted by mine host.

"Is my friend here?"

"Your friend, Lieutenant Briot, is expecting you in his private room."

"Conduct me."

In a sufficiently dusty chamber, Linio found a military gentleman with his heels upon the table, a bottle before him, and an "Acts of the Apostles," a peculiarly filthy and witty Royalist paper, spread out upon his knees. The stranger leaped up instantly.

"Lieutenant Briot?" demanded Linio.

"So my papers read," returned the officer.

The ex-Baron bowed. "At service, at service; but perhaps, for form's sake, I had better ask for your token."

Briot held out the half of a playing card, a "King" cut across irregularly. It matched precisely with the half which Linio produced from a greasy pocketbook. The messenger from the Tuileries thereupon flung back his coat, accepted a chair, sampled the bottle, and became ready for business.

"You are 'Lieutenant Briot' to-day?"' resumed Linio, eying the other closely so as to be sure to recognize him in case he parted with his heavy beard. "You were 'Captain Frenade,' I believe, some months ago when you passed through Paris and Chalons?"

"Briot, Frenade, two or three other *noms de guerre;* faith I've trouble to recall them all!" The tone was hearty and daredevil. "I think I've not met you in my other trips before Citizen—er, Ramel, though without that mustache, I'd swear that somewhere I'd seen you. Can't say that our saintly Abbé picked out a very fine inn for our rendezvous. Wine bad, food worse and enough things crawling about to grace La Force or the Conciergerie."

"But somewhat easier to depart from," remarked "Ramel"

dryly; "therefore the selection.—You can recall some narrow escapes, M. le Vicomte."

Laurent tapped his lips. "Best keep that title quiet a few months longer.—Well, some adventures there have been, no doubt. They suit my nature. That one at Chalons, whereof you must have heard, was the closest. I thought they had me there for a quarter of an hour.—Do ye know, Citizen, I'd give half the reward which I hope to get when France is righted to know how it all happened. My papers were perfect. Nobody but Vernet knew my errand. Yet snapped I was. If it hadn't been for staunch royalists at their Hôtel de Ville—I wouldn't be sampling the *Three Pigeons'* fleas to-day."

"Traitors grow on every bush," observed the other sagaciously. "It was luck enough that you got away with the King's letter. Most of the ladies and gentlemen named in that portmanteau which was seized are now snug in L'Abbaye.—Better fortune this time!"

"I have been taught by that not to reënter Paris. Vernet sent me word to expect you as a faithful and clever go-between. So war was declared to-day? I heard them saying that in the courtyard."

"To-day; the King asked it and our patriot deputies voted it in less time than they took in ordering a new impost. Of course, the Queen was very happy. I'm straight from the Tuileries."

"And the King?"

"Why, His Majesty seemed rather less delighted, but I imagine it was the usual case of his saying first 'No' and then 'Yes'."

Laurent frowned. "If the King could only say 'No' and always 'No,' needless, perhaps, that I were here. But you have the billet?"

Linio fumbled in his bosom and brought forth the packet. "This is what the Aulic Council will want in Vienna." He tossed the papers on the table.

The Viscount eyed them with unconcealed wistfulness. "The Aulic Council, the military brain of Austria, and I, a Massac, taking such a billet from my King and Queen to the age-long enemies of France! Three years ago—who would have conceived it possible?"

"All's topsy-turvy," remarked Linio, who hated the least approach to sentimentality.

Laurent started violently. "What's that noise outside?" he demanded, while Linio, pouncing nervously again upon the packet, crammed it violently into one of his top-boots.

The noise subsided. "It's only guests arriving in a carriage," observed Linio. "The innkeeper's the right sort of a man. All's safe." Nevertheless, Laurent observed that his companion suddenly was looking white and his voice was shaking.

"Give over the billet," ordered the Viscount. "I'm ready and must start immediately. I'll make Reims by morning."

Here, however, the agonized voice of the innkeeper sounded through the door. "Messieurs, Citizens. That room is private. I implore you——"

"Force the door," commanded a second voice.

Laurent dashed toward his great coat, drew forth a pistol and levelled it at the entrance.

"Betrayed! Trapped!" he called to Linio, "but we'll sell our lives dearly. There's still a chance."

The push of a powerful shoulder almost broke the weak lock. The Viscount saw with despair that there was only one window and only one exit, yet he beckoned frantically to his companion. "Try the window. Burn the packet if you can. I'll try to win you a start."

But Linio stood like a man paralyzed, ghastly and gibbering. "Another thrust!" ordered the voice without, and instantly the door crashed inward. The Viscount fired at the first figure in view, but the toppling door and his own excitement, disconcerted his aim. The ball tore into the plaster. Into the room, sword in hand, entered René Massac, side by side with Arnaud, who was brandishing a pair of enormous horse pistols. Directly behind them appeared the calm face of Father François.

Laurent flung the smoking pistol in the intruders' faces, sprang back toward the wall and whipped out a long dagger. In blenching astonishment, the two cousins confronted each other, while the sword and dagger first went out point to point automatically, then slowly sank downward. In this blank interval, indeed, Linio recovered himself enough to begin sidling toward the window, a movement instantly checked by Arnaud's "Halt!" reënforced by the muzzle of a pistol leveled at his head.

Instantly rose the clamor of the host outside the door. "Bandits! Violence! Help! Gendarmes!"

"Good friend," observed Father François, his arms folded peacefully behind him, "pray less noise. Keep quiet and your inn continues in business. Raise an uproar, and I promise that Procureur Danton finds your affairs to be vastly interesting."

The innkeeper slunk away, muttering, but Laurent at last found his tongue as he faced the intruders:

"Well, cousin, I knew that we would some time meet again, but not that we would have the actual pleasure of killing each other."

René, however, was the palest person in the room. "Before God, Laurent, I came out on sure information that this 'patriot' (he gestured with utter contempt toward Linio) was bearing a certain packet to a certain Lieutenant

Briot, otherwise Captain Frenade. And here I discover—
you. I pray heaven that it is all a ghastly mistake."

"Yes, yes, a mistake, cousin; what a coincidence, what a
strange meeting. Ha! ha!—What a fine talk we'll have."
But it did not escape René that, while Laurent emitted his
hideously forced laugh, he was edging to put his own breast
between Linio and Arnaud's pistol.

Again the sword blade rose. "These are bad times,
Laurent. This sight of you has unmanned me, but what I
have come for I must do. This fellow has received a certain packet. That packet I must have. Let him give it
over."

"No, no, no!" groaned Linio at length. "I have nothing.
Only a private errand to this gentleman. Most simple
business—we will explain——"

"After you have been searched," remarked Father
François, his hands still behind his back.

Laurent seized a three-legged stool, and brandished it
above his head as a weapon, shouting simultaneously, "He
has nothing. *I* have obtained the packet. You can take
it after you kill me." René wavered, irresolute, but Linio
beside himself with sheer animal terror, seized the interval
to rush now toward the door. Arnaud felled him with a
prodigious kick, which sent him sprawling on the dusty
tiles, and before he could rise, René was holding his sword
point at his cousin's breast.

"We Massacs are poor conspirators, Laurent, and doubly
poor when we have to lie. If he had not still the packet
himself he'd never risk that precious life of his by avoiding
search. Ha!—Just as I thought." Arnaud's gimlet eyes
had caught the white of the paper protruding above the
gambler's top boot, and his great paw had closed on it in
a twinkling. Father François' hand calmly received the

billet, while Linio rose to a sitting posture upon the floor, rubbing himself and moaning.

The beads of sweat were standing on René's forehead. "Bless heaven, Laurent, that you had *not* yet received the packet. Then, in very truth, I must have killed you. That swine was easy!—Now, what have we found?"

Laurent flung himself helplessly into a chair, and sat with his face buried in his hands, which rested on the table. His voice choked with his tears and sobbing. "Curse you, cousin, a thousand devils curse you! Oh, my honor, my honor.—That it should come to this!"

"Give thanks it is Father François and I, and not strangers; that Massacs are still Massacs. Your honor's safe.—But we must know the contents of this packet."

"By our old love, by your father's soul, do not open it!" implored the courier.

"By my duty to France I must open it." René motioned significantly toward the window, quite unguarded now; but the Viscount did not again attempt this escape. He raised his head and, horribly fascinated, gazed upon Father François as the latter slowly drew out a clasp-knife, cut the strings and began unfolding the papers. Linio by this time had staggered to his feet, and stood helplessly quaking and gibbering in fear of Arnaud.

"Scum!" taunted Laurent, "have you not a life to lose in the service of the King if I make the attempt with you?"

"A noble confederate, cousin," returned René; "I congratulate their Majesties on such a confidant as Linio!"

"Linio? Citizen Ramel, you mean.—*Bon dieu*, I recall your face now from the *Silver Swan* and before that.—To have put trust in such carrion; the King's lost!"

Laurent again bowed his head and wept aloud, while Father François shook out the billets.

"Listen, my children, and René will confirm whether these are the writings of the King and Queen. Listen to what God has permitted René and myself to prevent from being transmitted to Vienna"; the lecturer's voice was calm, but infinitely sad. "Here is the request in the Queen's own hand, asking the Emperor, while privately assisting the emigrés, to invade France, avowedly only in the cause of Austria. She begs that the first proclamations should be 'mild,' because vengeance can follow later. Here the King himself asks that Austria employ forty thousand more men than had been privately proposed. Here is the minute of the secret plan of the French ministers to detach Prussia from the alliance against us. Here are lists of regiments, sketches of fortresses. Here the declaration that the King and Queen may be compelled in public to denounce the Austrian attack, but that Vienna must not heed them——" [1]

"Father," burst from Laurent, "bid Arnaud to do me one last service—to blow my brains out."

René turned to his servant and to the whimpering Linio. "Carrion!" he addressed the latter, "do you see that door? Make through it. If found near Paris to-morrow at dawn your worst foe will pity your death. Neither King nor Nation will need you again."

"Thanks—thanks, Monsieur!" came in one howl from Linio, as he scuttled out incontinently.

René began taking the papers from Father François as, one by one, he turned them over. Then he approached his cousin, laying his hand upon his shoulder, while his own face was working.

"Laurent, as the heaven is over us, when I set myself to this business, the last person I thought to meet therein was

[1] That the King and Queen actually communicateed these matters in unciphered hand to Austria stands on the familiar record of history.

you. I had expected to take this billet, if it proved to be as I feared, to the Palais de Justice.—I cannot go through with it. I would die for the Nation, but, after all, I am a Massac and you are my cousin.—It may be misprision of treason, worthy itself of death—but see——"

He strode over to the fireplace, where a few embers were still gleaming, while outside the April day faded into a deepening twilight. "The plan of the fortress of Maubeuge —look!" The paper fluttered down upon the coals, immediately the room was lit by the bright, wavering flame.

"God bless you, cousin," came from Laurent hoarsely.

"You are a poor conspirator," pursued René, still with tense voice. "None of us take to that kind of work. Better fight more openly, then reckless courage helps better.— Well, here follows the garrison at Strasbourg; and there's the distribution of the fleet. *Parbleu*, when has a Frenchman had to soil his hands with such a billet before!—Tell them what you will at Vienna, but not that the Revolution will go down without a struggle."

"Here are the other papers, my son," spoke Father François in a strange, impersonal tone, handing them over.

"And yonder they are upon the flames—all!" René spurned the smoking pile that the fire might catch every sheet.

Laurent rose and gripped his hand. "You have given me a quarter of an hour in hell.—Now I can still love you."

René returned the clasp and then pointed earnestly toward the exit. "Some fool may break in upon us with questions. You are ready—ride. And swear me this, that if you fight against us, thenceforth it will be openly as a soldier."

"I swear it, cousin."

Father François lightly touched the Viscount's head. "Alas! my child, that you must fight against France."

"Alas, my Father," murmured Laurent, "but to me the King and the Queen are still France."

"God's will be done," answered the priest, casting down his eyes.

As Laurent flung out of the darkening room, the three others gazed after him vacantly, then Arnaud fumbled in his pocket and held out to his master an object that flashed in the last glow of the firelight.

"I knocked it from Linio's finger when I felled him," he explained, "and I felt that Monsieur would not blame me seriously if I failed to give it back when he made such haste to leave us."

René received the topaz ring and bent from the window to examine it. The "M. A." intertwined with lilies was plain upon the chasing, and the younger man gave a laugh horrid in its bitterness. "Yes, Arnaud," spoke he, pocketing the ring himself. "I dare to guess how Linio gained this ring; to-morrow let it reseek its owner."

.   .   .   .

Late the next afternoon a package was placed in the hands of the Queen, while she was in the private cabinet in the Tuileries awaiting the report of Linio. When she opened she found only the topaz ring, and with it these words in a hand she promptly identified:

"Adieu, Madame; eternally adieu. As I said with grief in the garden, all else becomes impossible."

.   .   . Only a little later the supper room of Virginie Massac was filled with her guests. All the old friends had been bidden. When the time came for the toasts, Virginie rose with spring flowers in her hair and the brightest blush upon her cheeks. She beckoned to her husband.

"Shall not the toast be 'Long live the Nation'?" demanded St. Just.

"René has found a better," announced Virginie.

"A better?" cried the whole table together.

"Yes, my friends"; René lifted his glass, as it gleamed red under the candles. "For there can be no other hope for France than this.—I drink now to the toast—'LONG LIVE THE REPUBLIC!'"

CHAPTER XXVII

THE MARSEILLAISE

From a letter of René Massac to Georges Danton, early in August, 1792:

". . . Wisely have you flown back to Arcis to provide for your aged mother before you lead us in forcing the crisis. I send you the latest tidings.

"You are right. Yours is the only way. On the frontiers are only defeats, panics, outcries, 'We are betrayed.' French soldiers are fleeing from the shadows of the enemy. Austria is invading. Prussia is invading. Lafayette and the other generals are at their wits' end. And oh! what boastful whispers drift now from the Tuileries, from Dreux-Brézé's companions, and (I fear me) from the Cabinet of the execrated 'Madame Veto,' the Queen herself.

"Poisoning uncertainty is everywhere. The helpless orators in the Legislative Assembly make it a mere Cave of the Winds. The King, if he cannot fight valiantly, should abdicate promptly. We know the force that controls him: he will not. So we Jacobins must save France by another method—a grievous one. There is no other way.

"All this you knew before departing. You also knew how great was the power which 'Monarchy' still held over the imaginations of France, how great would be the wrench to destroy it. You led and organized: we toiled under you, but still the task seemed insuperable. Take courage: Paris at last is ready.

"Two things have just come to aid us, a proclamation and a song. The proclamation came first; it was from the Duke of Brunswick, commander of the advancing Prussians and Austrians. In terms of naked brutality, we are warned to make no opposition to the invading forces. Those who dare to resist his horde of emigrés and Teutons are to be dealt with 'according to the most stringent laws of war.' Paris must submit herself instantly to the King. If the Tuileries are attacked, Brunswick will 'deliver the city of Paris over to military execution and complete destruction.' No line is drawn between champions of orderly reforms and extreme democrats: all alike are left hopeless should the Duke attain his goal. Did the devil perchance inspire some royal woman to instigate this folly?—Imagine how the boulevards are raging!

"But the song assists the most. Yesterday there entered Paris the Marseilles battalion, the 'six hundred men who knew how to die,' sent hither by our zealous Barbaroux—those 'Volunteers' come to strengthen the arms of our city patriots. Dark, unshaven men with bronzed cheeks and blazing eyes, they have come up from the South, tugging their cannon, waving their flashing bayonets, but above all, bringing us their song, composed, I believe, by Rouget de Lisle of Strasbourg, but now caught up by our champions from Marseilles as their own. It burst on us indescribably when they entered the city thundering from throats of iron:

> "Allons, enfants de la patrie!
> Le jour de gloire est arrivé!"

"Clear on to the chorus, which was like the roar over a storm-whipped ocean:

> "Aux armes, citoyens! Formez vos bataillons!
> Marchons! qu'un sang impur abreuve nos sillons!"

"All Paris is singing it after them. It takes men out of themselves: it makes them know how sublimely beautiful is death for one's country.

"Thousands now are enlisting. Above all public buildings float great white banners with the terrible black letters: 'THE COUNTRY IS IN DANGER.' Young men mount the recruiting platforms with a great passion in their eyes, but they know, alas! that before facing the alien invader there is a more fearful work awaiting them even here in Paris.

"Daily the tension increases. The city is orderly, yet every morning men shrug and mutter, 'Not yet.' Bankers are cramming their strong boxes. Pacific bourgeois send their families into the country towns. Around the Palace stand now the eight hundred Swiss Guards, alert, disciplined. 'France' to these mercenaries is nothing: 'The King' is everything. We must soon take their measure.

"In the Tuileries the King and Queen have just held what may be their last levee. Much splendor, gold lace, powdered perukes and hand-kissing; but can the double sentries keep out the howls from the Place du Carrousel, 'Dethronement! Dethronement!'

"Back, then, to Paris, our chief! The moment is nigh. We wait your coming. We know that we shall strike for the life of France. . . ."

CHAPTER XXVIII

THE TWILIGHT OF THE KINGS

SUNRISE, August tenth, 1792. Mme. Elizabeth, sister of Louis XVI, is rising in the Tuileries and lifting a blind. "Sister," she says to the Queen, "come and look at the dawn."

Queen and princess are looking forth upon the rose-colored sky of a perfect summer morning. At their feet, very quiet and empty now, spreads the Place du Carrousel. To those same windows some seventy-five years back, the Duc de Villeroy had lifted the young Louis XV to see the dense throngs gathered below to cheer him. "Look, Sire," spoke then the Duke to the little boy, "upon these multitudes. They all belong to you. You are their master."

Seventy-five years. The Tuileries palace is now virtually the only spot in France where the grandson of Louis XV can have a few Frenchmen obey him. "I wonder whether Brunswick will get well beyond the border to-day," whispers the Queen.

. . . René Massac had gone sleepless through all of the hot summer night which had preceded. At ten in the evening he had taken farewell of Virginie and the sleeping Henriette. He was going, he said, to assist Danton at the Cordeliers Club beyond the Seine. Virginie knew perfectly well what was intended: two days earlier her husband had accepted election, much more formal this time than before at the Bastille, to his old command of the battalion of the Cordeliers Section of the National Guard. Already, as soon

331

as night fell, the tocsins had begun ringing from all over
Paris, bell flinging out its challenge to bell with one set of
ringers relieving another; and Virginie, of all women in the
city, understood what that summons must mean. The salon
was empty, the candles burning dim, when her husband embraced her.

"To-morrow will be the day," she said, smiling up to him
proudly.

"To-morrow will be the day, my beloved."

"Then," her voice was firm, but she could not escape that
affectation which was the life of her age, "I give you the
farewell of the Spartan mother to her son, 'Return either
with your shield or upon it.'"

"And tell Henriette her father went forth to conquer for
Liberty or to sleep on the bed of honor."

"Go forth, best beloved—I shall pray for you." And
there was no affectation in their last farewell.

At the Cordeliers the leaders of the Club had thrown
open the hall of the old convent to the enormous companies
of waiting people. Desmoulins, Barbaroux, Fabre d'Eglantine and others of Danton's lieutenants had poured forth
their fervid oratory. Then the dark and sinewy men from
Marseilles had been admitted, had thundered out their
song, and Danton had addressed them.

"You have heard the tocsin, that voice of the people
which calls you to the succor of your brothers in Paris.
You have hastened from the extremity of the land to defend the nation from the conspiracies of despotism. Let
this tocsin now sound the last hour of kings, the first hour
of vengeance and of liberty. To arms and ça ira!"

"Ça ira!" shook the vaults of the Cordeliers. Then hours
were spent in the mustering of thousands, the rumbling of
cannon. Two enormous bands were forming, one at the
Cordeliers, one at the Hôtel de Ville. At the Hôtel were

Santerre and, of greater importance, a tall, blonde man of soldierly bearing—Westermann—an Alsatian officer of high ability, to whom the Revolution had come as a new evangel. In the two bands were twenty thousand men, mustering under the torches. They were no mob. True, half were without uniform; many a gun lacked its bayonet; privates contradicted sergeants and sergeants contradicted captains. But organization was there; a rude, flexible but effective discipline was there; above all, an unspeakable determination to end an intolerable situation and to save France was there. The attack on the Tuileries was to be quite other work than the attack on the Bastille.

The twenty thousand had gathered under the balmy summer night amid the tumult of the bells, the trampling of feet, the shouting and singing. It was known that the Palace was alarmed; that such companies of the National Guard as still seemed loyal to the King had been mustered; that some hundreds of gentlemen had gathered in the Tuileries to sell their lives in defence of the Throne. But it was also known that the old loyalist Commune, the City Government of Paris, had that night been swept from power by the new members named by the Paris sections, that Mandat, the royalist commander of the National Guard, who had sworn to hold the Tuileries for the King, had been arrested at the Hôtel de Ville and then (by one of those crimes inevitable when once the devil is unchained) had been shot dead whilst being led to prison.

So it had been under the cressets and the torches. Now the east was turning red, the towers of Notre Dame began to stand forth clearly against the dim blue, the gray line of the Seine began to shimmer. As the dawn strengthened the bells became more frantic and the trampling quickened. Massac, for the last time, went up and down his lines, looking every Cordeliers man in the eyes while the corporals served out the cartridges. At the Tuileries some of the National Guard had already slunk away from the defence, some were crying "Long live the People!"—but the Swiss were only glancing to their priming. Eight hundred professional troops, the best infantry in the world—in them stood incarnate the power of the Old and the peril of the New.

. . . Suddenly all the drums began beating together. Massac drew his sword: "*Allons, citoyens!*" he commanded, and the Cordeliers battalion (traders, shop-keepers, craftsmen of another day, who had just quitted mothers, sisters or wives) with faces set, moved slowly, unflinchingly toward the Pont Neuf, beyond which, half-hidden in the frond of its gardens, rose the spires of the Tuileries, the last stronghold of Monarchy in France.

The attackers moved slowly. No light thing they were undertaking and not by rashness must their purpose fail. But Paris (awake all night) was astir already. No shops were open, not even the wine-shops. Enormous masses of people, nevertheless, of every condition, were pushing along the Rue Honoré, along the quays on either bank of the Seine, were hanging over all the bridges, were loading to danger point the floating barges. The dice for the life of the Monarchy were about to be thrown before a hundred thousand spectators.

Four o'clock. The King, after a sleepless night, had retired at three to his chamber. The Queen, her sister-in-law, the little group of ladies who were ever faithful, the royal ministers who had sat up since sunset to give perfectly futile "advice," reclined heavily upon the benches or stools in the great ornate council-chamber of the palace. The enormous building now swarmed with armed men; Swiss, great nobles, gentlemen-in-waiting, a scattering of the National Guard. Weapons of every sort except cannon were in abundance. One great thing only there lacked—a commander who could infuse passionate resistance into the defenders, and Mandat was dead; none could replace him. Now Louis reappeared and never was figure less royal. His violet-colored suit was disorderly; he had lain down for a short time, and his hair, powdered and curled on one side, was without powder and flattened on the other. His pallid features, swollen eyes, trembling lips, told he had been weeping, but he still retained his vacant, good-natured smile.

Outside the bells grew, for the moment, less clamorous, but messengers were coming in. "The attackers are leaving their rendezvous. They are marching down Rue Honoré or they are crossing the bridges." Already in the Place du Carrousel, before the east front of the Palace, was gathering an unarmed throng, turbulent, unfriendly; brawny arms were flung on high; banners and placards were shaken; while the yelling rose unceasingly. "Down with M. Veto!" "Down with the conspirators!" "Long live the Nation!"

The din drifted in through the tall open windows. It became increasingly the howl of beasts. There were trembling lips in the Council Chamber, but the Queen's were not among them. She faced the King when he reappeared. "Monsieur, here we have troops. It is time to learn who will carry the day—the King or the insurrection." The King smiled vacantly and looked about him; Roederer, Recorder of Paris, the highest official present, a weak man whose one hope was to avoid bloodshed, bowed toward Louis and shook his head. "Sire, Madame, there is only one safety. The Legislative Assembly is in session. The people will respect their deputies. The deputies will protect the royal family. Retire, I beseech of you, to the hall of the Legislative."

The Queen's eyes glittered, but her husband only stood shifting from one foot to another and looking from face to face. Then into the circle burst a municipal officer. He forgot to congé to the King, and his tricolored scarf had almost fallen from his shoulders.

"They approach, Messieurs. The gunners on the bridges are unfaithful. They have drawn the charges from their cannon, and thrown open the bridges and quays to the insurgents. Soon they will be before the palace."

"What do they want?" spoke the Keeper of the Seals in ghastly whisper.

"Abdication, of course," faltered the answer.

"And after abdication, what?" The Queen's was the only firm voice in all that blenching circle.

The officer merely bowed in silence. All eyes went back to the King and to Roederer. "There are not five minutes to lose, Sire," spoke the Recorder jerkily; "the faithful troops are insufficient. The one hope is the Hall of the Assembly."

Marie Antoinette gave her head a royal toss. "The Swiss may be insufficient, Sire, but they are faithful. Hundreds of your nobles also have gathered to defend their King. You have the blood of Henry of Navarre. Put yourself on horseback; draw your sword. Call to your faithful men, 'Conquer or die.' Charge forth. Then, conquering or dying, to the end you are a King of France."

All eyes looked on her admiringly; even the timorous Roederer felt the thrill, then all eyes went back to the King. One word and the palace would have belched defiance from its hundreds of windows, would have charged forth to battle in the streets. Not till long afterward did the world know that an observer of the scene, a young officer, had said that if only Louis had shown himself boldly on horseback, the glory that still hedged about a Monarch would have swept all before him; his troops would have routed the insurgents. So spoke Napoleon Bonaparte.— But Louis only looked back at the Queen with uncomprehending, lack-luster eyes.

"It cannot be," he said hoarsely, as the silence lengthened. Then, after another interval, "Let us go."

Forth from the Tuileries they went, while the loyal guards and gentlemen stood sadly and wondered. The King walked with his ministers. The Queen, with a face of stone, silently took the arm of the Minister of Marine. The little Dauphin kicked the dead leaves as the company crossed the Tuileries gardens. "See," said Louis vacantly to his son, "there are plenty of leaves; they are falling uncommonly early this year." Once the Queen turned her head toward the palace, its windows crowded with hundreds of loyal defenders, sorely bewildered to see them go. "We will soon be back," dogmatized the King, walking on stolidly.

Thus it was the Legislative Assembly received them. "I am come," announced the King, "to prevent a great crime"; and huddled into the press-reporters' tribune, through all that sweltering day sat the father, mother, children who had been the Royal Family of France, while before them the pedants of the Legislative went through the motions of debating "The Regulation of the Negroes in the Colonies"— until musketry gave the most ponderous orator other matters to debate.

. . . The King had gone, yet the attack lingered. It was no light matter to muster twenty thousand along narrow streets and quays and set them in effective array. There was much shouting, ordering, counter-ordering, and thrusting aside of the multitudinous spectators. As the shadows shortened, it was known the King had taken refuge in the Legislative; but the Swiss still stood in their red ranks,

silent and solemn, and a victorious palace could still recall
its inglorious chief.

"Allons, citoyens!" once more commanded René Massac
and all the other battalion colonels.

The bells had seemed for an interval to have grown
weary; now they magically revived. The Cordeliers bell
(Danton himself at the rope) was calling recklessly across
the city. St. Roch, St. Eustache, all the rest were answering together, then closer to the Tuileries itself, St.
Germain-l'Auxerrois clanged from its steeple, with the self-
same voice that had flung the first summons to the massacre
of St. Bartholomew. The clangor blended with the shouting
of thousands. All the areas around the palace were black
with heads and tossing weapons. Nine o'clock.—Either
King or Insurrection was to collapse ingloriously, or here
was the death-grip.

The insurgents pushed boldly across the Carrousel, heedless of the windows of the palace, each garnished with
twelve frowning musketeers. The heavy gates of the Cour
Royale, directly before the Tuileries, yielded suddenly.
Still without firing, the insurgents poured into the inner
court. As often enough, before an incalculable act, the
thousands seemed to pause. There was much shouting,
"Down with M. Veto!" then presently the Marseilles men
and the rest in the van, pushed on slowly, without shot or
blow, across the vestibule itself, until they blinked into the
darkened halls and galleries of the vast residence and saw
at last the Swiss drawn up, step by step, on the grand
staircase and poising their muskets.

The defenders stood as rigid as the pilasters. Among
them moved an officer with drawn sword, giving his orders
in a low voice. During the involuntary hush, a voice was
raised, Westermann's. He was addressing the Swiss in their
own German: "Do not fire on your brothers among the

people. This quarrel is none of yours." For an instant the red ranks seemed. to waver, then from the balustrade above there rang a shout and a shot, from some loyal nobleman, no doubt, overwrought by the delay.

Instantly the sword of the officer waved aloft. "Fire!" and a terrific volley from the stairs crashed point-blank into the edging, hesitant intruders below. In a twinkling all the windows of the Tuileries belched flame. The vestibule was cleared, save for the stricken, while from the outer areas rose the screams of death and of panic. Then the Marseilles men found their cannon and roared back their fury, and the fate of France lay on the knees of the angry gods.

The fire of the Swiss was sustained, terrible. They volleyed with disciplined precision. The front ranks would fire into the dense masses, swing aside mechanically to make room for the second and third ranks, reload, fire again. From the palace windows, the counts, marquises, barons, all the gallant Noblesse who had rallied to sell their lives for an ungallant King, emptied pistols, muskets, blunderbusses. The cannon in the Carrousel thundered reply, but the palace walls were strong and the gunners fell at every discharge of the Swiss. The insurgent musketry produced a hideous crash of glass, but seldom hit a human target. Then all the portals of the Tuileries flew wide, and out poured the Swiss with the bayonet. "Hurrah! Death to the Dog-brothers!" came their gutturals. Simultaneously upon the central cupola, the Tricolor flag sank upon its staff, and instantly was replaced by the defiant White and Lilies of the old Monarchy, while from the windows pealed the loyal cheer, *"Vive le Roi!"*

The charge was irresistible. The Cour Royale was transformed into a litter of broken pikes, muskets, grenadiers' caps, with not a living attacker within it save a few wretches who ran behind the sentry boxes. The Swiss stayed not. With another deadly fire, they pursued straight into the plaza of the Carrousel, seizing the silenced cannon and dragging them back to the palace, while from the quays and streets there went up a hideous screaming, to be answered by the paean of victory from all of the shattered windows.

Ten minutes, during which the palace waited for "the mob" to dissolve, as all well-regulated mobs ought to dissolve after so complete a repulse. Ten minutes, while the news was brought to the refugees huddled in the reporters' box at the Legislative, news which sent back to the Queen's white face a little color. Ten minutes, during which the Colonel of the Cordeliers gritted his teeth, struck laggards with his sword, and told his men it was pleasanter to die by musket balls than by the King's hangmen.—And after that awful lull, to the consternation of the palace, the drums resumed, the pikes and banners tossed, and the attack swept back into the blood-spattered Carrousel.

Slowly, desperately this time. Reinforcements were in from St. Jacques and from St. Antoine. Santerre led up one column and Westermann the other. Again the fire from the windows smote on them; again the Swiss stood firing, loading, firing; but all fear had passed out of the attack. The White-and-Lilies flag on high had become oil on the blazing furnace. "Long live the King!" was drowned in the continuous and ever-fiercer, "Long live the Nation!"

Inch by inch across the Cour Royale, striving with all the furies set in the heart of sinful man. Inch by inch into the vestibule, the marble floor becoming one shambles. Inch by inch to the foot of the great staircase, the living stepping over the dying. That was the attack.

In the dense smoke René Massac (like all the rest) saw only the flashes and bayonet thrusts directly before him.

After he had rallied his men, he rushed forward recklessly
and the attack perforce took care of itself. Sense of time
vanished in that fiery inferno. Life, death, Henriette,
Virginie, heaven, hell, nothing now mattered save breaking
that line of the Swiss, still visible through the welter. The
Cordeliers battalion was unfaltering, it pressed the attack
to the left of the vestibule, while the black Marseilles men
stormed the center. The attack on the Bastille had been
child's play beside this—for the Tuileries was defended by
skillful and desperate men.

Still the staircase, the Swiss, the fire from the windows.—
Was nothing possible save frontal attack? Which side
would collapse the first? A little lull while Westermann
brought more cannon, an instant's lifting of the smoke cloud,
a lieutenant plucking at Massac's tattered shirt as he summoned, "Once more—citizens!"

"See, *mon* Colonel—the Galleries of the Louvre. The
Tuileries can be turned."

So it was. Beside the Seine and pierced beneath with
wickets, ran the long elevated corridor from the Louvre
connecting with the upper floor of the Tuileries. Carpenters had already torn away part of the planking where this
gallery entered the angle of the royal residence, but by
some blunder, the gap was still not too wide for heroic leaping.

"This way, citizens!" None could hear René in the re-
doubling din, but all the Cordeliers men could see him as
he led toward the south against the gallery. The battalion
followed to a man. Shattered timbers and comrades' shoulders made the ladders. From all the palace windows muskets blazed on them. What matter—to those who lived?
The gallery was mounted. The strength of giants, the
agility of satyrs crossed the gap in a twinkling; then
opened before them the glimpse of enormous gilded halls,

glittering chandeliers, far-flung tapestries, silken couches, glowing rugs—and white-faced women who fled back screaming.

The Cordeliers battalion went through the corridors as a living avalanche sweeping the defenders from the windows before them. From the Cour Royale below rose now the answering roar of triumph. Barred doors were being beaten down with inlaid sofas for battering rams; delicate page boys in corners selling their lives dearly; old nobles haughtily throwing away useless swords and folding their arms to the bayonets as they gave their defiant "Long live the King." Then the rear of the great central hall, the grand staircase burst to view, with the Swiss still holding the steps and keeping their thinning lines in the face of the pressing thousands.

"Long live the Nation!" from the conquered galleries above. "Long live the Nation!" in triumph from below. Suddenly a silence from the Swiss. They were falling back, in orderly platoons, disciplined to the last, retreating with soldierly dignity to the rear of the palace and into the enormous gardens. The cannon ceased. The musketry sank to a fitful rattling. Not till hours later did René Massac and the other victors know that, when the conflict first began, the terrified Roederer had persuaded the King to write an order for the Swiss to cease firing, but that the officer entrusted with the message had kept it in his pocket until all military hope of defending the palace had fled.

Massac saw only his small part of the things which followed. Four hundred bodies lay piled before the vestibule alone. Some National Guard companies had only five unwounded men left to cheer the lowering of the flag of the White-and-Lilies. The resistance of the palace had changed the attackers to devils, and like devils full many of them

acted. René was spared the sight of the massacre of many
of the Swiss after they were disarmed and unresisting. He
did not see the murder of the hall porters or how the very
cooks in "the tyrant's" kitchen were hewn in pieces. But
he did see the palace in the clutches of a swirling pack of
brutal men and more brutalized women, not the armed
attackers, but their foul parasites, the offscourings of a
great city, who had flocked to the spoil when others had won
the victory.

Fortunately the very vastness of the building wearied the
fury of the invaders. To smash pier mirrors, shatter price-
less vases, rip from the walls pictured tapestries and shred
them to pieces, fire pistols at statuettes, plunge swords
through silken pillows, all that was barbarous enough, but
it spilled no more blood.

The victory once won, and most of his own surviving men
dispersed in their triumph, Massac did what he could. From
behind an arras he dragged a shivering footman. "Where
are the Queen's ladies?" The fellow was too terrified to
speak, but he pointed toward the Council Chamber. A villainous band had already forced the high doors, and two
ushers who had courageously held the entrance had gone
down under the pikes and cleavers. What René did, he
knew he must do quickly. A score of Cordeliers men still
followed his "This way—to save our honor," and they
brushed aside the mob with their swords and bayonets,
until their colonel found himself face to face with a dozen
women, old and young, delicately dressed and with powdered hair.

The faces of these women were like death, but not one
of them was flinching. Massac's reach instinctively went
up to his hat; he had left it scaling the gallery, but he
could still put his hand on his breast. The old Marquise
who was confronting him dipped at once in a perfect cour-

tesy. It was as if two shades of a perished world were saluting one another.

"Kill! Hew in pieces! We want to eat Mme. Veto," bawled the voices behind, but René turned with his outstretched sword.

"The Queen, I tell you, has fled to the Assembly." And then, when he saw ugly fellows fingering their cleavers, "We give mercy to all women; do not dishonor the Nation."

The onslaught halted, but there still were menacing glances. René bowed again to the women. "Cry 'Long live the Nation.'—That alone will save you." "Long live the Nation," spoke several, although he knew that the words stuck in their throats. But the crisis was passed. "They cheer for the Nation!" declaimed a tall drayman. "That saves their hides. Here, comrades, is Mme. Veto's bedchamber—let's rumple her finery!"

A second swirl of feet. René heard the crashes and shouting as the chests and wardrobe flew open, as silks and velvets were tossed, tumbled and rent asunder by the plunderers. Massac gave his arm to the Marquise. Suddenly it came over him that he had also given his arm to her at a supper at St. Cloud four summers earlier, but it was no moment for reminiscence. "Mesdames," he said the ladies, "because we are Republicans, do not think that we are brigands. Permit us the honor——"

Knowing the palace better than the mob, and with his men stalking ahead with their bayonets, he led the women by a quiet passageway out into the gardens, where now thousands of people were scampering in and out among the chestnuts and the orange tubs, laughing, whooping, howling. The battle was completely over. The most distracting noise was from the incessant crash of the rare furniture and porcelains being flung from the upper windows of the palace upon the terraces below.

René led the way again as in a manner of dream, the stupefied women following. All the sentries by the garden gates had disappeared; they reached the Quay of the Tuileries with no greater peril than the jeers of a few "patriot" bands on their way to the loot of the palace. After crossing the Pont Royal, he found it quite prudent to dismiss his charges, a couple of the Cordeliers men warranting to conduct them to a small hotel in St. Germain, where there would be at least temporary safety.

The old Marquise courtesied again when he left her. Her grace was perfect. "M. le Chevalier," said she, with disarming irony, "thanks to your charming doctrines, we seem to have lost everything we possess, except our politeness. That we retain. Do us the honor of permitting us to thank you."

. . . It was mid-afternoon when René, having cared for his wounded, dismissed his unhurt and satisfied himself that order was returning about the palace, suddenly became conscious that he had problems of his own. He was still alive; the fact came to him as an actual discovery. He had witnessed the triumph of the cause for which he had staked his all. The achievement of the day overwhelmed him by its vastness. The sun was beating down with August fervor. Outside, however, of the shambles around the Tuileries and its great gaping windows, Paris seemed remarkably the same. The lesser shops were reopening. People were moving without fear along the streets. The deed had been done.

Massac knew now that he was not merely hatless; his coat was a tatter of bloody shreds. He had eaten nothing, he had drunk almost nothing since before midnight. And suddenly he knew that he was longing desperately for the cool quiet of Rue Leonard, for Henriette, for Virginie.

A big man with a bandage across his eye was standing

upon one of the stone pedestals along the quay. That morning the pedestal had upborne the statue of a Marshal of France; at that moment the marble was being shivered to bits by a score of men and women eagerly obliterating "the vestiges of tyranny." The man beckoned, then shouted, "Good news, Citizens! The sluggish Legislative has acted at last. M. Veto is suspended from office. He will be held a tight prisoner. Soon there will be a grand new Convention elected. It will give a Republican Constitution to France."

The destroyers of the marble all cheered. Next a brawny woman with a yellow handkerchief over her falling locks, seized a small man with a red cap, and he a dark woman with no head covering at all. From before some wine shop near the quay a viol began to squeak. The twenty all dropped their rude hammers, seized one another's hands and began a long gyrating ring. More and more joined; soon hundreds were swaying together with them; National Guardsmen in uniform, plunderers in gold lace coats snatched from the palace wardrobes, women of every stage of beauty or ugliness. René recognized one of his own sergeants; he had lost his bearskin cap and had replaced it with a beribboned bonnet that at dawn had called a princess its owner. The ever-growing company went hand in hand, whirling over the pavement by the quay, leaping, swinging about in animal triumph, while faster and faster went the impromptu song, led by a few voices:

> "Madame Veto you see
> Vowed she'd slaughter Paree,
> But our staunch cannoniers
> Made her quake with her fears;
> And her patriot foes
> Promptly smashed in her nose!
> Let us shout then and dance
> For the good luck of France!"

Then all the transported multitude bellowed its chorus together:

> "Dance we the Carmagnole;
> Hurrah for the roar, hurrah for the roar!
> Dance we the Carmagnole;
> Hurrah for the roar, the cannon's roar!"

At length many caught sight of René. He had been a conspicuous figure in the assault. More cheering. Women stopped their whirling long enough to blow kisses to "The gallant colonel! The heroic patriot!" Massac turned away, and shook off the firm endeavors to drag him also into the circle of the dance. The sun was still beating down from on high, but he neither sensed its heat, nor felt any exultation at the deed accomplished, only a complete weariness and a wave of still more intense melancholy. Before his eyes was floating the vision of that man and that woman now pent up in the Legislative while the deputies decreed their fate; the man and the woman who had been their own worst enemies, and whose downfall had become the price of the life of France.

> "Dance we the Carmagnole;
> Hurrah for the roar, the cannon's roar!"

"Oh, Liberty," he apostrophized to his own soul, "when I set out in quest of thee, how could I know thou must exact so dear a price!"

CHAPTER XXIX

THE VOICE OF DANTON

From a letter of René Massac to Virginie, September, 1792:

" . . . My Beloved, and you, my other Beloved, Henriette: Happy would I be to embrace you both a thousand times, and yet my satisfaction is great that you are now safe in peaceful, friendly Massac Chateau.

"After enlisting as many stout peasants as possible among our fellow citizens at Massac, after I brought you thither, you know that I proceeded to Ard with the Colonel's commission which Danton had procured for me. There, thanks to the patriotic fervor, I had little difficulty in recruiting up my entire battalion. The good people, furthermore, insisted on electing me 'substitute deputy' to the National Convention, which is to ordain the Republic for France. An empty honor: the Nation to-day needs not talkers, but fighters, and M. le Maire, the actual deputy, will never be disturbed by me in his new duty at the capital.

"Once more I am in Paris. The house on Rue Leonard is sadly desolate, and I am continually with my men. To his great scandal, I have named Arnaud a captain, telling him that the Nation requires now not so much gentleman officers as commanders who at least know how to deploy three files. Our Picard lads have indeed much of soldiering to learn—almost as much as their colonel; but they are hard and fit, can live and fight on a hunk of bread, and keep on marching after your Prussian's legs have broken under him.

"What shall I write of the public case? I know that you have sickened with horror at what you have heard of the massacre of the eleven hundred Royalists pent up in the prisons—the work of that hellish Marat. It has been the unspeakably brutal vengeance for the crimes of the Old Régime. I do not palliate it. I only say that one thousand years of oppression provoked the deed—its victims often the harmless and the innocent. Yet the life of the great city goes on calmly, although trade has sadly dried up, and people talk in whispers as the bulletins reveal the steady advance of the Prussians. More and more my thoughts are being swallowed up in the war. I cannot deny my ancestry. We Massacs were ever a fighting race.

"What are our hopes? Brunswick is over the Rhine. Lafayette (horrified at the deposition of the King) has fled into exile. Longwy has fallen. Verdun is falling. Yet we do not despair. All the spiritual and physical power in France is rising to bar the advance upon Paris.

"You know our leader, our inspiration, our colossal pillar which abides the shock—a gnarled and bruising mass of granite. This is truly the hour of Danton. In name only Minister of Justice, in reality he seems to be the entire government. He is terrible, inexorable in all he deems needful to save the Nation. 'I have been carried into office by a cannon ball,' he announced to his friends. When he heard of the prison massacres his laugh became hideous: 'When the house is ablaze I forget the knaves who pilfer the household goods, I rush to put out the flames. We are at crisis.' Then, with a snap of his big teeth, *'We must make the Royalists fear!'*

"To-day in his office I found him confronting that other great patriot and friend of ours, Robespierre, who commends the fall of the Monarchy and urges the Republic, but who is never a man of action. The two argued violently across Danton's table:

" 'I tell you, Danton, the first need of France is virtue.'

" 'I tell you, Robespierre, the first need of France is victory.'

" 'What use is victory without public character? On the ruins of Royalty we must erect a holy equality and the Rights of Man.'

" 'What use are equality and Rights if the Allies keep advancing?'

" 'Danton, you would corrupt the Nation.'

" 'Robespierre, you would leave no Nation to be corrupted.'

"My appearance halted them. Danton laughed, Robespierre smiled, their parting was friendly. But after 'The Incorruptible' was gone, Danton spoke of him as 'The greatest power presently in France; always in earnest, always dealing in generalities, always dogmatic like a theologian:' then added, 'and since I deal always with the concrete and hate dogmas I must look out! He will have all our heads—but not to-day!'

"Next he talked freely of the war, concluding with absolute earnestness, 'No, my friend, the Prussians will not get to Paris. I have just brought my mother here.—I will not let them!'—And he dismissed me with a great clap on the shoulder.

"This then is the man reared up to control our destinies. As for our former rulers they have vanished into the Tower of the old Temple. They can walk in the enclosed garden. They may have officious guards, but they are better lodged and fed than nineteen-twentieths of Paris. For the King I have profound pity. For the Queen I force myself to have pity too, though all the young manhood of France must pay the price for her purblindness and—error (I soften my words). Let this all pass. Louis Capet and Marie Antoinette his wife have vanished out of my life. I mourn them simply as I mourn other misguided and departed friends.

"Arnaud comes to tell me the battalion must soon march. We go to Champagne where General Dumouriez is striving to halt Brunswick near Valmy. Think of us as only a small, a very small part of an indescribable national uprising. Teach Henriette as her first words, *La République!* Greater than all disappointments, crimes, brutality rises now the vision of resisting France; Europe against her, but her sons leaping embattled to her aid. Disillusionments, anger, grief, all are banished by the sight of that Tricolor now whipping above me against the heavens. To me, René Massac, as to all my countrymen, comes the clarion call just flung forth by Danton:

" 'BOLDNESS, AND AGAIN BOLDNESS, AND EVER BOLDNESS— AND FRANCE IS SAVED!' "

BOOK IV
FRATERNITY"

CHAPTER XXX

HOW A SONG WENT FORTH TO BATTLE

EIGHT in the evening, October fifteenth, 1793.

The night was foggy, dark, chilly. The feeble camp fires were barely gleaming on the edge of the battlefield. Near by a wounded man was groaning, while propped against the timbers of a wrecked cottage, Colonel René Massac, commander of the Ard battalion of the Twenty-second demi-brigade, sat half length upon the ground, dog weary, and indulging for the first time that day in the luxury of his own thoughts.

Gone! Gone! Gone! The Old France of the first twenty years of his life. Gone into antiquity as completely as the pageants of Xerxes. Gone the levees and the couverts, the congés and the courtesies, the taboos and the etiquette, the diamond necklaces, the sham pastorals and all the rest of the tinsel that had been woven into the Nessus-shirt of France. Gone forever, as were gone the fireflies which made their gleams through a single night in a summer vineyard.

Gone Louis XVI, dying with a courage and dignity which cast the mantle of charity over the pitiful insufficiencies of his life.

Gone that vaunted Constitution of France, which the Constituent Assembly had given forth as the crowning achievement of political wisdom. In its place was now the provisional rule of the National Convention, too busy at present with saving France, to inflict "permanent" laws upon her.

Gone those elegant doctrinaires, the Girondists, from Mme. Roland downward, who had praised a Republic yet let others fling down the Monarchy, who had voted for war but failed utterly in the skill to conduct it. They were in prison now, preparing speedily to mount the guillotine.

Gone Marat, that gospeller of hate, whithersoever the dagger of Charlotte Corday had dispatched him.

Gone finally into the eternal eld, all those roseate dreams of 1789, of a world set free without bloodshed or bitterness, through the example of peaceful regenerated France.

Come now the Republic armed, terrible, preaching the gospel of the sword, "casting down (as Danton had shouted) before Europe as the gauntlet of battle, the head of a king."

Come such a war as never before in the annals of France. One nation against all Europe: Austrians rolling into Flanders, Prussians into Alsace, English seizing Toulon, Spaniards beating upon the Pyrenees, German and Italian princelets aiding the mightier Powers.

Come civil war: Lyons in revolt, Normandy and Brittany defiant, La Vendée (by the mouth of the Loire) blazing with insurrection to bring back a king. The Republic bleeding at every pore was defending itself like a wild animal. Bleeding but fighting still; the world against the Republic, and the Republic holding the world at bay.

Come at Paris the great Committee of Public Safety, a twelve-headed dictatorship, ruthless but marvelously efficient.

Come too at Paris the Revolutionary Tribunal, sending to Ste. Guillotine every Frenchman tinged with "moderatism" and failing in unswerving loyalty to the hard-pressed Republic.

Come finally new customs, new morals, new laws and

even a new calendar (with "decades" instead of weeks, and Sundays abolished as a memory of "slavery") along with a new religion of "Reason" in lieu of Christianity.

Come in short a new heaven and a new earth. Better than the old?—René Massac with millions of others deafened by the roar of the gigantic conflict dared not stop to answer. He only knew that at that moment he was ragged, filthy, unshorn, hungry, weary, slightly wounded (for the fourth time in six months) and passionately desirous of sleep.

His Ard battalion had fought in Lorraine, in Alsace, in Brabant, in Flanders, in Picardy. They had arrived just too late to share in that glorious repulse of the Prussians at Valmy in September, 1792, which turned back Brunswick's drive upon Paris; but theirs it had been to share in the victory of Jemmapes, and to cover the retreat from the defeat at Neerwinden. They had avoided being caught in Dumouriez's treason when he went over to the Austrians, and had just escaped from Mayence before the Prussians starved out its devoted garrison. Next they had been hurried into La Vendée to hold Nantes against the royalist insurgents.

Now they were back on the Belgian frontier. They had helped save Dunkirk from the English, but the new Austrian invasion under the Prince of Coburg was more deadly. Valenciennes and Conde had succumbed, Le Quesnay had succumbed, he was now before Maubeuge, the last French fortress on the straight road to Paris. Three weeks of siege and the garrison must have eaten their last horses, yet the cannon still were grumbling, sure sign that Maubeuge held out. But if this fortress fell not one military obstacle would check Coburg's march on Paris. The Revolution having braved all Europe through a fiery year, was thus in mortal peril of being snuffed out.

The last news at camp had been vile. The British flag blew above Toulon. The Vendean insurgents were defiant. The Prussians in Alsace were storming the lines of Weissembourg. With such news René Massac had little time for heeding a report from Paris that "the Widow Capet," (otherwise the ci-devant Queen of France) had been ordered to the Tribunal, and that probably the very next morning would make her submission to "the holy Guillotine." Massac's thoughtlessness was pardonable. He had just seen forty of his own men fall dead from bullets, and Paris seemed pretty remote.

The situation at hand was viler. The French had battled all day. To save Maubeuge the Committee of Public Safety had assembled every demi-brigade [1] available in northern France. To command this flung-together army was Jourdan, who had been a linen-draper in Lyons when the war called him back to his boyhood soldiering; but above him there was now the great Carnot himself, that engineer, quiet, hard, effective, the "war-member" of the Committee of Safety.

Carnot and Jourdan had been ordered to save Maubeuge. If the place fell, they knew that the guillotine awaited them in Paris. What results? A day of headlong assaults on the Austrian batteries before the villages south of Maubeuge. Desperate valor by the French infantry. Counter-charges by the Croat and Magyar cavalry. Villages taken, lost, retaken. Then, just as the October sun slanted downward, a false move exposing the flank of the extreme French left to Coburg's hussars. A crumbling in the line, panic, and the whole of Jourdan's army in jeopardy. Cannon lost. All the captured villages lost. The rout of the entire army saved only by the interposition of those squares of

[1] These organizations of five battalions had become the regular unit in the French Republican armies, replacing the old regiments.

the veterans against which Coburg's horsemen dashed and slashed in vain.

So all day that battle, in which no victory meant defeat; for Maubeuge must surely be very near its end unless relief broke through quickly. Now again it was dark, foggy, cold. Wounded were groaning; dying horses screaming, artillery and wagon wheels rumbling—all out in the great, black, murky void. Massac had had six hundred men in his squares when the Hapsburg cavalry beat on them. He had now perhaps four hundred who would not be too stiff in the morning to answer the summons "Fall in!" They had marched most of the night preceding. They had fought all day. They had no food except the pieces of hard bread left in their knapsacks. They had no drink but filthy ditch water. No tents. Almost no fuel for the bivouacs, and the Austrian cannon kept flinging random shots where-ever there gleamed a camp fire.

René had discovered a barn, and seen his worst wounded laid upon the hay. One of his surgeons had been killed, but perhaps the other had still a little lint and bandage left for a few very desperate cases. He knew that the battle was as good as lost. For the moment, however, that was to him a matter somewhat indifferent. He had long since made up his mind that never would he see Paris again, and never again the chateau which still sheltered Virginie and Henriette.

Weary beyond expression he dozed upon the moist ground.—The moans, the rumbling, even the bellowing of the Austrian twelve-pounders were dying away. He was seeing the supper table, the candles, the old Massac plate, the napery. Virginie sat opposite to him with some flowers in her hair. Henriette was in another chair perched upon a great cushion. What a great girl! Old enough now to lean her elbows upon the table and to pound with her spoon.—No! The pounding was only a jostling of his elbow.

"*Mon* Colonel," so a Captain Fargeau was reporting (more intimately René called him Arnaud), "the burial squad has finished. There were forty-two. Other orders?"

"No others except to throw out double sentries. I don't think those cannon balls can reach here dangerously: make bigger fires. Did I see a dead horse behind the hay-rick?"

"Two dead horses, fresh killed to-day, *mon* Colonel."

"Try to make them into hot soup. They will do for the whole battalion.—Yes, and if the carts have come up serve out more cartridges. That is all.—Hold, were you not wounded, Arnaud?"

"Only half an ear. A grape shot took it. Nothing. Has stopped bleeding already. But you—M. le Chevalier?"

"Only a spent ball grazed past a rib. Not to be mentioned."

"Very good, *mon* Colonel." Captain Fargeau saluted, disappeared and René Massac proceeded to gnaw his lump of bread, and again his head slowly nodded forward.—Once more Virginie in blue and Henriette drumming with her spoon upon the table.—No, he would never see them again. But after all his had not been an unhappy life. What scenes had he not been through since that hour of incalculable decision when he resolved to defy caste, tradition, court, family and to wed Virginie Durand. Would three score years and ten spent vegetating at the chateau or chasing golden will-o'-the-wisps at Versailles have been the slightest recompense? Why had no ball found him already in any of those dozen battles which he had been through? At least he had served his apprenticeship now, had earned that right which General Chancel had lately held out to his own starving troops: "Learn, my comrades, it is by a long course of labor, privation, weariness and suffering that

we must earn the honor of fighting and dying for the
Republic."

To-morrow? What would they do to-morrow?—Perhaps
Maubeuge had surrendered already. Not so; from away
beyond the dark horizon where the Austrian camp fires
were gleaming there came again a steady roaring, batteries
answering batteries. Maubeuge was holding out,—and
there were four hundred men still left in the Ard battalion.

Another jarring voice at hand: "Colonel Massac. Message for Colonel Massac." An orderly with a paper, guided
by one of René's sergeants, appeared under a faint lantern.
The orderly saluted: "To the Commanding officer, Twenty-
second demi-brigade."

"You seek General Motte."

"Alas! *mon* Colonel," broke in the sergeant, "it is just
reported that General Motte was killed in the last charge.
You are the senior colonel and the demi-brigade commander."

René rose heavily to his feet. A little matter like this
was far beyond troubling him just now. It was all in the
day's work. "Hold up the lantern," he directed, and read,
scribbled on the paper, *"All demi-brigade commanders to
headquarters immediately.* JOURDAN. CARNOT."

"My horse," he said, still in utter weariness.

The tired horse was brought. The tired officer mounted.
The tired orderly escorted him over founderous roads, past
a church ruined by the cannonade; through a spectral village so full of wounded men that it seemed one lazar house;
through encampments of sleeping figures lying stretched
under thin blankets upon the naked ground; through another village crammed with wagons, cannon and horses
rattling at their tethers. Everywhere the little red bivouacs, everywhere sentries leaning on their muskets and
fighting off sleep, everywhere the smell of fetid straw, foul

wounds, and the murk of death. Constant challenges and countersigns. Constant sputterings of muskets where the Austrian pickets were thrown out upon the not-distant hills. Occasional cannon boomings. The steady growling of the distant guns before Maubeuge. At last stronger lights. An inn surrounded by sentries. Hurried salutes to the arriving officers. The great room of the inn crammed with tricolor cockades and official scarfs of office.—And Réne Massac found himself dropping upon a bench beside an artillery colonel with an arm in a sling, and a cavalry general with a patch over one eye.

The general-in-chief and the representative of the Great Committee sat side by side behind a deal table on which sputtered two weak candles. Jourdan, in a very dirty uniform, showed a large round face under an enormous cocked hat with long, very broken plumes. Carnot, too, in an equally dirty civilian brown, sat there. His was the big ugly head, the flickering tapers not concealing an astonishing bulging of the forehead over which protruded a long wisp of black hair. Carnot's own hat lay upon the table, amid a heap of dispatches and requisition papers. Fully thirty officers were in that somber room, men who had fought all day and who had come straight from their commands. It was the last place in the world for oratory; for months life to every mortal present had been stripped down to its stark realities.

Jourdan rose, returned the salutes of the assembled council and stated the case with soldierly bluntness. The army, the only one covering the road to Paris, had fought hard since dawn. It had been spread out in a long irregular line of more than seven miles, attacking a wooded plateau held by Coburg as he blocked the relief to Maubeuge. The French had attacked with fury all along the line. On the right center they had almost stormed the village of Dourliers, but at the crucial instant the corresponding attack of their left wing had failed, then had been swept backward. The newly won positions had therefore become untenable. There was nothing for it apparently save to retreat to the old positions with the whole day's sacrifice wasted. The Austrians held the high grounds, they had great superiority of cannon, they were elated by victory—and Maubeuge was ten miles and more away.

"I have lost half my men. Maubeuge had better hold out a little longer," came from the cavalry officer with the patch across his eye.

"Maubeuge had better hold out?" Jourdan's wide lips curled terribly. "Rise, Sergeant Lejay."

A tall cadaverous dragoon rose and saluted with his left hand, his right was in a sling. His uniform was covered with mud: "I am from Maubeuge, I and twelve other dragoons. We set forth yesterday. We swam the Sambre and luck favored us. We got safe to Philippeville. We have brought the general and the Citizen Commissioner the news. In Maubeuge the last horses are killed: the last bread is nearly served out and soon there are only dead leaves, grass, straw. We of the army have learned how to starve, but already the women and little children are crying with hunger in the streets."

"Clearly, comrade officers," spoke the general calmly, "it is necessary that Maubeuge should be relieved."

A great muttering under the huge military mustachios answered him. A gray-headed general-of-division began gesticulating: "I was in Dourliers to-day with my men. Why did we have to retreat when the road was nearly open?—Because the demi-brigades to my left crumbled and ran away.—To-morrow let us fight again, let us take Dourliers again. But I shall leave another thousand of my children on those accursed slopes unless——"

A perfect growling from half a dozen officers interrupted; a veteran equally gnarled struggled to his feet. "How in the fiend's name were we to stop those hussars without artillery? Why were we of the left unsupported by proper cannon?—Because you had them all before Dourliers."

"Peace, comrade officers, peace," enjoined Jourdan, banging a great fist on the table. "We are here to plan, not to recriminate."

"Good," tossed back half a dozen, "back to the charge to-morrow."

"And be repulsed again to-morrow." This from Carnot, hitherto the most silent person in the room. While they listened, he proceeded: "What do we confront? An army nearly as great as our own, better disciplined, intrenched, with twice as many cannon. If we attack to-morrow as we attacked to-day, we shall be repulsed with greater losses, and Maubeuge capitulates the next day.—We are met to find a better plan."

Much speaking, foolish, wise, all of it inconclusive, then a general cast out a thought which made Carnot lift his great protruding head: "We have tried on the left and also on the center. Why not on the extreme right,—Wattignes? The Austrians will not expect us there. We can burst on them at first dawn, gain the high ground, turn their flank, open the road to Maubeuge."

"Why not indeed?" Jourdan's guffaw was fierce. "The whole army is now in position. The Austrians know it perfectly. We have almost no troops upon our right. If we draw battalions from before Dourliers they will counter attack instantly, crush our center, ruin the army. To take Wattignes needs seven thousand men. Where do we get seven thousand men? Out of the trees?"

"Out of the extreme left, *mon* General." René Massac was almost overwhelmed by his own boldness, but he per-

sisted. "I am the junior officer present. No matter; I can
dare to suffer rebuke as well as death for France. If you
attack on the right and your center remains strong, Coburg
will never imagine that you have weakened your left. The
demi-brigades on the left are overwhelmed with humiliation after to-day's misfortunes. Give them chance to
redeem themselves."

More muttering, some friendly, some resentful, and Jourdan shot back his sarcasm. "Does Colonel Massac remember that it is seven miles from one wing of the army to the
other? Is he so fortunate as to command men who can do
without rest and without sleep?"

René leaped to his feet. "Without rest and without
sleep; and why not, *mon* General? Why are resting and
sleeping always necessary for soldiers of the Republic, any
more than merely keeping alive when it is necessary to
charge a battery. We of the Twenty-second demi-brigade
are not soft Parisians; we are tough peasants. We know
how to march, to use our feet, to sleep standing up. Of
course, we are tired, almost spent. But that does not mean
that we cannot cross from length to length of the army and
at gray dawn fall upon the Austrians, where they think
only a screen of pickets is watching them. The Ard battalion can do it, my other comrades can do it, thousands
more on the left wing can do it. Only hasten your orders;
the way is long and the night grows old."

Carnot was upon his feet confronting Massac; eye to eye
two strong men looked on each other steadily. Then the
Commissioner's powerful hands crushed the papers lying
before him.

"Colonel Massac, bring up your demi-brigade to lead the
charge. General Jourdan, issue the needful orders for the
sustaining column. Citizen officers, to your battle posts.
We renew the attack at gray dawn."

. . . René Massac massed all the company and non-commissioned officers around him when he gained his own bivouac. The men were being roused from stables, barns, hay mows and the bare ground. The slightly wounded were groaning over their stiffness. All were cursing as can only veterans just deprived of precious sleep. Massac laid the matter before his group of shaggy upturned faces, as the sole lantern flickered over one dark countenance after another.

"We are exhausted; thirty hours and barely any sleep."

"Yes, *mon* Colonel," all in a chorus.

"Now again we shall have to march all night."

"Yes, *mon* Colonel."

"We will strike the Austrians by surprise just at the first mists of dawn."

"Yes, *mon* Colonel."

"Their fire will be terrible. Half of us will go down."

"Yes, *mon* Colonel."

"But THE SONG will help us very much."

"Yes, *mon* Colonel."

"The rest of us will march over the Austrians. By noon we will pass out rations in Maubeuge."

"YES, *mon* Colonel."

"To duty, then. A great honor is awarded us. Toward Wattignies, in all silence."

.   .   .   .

It was the first glimmer of dawn around the village of Wattignies, near the extreme right of the French and the extreme left of the Austrian line. The place had been held by three infantry regiments of the White-coats, by another regiment which wore red facings, and by a very strong artillery. The Hapsburg officers, comfortably billeted in the houses, were too seasoned warriors to be disturbed by the constant out-post firing and by the pretty steady exchanges of the cannon. The general in command, the Prince of Sondershausen, only turned over on his camp bed when a particularly heavy burst of firing set in, far away to his right near Dourliers.

No doubt (His Highness reflected dreamily) the French would renew their attack upon that ruined hamlet presently. They were a reckless folk, those Republicans, their atrocious principles seeming to fill them with a suicidal love of charging batteries; but steady discipline and Teutonic firmness assuredly would hold them in the morning, just as it had the day before. His Highness felt not the least anxiety as to his own position at Wattignies. Barely enough French were in position before him for a respectable demonstration. If only Coburg would send over two more regiments, Sondershausen hoped to seize the offensive, turn Jourdan's flank, and cover himself with glory. It would be pleasant then to march speedily into Paris to avenge the murdered King and the soon-to-be murdered Queen, and incidentally to renew acquaintance with a certain opera comet, from whom the Prince had taken a lingering adieu when he was at the embassy in 1789.

The guns at Dourliers had died down to a feeble growling. Another distant grumbling was coming from Maubeuge, but the commander was again clicking glasses with yet another bewitching lady—at Bad Baden this time—when an aid began wakening him most uncivilly.

"Oh, Serene Highness, the colonel of the Klebek regiment sends an amazing warning! His sentries hear a strange going behind the French lines; murmurs, trampling, rattling of muskets and bayonets. A great force is being brought steadily before Wattignies."

"Great force? Great devil! Where will Jourdan get it? We know that every demi-brigade of his was engaged yesterday. He's ruined if he unmasks Dourliers."

"Nevertheless, the colonel's warning is urgent."

"The colonel is an ass!" For all that, the Prince (a very seasoned warrior) had leaped out of bed, and his aid got him into his coat and greatcoat.

In the little market place before the headquarters, dragoons were mounting and a Croatian battalion was falling in amid the cuffs and curses of its sergeants. Another runner to the Prince: "Your Highness, the noise from the French increases. The colonel of the Hohenlohe regiment also sends the warning."

"A feint to stop our advancing, while they try the center." But the Prince himself had now caught "something" (he could not name it) coming down through the impenetrable mist. "Bring the reserve artillery to position," he ordered.

The Austrians and their allies were leaping from their bivouacs and were tumbling into line. The dawn was advancing, but still the white mist clung to the ground and thence upward to half the height of the church steeple. Above this vapor the trees, with their dead autumn leaves, rose like ghosts, yet the ground was completely shrouded. Now the guns, miles away to the center, all awoke, followed by heavy volleys of musketry. "Beyond a doubt it is the attack on Dourliers," one staff lieutenant was exchanging with another, when suddenly, out of the white mists right before them, out of the fog-wrapped hedges and the grayer void behind, came bugles, one, two, many. Then a French voice like a clarion, *"Advance!"* Then, following the bugles and the command, a roar louder than the cannon, seven thousand voices, rancorous, frantic, all bellowing together:

"Allons, enfants de la patrie!
 Le jour de gloire est arrivé!
 Contre nous, de la tyrannie
 L'étendard sanglant est levé.
 Entendez vous dans ces campagnes
 Mugir ces féroces soldats!
 Ils viennent jusque dans vos bras
 Egorger vos fils et vos compagnes!——
Aux armes, citoyens! formez vos bataillons!
Marchons! qu'un sang impur abreuve nos sillons!" [1]

"Fire, in the fiend's name! Up with the full reserve!"
bawled Sondershausen, vaulting into his saddle.

The first order was needless. The entire Austrian line
was darting flame. The guns were leaping on their carriages. Still the song, and now appeared the head of a
broad column thrusting out of the mists; a jagged line of
bayonets, the outline of a banner. Ever nearer.

"Que veut cette horde d'esclaves,
 De traîtres, de rois conjurés?
 Pour qui ces ignobles entraves
 Ces fers dès longtemps préparés?
 Français, pour vous, ah! quel outrage,
 Quels transports il doit exciter!
 C'est vous qu'on ose méditer
 De rendre à l'antique esclavage;
     Aux armes, citoyens!"

"Double shot with grape! Every gun! Mow them
down!" The Prince, with drawn saber, dashed behind his
artillerymen, slashing at every cannoneer who failed in the
most desperate energy. The head of the column seemed
sinking into a heap that reddened even under the twilight,
but that head was ever renewed. Now closer still:

[1] The Marseillaise seems to me to be untranslatable. But I defy
an American or English reader, to whom all other French is sealed,
to fail to get its power to send men into battle.

W. S. D.

"Quoi! ces cohortes étrangères
  Feraient la loi dans nos foyers?
Quoi! ces phalanges mercenaires
  Terrasseraient nos pères guerriers?
Grand Dieu! par des mains enchaînées,
  Nos fronts sous le joug se ploieraient;
De vils despotes deviendraient
  Les maîtres de nos destinées!
    Aux armes, citoyens! . . ."

Out of the mists came the impact of men. Ahead or beside of the infantry were running the French officers. They had set their great cocked hats upon the points of their swords and were swinging them aloft like standards.

"*Um Gottes Willen,*" groaned a veteran captain at the Prince's side, "we are not killing them fast enough! They are up to the entrenchment!"

The Austrian works now were one line of fire. The stone fences and barns, the dwellings of Wattignies were blazing death like an Inferno. Not one shot yet had the French fired. Now the column was scrambling up the slope. Again the head melted away, but Antaeus-like, the touch of Mother-Earth seemed to raise it with new ardor. From far back into the awful distance was again coming the song:

"Tremblez, tyrans! et vous, perfides,
  L'opprobre de tous les partis!
Tremblez, vos projets parricides
  Vont enfin recevoir leur prix!
Tout est soldat pour vous combattre:
  S'ils tombent nos jeunes héros,
La France en produit les nouveaux,
  Contre vous tout prêts à se battre.
    Aux armes, citoyens! . . ."

Mounting the slope and over, the fallen as stepping stones for the living. The Klebek regiment, the Hohenlohe regiment, the Stern regiment standing like the veterans that they were, to take and thrust with the bayonet. The Austrian gunners cramming home the last grape into their heated tubes, and sending it down the whole length of the column, now fair before the smoking muzzles. And louder yet:

> "Français, en guerriers magnanimes,
> Portez ou retenez vos coups;
> Epargnes ces tristes victimes
> A regret s'armant contre vous.
> Mais ces despotes sanguinaires,
> Mais les complices de Bouillé,
> Tous ces tigres sans pitié
> Déchirent le sein de leur mère.
>   Aux armes, citoyens! . . ."

"At them! For honor and Austria!" Sondershausen himself led the charge, his dragoons tearing behind him. The gunners were dropping their rammers and running behind the squares of the infantry. The horse piled upon the French column, striking, hewing, flinging themselves upon the bayonets. Once more the van of the attack crumpled, once more was miraculously renewed from behind. The dragoons recoiled decimated, shattered. The three infantry regiments stood in their squares like veterans, and beat back the first onset. Behold now an enormous tricolor banner emerging from the mist, with gilt letters visible through the powder smoke:

"LA LIBERTÉ OU LA MORT."

Thousands of voices still bellowing from the rear:

> "Amour sacré de la patrie,
> Conduis, soutiens nos bras vengeurs!
> Liberté, liberté chérie,
> Combats avec tes défenseurs!

Sous nos drapeaux que la Victoire
Accoure à tes mâles accents;
Que tes ennemis expirants
Voient ton triomphe et notre gloire!
Aux armes, citoyens! formez vos bataillons!
Marchons! qu'un sang impur abreuve nos sillons!

Up to the guns and past them. Up to the squares and
over them. The three regiments were a scampering pack
of fugitives, or of wretches dropping their muskets and
howling their German *"Gnade! Gnade!"* The great banner was floating in the market place of shattered Wattignies,
while the song died away into one fearful, exultant *"La
Victoire!"*

Yet not the end. There was one of Coburg's regiments
that had not run away. Onward it came, the red facings
of its uniforms matching the horrid redness of the trampled
soil. Above it blew another banner, not the tricolor, but
the old White-and-Lilies of Monarchist France. It was the
Royal Bourbon, the regiment of the emigrés. It charged
against the victorious column with all the courageous hate
which can surge up in the hearts of men.

"Vive le Roi!"

"Vive la République!"

"Rebel swine!"

"Bestial traitors!"

Frenchmen grappled with Frenchmen. One royalist
officer, of lordly pedigree no doubt, before all others was
valorous and reckless. He was seen through the sulphurous
murk dashing his sword amid the bayonets, as if by his
sole efforts to open the line and let his men force through.
—Now he was down; half of his men were down; the White-
and-Lilies banner was down. The remnants of the Royal
Bourbon went streaming off with the Germans, Croats,
Magyars. The great column had halted at last, where the

bullet-pierced tricolor wafted out against the gray October sky.

Coburg's flank was turned, and that general knew it. Hapsburg discipline held, nevertheless, and the retreat through Dourliers and far to the East was prompt and orderly. His troops were marching back to the Sambre and over the pontoon bridges, while the exhausted French were dropping in scores by the hedgerows to slumber in broad day. But the deed was done; Jourdan's other divisions and the cavalry were advancing unopposed.

By noon the hungry sentinels south of the besieged fortress saw a body of dragoons, muddy, tattered, riding toward them, brandishing their swords and shouting.

"*Qui vive!*" called the sentinels.

"France!" trumpeted the dragoons, "the bread carts are behind."

And the gate to Paris was locked against the Austrians.

.   .   .   .

Eight in the evening, October sixteenth, 1793.

This night was, if anything, more foggy, dark, chilly than its predecessor. René Massac this time lay upon a truss of dirty straw in a barn half way between Wattignies and Maubeuge. He was in that second stage of utter exhaustion when he was far too spent and excited to fall asleep. This time a ball had not grazed his rib, it had found his left arm. Jourdan's surgeon had put it in a splint, and had expressed the hope that it would not hang too stiffly during the rest of the owner's life. Massac was very happy. Still another time Death most unaccountably had decided to pass him by. There was beginning to be a real hope once more of seeing Virginie and Henriette. All around the barn sorely wounded men were groaning, but other soldiers were singing. They had found a small tavern, only half-plundered by the Austrians. René knew that he ought to forbid the bottles, but heart and flesh cried out against it. Captain Fargeau came in again with his report. Having exposed himself in the charge more recklessly than any other member of the battalion, by the law of the contraries he had escaped this time without another scratch.

"Well, how many of us are left, Captain?"

"One hundred and forty can still answer roll-call, *mon* Colonel; perhaps a hundred and fifty when they have slept out their sleep. I have had to bury only sixty more."

"Might have been worse. Where are those flags?"

"Corporal Jouve has the one from the Royal Traitors. Lieutenant Bourdon the one we took from the White-coat Klebeks. The Noyon battalion claims the Klebeks', but (with a snort) I said, 'Come and seize it.'"

"We must not be selfish, Captain Fargeau. One captured flag is enough for one battalion."

"I know, I know, *mon* Colonel, nevertheless——" and the Captain whistled through the place where his front teeth had been, before they were knocked out in an Alsace battle.

Other reports followed as to the state of the battalion. What a lucky day it had been on which to die! How could one ever hope for a better end?—Presently the Captain looked about him slyly, to make sure no unfriendly ear was eavesdropping in the barn; then he gave a louder whistle toward the door, and turned again to his commander. "M. le Chevalier," he said in his unofficial voice.

"What is it now, Arnaud?"

Before the latter could answer, René rose on his sound elbow as two bearers entered the barn; the lantern showed that they were conveying a man motionless on a litter of muskets. The instant they had set him down upon the straw beside the colonel, the Captain ordered them, "Begone!" and they faded into the dark outside.

Arnaud lifted the blanket he had thrown over the stranger's face and held up the lantern. "He is alive! M. le Chevalier," he announced almost gleefully, "see—he stirs."

René staggered to his feet. *"Ma foi!* It is Laurent. My cousin! How? Where?"

"Very simple, M. le Chevalier. When we searched the field I had with me Jacques and Pierre, the two brothers Carat, sound lads from Massac, who knew you and M. le Vicomte when you hunted frogs along the river. We were turning over the dead ones where the charge of the Royal Traitors burst and broke. 'Gone' and 'Gone' and 'Gone' we were saying; suddenly then Jacques cried out, 'Life in this one!' and then Pierre, all in an echo, 'Before God, it's M. le Vicomte!' And sure enough, he was wounded like the best of us, but the breath still stayed in him."

"Good fellow." René's unwounded hand pressed the horny palm of the veteran; "for this act I thank you from the bottom of my heart; but hear this, my cousin is an emigré taken in arms against France. His life is forfeit the moment a drumhead court martial can identify him, his life, and that, furthermore, of every man who assists to protect him."

"Why, so I knew, and told Jacques and Pierre, but we all agreed that after all he was a Massac and that there had been Massacs before there had been any Republic; and since to-day, the Citizeness Republic had done so very well—why, it would work her no harm, and so here we brought him!"

The Colonel bent over his helpless cousin. A year's campaigning had taught much rough surgery. Laurent was nigh dead from a cut artery, to which, however, Arnaud had already applied a tolerable tourniquet. The other wounds were not necessarily fatal. René assisted his follower to strip off the tell-tale white and red uniform, and throw over his cousin the blue and white of some fallen Republican.

"An officer on detached service from a distant demibrigade. Charged as a volunteer. Picked up on the battlefield"; that, they agreed, could be the story.

Laurent presently was returning to consciousness, was stirring, was beginning to groan and mutter questions, and Arnaud produced a black bottle that put a little more life into him. It was necessary to revive him carefully, however, to get him to the point he could be made to understand his position and answer to his part, before any strange surgeon handled him. The Captain had barely dragged him to the darkest corner of the barn, when a lieutenant with a second lantern entered, saluted, then passed to René, who was back upon his straw, a paper with the printed heading:

"IN THE NAME OF THE REPUBLIC, ONE AND INDIVISIBLE."

Below in firm hand was written:

"For services to the Nation, René Massac is named General of Brigade. Lazare Nicolas Marguerite Carnot."

. . . Four days later a small party of invalided soldiers approached Massac chateau. They escorted General Massac, who, doubtless, expected to find the Citizeness, his wife, and the young Citizeness, his daughter, somewhat glad to see him. With them, in a horse litter, was borne a comrade officer of the General's, seriously wounded and invited by his friend to recuperate at the chateau.

CHAPTER XXXI

THE NEW PARIS

RENÉ MASSAC, with Virginie and Henriette, reëntered Paris on November ninth, 1793.

More officially it was the 20th Brumaire, Year I of the Republic. The new calendar, "repudiating the vestiges of tyranny and superstition," was only a minor item in the changes which fifteen months without a king had already wrought in France.

The day before they entered, Citizeness Roland, not now quite Republican enough for the prevailing mood, had spoken from the scaffold her "O Liberty, what crimes are committed in thy name." A couple of days later, Bailly, president of the Third Estate when it took the Tennis Court oath, but now under indictment for "Moderatism," was scheduled to confront "the razor of Equality." A large part of Paris appeared to enjoy these things and to watch expectantly for the tumbrils rattling from the Conciergerie to the Place de la Revolution, the Place de Louis XV [1] in departed "slave days." However, between these two days of excitement, the Revolutionary Tribunal had rested and Citizen Sanson and his assistant, Citizen Thibaud Durand, had a little respite from their patriotic labors.

The Massac party instantly found that many of the street names were remarkably changed. Rue M. le Prince suddenly had become Rue de la Liberté, Rue de St. Louis was Rue de la Fraternité, the Palais Royal boasted itself

[1] To-day it is the Place de la Concorde.

375

now to be the Palais Égalité, and even as the coach turned down the quondam Rue Leonard, a fellow was nailing up a new sign board, "Rue de la Démocratie." Nearly half the men on the streets wore red caps and more than half wore long trousers. That was apparently the easiest way to proclaim your patriotism and to avoid open sneers or something much worse.

But if the Massacs' house now stood on Rue de la Démocratie, its friendly door still swung wide open. Inside all was homely and familiar. André had come on ahead and had made everything ready, although he complained vigorously because he was not allowed to appear in livery. René had been summoned to Paris as soon as his wound permitted, in order, with certain comrade officers, to present the captured battle-flags to the Convention and receive the formal thanks of that body of the victors of Wattignies. Laurent had been left recuperating at the chateau. Only a few devoted peasants knew his secret, and in any case, to take the Viscount to Paris had seemed madness. But at Massac there appeared to be little risk.

Barely had the house been reopened when, with a great knocking, there appeared a "Commissioner of the Section," an atrocious looking fellow with a broad sash and a huge plumed hat. With him came three members of the "Revolutionary Army," the new patriot patrol of Paris, "empowered to investigate papers and to issue cards of 'citizenship'." General Massac's name, of course, had gone before him. The Commissioner bubbled with enthusiasm for "the heroic patriot," nevertheless, his constant gaucheries and his crude commingling of servility and familiarity reminded Virginie all too clearly of the fact that she had once seen him flourishing a pair of curling tongs. The "Army" refreshed itself in the kitchen with eau-de-vie, while the Commissioner made out those cards, certifying to the name and description of each inhabitant of a house, which every person in Paris was obliged to carry. Then the Commissioners somewhat officiously suggested that good patriots often set the bust of "Marat the Martyr" in their windows, tacked a card with a list of all the denizens inside upon the house door, smirked at the Citizeness and departed.

Virginie wept that night on her husband's shoulder.

"I wish that I were back in the peace of old Massac."

"So do I, *ma vie*."

"Is it true that the prisons are still crammed, that every person with noble blood can be denounced as a 'suspect' to any Section in Paris, and then at once be imprisoned?"

"Have no fear, dear heart. I am in Paris on a mission of honor. I am privileged."

"Do you know, beloved, this changed air of Paris chills me already. On the campaign I knew that you daily took your chance with death, but I whispered to Henriette each night when I said my prayers by her crib, 'He perils his life for France.' But here, how is France profited by these hideous executions? How could Manon Roland 'imperil the Republic'?"

"Doubtless, doubtless (René's shoulder, if not his words, were comforting), there can be hideous blunders. Spies and traitors abound; hence the severities. But they cannot harm any of us."

"The good God grant it. But how now can the best of patriots feel safe? Promise me, surely, that we shall quit Paris the moment your mission here is ended."

"That I pledge right gladly." And indeed René had heard many things already, things which he had kept from Virginie, that made him mutter, "Life is cleaner on the battlefield."

. . . . He could not complain, however, of any lack of warmth in the reception awarded him the next morning at the Tuileries. That seat of "abolished despotism" had become the human arsenal and magazine of warring France. In the great northern wing, the Pavillon de Flore once, now the Pavillon de l'Égalité, sat the awful Committee of Public Safety, forging the thunderbolts against hostile Europe. In the old palace theater met the Convention itself, successor to the vanished Legislative and National Assemblies. To this high parliament, Carnot had generously and fairly recited the story of Wattignies, praising alike the dead and the living, and it had not lessened the cheering because one of the deputies' own vice-members had proposed and led the victorious charge.

Very properly, then, General René Massac and certain fellow officers from Wattignies, were conducted with all honor into the great, ill-lighted hall. Tier above tier, hundreds of faces rose above him as he was led before the tribune. Highest of all, he glimpsed a shadow-wrapped gallery, packed apparently with nudging and whispering spectators. Thanks to the illumination, only by sky lights, the features of the seated deputies stood out distinctly, yet shrouded by a kind of theatrical gloom.

Amid resounding bravos from Convention and gallery, he was permitted to drape the captured battle-flags upon the table before the high rostrum of the President. That functionary rose to acclaim "our heroes." All the deputies rose. A succession of orators mounted the tribune and spouted furiously about Thermopylae, Horatius Cocles— and Wattignies. Massac endeavored to sit with becoming modesty; to pick out familiar faces along the benches; to note that portentious gap where had sat those twenty-one Girondists who had preceded Mme. Roland to the scaffold. Finally, with a few becoming words, he accepted in his comrades' behalf, the tumultuous vote that "The Army of the North has deserved well of its native land."

All had been according to card. The acclamations at last ceased rattling the sconces, and the President was about to put the second vote (customary at such proceedings), "General Massac and his fellow officers are awarded the honors of the sitting and the Convention proceeds to the program of the day," when suddenly a great thrusting and protesting seemed descending from the hitherto applauding galleries, accompanied with amazing shouts.

"No honors to an aristocrat!"

"Down with all ci-devants!"

The President's bell clanged loudly, but the uproar from newcomers in the spectators' section continued. Instead of bidding the ushers to clear the galleries, the President only gazed about helplessly while the noise swelled louder. René at length comprehended that the cat-calls were aimed directly at himself.

"Massac's an aristo!" shrilled a strong feminine voice.

"Honors only for sans-culottes!" bellowed from an unseen throat.

"A deputation, Citizen President," quavered one of the doorkeepers, and the President ceased ringing the bell as if a deputation was very much of a routine performance. René, sitting at the foot of the tribune, saw some fifty persons, mostly men with red caps, blue blouses and baggy trousers, but with a sprinkling of women with red handkerchiefs pinned over streaming hair. They advanced, forcing their way up the central aisle as far as a great plaster Statue of Liberty, which rose as a kind of buttress amid the front benches. To judge from the uproar at the entrance, the sergeants were now having considerable trouble in keeping the fifty of the deputation from being reinforced by some five hundred equally ardent patriots behind.

The President, a small fidgety man, rose on the rostrum with a somewhat pained, official smile, and pointed to sundry pikes and muskets which the petitioners were flourishing.

"The Citizen Deputationers will cease to exhibit their weapons. They are patriotically aware the Convention must deliberate freely, without thought of coercion."

"The devil it will!" roared a very large man, waving a long steel skewer on which was transfixed a pig's heart.

"What have the Citizen Deputationers, in their Republican zeal, to lay before the National Convention to-day?" mildly inquired the President, with half a look toward the exit door behind him.

The man with the skewer and pig's heart had the grace to pull off his red cap.

"Hark you, Citizen President. We meant to get here an hour earlier. We're from the Forty-first section, the one they used to call St. Antoine. We've met and deliberated. We don't like to have any honors shown to this fellow called General Massac. He can't deny he's a ci-devant. All ci-devants are aristos. All aristos are traitors. The place for aristos isn't here, but in L'Abbaye or La Force, until the Tribunal can reckon with them. If he's seemed to fight for France, that's only another monarchist plot. We won't ask Ste. Guillotine for him to-day, but——"

Howls of approval from the over-crowded galleries here cut short his argument. Despite all past experience and all that he had lately heard, René's skin was crawling with anger and astonishment. The anger was inevitable. The astonishment was at the almost cowering silence of the seven hundred odd deputies who had just been praising him to the skies. The President, indeed, ventured with weak politeness to expostulate.

"But, Citizen Spokesman, General Massac has rendered a great service to France. His patriotism and gallantry are commended by Citizen Carnot himself."

"Hell swallow Citizen Carnot!" roared a gigantic figure at the first orator's elbow.

"Away with all suspects! Guillotine all ci-devants!" burst in a new broadside from the gallery.

"Citizens! Citizenesses!" implored the President, again jangling the bell, but with not one deputy rising to support him. Massac's forehead was on fire. "Wattignies was heaven to this!" he was muttering between clenched teeth, when there was a stir among the upper benches; some one, in fact, was descending to mount the tribune. The President stopped ringing, and now called with all his lung power, "Patience, patriots; Citizen Robespierre wishes to speak to you." An announcement at once followed by an amazing quiet.

The "first deputy" of Paris mounted the tribune slowly, with just the proper gesture of his lace cuffs to call attention to his blue coat, silvered buttons, nankeen small clothes and white silk stockings. No red cap and long trousers of Republicanism for him. His powdered hair could have graced Old Versailles. He carried his head loftily, awarding no glances of recognition. His little body seemed, indeed, to carry a soul that had barely consented to quit the clouds momentarily in order to deliver some incalculable message to his fellow mortals.

Instantly the galleries ceased howling, while the deputation looked sheepish. "The Incorruptible! The spotless patriot! Hush—listen to the great citizen!"—so in low murmurs they greeted him.

Robespierre stood quietly on the tribune with a calm, short-sighted stare, smiled urbanely, shook out a fine cambric handkerchief. "Heavenly man!" cried an ecstatic female in the gallery.

"Citizen President, Citizen Deputies, Citizens of the Forty-first section (the words came as coldly and clearly as a Euclid theorem), patriotism is admirable, but only the Supreme Being is denied the power to err. The enormity of the crimes of most aristocrats has blinded these incomparable Republicans to the fact that by an almost superhuman virtue, a few noblemen can actually rise above the iniquities of their caste, and prove themselves untarnished patriots and veritable Catos and Brutuses for the Republic. Such a one is General René Massac. His patriotism, his devotion, his heroism, have washed out the stain of his aristocracy. I know him. I vouch for him. I pronounce him to have deserved well of the Nation."

Jehovah thundering from Sinai could not have produced more instant conviction. Having uttered these curt sentences, Robespierre descended the tribune with precisely the same slow gravity with which he had ascended. The effect was immediate, astonishing.

"It's all right. We were mistaken!" blurted the man with the skewered pig's heart, like a whipped lad before his school-master.

"Brave general! Gallant hero! Pure patriot!" the gallery suddenly began echoing in a regular chorus. And at once the deputation shamefacedly filed out, but not before a short fleshy woman had bounced up beside René, flung her handkerchief over his head and kissed him smackingly on both cheeks.

. . . The instant that the sitting had adjourned, Camille Desmoulins (a deputy now himself) hurried his old friend through the crowd of jostling, bravoing parliamentarians.

"Why did we not all fly to your assistance? Why did we wait for Robespierre?" he was responding. "Parbleu! did you want us to be blackguarded and perhaps torn in pieces? These Section deputations come every other day. This one was mild."

"I prefer the Austrians," remarked Massac. "Where is Danton?"

"Danton is burned out, please Jupiter, only for the moment. You know his wife died, and that made his life stand still. Then, by her own dying wish, he married again. For months thereafter he strove and stormed for us like a Titan. Suddenly he announced, 'I am spent. I want some sleep.' And home he went to Arcis. He is there yet."

"I wish he had been here.—But I had not caught the power of Robespierre."

"Power? He holds us all in the hollow of his hand; or thinks that he does, and Paris agrees with him—almost the same thing."

"You do not seem so much his admirer as you were once, Camille?"

"I love patriots, I detest pontiffs and prophets; besides, there is coming to be too strong a sniff of blood about him."

"The sniff of blood?" But before René could drive home the question, a hand slipped under his unwounded arm. He looked into the face of the Greek god—St. Just.

The youthful prisoner of Vincennes had risen now to the seats of the highest. Not merely was he a member of the Convention, he was one of the omnipotent Twelve, of the Committee of Public Safety itself. René knew that he had proved himself a powerful speaker, a remarkably efficient administrator, but above that, France recognized him now as the most trusted lieutenant of the great Incorruptible himself. Desmoulins and St. Just exchanged glances not wholly friendly, while the latter tugged René away without a syllable of apology.

"How is Virginie?" the younger man demanded abruptly.

"She is well. The door at Rue Leonard is waiting to open to you."

"Rue de la Démocratie, you mean," corrected St. Just with a frown. The hardness, like whetted steel, about St. Just's manner was, in fact, more apparent than ever; it did not please René, but it lightened quickly into one of his disarming smiles. "Come," he commanded, "our friend wants you."

Massac found himself conducted into a great bare room in the Pavillon de l'Égalité. Upon the walls there still hung an elaborate tapestry portraying the Rape of the Sabines, but it was now heavy with dust and some patriots had enjoyed themselves thrusting bayonets through it. All of the carved and gilt furniture had disappeared in favor of a couple of long deal tables covered with green cloths, ink stained and strewn with papers and pamphlets. A number of plain, hard chairs were the only other objects, except a scowling bust of Marat upon a shelf between two high windows, and a smirking one of Rousseau between two others.

Robespierre, immaculate as upon the tribune, stood in the center of the wide space. He came three steps toward René, and held out his hand, smiling, as usual, a little vacantly.

"Welcome back to us, Monsieur." Massac doubtless betrayed a slight astonishment at not being saluted "Citizen," and the thin precise voice continued, "In public we keep the patriotic forms. In private I venture to indulge my personal prejudices. Our aim should be ever to avoid alike the reactionists and the 'extravagants.' Both are equally harmful. All things should contribute to the Reign of Virtue."

René was irresistibly reminded of Father François' manner to him as a little boy, when his friendly preceptor had become unusually didactic.

"You were my warm friend in the Convention, M. Robespierre," spoke the soldier. "I am sorry that my other friends seemed so slow to defend me."

"It is my privilege, General Massac, to be favored with the confidence of the sovereign People. For that reason I can assume a certain boldness perhaps not permitted to less trusted patriots. It will always be a satisfaction to testify alike to your services and to your sentiments."

René bowed. Robespierre had never been an easy conversationalist, and time had now made a familiar dialogue more difficult than ever. The statesman paused an instant, wiped his lips slowly and delicately, and proceeded:

"You witness great changes, General Massac. The Supreme Being does not permit us, of course, to approach our goal without certain painful acts of justice. But we progress. Effete institutions, ignorance, superstition are crumbling. The natural virtue of Mankind asserts itself. In another year, if our patriot army continues its victories, perhaps we can glimpse the approach of Utopia."

"I rejoice in your prophecy, Citizen Commissioner. I have learned a soldier's bluntness in the camps, and there sometimes angry opinions are uttered. 'In battle we kill Austrians and Prussians in fair fight. At Paris they kill weak women and old men who are Frenchmen, and who have their arms tied behind their backs.'"

Robespierre's smile tightened, while St. Just's marvelous face clouded palpably.

"Needful severities, General Massac. We cannot eliminate all enemies of liberated France, but we can at least hasten the reign of Virtue by putting aside false mercy;" the senior Commissioner's voice was keen as a blade. "The wise surgeon is not always the one who administers sugared medicines, but whose scalpel removes the cancerous ulcers."

"True, Citizen Commissioner; in the army we also learn not to cavil but to obey orders. After your good opinion uttered to-day, do not think that I have words of blame for those making possible the defence of France. I only hope the army will soon win such rest and security for the Republic that clemency and humanity can become universal."

"I agree with all such enlightened sentiments." Then, in terms stilted, but not unkindly, Robespierre asked for the welfare of Virginie and Henriette, cautioned René to take no liberties with his still bandaged arm, and promised to call at the Rue de la Démocratie. And so, with a certain high-strung cordiality, the interview ended. Massac quitted the Pavillon de l'Égalité with a conscious sense of relief, although he reproached himself for it. "Somehow the old days of comradeship have faded," he kept saying as he went homeward with a perplexed mind.

. . . Robespierre and St. Just had remained turning over an enormous quantity of papers. At last the younger Commissioner let their talk again become personal.

"What if we have lost him? He goes to the army. He sees a thousand men fall in battle, therefore he grows humane."

"His sentiments are based on ignorance," commented Robespierre.

"It is not enough to be devoted to the Republic; one must be devoted to the complete, the absolutely virtuous Republic."—St. Just flung a spoiled pen upon the floor and began to nib another.

"Allowance must be made for his natural kindliness. He must adjust himself. He must be taught that ruthlessness for the hour will be humanity for the centuries." Robespierre was tying up a parcel of papers and docketing, *"Indictments for the Public Prosecutor."*

"Yes, he can become useful; moderatism has not as yet captured him. Yet of one thing I am afraid."

"Of what, Antoine Louis?"

"Of this, my master. His wound is healing fast. You can see that he does not love the present state of Paris. His wife will be like him. As soon as possible he will say, 'I am needed with my men.' Then he will return to the army."

"It cannot be. He may become indispensable to us. All the others in our confidence are men of talk. As a soldier he has become a man of deeds. The need of such a man can come."

"Very right, my master."

The other presently reached for a piece of paper, scratched a few words, and tossed it to St. Just with a curt, "Take that to Carnot."

St. Just read immediately: *"I request that General Massac be honorably detained in Paris.—*MAXIMILIEN ROBESPIERRE."

CHAPTER XXXII

THE GODDESS OF REASON

"BUSINESS was looking up."

Never had Citizen Spartacus Durand felt happier about his professional prospects. "Citizen Thibaud" he had been until recently, when (like so many other patriots) he had "Republicanized" his name. "Spartacus," he vaguely understood, was some old worthy who had once done something to kill tyrants. "How admirably it sounded!" Spartacus, therefore, had been duly registered under it at his section headquarters amid much cheering, and so the matter had rested.

Spartacus was genuinely busy. The Revolutionary Tribunal had begun in April, 1793, with only a few dangerous traitors. Then, in September, it had been really oiled for action. The Queen had heard its verdict in October and immediately afterward there was a charming acceleration; the Girondists, Mme. Roland, Bailly, Philip Égalité (otherwise the ultra-liberal Duc d'Orléans), Barnave, the great foe of despotism in the old National Assembly, very many like them, all failed equally to meet the yardsticks of the New Orthodoxy. Citizen Spartacus next saw them all pass in intimate review before him.

In addition to these there was also a gratifying supply of everyday thieves, bandits and equally criminal speculators [1] referred to Citizen Sanson by the regular court. Citizen Spartacus thus found his fees mounting splendidly.

[1] "Profiteers" another age would call them.

He gladly complied with the usage that he should help to officiate in the height of fashion, red cap and long trousers, of course, but also broadcloth and velvet, fine morocco shoes, gold braid and the rest. His hair had been clipped short, as per reigning custom, but it shone with costly pomatum. He flaunted costly rings and a jeweled watch. In short, Spartacus proved that Republicanism was not merely patriotic, but profitable.

A certain day's work having ended, this vindicator of Liberty retired to refresh himself at the wine shop "Mucius Scaevola." The place was filled with red-capped members of the Revolutionary army, in convivial converse with red-capped and possibly tawdry citizenesses. By all of these Spartacus was highly admired. Many tried to catch the great man's condescending nod, and one fellow looked up from a big plate of garlic and ventured:

"Good sport to-morrow, Citizen?"

"Nothing at all, I'm afraid, with our Widow. Everybody'll be adjourned to the Temple of Reason."

"Oh, yes. Hébert's little affair.—It ought to be rich."

The Temple of Reason, of course, in slave days, had been Notre Dame, and Hébert was that semi-dictator in the city government, whose special enmity went out against "abolished superstition," in other words, against Christianity.

Spartacus found his accustomed shady corner, pot and cronies. They were beginning to discuss "who's next for the Tribunal," when Spartacus sprang to his feet. A very important figure was before him, Citizen Vernet himself, accompanied by a man in a long red coat, topped ultra-patriotically with a thick poll of red hair. Vernet coughed suggestively, the executioner's bottle companions promptly sought other tables, whereat the two newcomers took their places and Spartacus gasped when the red-headed man flung back his cloak. "Citizen Linio—of all men!"

"The wig's useful as I get back to Paris. Keeps some fool from remembering why I had to leave so suddenly."

"But where've you been all this time, Citizen——"

" 'Puget' you'd better call me now. Why, I've been mostly in Switzerland; it's full of emigrés and Republican spies. The Abbé has found me pretty handy there."

Vernet tapped on his companion's wrist. "Plain 'Citizen,' please. No more 'Abbé' or even 'Constitutional Bishop.' It's a month ago when, with Gobel, then Archbishop of Paris, and a whole platoon of his clergy, I appeared before the Convention, stripped off my cassock, tossed down my crucifix and renounced holy orders. I'm helping at the Festival of Reason to-morrow."

"Just as you like it," grunted Linio, "Abbé, Bishop, Citizen; all one to me. I'm again in Paris just to ask 'What next?' "

"Many things, dear Puget," rejoined Vernet, "but there's one item that may also interest Citizen Durand, that's why we seek him here. Is he aware that his niece and nephew-in-law are again in the city?"

"Curse those Massacs.—Yes, but what good can *they* do me?"

"Patience, my worthy Durand, General Massac is likely to stay in Paris for some time. He's not been allowed to rejoin the army."

Spartacus' eye brightened. "In L'Abbaye then?"

"Not at all. His prison has golden bars. The regular deputy from Ard falls seriously ill. It is suddenly discovered that General Massac must serve as his substitute in the Convention."

Durand merely growled. "Why'd you come here, then?"

Vernet shrugged tolerantly. "Citizen Executioner, pray to hear me out. As a deputy Massac cannot indeed be arrested on any ordinary denunciation. Still, if a very serious crime against the Republic were fastened on him, things would be different."

Durand merely eyed the former churchman with low cunning.

"Now, my friend," Vernet's voice sank to an effective whisper, "consider this. One of the General's soldiers from Massac, a Jacques Garat, was here in Paris on furlough. Our good 'Puget' got him drinking, got, in fact, certain confidences out of him. I am having them verified. If they are verified—well, let us await those chances. Meantime, consider one item. Massac's and his wife's properties have not shrunk any during the war. He had the good fortune to find a very competent man of business to handle his affairs."

"What's that to me?" demanded the executioner.

"Simply, good patriot, that if anything befell Massac, his wife and child would require a guardian for this property selected from among the nearest male kinsmen of undoubted devotion to the Republic."

"Aha! I see!" and Durand thrust back his pot with a snort.

"In other words," put in Linio, "if you'll go back into trade with us, will take up the old plot again, will trust our dear Vernet and myself—a delightful prospect again opens."

"Will I?" cried Spartacus. "Will a cat eat fish?"

"I think," observed Vernet at his blandest, "that a little later you can perhaps coöperate with us to admirable advantage."

"But mind," put in Linio, "this time the secret stays among ourselves. Olympie, that termagant of yours, shares nothing of it."

Spartacus' looks instantly clouded. "I don't like her," he asserted, "but why bar her out?"

"What happened at Massac?" retorted the ex-Baron.

"Never mind what. We quarreled hard enough, but we've made everything up. True, she jilted me there in the cottage and ran off with the girl, but you seemed very ready to cut our throats yourself—therefore, don't rake up that old story."

"Oh! let it pass then," growled the adventurer. "But how do you think Massac ever came to nip the Queen's packet at Sevran?"

"Kill me if I know," shot back the executioner.

"Well, I haven't been chewing all these months upon that vile failure for nothing. The packet was burned, but although Massac was fool enough to have qualms about betraying his swash-buckler cousin, that didn't prevent the information from being so stale, when it actually did get to Vienna, as to be worthless. And that's why I have to wear a red wig now and to put up with other inconvenient things."

"Citizen Durand surely understands," interposed Vernet, as gently as dropping oil, "that if it is only to ease our good Puget's suspicions, he will swear to reveal nothing of our present speculation. Citizeness Durand's help is hardly required, and the project remains strictly between ourselves."

Spartacus appeared far from happy. He realized perfectly well that he was being let in on the plot solely because some countenance by himself later might be required; he knew equally that without Olympie's worldly-wise head to guide him, he would be a veritable shuttlecock for two such practitioners as Linio and Vernet. How much of the Massac fortune he himself would ever touch if this newest undertaking prospered, was much more than a question mark. Still, the eyes of the others were on him. Undoubtedly Vernet had good hopes of fastening a real crime on the General, otherwise he would never have sought out Durand. And Vernet was reputed such a lucky man; always landing on his feet like a cat; ready, if the King had prospered, to demand the highest possible rewards; yet able, now that the King had made his long congé, to ascend steadily from one Republican glory to another, until he was only one stage under the Great Committee. Durand, therefore, with marked reluctance, nodded. "Very well, then; I swear in the name of all the sans-culotte virtues to say nothing to Olympie."

"The Citizeness herself will thank you presently," comforted Vernet, as he and Linio, after favoring Durand with a few more details, took their departure. The executioner watched them go with extremely mixed feelings. After all, if the Massacs were so rich, was not the next obvious move one of blackmail? But to levy that he would need the aid of Olympie, and he had just sworn an oath. Of course, oaths could be broken, but Vernet, if not the sans-culotte virtues, could breed all kinds of bad luck if he were flouted. It seemed best, therefore, to let matters drift, especially as——

"Citizen Spartacus, Citizen Spartacus Durand," ordered a voice at his elbow, "quit your wool gathering!" A lanky fellow with long, greasy hair and the clothes of a half-starved clerk, was standing over him. "I couldn't find you at Sanson's office. Citizen Hébert sends me. You are wanted to carry the bust of Brutus in the procession to-morrow. We can count on you?"

"Of course, Citizen Chaumette."

Durand flung an assignat on the bar and stalked homeward. He knew that admiring glances were following him. "Another civic honor! How well Republicanism paid!" Nevertheless, life retained for him certain perplexities.

"The moment has come to unnail Jesus!" So Manuel, one of the "moderate" Girondist deputies, whose own head by this time had fallen, declaimed as early as 1792.

By 1793 the anti-Christianity movement had become an avalanche. The Church had been the ally of the Throne. The Throne had fallen. Away then with the "fanaticism and superstition" that had been the ally of the Throne!

"The people," Chaumette had cried, "shall be our God; we need no other."

"We desire," shouted Hébert, whose indescribably filthy *Père Duchesne* was now the most widely read journal in Paris, "no religion save that of Nature; no temple other than that of Reason; no other worship than that of Liberty, Equality and Fraternity."

The Convention, however, had dawdled. It was even said that the Incorruptible actually believed in a Supreme Being himself, but the Commune, the City Government of Paris, had been more resolute. Dominated by Hébert, it had undertaken to dechristianize the churches, and to suppress as "fomenters of disorder" every form of religious service. Even the Jews and Protestants were in danger. The prisons were crammed with priests. Other priests of a different temper were publicly divesting themselves of their habits and were taking wives by the new Civil Marriage.

Long before René Massac had recovered his bearings in Paris, most of the church bells not needed for tocsins had been taken down as constituting "gewgaws of the Eternal Father" and "sugar plums for religious ears" and melted into cannon. The tomb of St. Geneviève, the patron saint of the city, had been enthusiastically smashed open and the bones and shroud publicly burned at the Place de Grève "to expiate the crime of having promoted error." All the plate and vestments from the churches had, of course, been carried off to the Hôtel de Ville to be sold by the

Commune. As for the destruction of saints' images, crucifixes, altars, altar screens and other tokens of an "abominable past," that had become too common for ordinary remark.

Of course "Sunday" had been formally abolished. Woe to the tradesman who closed his shop on that day, or to his wife if seen then in her best clothes. Woe just as much to the tradesman who failed to close his shop on the new "Tenth Days," and go then to some public hall to hear extolled "the Republican virtues." There was even brisk talk of pulling down all church towers, "which, by their height, contradict the principles of equality," and of inscribing at the entrance to all cemeteries, what they had already placarded at Nevers, "Death is an eternal sleep."

The climax to this brave work was now at hand. René Massac had taken his seat in the Convention too recently to be compelled to join with his colleagues, when, with angry protests in the hearts of many of them, they had marched in November to Notre Dame, to give official sanction to its consecration as "The Temple of Reason." That festival, however, had been so congenial as to demand repetition. All Republican Paris seemed to be delighted when another grand celebration was held in December.

A bright, pleasant winter's day. No snow and not too cold. All of the quays, the bridges, the avenues leading to the Ci-devant Cathedral, were crowded with excited men and still more excited women. A carpenter was dancing about in trousers made out of a plush dalmatic. A mason flourished around in a duster made from the alb of a murdered priest. A red-coifed, red-scarfed girl kept gyrating with a holy water sprinkler instead of castinets. Some brute of a porter flourished a thigh bone—boasting loudly that it was the relic of a "tyrant," plucked from the tomb of the Kings at St. Denis.

"It is a sight to make patriots rejoice and aristocrats grieve." Thus Citizen Vernet unctuously summed up the doings to Citizen Hébert, as they agreed upon the day's programme.

At length the organized procession marched down from the Hôtel de Ville and across the bridges. Patriotic clubs, sisterhoods of female Republicans, revolutionary committees, deputations from the Paris sections, deputations from almost everywhere in France, thronged, pushed and jostled after one another in a great patriotic confusion. Twenty anti-Christian songs seemed being roared at once. Six anti-Christian bands kept braying down one another. There was enough of tricolor scarfs, banners and bunting to make sails for a navy. Evidences of patriotic health-drinking in the wine shops abounded. "Reason" had, in short, had every cause for joy in her votaries.

Into the Temple next, amid cheerings that jarred the old Gothic vaulting. The sculptured saints, however, did not frown down from their niches for the good reason that the niches were empty, the "idols" having been already ground to bits. At last came a modicum of silence wherein to listen to the female chorus, decked out inevitably with tricolor sashes, as it sang the "Hymn to Liberty" with the refrain:

> "And the true religion is this——
> To love our Constitution."

Nevertheless, in the vast choir, where once the high altar had stood, there was now indeed a gleaming galaxy of candles, but they were set before a huge, ill-shaped pyramid of painted wood, crested by an empty throne. A throne not destined long to stand vacant, for borne on a litter lifted high by members of the Commune, togaed as "Roman senators," rode the Goddess of Reason herself—on other days Citizeness Candeille of the Opéra.

Continuous cheering accompanied her. "Hurrah for our Mother of God!" "Ah! What a fine Holy Virgin!"

"Reason" boasted a Phrygian liberty cap, a flowing and very diaphanous cloak of sky blue, and red theatrical buskins. What with her rouge and her voluptuous form, no wonder the plaudits. She gestured magnificently with a silver wand. The cheering pealed through the gray heights of the nave and transept as her cortège swept onward. Louder applause still, when she descended majestically from the litter, mounted her throne, then received from some follower in amazing pontificals an immense gilded torch. "Reason" set the flambeau in a socket, made a charming genuflection before it, struck flint and steel, and set the torch in a blaze.

Instantly Chaumette, Spartacus' acquaintance of yesterday and Reason's high priest to-day, received from two acolytes a smoking censer, which he waved with august solemnity before the goddess and the torch; when behold! as the torch gained strength at the very foot of the throne through the incense smoke, the thousands, with an excited gasp, saw the white marble of a mutilated statue of the Virgin, lying prostrate at the feet of enthroned Reason.

"Rise, image of Superstition! Rise emblem of tyranny!" rang Chaumette's apostrophe through choir and clerestory. "Deceive the people if thou canst!—Wait! Watch! She rises not.—Enlightenment banishes error. Priest-craft perishes with king-craft. Reason alone shall reign forever!"

"Vive la Raison," pealed from the upturned faces. Instantly the music resumed faster, faster. Wild hymns jangled together. The goddess was seen brandishing her scepter through the incense smoke, and swaying in graceful attitudes. Cannoneers of the Revolutionary army were bending before her with pipes in their mouths. One bearded fellow, with hairy breast laid bare, stood just below the throne, imitating by his gesticulations the celebration of the Mass. In the aisles men and women were already making dashes for the piles of sausages, pork puddings and pastries ready there on tables, cramming their mouths, then swinging out into the nave, and catching hand to hand; while all the music soon blended into the wildest of dances.

> "Dance we the Carmagnole,
> Hurrah for the roar, hurrah for the roar!
> Dance we the Carmagnole,
> Hurrah for the roar, the cannon's roar!"

. . . René Massac and Father François had been silent spectators from the safe shelter of a column. They turned away as women and men began flinging off their cloaks in order to whirl more madly. Religion for René himself had long since refined itself into a simple belief in a righteous personal God. Since 1789 he had never been to Mass, but the whole present spectacle sickened him. He left the outraged cathedral groaning in spirit.

"My Father," said he, "have I and my comrades fought only to bring to pass *this?* How can God suffer it?"

"My son, God in His balancings is forever just. I always told you that the throne, the nobility, and alas! the human servants of the church who condoned iniquity must pay their price.—To-day they are paying it! *Vexilla regis prodeunt inferni!*—The banners of the King of the Pit come forth."

They walked on in silence back across the Pont au Change; then Father François spoke again.

"My René, I have considered and my duty is plain. Not for years have I officiated as a priest. The altar had other ministers, and I had many duties and no liking for the subtleties of theology. But I have never been deposed by the Church. Now I must again celebrate Mass."

René instinctively halted. "Dear Father, are there not

dangers enough in France that you must go out of your
way thus to invite imprisonment and even the guillotine?"

"You say well, René; apparently we have 'liberty' now
only to be atheists."

"For my sake and for Virginie's, avoid this peril."

The lecturer took the soldier's hand. "My son, at Wattignies you did not say, 'For Virginie's sake I will avoid all
danger'; you said, 'It is for France.'"

Despite himself Massac smiled, then answered, "Warfare
is different."

"The duty of sacrifice is never different. Why should I
fear Hébert's prison and guillotine more than you did the
Austrians' grape-shot? Why is the Church in France to-
day sharing the fate of her rotten civil institutions?—Because the Church has shown of late to the world very many
sodden prelates and very few saints. We cannot now become saints of a sudden—the more our sins—but we can
still bear our witness as brave confessors.—Well then, to-
morrow will be Sunday."

. . . It came to pass, therefore, that two days later
Citizen Puget waited upon Citizen Vernet at the latter's
bureau in the Louvre, where the Committee of General
Surety kept its stronghold. The Commissioner seemed in
a genial mind. Everywhere he had been congratulated
upon his success as director of the Festival of Reason. Just
now he was jotting his approval upon a sample pack of
"Republican playing-cards" with "patriots" and "patriot-
esses" substituted for "kings" and "queens." Puget pulled
his red cap from his red wig.

"Good news," he proclaimed. "One stroke we can make
immediately."

"You look happy, my friend," spoke Vernet, looking up,
"what is it?"

"Our old acquaintance, Father François, celebrated Mass

yesterday at a secret conventicle, easily sworn to as treasonable. Shall I denounce him?"

Vernet rubbed his hands. "Good Puget," said he, "beside our larger plans, this pious François is only a trifle; yet trifles heaped all together make mountains. Swear out your papers. Take oath before my colleague Amar; I'd better not appear too openly. The arrest will be prompt, and I—ah! perhaps I can talk to Fouquier-Tinville or one of his assistant prosecutors in order that the reverend lecturer need not endure his imprisonment too long."

CHAPTER XXXIII

THE INCORRUPTIBLE

DETAINED in Paris sorely against his own will and that of Virginie, General Massac, nevertheless, accepted his seat in the Convention with tolerable grace. The deputies (he learned soon enough) were cowed. The Great Committee and its adjuncts dominated everything. Daily the deputies met, listened to the high-flying oratory of the Committee's "reporter," the theatrical Barère, or sometimes to the fervid demands of St. Just, or—on set occasions—to the cold, impersonal dogmas of Robespierre. Then the Convention after a little sputter of debate, voted usually whatever was requested, and adjourned. After the fate of the Girondists, who had defied the moods of Paris, it was clear enough that any deputy who made an unpopular speech might find himself half way to the Tribunal. The Convention seemed merely the thin veil for the twelve-headed dictatorship.

But not for an ineffectual dictatorship. The Committee of Public Safety was saving France—hence its justification. Wattignies had stopped the Austrian drive on Paris. Now came a whole string of other triumphs. Lyons surrendering, the Vendean rebels weakening, the Prussians being hustled from Alsace, the English quitting Toulon—this last, thanks partly to a certain young Colonel Bonaparte. All the valor of the armies, nevertheless, would have been futile save for the terribly efficient direction sent them by the little group of men who met nightly around Carnot's long tables in the Tuileries, read dispatches, drafted orders, demoted ruthlessly, promoted instantly, and made potent the will of the armed Republic.

Carnot added Massac to this staff of assistants, and, understanding campaign conditions as now he did, the young officer's knowledge was often invaluable. Along with the others of this little family of soldiers and technicians, many a night Massac would toil into the small hours, cast himself on a hard mattress spread under some wall-painting depicting outcast royalty, sleep a couple of hours, rise and resume his work at the long tables.

Carnot was saving France, and since he was saving her, neither René Massac nor many another soldier spent too much anger over various fearsome doings among the civilians, whilst they themselves struggled with the means of changing loose levies into disciplined battalions and providing them with guns, cartridges and food. "Terror" was being tolerated, because it seemed to be crushing out internal opposition and making France one living weapon against her encircling foes. Let rebellion and invasion cease, and Terror must cease also. That seemed the inexorable logic which comforted René as he went back to his toil in Carnot's office after the saturnalia of the Festival of Reason. "It cannot last much longer, and at least it will spare me and mine," he would tell himself when he could not fight away hard thoughts about many things.

Part of this grim comfort ended one winter afternoon when he walked home after four-and-twenty mortal hours in the War Commissioner's bureau. One click of the door, Virginie's embrace, and Henriette's coo and scamper, and the victualing of Strasbourg and the garrisoning of Dunkirk ought to fade for him like the ghosts of yesterday. The street scenes, however, offended him more than of wont. The theater billboards were announcing the new anti-religionist plays: "The Hypocrites Unmasked," and "The

Republican Sacraments." The day's ceremonial at the Place de la Revolution was just over. "Only four this time," a strapping girl in good clothes was lamenting, "and not one ci-devant or priest among them, only common assignat forgers." The lines were forming as usual before the bakeries, for Republicanism had not filled the larders. The journals hawked by the boys were uncommonly filthy.

Nevertheless, his troubles were only vague until he turned into Rue de la Démocratie, where he saw a familiar sight—a hackney coach containing three "Revolutionary soldiers" and some other figure, presumably of a prisoner. "An arrest," meditated Massac; "possibly another capture for counterfeiting." But a second glance told him that a little crowd of idlers was dispersing from before his own door, and he flew on to the entrance. It was flung wide, and before him, convulsed with tears, stood Virginie.

"They have taken him!" as she cast her arms about his neck.

"For God's sake who? How?"

"Father François. He came to dinner, then stayed to play with Henriette. Suddenly a great knocking. 'We want the ci-devant curé, Citizen Paul François. We've tracked him hither.' They forced their way into the parlor, those hideous men. They seized him as he rose from building blocks for Henriette. He only gave his little laugh and said, 'I have expected this courtesy ever since Sunday.' Then he kissed my cheek and Henriette's forehead, and they led him away."

Massac swore all the oaths which he had learned on the battlefields. They were many. At last he could articulate calmly. "I know what is the charge against him. I pleaded with that beloved old fool not to destroy himself. Now I have got to save him. Did they show a warrant?"

"Yes, some document signed 'Amar'."

"The most remorseless and active villain on the General Surety! I could demolish any private complaint sworn out before a Section President—but this one—well, it will be hard."

"Commissioner Carnot is your friend."

"He is deaf and dumb to everything not concerning the army. That is one of the secrets of his power. He will do nothing. There is only one man in France to whom that bloodhound Amar will yield. I will go to him, for the peril to the Father is great."

"You mean to Robespierre. Oh! hasten, my dearest—and I will pray; these are days when we women learn so well how to pray."

. . . The Massac coach horses had long since been requisitioned for the army, but André found one of the surviving hackney cabs, and in it his master raced to the Louvre. As René expected, the offices were nearly all of them closed. Amar had left, but a chief clerk was locking up the desks and strong boxes at the General Surety.

"You have copies of the latest denunciations?" demanded the flushed and panting visitor.

The clerk hesitated, but General Massac, familiar through Paris for his record at the Bastille, the Tuileries and Wattignies, was a privileged character not lightly to be denied. The papers were put in his hands. He ran through them hurriedly, selected one about which he penciled a few notes, then tossed down the packet.

"Number 366 Rue Honoré, the house of Duplay, the contractor," he ordered the waiting coachman.

It was Massac's first visit to the lodgings of the most powerful man in France. Robespierre had lived now with the master carpenter, Maurice Duplay, for two and a half years. The substantial bourgeois family had become devoted to him and did everything for his comfort, but even as he entered, René could not hold back the thought of how the surroundings of Power had changed. No Swiss guards, no double-bending flunkies, no magnificent doorkeepers, no sworded and bejeweled marquises-in-waiting. But here dwelt the only man in France who could save Father François from imminent death.

The General passed under a narrow archway and entered a small court smelling of sawdust and lumber. From the shop at one side there still came the noise of a hammer and a plane. A single burly, formidable "sans-culotte," a member of the Revolutionary army, lolled upon a bench in the courtyard. Beside him lay, not a gun, but an ugly-looking club. The fellow was obviously the guard whom Robespierre's admirers insisted upon inflicting on him ever since the murder of Marat. The rascal glanced twice at the visitor and subsided; a big brown dog emerged, however, from a side passage, then began a few semi-friendly barks, having met René on the streets when his master walked to the Convention. The barks produced, not a porter, but a plain, heavy-featured girl, somewhat dowdily clad, and the visitor knew that she was Eleanor Duplay, a daughter of the house, and to whom rumor said that Robespierre was in a way to be betrothed.

She recognized the officer and addressed him with a certain politeness: "What does General Massac desire?"

"I must see Citizen Robespierre on a matter of grave importance."

Eleanor Duplay frowned, for she and the dog were vigilant guardians of their distinguished resident's leisure. "The Citizen Commissioner has shut himself in his chamber. I think that he is preparing a speech for the Jacobin Club to-night."

"I regret the intrusion, Citizeness Duplay, but the case is so urgent I feel justified."

Eleanor bowed reluctantly. "Let the General follow then."

She led him up a narrow stair and knocked on a darkened landing. Robespierre himself opened. Never yet had René failed to meet him clothed, brushed and powdered. It was not otherwise that afternoon. His chestnut coat, gray kersey waistcoat, white embroidered shirt were as immaculate in the intimacy of his chamber as when he addressed the Convention.

The room itself was amazingly simple, though not quite austere; a well-worn desk piled with papers, most of them neatly bound with blue twine, three stiff wooden chairs the worse as to paint, an arm chair in dingy upholstery, a narrow cot-bed, an old wardrobe. That almost completed the furnishing, save for a considerable number of framed pictures, a good woodland print, a sketch of a dog, and several portraits in color or silhouette of Robespierre himself, the gifts of admirers; and these flanked by a couple of shelves of books in very frayed bindings, Rousseau, Voltaire, Diderot and similar late writers, but also Racine, Corneille and the other masters of French classical letters. Such the abode of the man whose speeches were brooded upon in every Ministry in Europe.

Robespierre bowed stiffly, but not repellently. The least curving of his lips showed he regretted the intrusion, and Massac made instant apologies. "I thrust myself upon you, Monsieur, because it is in your power to prevent a great crime. That is my excuse for interrupting your leisure."

The Commissioner silently beckoned the other to be seated, and René immediately began his errand. Father François had been arrested on the charge of uttering a prayer for the King at the time that he celebrated Mass in a hall privately hired. Only a few pious old women and humble tradespeople had seemed to be present, "but fortunately (affirmed the denunciation) one of these had actually been Citizen Puget, a devoted member of the private police employed to protect the Republic under the direction of that incomparable patriot, Commissioner Vernet."

Saying Mass, although not actually made penal by Convention, had been declared a crime by the hardly less authoritative Commune of Paris; while praying for "the King"—which could be none other than the miserable boy, "the son of the late tyrant," who was now confined in the Temple, was doubtless as treasonable as shouting *"Vive le Roi!"* before the Tribunal itself. Commissioner Amar had vouched for the seriousness of the crime, and for the responsibility of the complainant. He and Commissioner Vernet had joined in urging immediate action upon Public Prosecutor Fouquier-Tinville at the sitting of the Revolutionary Tribunal to-morrow. "Another speedy example of Republican justice would benefit the Nation, etc., etc."

When Massac had finished, Robespierre merely regarded him calmly, with his little nearsighted stare, and semivacant smile.

"Well, Monsieur," came at length, "this is very regrettable. But the case falls manifestly to the General Surety. Why am I honored with this visit?"

Fortunately the petitioner knew the petitioned; he had expected such an answer, and remained calm himself.

"Monsieur, you have been to my house. You have often met my old preceptor, Father François. You coöperated and served with him in the National Assembly. Churchman that he is, his devotion to Republicanism was well known when Republicanism was a danger. He may have celebrated Mass; you yourself have denounced the 'extravagance' of forbidding it; the absurd charge that he openly prayed for the King can only rest on perjury."

"I concur. Remember, nevertheless, that the Tribunal, in its impartial justice, can acquit as well as condemn."

René still curbed himself. "The Tribunal composed of fallible men can err. They will respect the behests of the General Surety, and Amar is among the fiercest of the 'Extravagants.' As for Vernet, I believe him to be Father François' personal enemy."

Robespierre, precisely as his visitor expected, simply repeated his old question: "Why are you here?"

"Because the Incorruptible delights in the vindication of virtue; because Father François is not merely innocent of the charge, but an old soldier in the struggle for liberty and humanity; because the First Deputy of Paris is never happier than when he performs an act of the highest magnanimity and patriotism."

The statesman deliberately frowned his best official frown. "General Massac speaks now with a man impervious to flattery."

"General Massac speaks with a man whose love for justice and humanity will reënforce any poor arguments of mine."

The other now as deliberately smiled. "You are an old acquaintance, Monsieur. You know how to disarm me. What then would you?"

René also smiled. "Citizen Commissioner, the General Surety is under the orders of the Public Safety. No other name in the latter compares with your own. I beseech you to write an order to Fouquier-Tinville, directing him to quash the denunciation of Father François and set him at liberty."

Robespierre reached very slowly toward his pen, in the manner of a man struck by a new thought. "You overpersuade me, General Massac." Then, with a studied pause, "It was agreed that the orders of the General Surety should only be superseded by a two-thirds vote of all the Public Safety. You ask an irregularity."

"Surely," began the soldier in dismay; but his host had commenced to write rapidly, calmly observing, "An order for your unfortunate friend's freedom would be improper; but a personal request to the public prosecutor—ah! that might well be forgiven." And he put the writing in René's hands.

"To Citizen Fouquier-Tinville. I request you earnestly not to place the ci-devant curé Paul François before the Tribunal until I have been personally consulted."

René bowed, for he realized that to press for a greater favor was useless. Father François (he felt) could hardly be imprisoned very long.

"I thank you, Citizen Commissioner," he said, extending his hand.

Robespierre received it, but commanded, "Remain seated, Monsieur. This act gives me sincere pleasure. It makes me partner in the sublime justice of Nature. I respect your friend's belief in a deity, although I reject his outworn theology. The atheism of Hébert and Chaumette repel me. In due time I shall deal with them. We must set up the pure, uncontaminated worship of the Supreme Being, tolerating certain passing extravagances as little as possible."

The deep, hard eyes were taking a kind of fire; the precise voice had assumed a certain vibrancy.

"We endure much for the sake of the Republic," rejoined the soldier.

"But not merely for a Republic of unbelief, vice and sordid pleasure, but for a Republic destined to be a superior Rome, a worthier Sparta; a Republic of chastity, sublime virtues, unsullied religion." The tension behind Robespierre's tones steadily increased. Massac grew uncomfort-

able as the First Commissioner addressed him directly:
"Go on; win more victories over the armies of tyranny.
But fail not, that we may win greater victories over error
and ignorance here in Paris. There comes soon an hour
when to be mistaken is to become vicious, to become vicious
is to become a danger to the Republic. Such dangers the
Tribunal is set up to eliminate."

René in politeness bowed again, while the oration (for it
was nothing else) completed itself: "I forgive mistakes of
the head. I were not the Incorruptible if I could condone
mistakes of the heart. Many pure patriots like St. Just,
Couthon, and others think with me. We are being com-
missioned by the people to abolish presumption and false-
hood, and a certain ruthlessness can be the only means of
achieving the reign of Virtue.—I am glad that to-day you
presumed upon my friendship; in return your own aid will
doubtless be counted upon when the supreme moment for
setting up this reign of Virtue is at hand.—Good then;
commend me to your amiable wife."

The General walked out through the darkening courtyard, and rumbled immediately in the hackney coach to
the Palais de Justice, where, in a murky office, the public
prosecutor and his staff were making up what was cheerfully called "to-morrow's honor roll." Fouquier-Tinville,
a hard, repellent man whom the welter of the Revolution
had lifted from a clerk's desk in the police office to the
most terrible duty in Paris, scowled when the General's
epaulettes thrust past the protesting doorkeeper, but put
on his best professional smile the instant he caught the
familiar, neat handwriting flourished under his nose. One
penstroke crossed off a certain name on the list spread out
before him.

"What a pleasure to accede to the least wishes of such an
incomparable patriot as the First Commissioner! Certainly

the· ci-devant curé was to enjoy every indulgence short of
liberty. Certainly he was about to be transferred to the
Luxembourg—most commodious of all the prisons."

The Citizen Prosecutor in person escorted General Massac
through the ante-chamber, past the smirking clerks and the
quavering petitioners. René shook hands with him cordially, knowing perfectly well that, without Robespierre's
letter, the next morning Fouquier would be shouting his,
"I demand death" to a wildly applauding courtroom.—The
Rue de la Démocratie at last; the opening door; the white,
inquiring face of Virginie; the joyous "I have saved him."
And René Massac fondly imagined that his troubles for
that one day were over.

. . . Unfounded hope. Virginie indeed voiced her relief
that their friend was in no present danger, but her husband's knowing eye instantly caught new tokens of anxiety.
She chattered in a forced manner before a strange young
lackey whom they had lately taken to assist André, then
led her husband up the stairs and into an unfrequented
chamber. Flung upon the bed, with a single candle burning beside him, was a man who raised himself on an elbow
as Massac entered, tried to laugh, but only groaned.

"Laurent—in the good God's name!" burst from his
cousin.

"Parbleu," vowed the Viscount, "you aren't over pleased
to see me! I don't blame you. My fault. Should have
thought straighter. Slip away to-morrow, as soon as this
damned——"; another groan.

"Tell me," commanded René in a voice of enforced
calm, "how came you here? We left you recuperating at
Massac."

"Why because, dearest fellow, if you are an ass, my own
ears are twenty-fold the longer. I seemed to be getting
better. The idea popped into my head, 'With the papers

which René provided and with a new disguise, how easy to get into Paris.' I thought of our little King in the Temple. Your charming friends have killed his parents, and now they say that the good citizen Simon, his keeper, has very curious ways. I knew of a Royalist refuge hole in the city. —Came hither, therefore, to make a stab at rescuing the little King. Not a chance. A fool's errand.—Should have known it."

"But why in this house?" pursued the General in tones of indescribable gravity.

Laurent forced himself hard to speak with his old bravado. "Why, you see our refuge got a bit hot for us. That devil's spawn Linio, who thinks that for the present Satan loves your dear Mme. La République the best, and so is keen for her himself, popped up, and got smelling around our way. I had to move. Of course, I intended to quit Paris. Then worse piled on worse. My old wound burst out, for I had left Massac too soon. The fellow I was with this afternoon (you knew that daredevil Marquis de Lanormy) refused to abandon me in the streets. 'Your cousin will take you in,' said he. I protested, but was just about fainting. Lanormy dragged me to your door while I was too helpless to resist. 'An old comrade of the General's—very sick,' blurted he, when they answered the knocker. So he thrust me inside and I tumbled on the floor while he made off.—Lanormy's well out of Paris and on his way to England by this time."

René made a gesture of intense anxiety. "Leave us together," he commanded Virginie. The instant that his wife was gone he seized one of Laurent's hands, then said with forced formality: "M. le Vicomte, any time you wish to have me mount the scaffold with you, I will esteem it entirely an honor; but in the meantime, permit me to think somewhat concerning the safety of my wife and child."

Laurent withdrew his hand and pressed it to his fore-head. "Maledictions upon me! We Royalists deserve the guillotine, all of us, for one rope of blunders ever since that old fool Necker first blurted out 'States General.' I demand death for myself for sheer imbecility. After you saved me at Wattignies, I made the vow, 'King, Republic or Inferno— I devote my life to my cousin hereafter.' When I came to Paris I never dreamed of going near you.—However (with a harsh laugh)—no harm's done yet. I'm stronger. Let me out on the street."

He staggered to his feet, began struggling with his clothes, then reeled back upon the mattress in a white heap. With a strong hand René compelled him to lie quiet.

"You are correct, Laurent. You are the greatest fool in our family. Now if you keep a spark of compassion for your wife in Coblenz, for your parents, for Virginie and for me, at least do this—do not stir from this room until I give the word."

"I promise, cousin," almost wept the Viscount. René was readjusting various bandages upon the reopened wounds. The latter did not seem dangerous to their victim provided he kept reasonably still. Going into the dining room, the General at once found André, who comprehended the case perfectly. It was agreed that the strange lackey should be sent away as speedily as possible, and that "the General's sick comrade" should be cared for with all desirable quietness.

But despite all timely precautions, there was a long silence between Virginie and her husband while, arm in arm, they bent over Henriette's crib that night. The law against harboring emigré spies was terrible. There was no need to tell each other of their danger. Linio, it was plain, was again in Paris. He had struck against Laurent already; he might have been behind the attack on Father François;

he could set a watch upon Rue de la Démocratie. Why, oh! why had fate again sent Laurent to them?

"Best beloved," whispered Virginie, as her husband kissed her, "I knew that my joy, when I wedded you, was too great to endure. Except now as God may guard us because He guards Henriette, what evil cannot befall!"

CHAPTER XXXIV

ST. JUST

VIRGINIE MASSAC was sorely perplexed. That astonishing youth, St. Just, had always been a law unto himself; now he had become his own law more than ever.

By common report, he was the most powerful member of the Committee of Public Safety, barring always his adored master Robespierre and the great Carnot. As soon as the Massacs returned to Paris, he resumed his constant visits to their home, but the old delightful suppers could not be renewed. Desmoulins and St. Just now would barely speak on meeting, and the latter seemed studiously rude to gentle little Lucile. After the first, Virginie managed with her perfect art that evenings the Desmoulins stayed to supper were never the evenings when St. Just walked confidently into her little salon, tossed his big plumed hat on the sofa and stayed to supper. The division now between the resolute Terrorists and their critics, the "Indulgents," was snapping old and intimate friendships.

St. Just seemed a being of no vices, no gross instincts, no masculine passions. His one enjoyment was apparently the perusal of endless pamphlets. Like Robespierre, he lived in two small rooms of Spartan simplicity on the Rue Caumartin. The third member of a mighty government, his clothes were barely tolerable, and money was to him the least consideration in the world.

During this hungry winter of 1793-94, St. Just had just returned to Paris with enhanced reputation. He had "gone on mission" to Strasbourg and had found supplies for the Army of the Rhine and restored discipline by methods brutal perchance, but effectual. He hated formalities. "Caesar (he would tell his friends) was not put to death by 'the forms of law,' but simply by thirty-two dagger thrusts." He dealt always with stark realities. His friends admired with trembling; and trembling still more, his foes now feared him.

At the Massac fireside St. Just betrayed an intense desire to banish all suggestions that he was a political leader. Theories he would discuss readily, but he avoided the least reference to current events. He even winced if René told stories of his late campaigns. When he spoke himself (which was seldom), it was only to repeat anecdotes of his boyhood in the Nivernais, anecdotes betraying a keen love for green woodlands and smooth meadows, or to plunge into some abstruse argument about "justice" and "absolute rights" in language filched from the metaphysical dialogues of Plato.

Most of the time, however, St. Just would merely sit and listen with eyes half closed, only the slight twitching of his delicate nostrils betraying that he heard. To all kinds of non-political discourse apparently he hearkened with delight. Absolutely unmusical and never darkening the doors of the opera, he would, nevertheless, sit for hours while Virginie sauntered through good classical music upon her harpsichord. Once as she thus played, he suddenly made a most unprecedented remark: "How beautiful your hands are, darting over the keys!" Words followed at once by a blush becoming a young girl, and then by absolute silence for the rest of the evening.

The Massacs always welcomed him. The General was not too unworldly to forget that Commissioner St. Just's frequent appearance at his door added his protection against the rabid suspicion of all ci-devants. Virginie would have been less than a woman if she had repelled the homage proffered apparently by a worshiper to a goddess upon some distant star. They both had the delicacy never to trade on St. Just's high influence and to respect his banishment of political allusions, although René often looked upon that tall youth gazing vacantly upon his pale glass of wine and water, and compared him with the perfervid orator of a few hours back, thundering before the Convention upon the need of "the perpetration of the Terror and the extirpation of the Republic's enemies."

So this tense, painful winter waned. It was Ventôse, in other words, late February, and the first buds were imagined to be swelling in the Luxembourg gardens, and on a certain day St. Just turned in again to the Rue de la Démocratie. The Convention was not in session, and René was either at Carnot's war bureau or (so Virginie imagined) had gone to inquire concerning the welfare of Father François.

The gentle lecturer was still a prisoner. All efforts for his release had halted against some filmy barrier, but Massac consoled himself that the Luxembourg was no dungeon, and that the prisoner was being kept from any more brave indiscretions which might have been grist to Vernet and Amar. Virginie watched her other guests depart after a very simple dinner, for all Paris was on war rations; but St. Just still sat in his low chair before the smoldering log in the salon, staring moodily at the embers and fingering his loosely tied cravat. His hostess, a good bourgeois in everything, took her sewing basket to complete some trifle for Henriette. St. Just that day had been more moody than ever. Something about him was unfathomable, and she would hardly regret his departure. Suddenly a gleam leaped into his deep-set eyes, matching a dying gleam from the fire. He spoke, and immediately she knew that his tones were charged with intense emotion.

"Virginie, have you studied Greek? What means ANANKÊ?"

"I have no Greek, Antoine Louis, but is it not 'Fatal Necessity'?"

"Yes. It was the irresistible force from the gods compelling a man to act against wisdom, custom, all the laws which should govern his being."

"So I've read." Virginie could see his hands clinching and unclinching. Suddenly she began to desire ardently that René might come.

"Virginie," St. Just's voice was very deep, "I am being conquered by ANANKÊ."

She snipped her thread and yawned studiously; "Antoine Louis, a good friend has a right to become boresome. If you were not a good friend, I would say, 'St. Just can ramble foolishly'."

He folded his arms, stared into the fire, then at length: "Yes, of course—foolishly. But tell me, has your 'good friend's' name ever been coupled with that of any woman?"

"Stories will spread. One is that you care for the sister of Citizen Lebas, your master Robespierre's old schoolfellow and present friend."

"A lie!" shot the young man sternly toward the fire. Suddenly, however, he leaped to his feet and nervously paced the floor.

"Yes, Robespierre is my master, although his Supreme Being seems too much like the old Christian God in new clothes. God to me is only impersonal force, of which we are all the playthings—of which *I* am the plaything to-day."

Virginie's laugh was too compelled. (Why did not René come?) "*You* a plaything of force, when all Strasbourg and half of France has been trembling before you? What have we had for dinner?—Do make a better jest!"

St. Just apparently heard not. "It's a lie that I cared for Henriette Lebas. I have sworn that I would never care for any woman; that women were merely a type of human bipeds, to which I would be eternally indifferent. But that oath too was a lie."

Phidias or Scopas never had nobler model than the youth who stood now with kindling eyes before Virginie Massac. Glance, gesture, all told her "danger." She watched him narrowly.

"We are all creatures of fate," he pursued in the same hard voice. "I believe this more truly than any Moslem santon. Why do Desmoulins and Danton (who's just returned to the Convention) demand halting the guillotine? Can Fouquier-Tinville send to the knife one wretch whose doom is not destined irrevocably? Am I not fated, just as much, to say what I must say to-day?"

Virginie knew that she herself was turning pale, but with a deprecatory smile, she rose: "I'm a poor philosopher, Antoine Louis. I can't follow you.—Some directions to André——"

The young Commissioner placed himself directly before her door. "I have fought against this with all my powers. No use. *Necessity*, the Necessity of the old gods.—I love you."

He did not attempt to seize her in his arms. On the contrary, he stood leaning upon the carven top of a cabinet, his head hung low, his long fair hair streaming as might a criminal's after a hideous confession. Seeing he did not approach her, Virginie, though pallid enough, stood her ground. "I have known you so long, Antoine Louis, that it is plain that you are very ill. Incessant work has un-

balanced you: that is all your words convey to me. Your
labors for the Republic——"

"For the Republic?" his words came back in a measured
wail. "Know then that I, the sworn member of the Great
Committee, am now keeping back the fact that you and
your husband protected here in this house an emigré emissary who has fought against France."

Virginie reeled as from a bullet, while no sound came
from her barely moving lips. St. Just's own tone became
a shade calmer.

"The lackey whom you discharged was a secret agent of
the Public Safety, for we do not trust the spies of the
General Surety too confidently. God or blind fate made
the fellow report directly to me. Any other household——"

But Virginie found her tongue. "This is the household
of General Massac of the Bastille, the Tuileries and Wattignies. Search this house from garret to cellar. You find
nothing."

"True, for I guiltily closed my eyes to the information
that after the ci-devant Vicomte de Massac recovered somewhat from his wounds, he disappeared from this domicile,
whether to quit France or still to lurk somewhere in Paris
my agent could not discover. Nevertheless, his actual evidence against General Massac would more than satisfy the
Tribunal. Services to the Republic do not pardon crim-
inality. General Houchard won a great battle, but in his
other duty he failed: he was guillotined."

Virginie, wholly recovered, regarded him with perfect
steadiness. "Very good, send your friend to the Tribunal.
I swear, however, that I will cry in the judges' faces '*Vive
le Roi!*' as other wives have done, just that I may accompany him."

St. Just's eyes now were glittering with consuming admiration: "I know that you would. That's what keeps me

back.—Never can the harshest fate make me your murderer."

"Antoine Louis," ordered Virginie, summoning all the powers within her; "go home. Rest calmly. Sleep. Then you will be once more yourself. I promise to forget all this wildness. Only do not stay with me again while I am alone."

He lifted his face, which was convulsed and working. "While you are alone?—But do I not love you? Have I not loved you from the first, only never understood my own soul until that accursed spy reported. I have stifled my duty for your sake. Of course, I ought to be guillotined. But how can I fight against destiny?—Oh! give me a little hope, Virginie. Hear this. Robespierre even to-day meets with his closest friends to decide whether to end or to intensify the Terror. Acts are proposed which would make the ears of every Frenchman tingle. I can avert them. I can swing the Incorruptible to mercy. Only a little hope. Promise not to say 'my husband, my child, my duty,' and turn me utterly away—and I——"

"No, no, no," burst now from Virginie, almost in a scream.

"Then be it so!" And St. Just's arms fell by his side, and his head bowed, like a man standing helpless under deadly blows. Then to the woman's unspeakable relief, the door clicked, a martial step sounded, and the General, hale and hearty in his blue and white uniform, entered with outstretched hand.

"Well met, Antoine Louis. You have doubtless kept my wife from being too lonely while I was detained.—You'll not stay for supper? More of Barère's interminable reports to digest?"

St. Just drew himself together with a jerk. Apparently he did not see the proffered hand, while Virginie retreated momentarily behind an arras: "Yes, more of Barère's long

words," he contrived to utter. "Virginie and I have had a
long argument about old futile theories of the nature of
human happiness. I'm late at the Tuileries.—Adieu!"

And out he went, nor, knowing his peculiarities, was
Massac astonished at his abrupt conduct. When, however,
he embraced his wife, he discovered that Virginie seemed
pale and fluttering. The matter?—Merely that Henriette
had been suddenly ill, although now as suddenly recovered.
René himself was fairly cheerful. Father François enjoyed
decent comforts and books. He was writing a *History of
Republicanism in Antiquity*. The war news was excellent.
Carnot's new armies had won more victories. Desmoulins'
boldly published criticisms of the continuation of the
Terror seemed to be gaining impetus. People were saying,
"the emergency is passing, let the Terror cease also."
Danton was back in Paris. He had recovered his health
and energy. He would conduct a campaign against the
abuses of the Tribunal. His old influence with the Convention was partly gone, nevertheless—etc., etc.

Virginie listened, but René sensed that her mind was
wandering. Henriette was sleeping in perfect health and
peace. The General regarded his wife closely, then asked a
question: "What was that argument you had with St.
Just?"

"His mind seemed wandering. Nothing but Greek words
and flighty ideas. I wonder is he wholly sane."

"At the Pavillon de l'Égalité he's terribly sane. He is
Robespierre's most trusted lieutenant."

"Best beloved," Virginie changed the subject suddenly,
"are you sure now of Laurent's safety?"

"Sure," vowed her husband. "No refuge within Paris
could be better. We agreed as to that when he left us.
Why, what has shaken your confidence?"

"Nothing," answered his wife. Yet, for once in his life,

he almost believed that she had answered him with a white lie.

. . . .

St. Just walked from the Massacs to the Tuileries, picking his way safely along Rue Honoré, yet consciously seeing nothing. Half of Paris had come to identify his terrifyingly beautiful features. Greasy caps were pulled off to him with "Good afternoon, patriot!" Delicate women shrank into doorways in dread of him, murmuring, "It's he who keeps Sanson so busy." St. Just merely walked straight ahead, his face as rigid as a sword of glass.

In Robespierre's bureau at the Tuileries, awaiting him, was the Incorruptible with three others, innermost initiates to the high mysteries of Liberty. Here was Couthon, a fellow member of the Great Committee, a paralytic in his wheel chair, albeit a man with a quick, dark countenance and a voice of singular power and beauty. Here was Lebon, fair and blue-eyed, one of Robespierre's most ardent supporters in the Convention. He had just returned from Cambrai, where, in behalf of the Great Committee, he had unflinchingly sent one hundred and fifty suspects to the knife. Here, finally, was a man, in uniform, of squat figure and haggard countenance, the worse for drink. He was Hanriot, commander of the Paris National Guard.

Barring Hanriot, nothing in these calm-eyed, gently speaking personages suggested that they had met to decide on the bloody deaths of scores of persons who had hitherto been their comrades, coadjutors and even their intimate friends. Robespierre sat quietly behind his desk, looking about him with his pinched little smile; his light green eyes glistening now behind blue spectacles. The others were obviously waiting St. Just, who dropped in a seat with merely a nod to Robespierre. "Pardon my delay, my master."

The First Commissioner rattled his blue papers: "I have invited you, my friends, because I know your pure intentions.—I was to see Danton.—Well, I have seen him."

A slight stir through all present as Robespierre continued:

"I met him last night at a supper party. You know I have never trusted Danton; he may love a Republic, but not our ultimate Republic of Virtue. Never mind. I tried to suppress personalities. We conversed at first even cordially. He praised my former doings, but grew cold as I pictured the future. 'I created the Tribunal myself,' he boasted. 'It was to be a bulwark of Liberty. Take care lest you make it a slaughterhouse.' 'Who has perished without a trial?' I demanded. Whereupon he rolled his gross, disdainful head. 'Trial!' he cried, 'you jest, Robespierre. You take criticism of yourself for a crime. You declare all your critics to be guilty'."

"And you answered the insult?" growled Hanriot.

"Very calmly, as became my patriotism. 'No, for the proof is that you are still alive.' With that I left him." The First Commissioner paused, smiled, folded a paper, then concluded, "The man, my friends, has become a menace.—He can corrupt the Republic."

Couthon at length broke the tense silence which followed. "Danton is the Man of the Tenth of August. His best friend, Desmoulins, is the Man of the Bastille. The one made Monarchy to totter, the other destroyed it. No light thing it can be to turn against them."

"The patriot of yesterday can be the traitor of to-day," affirmed Lebon.

"True enough. Moderatism's become treason," growled Hanriot.

But the First Commissioner's eye was seeking St. Just. The latter's cheeks had mantled red, and now he spoke rapidly, out of deep emotion.

"My master, my comrades, we approach the crisis. The war will cease to be dangerous within six months, and then there will rise the outcry against the dictatorship. 'Disband the Committee!' even patriots will begin clamoring. Reaction, selfishness, the old tyranny in new garments will recover strength. It is now the edge of spring. By the end of summer either we shall have changed 'Liberty, Equality, Fraternity' from an acclamation into a reality, or we shall be sleeping our untroubled sleep."

"Noble sentiments! Perfect Republicanism!" applauded Hanriot, as always after a speech he could not quite understand.

"Then you advise?" asked Robespierre mildly, while the others looked on St. Just intently.

"Past services to the Republic may give us the right to weep, but not the right to spare. We must use the next few months. The rest of the Great Committee think only about the war; they will let us deal freely with Paris. All obstacles we must conquer ruthlessly. Carnot and his colleagues can wait the final operation. We must deal with nearer foes. Let, however, our justice be impartial. Hébert and his atheistical 'Extravagants' are dangerous and detestable.—Let them disappear."

The others simply nodded and Robespierre's pencil became very busy upon the blue paper, until St. Just resumed:

"Danton, Desmoulins and their faction are less detestable personally. They are even more dangerous to the perfect Republic.—Let them too disappear."

Silence next, broken only by the dull rubbing of the pencil, and then by the wonderful voice of Couthon. "General Massac is a friend of Danton's—what of him?"

No one noticed how St. Just whitened again suddenly, for this time Robespierre's answer was prompt. "Detached from Danton, he is harmless and we may perhaps find him useful. I think I may omit his name, for the present, from our entry. I always approve of leniency when there is no betrayal of principle."

Prolonged conversation in similar vein, with more names added or rejected. At last all the others had departed, but St. Just lingered beside the desk. "A question, my master." Robespierre looked up, regarding him indulgently. "A subordinate came to me with this problem. He gave me no names, but said that a soldier who had done brave service to the Republic is suspected of having condoned the escape of a kinsman who is an emigré spy. Is it the duty of a very close friend to lay his suspicions before the prosecutor?"

The stare behind the blue spectacles betrayed obvious surprise. "Of course, Antoine Louis. How could his duty be otherwise?"

"But if the friendship is very close, and the spy has probably been rendered harmless?"

"Brutus the Elder put to death his two sons," the Incorruptible's voice was official and formal, "for their crimes in favor of tyranny, although the tyrant had been already overthrown."

St. Just bowed. "I will so answer my subordinate, my master."

The next morning St. Just appeared in the Committee rooms pallid and heavy-eyed. This fanatical defender of the Terror, this judge who at Strasbourg without qualm or flinching had sent hundreds to the guillotine, this "mind of fire with a heart of ice," had not slept one instant all of that night.

CHAPTER XXXV

SATURN DEVOURING HIS CHILDREN

On the tenth of March, Paris was astonished.

Hébert, the darling of the Commune, the dreaded Pope of the Goddess of Reason, and almost all his acolytes, had been arrested in their beds. The trial of these "Extravagants" was perfunctory, even for Fouquier and his Tribunal. The defence was pitiful for its groveling cowardice. On the twenty-fourth of March, five tumbrils laden with Hébert, his next hierophant, Chaumette, and a whole pack of their disciples, rolled through the brawling streets to the altar of Ste. Guillotine.

The crowds reviled them just as heartily as ten days before they had cheered them. Thousands of foul-mouthed atheists suddenly became vociferous deists all overnight. The Incorruptible had struck.

On the thirtieth of March, Paris was electrified.

At gray dawn Danton, Desmoulins, almost all of their conspicuous friends, barring René Massac, had been seized in their homes and flung into the Luxembourg. The Incorruptible had struck again.

The Dantonists had received some little warning of their fate. That Danton had openly spoken for "Mercy," and that Robespierre, after an ominous interval, had failed to second him, was known to all Paris. One day Hérault de Séchelles, a member of the Great Committee himself, but an intimate of Danton, sat at his desk in the Pavillon de l'Égalité. Suddenly he beheld the greenish eyes of the

First Commissioner intently fixed upon him. Hérault went home at once and put his affairs in order, little doubting what his doom was to be.

Danton had been told that his one-time allies were plotting his destruction. "They will not dare," he had asserted; but even when the warning continued, he steadfastly refused to fly, demanding, "Can a man carry away his native land upon the sole of his shoe?" His fearful energy, which had vitalized France and fulminated over Europe, could not be recalled. He had created vast engines of destruction; now, when he wished to halt them, they simply crashed onward, adding their author to the victims strewn along their way. He had pleaded for clemency and earned only the murderous anger of the men he had lifted to power. Vast weariness no doubt possessed him when he said, "I would rather be guillotined than guillotine others . . . besides, I am sick of the whole human race."

So, instead of entering the Convention, denouncing the ever-increasing Terror, and putting courage into all the shivering, white-lipped deputies to face their tyrants, he had waited almost passively for the blow; waited unresisting while St. Just announced to the whimpering Convention that "What constitutes a Republic is the destruction of everything opposed to it. A man is guilty who takes pity on prisoners, who has no desire for virtue, who opposes the Terror." And even while that fearful youth spoke, all eyes had gone over to the small smug form of the First Commissioner, sitting at the foot of the tribune, and had noted how his powdered head nodded its approval. Every sentence of St. Just was to mean the fall of twenty heads.

There had been a sign of protest in the Convention on the day of the arrests of the Dantonists. One deputy had dared to ask for an 'explanation.' René Massac vainly waited a second; he (though only a substitute) would have arisen third. But at the first murmur the Incorruptible had risen himself: "We shall see this day whether the Convention will be able to destroy a pretended idol," adding with a barely veiled menace, "The man who trembles is guilty." The demand for 'explanation' died into a scared apology. St. Just read out the indictment which Robespierre himself had framed for him, charging Danton, Desmoulins and their associates of "plotting to destroy the Republic" which they, of all men, had created; charging them with other "crimes" to which Robespierre had consented, and of which he often was the joint author.

The indictment was voted. The Tribunal began its destructive grinding. No greater farce had disgraced the cheapest puppet show upon the boulevards. Danton's great voice would boom out, nevertheless, intimidating judges, jurors, prosecutors and even guards. "Danton an aristocrat! France will not believe that story long!—My name goes with every revolutionary institution—the army, the Committees, the Tribunal!—Why, I have decreed my own death!"

The great voice must be silenced. The jury was not to be relied upon; Fouquier's nerves were being shaken. What of the Great Committee itself now, if Danton were acquitted!—Robespierre and St. Just, therefore, played their last card. The terrified Convention was browbeaten into voting that since the defendants had "insulted national justice," they had forfeited their right to argue and submit evidence. The crowd in the packed court room roared—but not against the prisoners. Despite the vituperations of the prosecutors and the direct mandate of the judges, that jury, wont to decide in a twinkling, debated for hours. At last they voted a hesitant "guilty," after the prisoners had been haled back to their cells.

It was the afternoon of a glorious spring day, April the

fifth, 16th Germinal, the trees in blossom, all Nature bursting into its joy, when the verdict was brought to the fifteen prisoners in the guard room of the Conciergerie. René Massac was with them; he had already seen every member of the Great Committee who was not a lieutenant of Robespierre. One of them, Lindet, had frankly sympathized, "I am on the Committee to feed the citizens, not to kill patriots"; but the others had been calloused or craven. Some, like the brutal and inefficient Collot d'Herbois, Billaud-Varenne and the tonguey Barère, had refused to save the men who had sought to end their own authority and chance for aggrandisement, others had been as the adamantine Carnot, who shrugged when René pled with him: "We are still in deadly warfare. Victory still rests on the unity of France. If Danton survives now to combat with Robespierre, that unity is broken. I mourn, but I can do nothing. We can fight Austria and Prussia, but not at the same time that we have to fight also against the Incorruptible and St. Just."

Massac regained the Conciergerie and procured speech with the prisoners. Sanson's men were already pinioning their arms behind their backs and snipping short their hair. The carts would soon be ready. Desmoulins, overwhelmed by the thought of quitting the wife of his love, was in an agony of tears. Westermann, that good soldier who had led the storm of the Tuileries, was standing silently like a Stoic. Of the rest, some were steadfast, some were near to collapse; but the great form of Danton rose like a calm fortress among them. He was delivering fearful comfort to his companions.

"As for me, I laugh at it. I have enjoyed my moments of existence thoroughly. I have made plenty of noise upon earth. I have tasted well of life.—Then let us go to sleep."

René made his way beside him. "There is still a chance,"

he whispered low, for Sanson was approaching with his cords. "The boulevards are murmuring. The old Cordeliers section, those men who followed me to the Bastille and the Tuileries—they will hear me. I will go out, ring the tocsin, cry 'Rescue.' There is a chance."

"There is no chance," came back the deep tones of Danton; "not with Hanriot's lousy guards lining all the streets. Swear to me that you will not throw your life away. Give me one last solace—the knowledge that René Massac survives to help pull down the Incorruptible. Commend me to Virginie." Then he raised his voice, "Vile Robespierre, in three months he will follow me!—And so adieu, my friend." He cast his arms about Massac, gave one crushing embrace, then submitted quietly to being pinioned.

. . . "Big game to-day," the turnkeys were joking to Sanson's men while they checked off the prisoners. Massac could not force himself to follow the tumbril, when crowded with its fifteen victims it rattled away. How green and golden was the afternoon! And the noise of the people along the route, how different from their wonted hoots and cheering!—Only later he learned those sayings which were to become part of world history, uttered as they were while the Revolution, like another Saturn, was devouring the greatest of its children. How Danton calmed the distraught Desmoulins. How his unnerved friend, Fabre d'Eglantine, bewailed, "I have written a play. Some one now will steal it and get the glory," to which his strong comrade made reply, "Be silent. In a week you too will be poetry." How when Hérault tried to embrace him, and the executioners interfered: "Fools, you won't prevent our heads from kissing in the basket."

He died the last. "My wife, my beloved! I shall never see you again. . . . Come Danton, no weakness"; and at the very end to Sanson: "Show my head to the People. It will be worth the seeing!"

. . . When René went homeward, fighting with hellish thoughts, little knots of people were gathering in the fine weather upon the street corners. There was something about them, their manner, the tone of their mutterings, not heard in Paris since the day of the Bastille. Was the Incorruptible still the civic idol?

A boy was hawking a ballad, glancing about him to avoid officious gendarmes, but taking many a copper whenever traffic seemed safe. René squandered a liard also. Thus read the hastily printed sheet:

"When Desmoulins, d'Eglantine and Danton
    Together reached the stream of Phlegethon,
    They paid their passage to the other side
    To Charon, honest ferryman, who cried,
    'You've given me too much; 'tis double pay.
    Here, take your change.' 'Nay' answered Danton, 'nay
    We've paid for six; three more will soon appear,
    Couthon, St. Just and—hark ye—Robespierre!' " [1]

[1] Latimer's translation.

CHAPTER XXXVI

VERNET AGAIN BURROWING

"Business was better still."

Citizen Spartacus Durand continued to find Republicanism extraordinarily profitable all through Floréal and Prairial. True, his tongue sometimes tripped and would say "April" and "May," but then the best patriots in Paris were doing the same thing. "It was hard" (so he heard at the Jacobin Club) "to dismiss at once all the evil vestiges of tyranny."

Shortly after Danton and the other "Indulgents" perished, Citizen Durand indeed had suffered from a mild panic. They had been drowning anti-patriots by barge loads at Nantes. They had been shooting them by hundreds at Lyons. What of his professional gains, if like practices extended to Paris?—This peril passed, however; Ste. Guillotine seemed far too acceptable to her local votaries to be abolished. On the contrary, she became more active than ever.

During the winter, according to Durand's rough and ready account, "The Widow" had barely averaged seventy political victims a month from the Tribunal, not counting, however, the fairly numerous common thieves, counterfeiters of assignats, and "speculators" that the ordinary courts handled; but no sooner had Danton gone than her employment quickened enormously. Well over a hundred in Germinal, over two hundred and fifty in Floréal, and

433

Prairial promised to supply more than three hundred and fifty. What a distinguished company! All of the high judges of the old Royal Parliament, any quantity of ci-devant nobles, all of the old Farmers-general, and mixed in with them a big supply of ex-patriots, of Republicans who had fallen from grace, or of ex-priests who had committed the blunder of not merely stripping off their cassocks, but of also following Hébert into strident atheism.

"One ought to know just how religious it is safe to be these days," Spartacus would tell his friends. "Hurrah for the Supreme Being!"

Yes, and there were now plenty of women too; old ci-devant Countesses and Marquises, a fair sprinkling of nuns, the widow of the atheist Hébert, who doubtless partook of her husband's atheism, though an ex-nun herself, and finally the Citizeness Lucile Desmoulins, guilty of the crime of having "conspired" (feeble patriots whispered "begged and prayed") "for her husband's acquittal. She had, indeed, gone to the last scene very gladly. "Perhaps," she told her friends, "I shall soon see *him!*"

Durand, in fact, had the weakness to admit that "if she had not been such an abominable anti-Republican, I might actually have felt two grains of pity for her."

All this made the worthy citizen's affairs prosper, and things were more helpful yet, now that the Incorruptible had announced his great general programme of *"Virtue,* apart from which Terror is baneful; *Terror,* apart from which Virtue is powerless."

Citizen Durand had long since ceased to live in the cheap garret which he and Olympie had inhabited while they did their first spy work for Linio. A steady income enabled them to hire a snug apartment on the Rue Paul (lately the Rue St. Paul) near Place de la Bastille. A most Republican quarter, and in the same building was printed the

Journal des hommes libres, the most abusive, patriotic and filthy of all the Jacobin sheets, now that Hébert's journal had vanished into silence. Spartacus and Olympie had furnished their rooms with heavy, over-ornate furniture because so many households were being broken up (their owners being either in prison or emigrated), that fine furniture was almost a drug upon the second-hand market.

There was a little mystery, however, about this apartment and Spartacus vaguely realized the fact. He had a strong feeling that between their living room and the printing office there was a space partitioned off and entered only by a small door well concealed in a panel. He never dared, however, to ask Olympie too closely about this. "You won't tell me what Linio and Vernet keep spilling in your ears," she informed him. "Leave this matter alone!" And he did so; especially because Olympie seemed suddenly possessed of a delectable quantity of assignats. Probably, Durand admitted to himself, Olympie was concealing some one behind that partition, and that some one was very likely an emigré, unable to get out of Paris. However, since the assignats were so abundant, it was not well to be too prying. Money was money; La Guillotine might suddenly slacken and the risk?—*Peste!* who would suspect one of Sanson's best helpers? If at any time the poor devil, presumably under concealment, became a real danger, it would be easy enough to betray him.

Spartacus consequently watched Olympie adorn herself with cheaply bought satins, and earrings of ci-devants now under La République's displeasure, and reminded himself that silence usually was golden. Affluence had rendered the couple good natured; they quarreled much less than formerly and Olympie often condoled with her spouse over his labors.

"Yes," he complained one day, "they are dividing up the

Tribunal now, to make it work faster. Citizen Fouquier is getting to be the most driven man in Paris. They say the aristos soon won't be permitted any defence whatever."

"Don't the jury ever acquit?" asked Olympie, fingering the bejeweled locket dangling from her ample neck.

"They used to once in a while, just hit or miss. 'For the sake of the impression,' so Cato Salles, who's on the jury, told me. But now it's almost never. All suspects are guilty. You can't make a mistake. Well," he pulled out a heavy repeater, two years earlier in a lieutenant-general's pocket, "I'm off again to business; a new rope and pulley to fix before the carts arrive.—What a dog's life!"

Olympie saw him go unquestioning, then went to the smoking hob, took thence a gridiron of well-browned cutlets and filled up a plate, which, with a demi-bottle she set next the wainscoting nearest to the printing office. Lightly she tapped thrice, then quitted the room. Presently the woodwork slid aside quietly, a hand extended, plate and bottle disappeared.

Olympie, paying not the least attention, put on most of her finery and went out. She was, in fact, bound for her club, "The Society of Human Rights," composed largely of market women. This "noble and patriotic organization," "a true assemblage of Aspasias and Cornelias" (to quote the eulogiums regularly handed them by Section orators) was especially intent on saving the Republic by crowding the benches of the Tribunal and cheering every time the Prosecutor called for "death." Some of the members, too, religiously attended La Guillotine with their knitting, but Olympie hardly cared for that. "One pigsticker in the family is enough," she said bluntly. To-day, however, there was a regular meeting of the club. President Rosa Lacombe would give another fine long harangue on the wickedness of Moderatism, and the need of the "complete"

Republic. Citizeness Durand, therefore, departed to be gone for some time.

She was still away when her consort returned and actually brought two fellow Republicans with him. The guillotine had just been moved to the Place of the Over-Turned Throne,[1] because unpatriotic shopkeepers on Rue Honoré said that the executions were getting on the public's nerves and were hurting their trade. Durand could, therefore, get back to Rue Paul promptly, and on this day the Tribunal had been almost slumbering. "Only one cartload; though there was good promise for to-morrow." His companions were Citizen "Fabricius" Puget, as Linio liked now to be called, and the great Commissioner Vernet himself.

"We wanted a quiet talk, Citizen Spartacus," explained Linio; "we understand that the Citizeness is now away, and every room at the Louvre has too many ears."

Durand, in a surly fashion, did the hospitalities and set out a dark bottle. Linio partook; Vernet partook not and merely rustled the lace on his sleeves. The executioner indulged in a pull himself, and then looked cunningly at his companions.

"I've been wanting to see you, too. Where's that emigré evidence against Massac?—Saw him only to-day walking bold and uppish as ever toward the Convention."

"We desired to explain," smoothed Vernet. "Very unlucky delays, but not unsurmountable. In a word, our good Fabricius Puget here at last has the evidence that at Massac chateau the ci-devant Chevalier harbored his cousin the ci-devant Vicomte. The latter disappeared, probably to go to Paris. Never mind; the evidence could be made good enough ordinarily to satisfy the Tribunal."

"Fiends below," burst in Durand; "why not an arrest then?"

[1] To-day the Place de la Nation.

"Good enough if—if my worthy patriot, General Massac, were a common suspect, an everyday ci-devant, a priest, a nun, a speculator, or just a girl with aristo parents sent to the jury to make up the day's quota.—But General Massac, hero of Wattignies, member of the Convention—of course, you see the difficulties."

"Bah!" spat Spartacus, clearing his throat.

"I broached it to Amar. He shook his head, 'Not so soon after that Danton business. The General Surety can't touch Massac.'"

"Bah!" spat Spartacus again.

"Besides," pursued Vernet, "there's something else. Suppose Massac is condemned.—But naturally you read the journals, Citizen?"

Citizen Durand knew well that Citizen Vernet knew well that French and Russian were equally illegible to the former; and he added a muttered curse while confessing, "He'd no time to read all of 'em."

"Perhaps, then," Spartacus kept looking hard at the neat white frills around the speaker's neck, and thinking how easily a certain knife could crash through it; "you have not realized that a decree has just passed the Convention ordering that all the property of convicted anti-patriots should not go to their heirs, but be confiscate for 'indigent patriots.' You confirm this, Citizen Puget?"

Linio nodded, and Durand now swore vigorously; the hole in the ladder before him was perfectly visible.

"Then if Massac's head drops, we will get——"

"Nothing," completed Vernet in accents bland as balm of Araby. "That is, unless the case were handled by some representative of the highest influence and delicacy." He began taking a long stamped paper from an inner pocket. "You understand, Citizen Durand, that as a busy—ah! let us say—public functionary, you cannot push your interests

as the Massac's uncle properly. Now, if you will only con-
stitute me as your attorney, if you will only put your name,
or if out of practice, your mark to the place where I am
pointing, I engage to act for you, to arrange faithfully with
persons of the highest patriotism and authority, in short, I
think I can promise that if—I say *if* General Massac
should be convicted, the control of a large part of his property falls into your hands."

The executioner glanced about with the uttermost suspicion. "I don't like long papers. My eyesight's bad. I
can't read these hen tracks. Leave the paper. I'll answer
to-morrow."

Vernet calmly began folding up the paper, but Linio laid
a lank, bony hand on Durand's thick and fleshy one. "Don't
be a fool," he enjoined. "We're all in this boat, and Vernet
alone can row us to land."

"Of course," completed Vernet suavely, "somebody else
is very likely to get convictive evidence against Massac.
Then his property will be absolutely confiscate. And at
the trial it could easily leak out that his wife's uncle suspected his crime, yet failed to denounce him."

The dark burly man suddenly turned white. "Not that!
No, never that!—I'm the very best of patriots."

"Perhaps," mused Linio slowly; "but half your 'patients'
of to-day were called 'good Jacobins' yesterday. One little
slip in these times and you give them 'the fillip on the
neck,' as you like to call it.—Awkward for you, Durand,
awkward."

Spartacus uttered an unprintable curse and almost frantically turned on Vernet. "Let's see that paper." He
seized it, unrolled it upside down and scanned intently.
"Reads fair enough," he growled. "What'd you have me
do?"

Vernet deliberately produced an ink horn. "Just make

a cross—here. Puget can sign as witness. In a couple of
months, Citizen, you can perhaps pass for a handsomely
rich man."

"The devil I can," was all the thanks which Spartacus
gave him. After a little more cajolery and firm warnings
as to secrecy, the pair took themselves off, not greatly
troubled because the executioner was still angrily suspicious. The two kept close together until they were well
down upon the Quai des Ormes, where they could talk
without peril of being overheard.

"We've got his cross," observed Linio.

"The only 'cross' of great value in these non-religious
days," returned the ex-Abbé calmly.

"Now what'll you do next?" demanded the ex-Baron.

"See if I can break down that mysterious protection now
thrown around Massac. I'll try to work on the Incorruptible or more readily upon St. Just.—I think you told
me that St. Just was no longer calling in Rue de la Démocratie."

"That's what I and my fellow spies of your bureau observed."

"Spies, spies!" Vernet permitted himself the luxury of
the ghost of a chuckle. "Where are any two of us these
days who haven't set spies upon each other?—Well, why
did our virtuous St. Just stop visiting at the Massacs?"

"Because they were friends of Danton and Desmoulins,
of course."

"Doubtless, doubtless. And yet——" suddenly Vernet
tapped his forehead, then stood stock-still, as if smitten
by some revelation; "my dear *confrère*, do you not sometimes feel yourself inspired? Something comes to you as a
flash, as a message from the gods. Am I wrong? Dare I
tell you? Hear this, then—St. Just, the impenetrable, has
melted at last to the fair Citizeness Virginie. *Voilà!*

That is why he left the Massacs. She dismissed him, and he's a baffled man. That fits in divinely with many things I've noticed and heard. Henceforth I will work with him upon *that!*"

Linio pulled off his hat, and made a bow half sincere, half sardonic. "Citizen Commissioner, it is the satisfaction of my life when I am permitted to coöperate with a man of supreme genius."

. . . That evening, when Spartacus had gone off again to the Mucius Scaevola to fume over his problems, the panel in the wall opened quietly and Laurent, pale with a long confinement, told an interesting story to his protectress, Olympie. He had been secreted in the apartment ever since that night when he had been well enough to be moved thither from the Massacs by René and André. Repeatedly he had striven to leave Paris, but only recently had his wound completely healed, and the risks of the attempt still seemed unsurmountable. Olympie (very well paid) had, however, been friendly and faithful, and his strength was at last coming back.

Now he could stretch his cramped limbs, and, thanks to a second hidden door, could wander about a little in the deserted printing office. While thus he exercised, the firm jaw of his protectress was dropping lower and lower.

"That sheep, to keep such a secret from me about the husband of my White Bird!"

Spartacus slept the sounder when he tumbled in that night, because he had not seen his helpmeet's countenance while she uttered this.

CHAPTER XXXVII

THE FESTIVAL OF THE SUPREME BEING

PARIS was gay, viciously gay.

Nobody talked about the Terror—except as ultra-enthusiastic patriots. Everybody thought about it.

The theaters were crowded, although no piece that was not directly laudatory of "Republican virtues" escaped an Argus-eyed censorship. The restaurants were crowded. The new gambling hells around the ci-devant Palais Royal were still more crowded. Never before had so many citizenesses averse to prudery been seen upon the streets. The shops all did a rushing business. If you had a roll of assignats you spent them immediately, for of what could you be sure on the morrow?

The sans-culotte gendarmes swaggered everywhere with their tall plumes and tricolored cockades. If they accosted a man at the next table to you in the café, flourished a paper, then led him away, you took pains not to notice, but studied to-day's docket for the Tribunal.—They had not arrested *you*—as yet.

René Massac went through these early summer days feeling himself more than ever in some prolonged lurid dream. Why could he not compel himself to waken and get back to what ought to be realities? But Carnot was still trusting him with most important duties. The war was prospering. France was flinging back her enemies; the enormous sacrifice in the armies had not been in vain; the Revolution seemed daily to be less in danger.

But if the foreign danger lessened, the Terror, for which it had provided the justification, only quickened. Batches of forty or fifty victims now. Talk of needing a second guillotine. And still the wholesale arrests, and the prisons filling by one door as they were emptied by another. Girls in their teens were being pounced on as "potential conspirators" or as "imbibing aristocratic opinions from their parents." Virtue, apparently, was conquering by the very simple process of eliminating all the conceivably nonvirtuous.

Massac knew how the cord everywhere was tightening, and yet it did not snap. He knew that even Carnot's and all of Robespierre's other associates on the Great Committee (barring Couthon and St. Just) showed strained lines about their eyes. One day Carnot gave him an order for drafting. He conned it twice, then took it back to his chief. "Do I read this aright? It sends to the front half of the gunners of the Paris National Guard. Hanriot will be furious at this pulling of his teeth."

The war chief regarded his lieutenant steadily. "General Massac, I intend that he shall be furious. Draw your own inferences." And that noon René returned home two shades happier.

Virginie was alone, yet apparently agitated. St. Just had abruptly ceased his visits just before the fall of the Dantonists. No doubt (surmised Massac) he had realized that this deed must set blood between them and render social intercourse impossible. Massac, on the whole, was glad that Virginie had been spared a formal break in an old friendship. The Incorruptible, too, never came now to Rue de la Démocratie. He had chosen his path, and never again could it lead to Virginie's salon. The salon, in fact, was empty, and very seldom in these days did she stir from her house and garden. True, with a little trouble, she could escape meeting the death carts on the streets, but other unavoidable sights were often painful, and boisterous sans-culotte patrols took easy liberties with pretty citizen-esses. Even in their own home Virginie and René talked of the public case only in whispers, and to-day she rested tremblingly on his arm as if some new fear possessed her.

"How much longer can it go on?" at last she questioned.

"God knows, my beloved. Robespierre seems stronger than ever. The deputies are rabbits flying before his frown. He thinks to make France virtuous; but he only makes those of us whom he spares cowardly."

Virginie's white hands closed hard. "Oh! If I were a second Charlotte Corday!"

"I rejoice that you are not. Robespierre is still the idol of three-fourths of Paris. If he were illegally done to death, every suspect in the city would perish in an avenging mas-sacre. It is this which keeps him alive."

She looked up at her husband with wide, frightened eyes. "Tell me, best beloved—I know that you have thought about this—what finally *can* end the Terror?"

"Yes, I have pondered for days. I know the Committee, the Convention. The Terror will end when the men who now crawl before Robespierre for safety, know that only boldness can save their heads. The feeblest animal can grow terrible defending its own life."

"I thank you, my dearest." He was frankly puzzled at her manner, but she vouchsafed no explanation and he did not press her. The times, of course, were fearsome enough to excuse jumpy nerves in a marble image.

.   .   .   .

Extract from the diary of René Massac, about this time:

" . . . . These pages I must keep from Virginie. I can see her distress already.

"To-day befell what I had vaguely sensed was coming. The Convention was not in session. I was drafting orders in the Tuileries when Robespierre summoned me to his private bureau. Since the death of Danton I have avoided him, being determined to do nothing to stultify myself; yet for Virginie's sake, not willing to cast away my life by futile bravado.

"Most of our interview was courteous. Robespierre flattered me in respect to my services; regretted he had been driven to 'certain painful severities'; said that I had committed 'a pardonable error' in behalf of unfortunate friends, but that 'a philanthropist should overlook much.'

"I told him that I was now only a soldier and that I never spoke in the Convention except on military topics, pretending not to understand his drift. Then, with his thin lips tightening and his eyes dry as a snake's, he opened his business. Briefly it was this: the foreign peril was passing, yet the true crisis was soon at hand: speedily the Friends of Virtue would have to give the 'last purification' to the Republic. For this task they needed a general more competent than Hanriot, to set over the entire armies of France. Such a man, however, must agree to take his orders absolutely and under all circumstances from Robespierre himself, and not from Carnot or anyone else. For this general would then await the glory of a Cincinnatus, of a Fabius, etc., etc.—An impressive pause, a hard look in my face and then: 'General Massac, do you now give me such a pledge?'

"I know that my blood half stopped in my veins, just as in some supreme peril in battle, before the mind can dominate the shrinking body; but I think that I answered him with thanks and a cold politeness, 'A soldier obeys his orders, and my lawful orders are now from Carnot. When *the Convention* makes you my chief, my poor abilities are all at your command.'

"I saw his face twitching when I said 'Convention'; his lips moved, he grew pale, then he merely said, 'I regret your decision.' We bowed very conventionally—and I found myself in the ante-room, turning hot, then cold.

"The most powerful and ruthless man in France undoubtedly is now my mortal enemy. He will bide his time, but at any instant the blow may fall. I have answered, nevertheless, in a manner worthy of my manhood and the love of Virginie, and I can at least go down fighting. I will now visit the place which I never leave without being a stronger and happier man; I will go to Father François at the Luxembourg."

.   .   .   .

The physical lot of the prisoners in that old Luxembourg palace was not wretched. The rambling building provided a vast number of tolerable cubicles. The halls, with their antique carving and gilding standing out in dusty magnificence, afforded room for social intercourse and exercise. The enclosed garden-court even permitted a little promenading, hand ball and a kind of tennis. Decent food was sent in by a restaurateur, the richer prisoners being arbitrarily taxed to pay for their poorer companions.

All this made outward existence endurable. An inmate, furthermore, mingled in the best of cultured society; all shackling etiquette and formalities were at an end; he enjoyed endless leisure; he could talk philosophy, natural science, or belles lettres to his heart's content. There was an endless round of cards, charades and theatricals. The ladies kept their lap-dogs. Flirtations between the sexes abounded; even love intrigues, not the most decorous. The well-fed jailors were usually proud of their "superior inmates," and gave many small privileges.[1]

The one great fly in the ointment would show itself every afternoon; "Daily honor list!" the head turnkey would shout in the main hall, then read off the list of his guests summoned to explain next morning to the Tribunal the reasons for their unfortunate detention. Next followed the hurried farewells, the stoical nonchalance, the "best wishes" from friends—wishes of a value precisely understood—and

[1] Conditions in the older prisons, ordinarily reserved for criminals, seem to have been far less tolerable.

the departure in hackney coaches to the Conciergerie. For the persons thus summoned, mortal troubles would then adjourn forever within four-and-twenty hours.

Father François had become reconciled to his captivity. "After all," he would remark, "there is a decided gain in not having to plan about one's future." He had made many friends, most of whom had quietly disappeared and been replaced by new ones. He would listen to all that René, a privileged visitor, had to tell him of public affairs, and always responded with shrewd comments of hope; but he was happiest when told at length about Henriette and Virginie.

This afternoon René could not bring himself to breathe a hint of his passage-at-arms with Robespierre, implying, as it doubtless did, that the protection which had hitherto kept the lecturer from the Tribunal might at any instant be withdrawn; but otherwise the young deputy went at length into the public situation, and in response Father François spoke with even greater candor than was his wont, analyzing the whole situation shrewdly, then concluding, "I think that in six weeks you will see the end." (For he always said "weeks" and not "decades" as by the new calendar.)

"Six weeks, Father? The thing has lasted already so long that I dare not believe even 'six years'."

"No; six weeks. I had a dream. I am coming to believe in dreams and many other unlearned fooleries. I seemed to be overlooking Paris. The city was under an enormous thundercloud. The sky was black; the sun was darkened; thunders roared; the lightnings of an indescribable tempest darted. Men looked on one another in anguish. 'The world will shrivel now in Thermidor,' they moaned, 'under the fury of God.' Then, in a twinkling, the skies were cleared. The thunders died. A great voice seemed to be sounding from heaven, 'It is finished.'—And next I saw your garden, the old chestnuts, and the birds singing among them; Henriette was playing on the turf, and Virginie was going to meet you, white roses in her hair, while you were entering with joy upon your face; and you said, 'The Terror is ended. All is well.'"

"Oh! if I can believe it. Thermidor—late July? But surely you were with us to share the joy, my Father."

"Somehow I did not seem to be sitting in the garden. I seemed to be blessing you all from far off. Somehow I do not think I shall see that happy moment with these mortal eyes. No matter—all will be well."

Profoundly impressed, gladdened yet saddened, Massac, a little later, was quitting the prison when, in the corridor nearest the turnkey's guardroom, he was saluted familiarly.

"Good afternoon, M. le Chevalier."

"Dreux-Brézé, as I live by bread!"

The ex-Master of Ceremonies was extremely friendly. His coat was frayed, but still immaculate. His cheeks betrayed a touch of rouge.

"I did not know that you were here," confessed René.

"About a month," drawled the Marquis, proffering his snuff-box. "Much pleasanter than my 'hide-and-go-seek' before they caught me. Charming society; witty conversation; never a minute for boredom.—See how I was amusing myself."

He exhibited a large volume under his arm. "Comte de Roux had it before he had to move to the Conciergerie yesterday. You knew de Roux—delightful fellow, my old mentor on etiquette. He passed me this book upon leaving —plates, you see, showing how to dance, wear your clothes, make your bow, doff and hold your hat. Invaluable authority!—I've found already that I made two errors at the last Tuileries levee."

"Dreux-Brézé," spoke Massac, not unmoved, "I pray God that if put in your place I can carry things as bravely as you can. Is there the least thing I can do for you?"

"Nothing, M. le Chevalier, nothing I assure you, except the small item of freedom, about which there seems to be a trifling difficulty. Otherwise, I seem absolutely content."

"A bitter climax this to an old friendship! We always liked and respected each other. You have no grudge against me, I trust?"

"Nothing in the least personal. Of course, I'd pass a rapier through you with the greatest of satisfaction because you took up arms against the King; otherwise, I bubble over with cordiality."

"I will not moralize," pursued the soldier. "My visits to this prison at least do me this good—they make me the less sorry that despite everything, I must claim noble blood."

"Why there *are* advantages in a certain breeding, after all," soliloquized the Marquis; "as de Roux said yesterday, after they called out his name, 'We nobles may be lacking in other things, but at least we must know how to bow ourselves out gracefully.' That's all we can do at present, and then, when everything's said, La Guillotine is far less boresome than gout or a consumption."

"I'll do what I can," vowed René clumsily, "perhaps a chance soon——"

"But hardly to-morrow, M. le Chevalier, and you see I've had a broad hint that I'll be on to-night's tally sheet. —So think of me kindly. Not all a cockscomb!—Now I must· have a little tête-à-tête with a certain Mme. la Duchesse; a few confidences you will understand——"

Versailles had never seen a more courtly sweep of body and hands. Massac walked out past the guards into the green pleasance of the Luxembourg gardens. Early summer was bursting. Every leaf, shrub, flower was crying its fragrant "Joy!" but in his head there was only a grinding summons, "How long? How long? How long?"

.   .   .   .

Two days later came the eighth of June, otherwise the 20th Prairial.

Paris was en fête. By decree of the Convention, acting at the behest of its lord and master, the capital celebrated now the Festival of the Supreme Being. Atheism was to be abolished by official mandate quite as emphatically as had been decrepit Christianity.

It was a perfect day for the early summer. An immense amphitheater had been arranged in the rear of the Tuileries. In the center rose a lofty tribune, likened by the envious (for a few such creatures still existed in Paris) to a "throne," the throne for the Incorruptible, with the abject deputies on benches behind him.

. . . Robespierre at last. The Incorruptible mounted his pulpit. He wore a coat of paler blue than did his fellows. His white waistcoat, yellow leather breeches, and hat overwhelmed by tall tricolor plumes, were conspicuous to the wide assemblage. He held an enormous bouquet of flowers and wheat ears—the first fruits of the year. No carmagnoles in this ceremony; no tumult; no lack of dignity. Amid measured but prolonged acclamations, such as might have befitted a Caesar, the First Commissioner rose, bowed solemnly, then delivered his set oration in praise of the Supreme Being, concluding:

"He did not create kings to devour mankind. He did not create priests to harness us like vile animals to the car of kings; but He created the universe to make known His power. He created men to aid and love one another, and to attain happiness by the path of virtue. . . . Being of Beings, the hatred of hypocrisy and tyranny burns in our hearts, with the love of justice and of native land. This is the worship which we proffer!"

Loud music next, many voices and a grand choral written for the occasion.

> Mighty God of a fearless people.

And so through the last thundering refrain:

> Thus we sheathe our triumphant blades,
> Having sworn to destroy all crimes and tyrants.

As a last scene, the Incorruptible descended from his tribune, received from an obsequious hand a torch, and, while incense smoke rose around him as if surrounding a high priest, set fire to certain sad looking wooden images of "Folly" and "Atheism." Who cavilled aloud over the omen because "Atheism" unpatriotically refused to catch, and the flames singed "Wisdom," placed triumphantly above her? A loud salvo of artillery concluded the scene. The hundred thousand spectators dissolved, while the Arch-pontiff calmly walked homeward toward the Duplays, surrounded by his sycophants, and himself smiling, ignorant that under the deputies' cocked hat, tongues at last were wagging. "There are Brutuses yet," Massac actually caught from the time-serving Barère. But stranger still was the word echoed from one member to another, "Robespierre's Supreme Being *bores* me."

René Massac began hoping against hope for France.

. . . .

Whatever the murmurs, the festival had been an enormous outward success. Never seemed the Incorruptible's priestly domination greater. But his prime lieutenant had not shared in his triumph. As his master descended from the Tuileries to ascend the tribune, St. Just had tossed out abruptly, "I am not well," pulled his hat across his eyes,

held down his head and walked straight to Rue de la Démocratie.

André, wondering at his reappearance, informed him,
"Citizeness Massac is in the garden"; and the young Commissioner, without a craved permission or announcement,
strode through the familiar house, and betook himself
thither. Virginie was seated under the largest chestnut, a
broad white seam spread out upon her lap. Her dress was
very simple; her hair in a charming disorder. On a small
mattress upon the bench beside her, Henriette rested in
chubby sleep. A tame starling was running back and forth
upon the grass, making random stabs for food. The summer lilies were all aflame in a long narrow bed; there was
a drowsy scent from the rose bush. The garden walls cut
off all of the noisy, evil world beyond. Here in its microcosm
lay the earthly paradise.

St. Just's boots rang harshly on the flags, yet his step
slackened involuntarily as he saw the filigree of sunshine
through the boughs upon the greensward. Doubtless he had
prepared some speech, but as Virginie, with ever-widening
eyes, silently rose and confronted him, the Commissioner
stood stock-still and for a good half-minute in perfect silence
they looked on each other. Then he held out his hand.

"I come as a friend," he began awkwardly.

She shrunk back from his hand. "No, Antoine Louis;"
her tone was low, but decisive; "there's blood upon it,
Danton's, Camille's, Lucile's blood." Then after another
instant, "Why have you come?"

He had turned white, next red, next white again—at last
he forced his speech: "I knew that your husband was sitting with the deputies. I would not find him here. I would
only find you. It is more than two months since we have
met. You did not dismiss me, but I knew I would be unwelcome——" Then, slowly raising his hand, as might a

man awakening, "Well—I have tried hard. Striven and failed. Now I am being driven to bay."

"Striven? Failed? Driven to bay?" Virginie would have been less than a woman, if into fear and repugnance there had not intruded curiosity.

"Yes. Striven to banish you from my thoughts. I see you every midnight, when I sit in the rooms of the Great Committee turning those endless papers. I see you in the Convention behind the president's tribune. I see you in the bureau of Fouquier while I con with him the mandates of death. I see you when I demand sleep; when I dream, when I wake.—What can be the end? The thing is too hard for me."

Virginie knew the house was then vacant, save for André and Henriette's *bonne*. She must rely on herself, and "herself" did not desert her. She pointed to a seat.

"You have been turning mad, Antoine Louis. That explains much; that pardons much. Who of us these days can remain sane? Now, since you profess to be a friend, compose yourself, explain."

He sat down slowly, laid his hat upon his knees, studied with compressed brows the little herbs at his feet. At last he resumed, breathing heavily: "I have sought solace through incessant toil for the Nation. 'Power,' 'Success' cry envious tongues. Ah! what success when René Massac walks home to his heaven on Rue de la Démocratie, and I to my gehenna fires on Rue Caumartin. Yet I was holding out. I was saying, 'St. Just, your only bride must be La Republique,' when as I told you my hand was forced. Now I see hell opening before me."

"Again, Antoine Louis, unless your old friendship was a lie, explain!"

He twisted off the tricolor cockade on his hat and very deliberately tore it up to bits. "I will explain. I told you that the suspicion of helping an emigré rested on your husband. You defied me to do my duty. You did well. For your sake I have sacrificed my duty to the Republic to preserve the man who destroys my own happiness. I told my spy, 'Keep quiet.' Now yesterday there comes to me another trusted servant of the Nation, not quite so powerful as myself, but with his own corps of spies. He tells me, 'General Massac has enabled his cousin, the ci-devant Vicomte Laurent, to escape the guillotine. I give to you the honor of denouncing him.'"

Virginie did not startle as he had expected. "And what did you answer Commissioner Vernet?" was her collected query.

"Vernet? You knew that it was he?"

"Don't wake Henriette, Antoine Louis. Yes, I know many things. I have not told René of your avowal to me. I feared lest he might kill you, but I have long since prepared myself for anything. I can mount the scaffold just as calmly as did poor Lucile Desmoulins, whom you murdered."

St. Just's face worked convulsively. "Speak not thus of dying. At the worst, I can still save your life. We can fly—to Bourbon, to Otahaite, to some other distant isle in the vast wide sea—where all this jumble in France can be forgotten, where our lives can all be begun anew."

The woman rose and stood firmly before him. "If I did not know that you were mad, it would indeed be my duty to tell René, and to let fate take its course. Know this now, that I shall decline to live without him. Save him, therefore, if you desire to save me."

"And if I do, you promise?"—his eye gleamed with half-insane hope.

"I promise you nothing, save the consciousness that if René and I perish, though you may disbelieve in heaven, you shall endure a lifelong knowledge of hell.—In my way, without telling him, I am striving to save my husband. Do not thwart me.—Now go. If you stay, I see that in your face forecasting words and deeds that must put an eternal gulf between us." Firm as a goddess, she pointed toward the doorway.

He rose, gazed on her with fearful intensity, then apostrophized the empty air. "I knew it was madness to come. What is that thing in women which destroys men's reason, duty, virtue?—How much longer can I hold off Vernet?"

"You can still hold him off, for you would not be my destroyer. Now, for the safety of us both, for mine, for yours—if that thing weighs with you—depart!"

Henriette was starting up in her sleep. Her fists rubbed at her eyes. St. Just gazed at her long in a kind of catalepsy, next darted, rather than reached for, Virginie's unwilling hand. The lips she felt upon it were icy cold; then he jerked himself away. "I go. Once more I will fight against myself, against Vernet. But if I fail—if he, wearied with me, should appeal direct to Robespierre—come life, come death, I will try to save you from the worst."

His look, as he turned, bespoke a soul in fiery torment. The door grated. His steps died away through the house and the little garden was vacant. Virginie caught up Henriette to her breast, and shook with sobs and tears. "My little one! We dreamed we were bringing you to dwell with us in a new world of gold.—Now has your mother left her even the right to go on living!"

When René himself returned, husband and wife embraced each other with more than their wonted tenderness. Each was conscious that something serious had happened. Each as carefully refrained from questions which might add to the other's pain. Nevertheless, René delivered tidings which brought to Virginie a little of comfort.

"*Ma vie*, here is news. I have just learned that besides sending away part of Hanriot's men, Carnot has ordered a demi-brigade of veterans up to Paris. What do you guess? It is my own staunch Twenty-second, and I am again to command it."

CHAPTER XXXVIII

"NECESSARY SACRIFICES"

"Let us go to the altar and attend the Red Mass." So exhorted Amar, chief spokesman for the General Surety.

The Red Mass, however, seemed in some danger from that familiarity which breeds contempt. A few optimists had dreamed that the latest Festival would mark the slackening of the Terror. Instead, two days later, on the 22d Prairial, Robespierre in person laid a new decree before the Convention. Once more the thin, clear voice, unpolluted by the slightest humor: *"Every delay is a crime. Every formality is a public danger."* Therefore, ran the mandate, before the Tribunal, let the defence be denied any cross-examination or advocates; let juries convict in whole batches on "moral proofs." No more witnesses! More serious yet, even the actual members of the Convention were to be tried upon mere accusation by the Public Prosecutor, not on the vote of the entire Convention.

Even the chalky-faced deputies protested. There was debate, delay; but Robespierre put all his cold, vague influence behind the decree. It was voted. At once "the Virtuous" were delighted. Fifty, sixty eliminations per day. "Heads are falling like slates!" openly rejoiced Fouquier-Tinville.

Spies, suspicion, fear now everywhere. The theaters were hopelessly dull; the new Republican dramas were stupid preachments, the old comedies and tragedies were barred if they mentioned kings, nobles or priests, except to revile them. In the cafés people talked in whispers, yet each man dreaded his bosom friend. "He might go to his Section center and denounce me." Prior to Danton's fall, it had seemed sufficient to be able to answer confidently the test question, "What have you done to deserve death should the Royalists be restored?" But now—who *was* safe? What sublime standard of patriotism could possibly satisfy the Incorruptible and all his neophytes and catechumens?

Yet, day after day, in this torrid summer, the most important man in the Republic was to be seen walking calmly to and from the Duplay home and leading a very conventional existence. He seldom went now to the Great Committee— St. Just and Couthon delivered his behests. Even the Jacobin Club heard him less frequently. He took his usual morning walk, met his few friends, sat over his papers, drank a glass of milk, strolled out to the hairdresser, sauntered out later with Eleanor Duplay and the big dog through the Tuileries gardens.

What life more peaceful? Of course, sycophants high and low haunted the Duplay house, offering even to peel the Citizeness' potatoes—all to get a nod from the great man. This profited them very little.

Prairial faded into Messidor, and now had begun Thermidor.[1] The summer became ever more hot and sultry. As the heat increased, Robespierre's retirement increased also. It was said that the high priest was preparing some grand pronouncement against the non-Virtuous, preliminary to setting up the glorious Complete Republic.

Upon a certain peculiarly torrid afternoon, not a breath seemed stirring; the great tricolor flags trailed motionless. Only a thin crowd watched the daily tumbrils, and Spartacus Durand and his comrades sweated and swore more than

[1] Thermidor began on July 19th.

ordinarily at their task. In his room at the Duplays' the Incorruptible sat in his stiff, hard chair and on other stiff, hard chairs were now St. Just, Lebas and the sodden form of Hanriot. Couthon apparently was indisposed. The visitors were stripped to their shirts and perspiring, but their host still was clothed, well-starched and immaculate. The great pile of documents before him on his desk suggested an important discussion.

"I had hoped we could delay a little," Lebas was saying.

"No time like the present," puffed Hanriot.

"Conditions force us," completed St. Just.

"No doubt, my friends," took up Robespierre, "we have all desired to wait. Matters are not wholly ripe. I confess that many citizens of excellent sentiments do not as yet exhibit the purest virtue in their lives. We must deal gently. We must be patient. But it is as Antoine Louis says, events sweep us on. The war made the Republic possible. The sudden end of the war can make the perfect Republic impossible. Barère has sadly disappointed me. I directed him not to spread before the Convention the fact that our last victory at Fleurus has rendered it unlikely that the foreign despots can destroy the Revolution. He has defied me. He has sounded out one long paean of victory. Now the anti-patriots, the impure will say, 'What excuse for the Terror?'—What indeed, except that having destroyed our foes without, we have not yet destroyed all our foes within."

Robespierre spoke to the three precisely as he might speak to three hundred. Now, as usual, he checked his oratory and looked toward St. Just, who resumed the argument:

"Therefore, I say, my master, 'Conditions force us.' I fear the worst in another month, as the story of victory works its way among the people and the armies. To delay now is more iniquitous than cowardice; it is a betrayal of the Republic."

"I'm with you, of course I'm with you," grated Hanriot, knocking his scabbard between his knees and the chair. "All the patriot National Guardsmen are with you. What if Carnot *did* order off half of my gunners? I've plenty of smart boys still left to clear the Tuileries!—Say the word, just a little warning, and Burr-r-r!" He drew a finger across his throat.

The shadow of a sneer crossed the chiseled face of St. Just. "I wish, nevertheless, that we controlled regular troops. Probably the thing can be safely accomplished, but for all that, a military leader with battle experience (Hanriot scowled, but St. Just ignored him) would prove useful. Did I understand you, my master, to say when I entered that you were disappointed in General Massac?"

"Disappointed," Robespierre's tone was more constrained than ordinarily. "Yes, that is correct. We dismiss him from our plans.—A word to you about him later."

Hanriot might have noticed St. Just changing color just then, but Lebas was interposing:

"We come now to final action. We are resolved. It is needful immediately to prepare the list."

"Leave the list to me, to me and Fouquier-Tinville! The finest Carmagnole yet——" But Hanriot's chuckling proffer died away while his superior's green eyes fastened on him.

"I reject all levity," observed Robespierre, creasing his lips. "The vengeance of the Republic must be measured, orderly, merciful in its selection only of incorrigible offenders. We must destroy no one innocent, just as we must spare no one guilty."

He opened his desk, took thence a sheet of the blue paper,

tested a pen, selected a better one, wrote a few lines at the top of the sheet, then looked up calmly.

"With whom shall we begin? When Antony, Octavius and Lepidus founded the Roman Empire, they began by compiling a list of Republicans whom they honored with death. It is fitting that we, founding at last the pure Republic, should also prepare a proscription list of the defenders of moderatism and tyranny."

"Carnot," spoke Lebas incisively, "has been invaluable against the foreign enemy, but is becoming too clearly an opponent to the triumph of Virtue. The Republic demands an act of preventive justice."

The pen scratched, the powdered head was lifted. "What others?"

"All of our colleagues on the Great Committee," St. Just's voice was hard, even reckless; "barring our Couthon. Some are corrupt; some are merely lukewarm, but I loathe my daily contact with all of them."

"No uncharitable judgments, Antoine Louis," corrected Robespierre. "We may be severe, but never uncharitable. Nevertheless——" and the pen scratched again. Then again the powdered head was raised. The others were hot now with suggestions. "Barras; taking Toulon has made him arrogant." "Tallien; at Bordeaux he took bribes to save from the guillotine." "Fouché; his Republicanism only masks hypocrisy." Many more names, of great villains and corruptionists, of honest men who had dared to face the Incorruptible, of old friends of Hébert. or Danton. Thirty-odd leaders, evil and good, who were obstacles to the nearing Utopia.

At last the pen ceased scratching near the bottom of the sheet. The First Commissioner looked away from the table.

"There are other enemies of Virtue," suggested Lebas.

"My friend," Robespierre's voice came with thin gentleness, "I demand Terror only where Terror is necessary. Let us always err on the side of clemency." Then interrogatively, "This list then is agreed?"

All nodded silently. The blue sheet was next folded very carefully, endorsed, dated, and Robespierre merely lifted his desk cover and laid the paper inside. It might have been a memorandum about new uniforms for the infantry. Then the talk at once shifted to tasks directly ahead.—The existing Committees must be swept from power, the Convention again "purified," a dictatorship proclaimed. Robespierre would take supreme office, and St. Just replace Carnot over the armies. If the Convention hesitated to vote the proposed decrees, Hanriot would ring the tocsin, raise Paris, clear the Tuileries. The Convention had no effective guard, and the glint of the bayonets of Hanriot's militia surely would make the deputies vote anything. Their cowardice could be assumed.

"The day?"—Robespierre could give a speech of formal warning on the 8th Thermidor. St. Just could fling down the gauntlet on the 9th. Hanriot had better be ready then.

Lebas and the guard-commander presently took leave to pass on the secret word among their lower initiates. St. Just rose also when Robespierre detained him. "I must see you alone."

"What is it, my master?"

"You heard me say that General Massac has disappointed. Alas! it is far worse. Not merely has he shown himself useless to us in our plans for the Reign of Virtue, but now he has brought himself within reach of the Tribunal as a common offender."

The fine lines in St. Just's forehead contracted, and his face worked with a distress patent even to Robespierre.

"You may well be in anguish. He was recently our

friend. We trusted him; we had hopes in him; we defended him before the Convention. He has betrayed us."

"What has he done?" repeated St. Just in a tense whisper.

"First as to my own disappointment. Over a month ago I may tell you now, I gave him my confidence and he spurned it. His regrets are still for Danton and for the other impure. Of course, at once I dismissed him, telling him the glory of the completion of the Republic must belong to others."

"Why then, my master," St. Just spoke through set teeth, "is not his name upon our list?"

"Alas! Antoine Louis. This is not the worst. He has not merely dared to mourn these nefarious Indulgents. I find that he has descended to the acts of a common criminal and must suffer immediately."

"A common criminal? René Massac?"

"Hearken then. Only this morning Vernet came to me. You know what an indefatigable patriot he is, destined to a great place in our Republic. In his zeal so simple, so sincere! He has completely obliterated all the vestiges of his old sacerdotalism.—Well, he revealed to me a terrible fact. There is evidence that Massac assisted an emigré who has actually borne arms against France.—Look at these papers."

St. Just rattled over the dossiers. Had not Vernet laid these very documents upon his desk over a month ago, and had he not, upon some shadowy excuse, directed "take no action."

"Rightly you turn pale, Antoine Louis," pursued his senior. "This one-time friend of ours has put himself beyond the pale of mercy.—Considering our former relationships, it indeed was delicate of Vernet to come to me thus privately. I said that the case seemed plain, but that I would consult you. Will you now take the denunciation yourself to Fouquier-Tinville?"

The papers shook in St. Just's hand. "Yes, René Massac was my friend. I am forced to confess my presumption, my master. I have known of these accusations, but believed a certain allowance was permissible. This emigré was René's own cousin——"

The greenish eyes deepened with astonishment. "You have known and you have not denounced?"

"Yes, my master," in the barest whisper.

The Incorruptible's little form heightened, as his thin voice came sternly. "When before has the purest of my friends sunk before necessary sacrifices? What is friendship before the absolute Virtue demanded for the nobler Republic?"

St. Just sat bowed in silence, his hands twisting and untwisting, but Robespierre extended his own hand. "Pass back the paper," he commanded in a tone of ice. "My most trusted associate has lapsed. I give him now the chance to undo his error. The case being as it is, we dare not refrain from the most sweeping justice. By these reports Virginie Massac must also have had guilty knowledge that her husband assisted an emigré enemy."—The pen went again to the inkstand, then wrote a sentence on the principal document. Robespierre sanded this carefully, then returned the papers to St. Just without the slightest comment. Next he rose stiffly, and sought his hat, remarking, "Couthon is not well. I must go and see him about many things."

St. Just, with a face of marble, walked with him out into Rue Honoré, where the two parted silently. Instantly the younger man devoured the new indorsement: *It being evident that the Citizeness Virginie Massac must have been cognizant of her husband's crime, she should be included in the denunciation.* MAXIMILIEN ROBESPIERRE."

The writing (St. Just realized) could not be erased without mutilating the entire paper. He did not turn toward the Palais de Justice and the prosecutor's office. Instead he wandered in a daze until suddenly he came to himself standing on the Pont de la Revolution, west of the Tuileries. The warm wavelets in the Seine were glancing upwards toward the relentless sun, and the heat was driving all strollers into the shadows, but St. Just knew that he was leaning on the parapet regardless of the sweltering rays. Suddenly, without conscious impulse, his hands reached out mechanically, then released something. Had any stranger been near he would have heard a repressed cry from a man astonished at his own action.—A crumpled white object was drifting away in the mid-current of the Seine. It was the dossier from Vernet.

. . . At length, as he walked from the bridge toward the Tuileries, St. Just realized that persons were gazing at his well-known figure and that some few were saluting him. By a great effort of will, the Commissioner pulled himself together and returned the greetings perfunctorily. "At least," the thought raced through his head, "this madness has gained me twenty-four hours. Well," he then added to himself, "what must be, must. Where is the alternative?" Thus he regained his bureau in the Tuileries.

Thanks to his position, he had, as already stated, his own detachment of agents and secret emissaries. For one of the most reckless and personally devoted of these, a certain Laclos, he now sent, and was closeted with the fellow for some time.

Ten minutes after Robespierre quitted his room, it was entered by Virginie Massac herself.

For over a month now she had known that both she and

her husband were in extreme danger. After Laurent's revelations of the overheard plot against the Massacs, Olympie had speedily wormed certain additional items out of her unsuspecting consort, and needless to say, she had gone straight to Virginie. But Virginie had not told René. The latter, she knew, was under extreme tension, and she feared that any new revelation might lead to some tragic deed of desperation. So she had borne Olympie's report and the dark warnings of St. Just in her own breast, and in silence had used her woman's wits to find some way of safety.

To-day, however, she had come to the Duplays' on a reckless, but not, she tried to tell herself, a hopeless errand. Of course she was unaware that Vernet, suspicious and at last angered by the unwonted faltering of St. Just, had finally carried the case against René straight to the Incorruptible, and her visit now rose from the fact that Olympie had picked up a firm rumor that Father François was likely to be sent to the Tribunal, Robespierre having somehow weakened in his protection.

Virginie had not dared to pass this report on to her husband, and she had screwed herself to a bold resolution. Robespierre for long had been her guest. To-day she abhorred the name of him, but there had been no personal breach, and René had never informed her of his rejected proffer of the First Commissioner's advances. Virginie thought that she understood Robespierre's weak side. She would stifle her antipathy, visit him privately, and make an appeal in behalf of Father François. At worst it could probably do no harm save to her own pride. At best, it might save a life dear and precious. So she had taken her parasol and unattended sought the Duplays'.

The sans-culotte guard had sauntered away from the house, following the First Commissioner at a protecting distance and blowing and cursing that the great patriot should choose such a time for a walk, but Eleanor Duplay still kept her watch in the courtyard. Virginie knew this pale, plain girl slightly; "Mademoiselle Shavings," Danton once had sarcastically called her. She scrutinized Virginie severely, for only a month earlier a Cecile Renault had called at the house, asked for Robespierre, acted suspiciously, had been seized, searched, discovered carrying two knives, and then had been promptly guillotined. But Citizeness Massac was recognized by Eleanor, and in the latter's belief the Massacs were still on fairly friendly terms with the Incorruptible.

The two women, therefore, conversed amiably:

"I should be glad to see the Citizen Commissioner."

"The Citizen Commissioner has gone out, Citizeness."

"For how long? The matter is important."

"To Citizen Couthon's lodgings, I think. He may return soon. He may be gone two hours."

"Permit me, good Citizeness Eleanor, to wait. See him I must, and it is better to wait than come a second time in the heat."

Eleanor Duplay made no great difficulties. It was usual enough for persons to wait patiently, even for a very short interview with Robespierre. His bureau at the Tuileries was the usual place, with a competent gendarme in the corridor, but Republican informality forbade that he should make himself too inaccessible. However, Eleanor felt required to watch the entrance to the court, and did not care just then for her visitor's company.

"You had better wait then in Citizen Robespierre's room at the head of the stairs, Citizeness Massac."

Virginie mounted. She had heard of Robespierre's room and was not surprised at its simplicity. The windows were open; blue-bottle flies were buzzing in and out of the little plants set on the casements. A clock wedged between two piles of books upon the shelves, ticked off the seconds of eternity. From the court below came the drone of voices; one of Duplay's workmen had knocked off work, thanks to the heat, and was chattering idly with Eleanor. The big brown dog sauntered up into the room, knocking the chairs and table with his tail. At sight of the seated woman he gave a low growl, but Virginie remained perfectly quiet, and after two sniffs he decided that she was harmless and retired peacefully.

The stiffly appointed room, the well-worn carpet, the books in frayed bindings, the solemn ticking of the clock all at first had a soporific effect. Could this indeed be the habitat of the man who (Virginie knew it well) was to be written down in history with Phalaris, Nero, Alva? Was it possible that death could be scattered broadcast by the user of that narrow bed, those uncushioned chairs, those well-thumbed volumes? Was not the thing grossly unreal, impossible?—Yet here she sat waiting an interview concerning life and death! And as she looked on those hard, austere objects, so fitting with their owner's life, it came over her with disheartening force that her appeal would be useless. One might turn the heart of a dragon; but who could wring mercy from granite?

Yet the occupant of the room came not; the blue-bottles still buzzed; the dog gave low barks now in the courtyard, while Eleanor and the workman condoled with the animal about his thick fur and the oppressive heat. Doubtless, despite her care, Virginie nodded. At least her thoughts drifted confusedly across many things; she saw cool meadows, running water, then of a sudden she was back in the room again, and some voice was speaking close to her ears.

Eleanor was not present, nor anyone else, yet Virginie

heard perfectly clearly, *"There."*—And Virginie knew that
she was sitting bolt upright; that her eyes were wide open;
that she was gazing straight across the room upon the writing desk.

Nothing about the desk to startle; a plain, sloping sur-
face of wood upon four solid legs, the paint considerably
worn, upon its top a dirty leaden inkstand and a sand
holder bristling with quill pens. But Virginie knew that
she was gazing upon that desk cover as the fabled victim
upon the charming snake.

Why did René's answer to her question come ringing back
to her? *"The Terror will end when the men who now crawl
before Robespierre for safety, know that only boldness can
save their heads."* What connection between these words
and the mute, unmoving fabric of the wood?

"Yes," the dull tones of Eleanor Duplay rose through
the casement, "Mother says that he eats too little these
days; partly it's the heat, but partly his great plans for
the Republic. She says that he dotes upon oranges. Hard
to get now, but we will find some."

Virginie's eyes were searching that desk cover inch by
inch—every crack, chip in the paint, inkspot. "Locked?"
No, a thin pamphlet was protruding beneath the cover.—
*"But he must keep all his public papers in his guarded
bureau at the Tuileries, not here?"* Was Virginie saying
all this in her own breast, or did some one speak beside
her? The room was perfectly empty.

*"When men know that only boldness can save their
heads."* But the room was still empty.

"Such an opportunity can never come again." But the
room was still empty.

"Robespierre can return any instant. Then too late."
But the room was still empty.

"You have never stolen a sou in all your life, neverthe-

less, for the sake of France DARE." But the room was still empty.

Virginie arose without a sound. Hands and feet worked silently, dexterously as if independent of brain. What she could actually find under that cover she had not the least intimation. To rifle a desk, to go through papers was beyond all her conscious reasoning. As if witnessing the act of some stranger, she knew presently that a woman looking like herself was lifting the desk cover, was examining the neat piles of pamphlets, and the packets of letters tied with red string. She saw the blue sheets of compactly arranged notes, doubtless for a prepared speech, but lying above these still another blue sheet folded, but not yet filed away.

The clear, small script on the outside seemed to Virginie to be burning her eyes as she glanced on it.

Thus ran the memorandum: "NECESSARY SACRIFICES FOR THE WEAL OF THE REPUBLIC. THERMIDOR 7TH."—Quite as involuntary as her other acts was the opening of the paper. It rattled slightly, her heart jumped, but she went on opening. There, in a handwriting unmistakable, spread out a list—thirty names—all of them great in France.

"When men know that only boldness can save their heads." But the room was still empty.

. . . The desk shut noiselessly. Nothing within was disturbed save that the folded paper was no longer there. Perfectly mechanically, Virginie took up her parasol and sought the door. She descended to the court and was greeted perfunctorily by Eleanor Duplay.

"So you'll wait no longer, Citizeness Massac."

"No. I fear that he will not come."

"You are probably wise. Often he goes direct to the Tuileries and remains all night."

The streets were still very empty, thanks to the heat. No

one noticed Virginie except that in a sans-culotte patrol one fellow turned to remark, "Devilishly pretty titmouse, but why in such a hurry?" Suddenly, then, she knew that she was almost running, and dropped to a safer pace.

She had sacrificed Father François.—But had she? What possible chance could her appeal have had with the Incorruptible? What joy to the gentle lecturer could he know that she had dared this thing for France.

As she neared Rue de la Démocratie, her hands went to her bosom. The blue paper was safely folded away.

CHAPTER XXXIX

NEARER THE UTOPIA

LAURENT'S wound at last was healed. His hiding on Rue Paul had not been violated;[1] Olympie had taken her assignats and Spartacus had remained in studied ignorance of how she came to have them. He had not even raged excessively when all of a sudden his consort put him through such searching questions, that all he knew about Linio, Vernet, and the new plot against the Massacs was soon squeezed out of him. He was really relieved. "His oath?" —How was *he* to blame if some bird apparently had told her what to ask him?

"Lump," Olympie informed him promptly, "so you put your mark on that paper? You'll not touch enough Massac property now to buy one lettuce leaf."

"You're fiendishly right," had been his affectionate answer, "but how could I help it?"

For a long time, however, things were calm. Olympie told Virginie, and Virginie commanded, "Not a syllable to René." The latter continued at the Convention and the War bureau. The Twenty-second demi-brigade had been recruited to full numbers and would soon now be in Paris; then René would make a desperate effort to get himself sent back with it again to the front—"unless something happened."

[1] He was by no means the only Royalist fugitive who was concealed successfully in Paris through the entire Terror, in exactly this manner.

"Something" was certainly in the air. "Something," however, could scarcely be greater work for La Guillotine. Fouquier was already sending up his daily quota of forty to sixty, selected almost at random from the seven thousand suspects in the prisons of Paris. "Depraving public morals" had now become the standard charge; it saved so much clerical labor for his overworked clerks. The only important thing was an imposing daily list.

Thermidor, as it advanced, was genuinely vindicating its name. "When had there ever been so hot a summer!" Shriveled leaves, parching dust clouds, even the current of the Seine seemed to be shrinking.

Now that Laurent's strength was returned, he resumed his flirting with destruction: for hours he would range the streets by night. Olympie had procured for him (or rather assignats to an easy Section president had procured) a proper "card of citizenship," and the nocturnal patrols at length gathered that he was some kind of a government clerk at the Tuileries, obliged to do night work. At rare and safe intervals he met René.

"A few more days," was at length the General's quiet promise, "and we will smuggle you out of Paris."

"I confess to a hankering for daylight promenades," admitted the refugee, "but I'm coming somewhat to enjoy your night life. It's like watching from the grand terrace at Versailles before they started the fireworks. The latter seem about to go off."

"How can you learn anything?"

"Partly from overhearing my courtly host Spartacus' genteel remarks; partly from dropping in at various cafés that keep open all night.—Your dear Incorruptible apparently wanes in his popularity."

"Would to God that I could believe it."

"You can believe it now all right. 'Virtue' and the tumbrils clearly cease to amuse. Your Republicanism is, of course, a game; and the best of games in time gets stupid."

René made no answer. Like every conspicuous man in Paris, he was steeling himself for the worst. They had all become fatalists. To take one day at a time; to say at each sundown, *"Thus far I have lived"*—that seemed the only formula. Every knock at his door might mean the sansculottes with their warrant. At night, when his arms clasped about Virginie, it was always to think, "Our love has been pure. Our life together has been of heaven. Nothing, nothing can take this eternal fact away—though death come to-morrow."

But the life of Spartacus Durand was not of heaven, although old cronies still bowed down to him, pert women ogled him, and boys ran far to escort "the patriot hero." Why no move against Massac? What of Linio, or of Vernet? How were they practicing?—Also a curious atmosphere was actually creeping into patriotic meetings. Spells of silence; fewer cheers for the Incorruptible. And at the Red Mass no longer frantic applause, but even a loud pity, especially if the "sacrifice" happened to be a young girl, or somebody old and feeble. The executioner even sensed that he was growing slightly unpopular.

All this troubled Spartacus not a little. Was it not the gift of every successful gamester to know the right instant for dropping the cards, and bagging his winnings? Was not this the instant? At length, on the afternoon of 8th Thermidor, he said as much to Olympie, after returning from his daily toil:

"Wish we were back in Ard. Our money could open a fine wine shop."

"What will Sanson do without you?"

"The devil can help him. I need a holiday."

"A holiday?" chuckled Olympie. "What, is La Guillotine herself weary?"

"The trade's a good one, but I've enough of it. I want La Guillotine to stop before—well——"

"Well what, you zany?"

"Before she kisses me herself. One can't help thinking."

"Thibaud Durand;" Olympie seldom said "Spartacus"; "Don't you *dare* to think. In these days it's perilous."

She fanned herself furiously with a tattered hat. Spartacus was making suggestive glances toward the supper table, when a rapid step came clattering up the stair; then the door was flung open without rap or warning. Linio himself whipped into the room, and one glance revealed his disordered state. His smart clothes were in disarray; he was pale and panting; more marvelous still, he was hatless and had lost that red wig which had been his mark in Paris since taking his last alias as Puget. Host and hostess surveyed him with silent wonderment. The visitor closed and barred the door in a twinkling, dashed to the casement, shot one glance down into the street, seemed momentarily reassured; next he mopped the great drops from his brow.

"*Bon Dieu,*" came between his gasps, "but that was an escape!"

Spartacus and Olympie still gazed on him transfixed, then the woman spoke first: "Pick up your wits, you rabbit. What's chasing you?"

Linio seized the water pitcher at hand, raised it directly to his lips and took an enormous pull.

"Vernet!" he spit out at last. "He almost had me. I am sold. You are sold. How can we all get away?"

"Put your brains back in the basket, man," commanded Olympie, while her spouse whitened and gibbered. "You'll surely rot unless you can speak six plain words."

Linio had recovered breath and a certain calmness. He

subsided into a chair and spoke connectedly: "Hot as hell, and I had to run for it! Lucky that the heat kept the streets well emptied and that I knew all the back lanes.— I was at the Louvre. For days I had been doing filthy work for Vernet. Some big plot's afoot. He's been setting spies on all his colleagues and even on the Great Committee. I'd been ordered to watch Carnot. Out of his bureau I saw coming Massac. That put me to thinking: 'Why was Massac still at large? Why wasn't our fine plot progressing?' I went over to the Louvre to report to Vernet; after I'd told him the little I'd picked up about the War Commissioner, I thought it was a good time for a few words on a more private matter. So I edged up to his desk. 'Citizen Commissioner, just a civil question?' 'Ah! my dear friend, always at your service'; you know how he rubs and smooths, and his voice was like a honey jug."

" 'Citizen Commissioner,' I said, 'how do we stand about Massac? Why is he still at liberty?' "

" 'Citizen Puget,' he said, 'at last we are making progress.' He held up a paper; it read *Indictment of the ci-devant priest Paul François.* 'This goes to the Tribunal to-morrow. The Incorruptible withdraws his protection.' "

" 'Very good,' said I, 'but he's mighty thin soup beside what we're really cooking. What's to happen to Massac?'

"Vernet smiled in that way that always makes your bile rise. He seemed to hesitate, then made his hands go something like a priest's administering holy unction. 'Well, my friend,' at length, 'I believe it can do no harm now to tell you. Massac ought to have been arrested yesterday; but in fact he is to be seized at his home to-night.'

"His smile, his hands, everything made me bristle. 'Fine news indeed,' cried I, 'but why do I have to wing this out of you so slowly. Is this the treatment for an old comrade? Damme, if I always trust your game.'

"And still he smiled, and suddenly I thought of a cat looking straight at a fine fat sparrow, but I stood my ground, and he began again, with more honey than ever: 'Perhaps I betray a private confidence, but to-day I could laugh even at our incomparable patriot St. Just. It was just as I surmised; outwardly all ice, inwardly like any of the rest of us, the victim of the tender passion. What happened? Why, getting weary of further delay in the Massac business, I went straight to the Incorruptible. "But I gave St. Just the denunciation," spoke he, "and added the name of Citizeness Massac. She was plainly implicated. Have they not both been arrested?" "Not in the least, Citizen Robespierre," said I, and back then I went to St. Just.— What embarrassment, what distress on his part! As a man of delicacy, I forbore to press him. "He had lost the papers." "No matter," said I, "we will draft a new set immediately. You can sign them along with Robespierre and Couthon." I could see him hesitate, but I stood over him while they were rewritten and he put down his name. Then I took them to Couthon and Robespierre—three members of the Great Committee, since a deputy must be arrested. *Ma foi!* but St. Just was white and trembling. Evidently a liaison, and what a pity that our pretty Citizeness is implicated! But official duty is duty. I've kept the service of the papers for my own men. They will be at the Massac home to-night, when the General comes home, away from the protection of the Tuileries. And that, my friend (quoth Vernet) is the whole of that story.' "

"Bah!" interpolated Spartacus. "I don't see but what all's coming right at last.—But what came next?"

Linio took another glance from the window, seemed reassured, and resumed:

"As I was leaving the Louvre, Vernet shook my hand with unwonted cordiality. 'My good confrère,' spoke he, smiling from ear to ear, 'perhaps, as the world must change, we near the end of our association together. I hope you have enjoyed our intimacy. After all, even my detractors must render me a certain homage. I have been favored with the confidence of the late King and Queen. If they had prevailed, I might even have expected a cardinalate. Now, however, I may humbly claim a certain partnership with the Incorruptible himself. If the Republic is reorganized tomorrow, barring Robespierre and possibly, for the moment, St. Just, what influence will exceed that of your humble servant?' And he bowed me out with his hand on his breast."

"Get ahead!" ordered Spartacus. "I don't follow all this fine rigmarole."

"'What's the fellow up to?' wondered I. 'I'd better watch for something funny.' Then in the doorway of the guardroom of the Louvre I saw my old crony, Sergeant Girardin, and thought I'd make an inquiry. 'Have you got a warrant for the Massacs yet?' I asked. He smiled, showing all his big white teeth. 'Here's the order for those top-lofty ci-devants,' said he, 'but I'm glad to see you at present about another trifle.' Then he laid out a second paper, adding 'Devilishly kind of you, Citizen Linio, to drop in now. Saves a lot of trouble this hot day.'

"As he said 'Linio' and not 'Puget,' I felt my flesh creep. I glanced at the paper: *'Order for the arrest of the Ci-devant Baron Eugene de Linio, alias Puget. Crime—entering Paris under a false name and concealing his former nobility, contrary to Law 983, Nivose 17, Year II of the Republic. Accuser,* ETIENNE VERNET.' 'So you see,' went on Girardin, sidling toward the door, 'with infinite regret, I'll have to conduct you very gently and politely to the Conciergerie, for you read the note: *'For Citizen-Prose-cutor Fouquier-Tinville immediately.'* "

Spartacus leaped from his chair, blind fear possessing him. "Why in hell's name are you here then? Off! Off!"

"Sit down, pig!" ordered Olympie, her jaw squaring steadily; "hear him out, if you'd have a chance left."

"I confess that I am," continued Linio, with a melancholy complacency, "a man of some presence of mind. I saw everything. Vernet had first induced you, my good fellow, to put your cross on that paper. It was not quite explained to you that it formally assigned to him all interest which you might enjoy in the control of the property of the unfortunate Massacs. Then he had worked on Robespierre to include your niece with her husband in the accusation. That simplified any claims. Finally, he would dispose of me—the companion who might ask an unwelcome share.—I comprehended the entire case. What a masterpiece of the Devil's own villainy! I retained, nevertheless, my presence of mind. I glanced about me, although pretending to read the warrant with care. Girardin was alone in the guardroom, although two gendarmes lolled on the bench just outside. At last he began to rattle his scabbard. 'You'd not arrest an old comrade,' I began. 'Duty's duty,' answered he, and was about to snap his fingers for the gendarmes, when, with a dart, I seized the light stool before us and flung it fairly at his head. He toppled in a heap with barely a cry, and I shot past and was out into the alley, while the two sansculottes ran inside to ask about the crash. Girardin must have been well stunned, and taken a minute to come to and order 'After him.' I made Rue Honoré, and was just across it when I heard a running and shouting coming down the alley."

Linio paused to mop his face once again, regained his breath, and concluded: "If the streets had been crowded and the hue and cry caught up promptly, I'd have been lost. Thanks to the heat, very few saw me, still the scoundrels chased me from street to street. They pressed hard, but they weren't like me—running for their skins. My lodgings, my regular places, of course, they'd search immediately, but how could they think of the apartment of that incomparable patriot Spartacus Durand? I doubled twice. I shook off pursuit. I came hither. *Voilà!*"

Again Linio seized the water jug and this time drained it, but once more Durand bounced to his feet. "Off! Off!" he kept commanding thickly. "Do you want to murder us all? What if you were found in my house?"

The fugitive regarded him patronizingly. "Why then, of course, you'd be guillotined along with your humble servant. So you'd better take the best pains to conceal me."

"It's every man for himself these days," mouthed Spartacus. "Friendship can't count. Go—or I'll call for help from the window."

Linio flung one leg over the other, and rested back in his chair, once more wiping his face. "Oh, nothing of the kind! If I'm seized, be sure I'll have quite enough to say about *you*. You're none too popular, my man. Plenty have come to envy your airs and your prosperity. Sanson's best hand taken!——" He doubled at the jest.

"Quit my house, will you?" ordered the executioner, getting ever more desperate.

"My worthy *Thibaud*," observed the intruder never stirring, "I always said you were no ordinary fool but pray to observe—these rooms are comfortable, they are safe, and in them I stay."

"By God you shall not!" Spartacus was ashen now. He looked appealingly toward Olympie but she only sat silent, her strong hands folded, her face lined mysteriously. Driven to bay her consort began moving toward a heavy iron bar resting in one corner.

"Yes, M. le Baron, Citizen Spartacus is right; only he also shall test out the fleas in the Conciergerie."—A pleasant voice with a touch of bravado. Laurent de Massac had emerged noiselessly from behind his door panel, unobserved by the two men as they glared and threatened. He was still pale from his long confinement, but he stood erect, alert and smiling. He was dressed like a perfect sansculotte,—red cap, baggy trousers, tricolor sash, short hair, heavy mustache. In each hand he held a pistol, and in his sash slung a naked rapier.

Whilst the three gazed petrified, Laurent calmly swung himself to a position across the exit yet near to the open window, then he spoke again: "Your conversation is interesting, Citizens, but threatens to become acrimonious. The Citizeness must be sadly disturbed (with a devil-may-care smirk toward Olympie.) Pray now remain quietly while I invite in your acquaintances."

Linio's hands reached vainly toward an empty pocket. Durand mustered leg power enough for a step nearer the iron bar.

"Spare me trouble, Citizens"; Laurent's tone was almost rollicking in its abandon. "If you interfere the results to both of you may be slightly disagreeable."

"Massac! That other Massac, the emigré, the outlaw." Linio at last found tongue; looking from Spartacus to Laurent, from Laurent to Spartacus, and wondering which one to fear the most.

"Laurent, Vicomte de Massac at your own M. le Baron's humble service. I know I'm taking the chance of bidding this topsy-turvy world farewell, but in René's behalf I'll not deny myself this fling of adventure.—Good! The presses are still clanging in the printing office—many people will hear me. So then!"—He fired a pistol through the open window.

"We're lost!" screamed Linio, rushing in frenzy toward the door, to be stopped short by the Viscount's rapier point straight against his breast.

The printing press beyond the partitions ceased clanging; voices were soon rising below in the street.

"Heard us already!" Laurent jauntily twirled the rapier, while his left hand drew a second pistol. "Only a moment more." And he called aloud "Help! Help! in the name of the law!"

Linio turned upon the quivering Spartacus: "At him, you rabbit! It's now his life or ours!" And he seized the heavy poker.

The gambler and the executioner leaped forward together, each brandishing a clumsy weapon. Laurent deliberately fired the second pistol into the street, and tossed the smoking weapon through the window. His own thin blade flashed about in lightnings. His attackers' ponderous blows beat the empty air or crashed upon the paneling. In a twinkling Spartacus dropped his bar with a howl and his right arm hung helpless, the blood gushing out upon his shoulder; whereupon Linio ran back into the room in abject terror. The Viscount calmly put his left hand behind his back and faced the demoralized pair, making passes at them with his sword point.

"No," he harangued them, "on the whole I prefer not to kill you. Death by the rapier is only intended for gentlemen.—Yet to be a good fencer has sometimes marked advantages.—Ah! at last—footsteps on the stair. Many voices.—*Help in the name of the law, Citizens!*—" His own voice went out like a trumpet: "Help in the name of the Great Committee.—I'm flinging back the bolts for you. —Seize the miscreants. Summon the patrol.——Hei, you fellow just entering, you seem to be a Guards' corporal. Put that ci-devant and his accomplice here under guard.

The patrol is chasing them with a warrant.—I am Jean Debray, emissary of the Great Committee.—My credentials if you demand them, but first seize these men."

Laurent's ease and swagger were inimitable. Printers, idlers, tipplers from the nearest wine shop, a shoemaker and his prentices, all had heard the shots, the outcries, and had come piling up the narrow staircase and into the little living room. Women below were rushing from their houses and screaming. Two dogs were barking as if to save their lives. Through all this came the clatter of a sans-culotte patrol. Laurent, the only self-possesed man in the twenty present, leaned from the casement:

"Ho there, sergeant! If you're seeking that ci-devant Linio or Puget, here he is. I've just arrested him myself."

"Patriot's work, Citizen," called back the sergeant; "we're up in a trice. We've searched every street."

The patrol forced its way up through the gesticulating press and banged into the living room. Spartacus, his fine coat turning red, was writhing in the clutches of two men. Linio, unhurt, was held by three others. The sergeant identified the ex-baron with one hawk-like glance; "Our meat all right! Pinion him snugly.—We're grateful to you, Citizen—Debray, did you say?—But who's this other prisoner?"

"Why they've seized Citizen Durand, the great patriot, Sanson's helper. Some mistake—" began a saucer-eyed woman.

"Yes, yes, Citizens," howled Spartacus; "I'm innocent. Seize that fellow;—emigré, refugee, outlaw!"

"Sergeant," interposed Laurent as coolly as he might have led a minuet; "this ci-devant nobleman here naturally fled to his confederate Durand for refuge. They share in the same crimes. I was on the investigation for the Great Committee. They are equally criminal."

"Yes, yes," swore Linio beside himself, "he knew everything. He can't deny me now. It's both or neither of us."

"Liar—I'm betrayed, slaughtered. Patriots, help!" exploded the executioner; to be met with "Hear the bloody wretch!" from one of the now tittering women.

Laurent slowly dusted his coat, rearranged his sash and reslung his sword. "Remove these malefactors, sergeant," he ordered. "Tell the Prosecutor that I will, if possible, come to the Palais de Justice to swear personally to the denunciation of this Spartacus Durand. I must, however, first report my success to the Tuileries. You are witness in any case, that Durand's accomplice has already implicated him. Such evidence always is more than sufficient for the Tribunal."

The sergeant saluted. So magnificent and commanding an agent of the Great Committee could only speak directly for the Incorruptible. The only thing to do was to obey implicitly. "And this woman, Citizen Emissary?" the officer's thumb jerked toward the utterly bewildered Olympie; "do we take her along also?"

"For reasons not wise here to divulge," Laurent's tone matched that of a state minister, "I request you to overlook her. Have the goodness to let me confer with her apart, before I am compelled to go to the Tuileries."

The prisoners were dragged away, the air ringing with their protests, curses and threats against one another. Men from the wine shop shook their fists at Spartacus: "Ei, ho! fat butcher—you'll make fine sausages."

Rue Paul after that lapsed into a sultry quiet. Only a boy, at length peeking from behind a rubbish heap, saw Citizeness Olympie walking very rapidly in one direction, and then "Citizen Emissary Debray" walking also rapidly but with complete self-possession in another.

Five o'clock, 8th Thermidor. René Massac was quitting the Convention to go to the War bureau in the opposite end of the Tuileries. Robespierre had just delivered a long speech, carefully prepared in the Incorruptible's most characteristic style. Vague threats and insinuations in every sentence, specific accusations very few. Soaring apostrophes to Virtue; scathing denunciations of Vice.—The needful step? To punish the traitors, to purify the Convention, and even the Great Committee and "to raise on the ruin of faction the power of Justice and Liberty."

Dead silence when Robespierre ended. Couthon at length moved that the speech be printed. Motion accepted without murmur; then a sudden boldness among the deputies. Answering voices from the tribune; "Whom was Robespierre accusing? Let him name the traitors." A demand which met with fatuous refusal, making every deputy who *might* have been named, ready to feel of his head to make sure that it was still on his shoulders. Then adjournment, while nerves were high strung, and after the Convention had deliberately rescinded its vote of "printing."

Such a rebuff had not been for the First Commissioner since the early days of the Terror. A great buzzing while the deputies dispersed. What was about to happen? Robespierre walked out surrounded by St. Just, Lebas and others of the Faithful, evidently bound for the Jacobin Club, there to repeat his oration before a more congenial audience. In the foyer he came face to face with René Massac. The greenish eyes behind the blue spectacles regarded the younger man with barely a glint of recognition. St. Just nodded slightly, then the group passed on. Massac with an outward composure which he did not feel, had walked slowly toward the great offices of Carnot, when a man with the sash of a sans-culotte emissary stepped suddenly from behind a pillar:

"A word, General."

All the color left René's face. Half conscious of what the other was doing, he let himself be led into a secluded alcove.

"Laurent," at last he could say, "are you weary of life?"

"Not so fond of it, dearest of cousins, that I'm not in a mood to risk it a bit, this time in order perhaps to do you a service.—Hark!"

And his tongue went swiftly, ending, "You know that the plans were all ready that to-morrow I was to flee France. I have considered. The plans can be hastened. They will not expect to catch you at your house before dark. You've two hours—perhaps three. Your own papers are ready. Get a coach. Drive to your home instantly. We can all fly together—Virginie, Henriette, you and I. Three days and we are all safe in England." Laurent's grip on his cousin's arm tightened.

René put him aside very gently: "Bravest fellow, you can call me a fool, but England is not France. I have no more right to flee from Robespierre's sans-culottes than I had to flee from the Austrian cannon.—Listen. To-morrow is the crisis. The cowards among us deputies have suddenly become courageous; never mind why. Either France is at once rid of the Terror, or I have no wish to survive this pollution of my country.—The Twenty-second demi-brigade encamped this morning at the Invalides. I think I know the way by which lawfully I can defy arrest until to-morrow."

"And Virginie?"

The soldier's head bowed but he did not falter: "Virginie too belongs to France. She had just shown courage beyond any of mine. How can I sacrifice my duty by going now for her at Rue de la Démocratie? You said that Olympie had started to warn her. Dare you risk the streets again, and take her a message yourself? Yes?—Come then to my own bureau, and wait until I rejoin you."

Leaving his cousin, René strode straight to the inner office of the War Commissioner himself. Carnot was bending over a map of Flanders, shifting the pins that marked the opposing armies. At sight of his favorite aide he smiled his firm military smile, and gestured affably while the officer saluted:

"Citizen Commissioner, I am informed that you are about to lose my services."

"Parbleu—how is that?"

Concisely, unemotionally, Massac repeated the substance of what had just been told him withholding merely his informant's name. As he spoke the strong lines on the ugly face before him deepened, then suddenly the pen dipped, traced over the paper, and the hard efficient voice sounded again:

"General Massac, whether by to-morrow night I am still War Commissioner or guillotined ask of the Devil. Till then I determine the fate of my officers. From this instant your orders are these: *'Ride immediately to the Twenty-second demi-brigade. Resume command. Put the whole force in readiness, and to-morrow bring up two companies to protect the Tuileries. And whosoever, whether sans-culotte gendarmes or Hanriot himself, seeks to arrest you, clap him in double irons.'*"

CHAPTER XL

"A BAS LE TYRAN!"

SIX A. M., 9th Thermidor; July 27th, 1794.

Still the relentless heat. The evening before the Incorruptible had repeated, in the more congenial atmosphere of the Jacobin Club, that speech which had been received so dubiously by the Convention. By his second audience he was wildly applauded. When he exclaimed theatrically while denouncing his enemies, "If I must drink hemlock I will drink it!" admiring voices called back "We will drink it with you!"—He returned home after a great ovation.

Very early on the following morning Robespierre had arisen and dressed with all his wonted fastidiousness, putting on the famous light blue coat that had graced the Festival of the Supreme Being. The honest Duplays, conscious that something was in the air, were all up before him, and shared his simple breakfast. After that he walked out with the devoted Eleanor into the garden of the Tuileries. His talk was gentle. Later Eleanor could recall that he made snatches at swarms of flying midges and laughed (as much as he ever laughed) when the insects eluded him.

Workmen and clerks were passing through the gardens on their way to their tasks. At sight of the light blue coat and of the big sans-culotte guard with his club trailing respectfully behind, they would make way on the paths, shrinking almost timorously, but sometimes their talk could be overheard: "Capital joke! One of Sanson's best hands got caught protecting a ci-devant. Goes to the Tribunal this morning. So the barber gets shaved himself—eh?"

Presently companions joined Robespierre, and Eleanor, (who never intruded in political talk) carefully dropped back beside the guard. St. Just appeared the first. If the master was immaculate, not so the pupil. Even Robespierre looked twice at the disorder of his dress, his pallor, his haggard appearance.

"You have slept little, Antoine Louis?"

"How could I sleep, my master? All night long I worked on the speech which I am to give to-day in the Convention, setting forth our final project. But our colleagues on the Great Committee have become suspicious. Collot says that we insulted him at the Jacobins last night. Billaud is equally furious. Carnot actually sustains them. They may try to defend themselves and make us trouble.—We must silence them."

"Do not fear, Antoine Louis. All the Virtuous will be on our side. It is natural for Vice and impure Republicanism to seek protection.—But tell me this; did I not put that list of enemies of Virtue back into my desk after I completed it?"

"I think you did, my master."

"I surely mislaid it. I can find it nowhere."

St. Just smiled like a beautiful demon: "How does it matter? *I* remember every name."

They had reached the end of the gardens and were turning back toward the Duplays. Down one of the walks now lumbered the burly form of Hanriot, who vouchsafed an uncouth military salute. His breath reeked with brandy, his eyes were unsteady, and his scabbard was banging against his legs. An orderly was holding a horse for him just outside the gates.

"All's prepared, Citizen Commissioner, up our way,"

came his thick speech. "Damme, if the spirit of our sans-culotte boys was ever better. Coffinhal has stirred up the faubourgs, Payan has convened the city council and given a rousing speech while I was getting out my National Guards. We'll hold the Hôtel de Ville in force, and send out my gunners on all the bridges and into the Place du Carrousel. Let those deputies (his epithets were sulphurous) dare to cough and spit once after you talk to 'em, just speak the word to me——"

"Peaceful measures will suffice, General," Robespierre in mild voice deprecated. "Merely the *suggestion* of force is enough: hesitation will disappear instantly."

"Paris speaks for France," completed St. Just, more emotionally. "The deputies are the servants of the Republic. Every insurrection by Paris has succeeded; the Bastille, the March to Versailles, the Tenth of August, the attack on the Girondists—all of them succeeded. Resistance to Paris is insanity."

"Humph!" belched Hanriot, "there's some maniacs left in the Tuileries for all that. Know what happened with Massac?"

"What?" from Robespierre and St. Just alike, but from St. Just the first.

"Of course you both, and then Couthon, signed the warrant. I sent a strong patrol to Massac's house last night. 'The General is at the Invalides,' whimpered the servants. To the Invalides then. Of all treasonable defiance—the officer who met my patrol clapped every man of them in the guard house! 'Carnot's orders. No interference with the regular army.' My men are locked up still, and I can only get 'em out after a battle. That's some slight 'insanity'—eh?"

Robespierre grew redder, St. Just whiter. The former's hands twitched slightly but he merely said, "Massac is unimportant beside Carnot. If he comes to the Convention to-day, seize him before he enters the Tuileries." Next adding, "Citizeness Massac of course is now in the Conciergerie."

"Entrails of Satan—no!" Hanriot's snort was hideous. "Our patrol couldn't find her. 'Another patrol came and arrested her over an hour before'; that's what was shaken out of her servants. Arrested by whom? By none of my men. She's in none of the prisons. Curse me, if it isn't some aristo trick!"

"We must probe this," remarked Robespierre, biting his lip but not remarking that St. Just was saying never a word. "These, Citizen General, are the last subterfuges of the Impure faction. Trifles at this stage must not disconcert us. To-morrow the rescued Republic will reward your zeal."

Hanriot nodded with his big plumed hat, and swaggered away, puffing and swearing at his orderly while he mounted. The First Commissioner turned back to St. Just, but that terrible youth was already striding off with passionate energy in the opposite direction toward the Demi Lune at the end of the Gardens.

.   .   .   .

Twelve o'clock.

High noon and the heat unabated. The sun, however, was red and hazing, and the ushers on duty around the Tuileries said, "There's the smell of thunder in the air." The seven hundred deputies were straggling in toward their hall.

Always silent and thoughtful in these days, they were now more silent than ever. They walked in little groups of threes and fours, talking only in whispers. "Was your name on that list?" some might be heard asking. "No, but I know that it can be to-morrow"; or "Yes, just as I expected," were then the standard answers; and everywhere there were winks, nods and the muttered, "Yes, we understand."

The rising seat tiers of the one-time royal theater filled slowly. The Incorruptible had not come. Couthon had not been pushed in as yet in his wheel-chair. But outside the Tuileries there was plenty of evidence that the friends of Virtue were already moving. The tocsins had not begun to ring, but drums were beating in all the swarming eastern quarters of Paris, in old St. Antoine and all those other crooked, foul faubourgs which filled up Hanriot's "Revolutionary Army." Along the eastern quays came rumblings; long ropes of men tugging the eight pounders to sweep the approaches to the Tuileries and the bridges. Deputies arriving from the Hôtel de Ville and the Palais de Justice knew the plazas there were swarming with red caps and bayonets. Unpopular representatives were insulted, as they passed these National Guard companies cooling themselves before the wine shops. "You'll be in the cart to-morrow!" "Cast your vote for Sanson!" were the yells, and things much worse.

Along with the deputies, there, furthermore, appeared a whole pack of ragged, half-shorn fellows and equally unkempt women, who packed into the Convention galleries, stamped, whistled, jeered the hesitating ushers and shouted, "When does the Carmagnole begin?"

Suddenly, however, another drum beat. From across the Seine at first. A single drum coming on confidently, and behind it a short column of men in white and blue, swinging across the Pont de la Revolution west of the Tuileries, and then moving up through the Gardens to enter the palace on its rearward side. Not Sans-culotte Guards; these fellows were not beefy and greasy enough. They were lean, gnarled, living masses of wiry sinew. They had great drooping mustaches. Many had foreheads slashed across with scars, and hands lacking a pair of fingers. A hundred and fifty, about, they moved with the quick springing step of veteran French infantry. At their head, under his tossing shako, marched a high officer wearing his sword.

The street boys, enjoying a scampering holiday, suddenly drew back in a kind of awe. They had never feared to hoot and jeer at Hanriot's battalions, but these troops advancing from the great barracks at the Invalides—were they not the genuine fire-eaters, the veritable "Wattignies men?"

All the power of embattled France, the France triumphant on the frontiers and sorely misdoubting the use made by Paris of its victories, was behind that short, grim column, and the street crowds knew it. The drum advanced, pounding, pounding. At the façade of the Tuileries it stopped. "Ground arms," shouted the officer. One hundred and fifty butts rang on the pavement together. The officer turned to his chief subaltern. "You will remain here, Captain Fargeau—unless you are needed."

The officers exchanged salutes; the commander turned to enter the building, when a corporal with the sash and feathers of the Sans-culotte Guard with three more of his irregulars shuffling behind him, approached him awkwardly and barred his way. "General René Massac."

"That is my name, Citizen Corporal."

"I am ordered to place you under arrest. Three members of the Great Committee sign the warrant——"

He had proceded thus far when a heavy hand fell on his shoulder.

"Does Citizen Carnot sign that paper, mon General?" demanded Captain Arnaud Fargeau.

"He does not, Captain," spoke René, with a shrug.

"Then, sirrah," announced the Captain, "orders are orders. Don't be a fool, my friend."

The Corporal glanced at the platoon of infantry. A deep growl was coming from under the mustaches. "Send *our* General to the chopper?" "Take him under our very eyes?" "What'd we win Wattignies for?" In a twinkling the entire patrol found itself disarmed, and standing sulky and sheepish inside a square of ferocious looking veterans who were fixing extremely sharp bayonets.

René Massac silently saluted a second time, and passed inside the Tuileries, where, even now, since he was a deputy, no writ, unless voted specifically by the Convention itself, could avail against him.

Most of the members were entering by the great eastern façade of the Tuileries from the Place du Carrousel, where Hanriot's men off duty were pressing into the square, catcalling, menacing, and very few had seen the column that approached from the garden front. At last, however, the great hall of the Convention was filled, with gaps only in those ill-omened places which former occupants had exchanged for the tumbrils.

The galleries burst into furious applause when the powdered head and the light blue coat of the Incorruptible moved to its wonted place at the very foot of the tribune. Almost equal applause echoed when the fierce glare from the skylight struck down upon the streaming locks of St. Just. He had changed his dress, and now was spotless as his master. The chamois colored coat, the white waistcoat, the pale gray breeches, all of unusual neatness, set off his pagan beauty. He was still deathly pale; his eyes were like coals in their sockets. In his hand he fingered the manuscript of the speech arranged with Robespierre; the speech laden with the destinies of France.

The formalities began. The president for the day, Collot

himself, the Incorruptible's late friend and present enemy, rang his bell. The secretary droned through the roll call. René Massac, from his seat high up upon the left among the Substitutes, could detach himself enough to try to study the scene before him, the narrow tribune facing the wide writing table; the President's chair higher still; the portrait of Marat the Martyr lowering above the president; the big ungainly statue of Liberty rising amid the front seats of the deputies; the unnatural light throwing foreheads and eyes into clear relief and hiding all the lower faces; the murmuring, shuffling, barely contained outbursts of the groaning galleries; the straining excitement on every visible countenance. René had witnessed the beginning of mighty battles; he had never awaited an onset more deadly, more decisive than this.

. . . . . .

Half past twelve.

St. Just mounted the tribune, tossed back his wonderful head, "which he carried like the Holy Sacrament," as once had jibed Camille Desmoulins, spread out his sheets; began his "Citizen Deputies."

Ere his high, hard voice had gone two sentences, lo! an uproar in the seats beneath him; a figure leaping, bounding up into the tribune, and a stentorian shout pealing through the entire theater.

"Tear the veil aside!"

It was Tallien, bitterest of the secret foes of Robespierre.

A greater wonder, a thunderous echo from all parts of the Convention. "It must! It must!"—A greater wonder still. Collot, the President, was proclaiming, "Deputy Tallien has the tribune." And in the sheer shock of surprise, St. Just found himself hustled from the rostrum, while from its height, Tallien was pouring forth a stream of perfervid oratory—desperately eloquent, as it was shot through by fear and hate.

Tallien raged. The benches thundered. The anger, the anguish, the haunting terror, which for months had possessed nearly every deputy save the inner initiates of the Incorruptible, sprang flaming into action. The greenish eyes at the foot of the tribune at first were lit by astonishment rather than by fear. No such revolt had been in calculation. The cold, complacent logic that had carried the avocat from Arras to the very portals of Utopia had provided for no such explosion as this.

Open threats had been flung against the "Impure" at the meeting of the Jacobin Club the preceding night. Terribly they were retorted now. From his seat rose Billaud-Varennes, the special object of Robespierre's menace. While Tallien still clung to the rails of the tribune, Billaud denounced the menaces against the deputies who had failed to cringe before the Incorruptible.

"The Convention will perish if it is weak!"

"No! No!" came back the roaring chorus.

The galleries began hooting the attacks upon their idol; but with his face lurid with passion, Billaud openly pointed toward one of the most strident intruders. "He dares to threaten the representatives of the people!" "Arrest him!" rose from the deputies. And the ushers, grown courageous in an instant, dragged the cursing, protesting wretch away, while over the close-packed, steaming gallery there spread the silence of just fear. The darling of Paris, the high priest of Liberty, Equality, Fraternity was being baited in his own Holy of Holies. Not one voice was being raised to defend him. What did it all mean?

Lebas struggled from his seat; made for the tribune; was seen standing in the center aisle, gesticulating, mouthing. Not one word from him could be heard. His enemies knew their part. Robespierre and his following had won their power by stifling almost every word of resistance. Not one speech of defence should they make now. Tallien stood in the tribune, with St. Just, dumb and wonder-eyed, still lingering upon its steps, while Billaud's deep bass simply silenced Lebas' weak treble amid the rising clamor.

At last an instant of partial hush. Lebas had subsided; but the powdered head, the light blue coat were moving upon the bench, were rising, were making a sudden dart toward the gangway to the tribune. Then, like one voice, hundreds of voices rose together, bursting fury behind them.

"A bas le tyran!"

An expression never there before, swept over the Incorruptible's face. For the first time his lips lost their inevitable smile. He halted. He groped back to his seat like one suddenly struck blind, while all around him the tempest raged, fierce and ever more fiercely.

Speaker after speaker, but always on one side; all the resources of rhetoric, of fury pouring over the human tongue brought to bear to whip the Convention to that point where it would pass from shouting to voting the irrevocable. One o'clock, two o'clock, three o'clock, and still the whirlwind blew; and still the Incorruptible and his few sustainers battled to obtain the tribune, and still they were swept aside.

René Massac had closed his eyes; was trying to contrast this scene with the charge on Wattignies, when the hand of an usher touched him. "Come this way, General."

In the lobby, where excited figures were passing and repassing, he saw the smartly dressed Emissary of the Great Committee. Some of René's own men, with bayonets significantly fixed, were now standing by the entrances to the Tuileries, beside the handful of doorkeepers. Hanriot's men, in brawling squads, were surging up as if to rush the portals, then at sight of the rakish steel of the veterans were falling back. As for Laurent's swagger, it left him the instant he had drawn his cousin into a safe recess.

"Bad news," he said abruptly, with a kind pressure of the hand.

René's form stiffened. "You mean that Virginie has been arrested. Well—tell me how it happened. I am ready."

"Arrested and yet not arrested. I know not what to say."

"And I do not know what to understand."

"I'll tell as well as possible. You instructed me to set forth for your house instantly, to tell Virginie that her father's old procureur, Gresset, although a legal pedant, was an honest, friendly man, and to take Henriette and flee to his house. He would shelter her for at least four and twenty hours."

"You did so; and of course it was too late."

"Yes and no. I found Olympie running from your house in an agony. A party of sans-culottes had just come and gone. They had taken away not merely Virginie, but Henriette also. They had brushed past and overpowered André, although they showed no warrant. Olympie got a glimpse of their leader, a Laclos, whom she knew was on the secret staff of St. Just."

"Of St. Just," echoed René mechanically.

"Yes, but hear this; an hour later another patrol visited your house. A regular patrol this time and with a formal warrant. Knew nothing of the earlier arrest. Searched furiously. Cursed the servants for spiriting off their mistress. Went away plainly baffled."

René's face was one of blank wonderment, while Laurent pursued: "Olympie and I have dared greatly. We have been to all the other prisons, not merely to the Conciergerie. Virginie is not in any of them. Besides, why did the first patrol take also Henriette?"

The two men stared at each other in silence, then Laurent smote his hands together. "Cousin, you know what I overheard at Spartacus' rooms. Where now is St. Just?"

René's smile became diabolic. "Within, listening to the speeches of—his friends."

"Where was he yesterday? Last night?"

"Part of the time here. Otherwise I do not know."

Laurent's fingers slid into the other's, and the clasp tightened. "Cousin, my side of the family owes some slight reparation to your wife. I'll find Olympie again.—What we can do, we can do."

And before René could speak another word, he saw the Viscount worming his way out among the brawling throngs crowding the Carrousel. The General himself returned slowly to his seat in the Convention; to himself he was saying, "You prove a harsh mistress to me to-day, *ma belle France*."

.   .   .   .   .   .

Four o'clock.

The carts were rattling off to the Place du Trône Renversé, half an hour after the jury had brought in its blanket verdict for the day.

Forty-five for the Red Mass this time. Despite the heat, patriot Fouquier, the Prosecutor, and patriot Dumas, the chief judge, would not slacken in their devoted toil. "The Incorruptible seems to be in difficulties. Queer stories from the Convention," remarked some of the clerks around the Palais de Justice. No matter. Sanson's men (minus one conspicuous member) would be waiting. The crowd in Rue Antoine must not be disappointed.

The crowd in Rue Antoine, however, was in curious

humor. Some were shouting "Shame!" some "Pardon!"; some anti-patriots were actually daring to cry aloud, "We've had enough! Stop the butchery."

Stranger still, Citizen Sanson himself ventured his inquiries. "Go on with your work," ordered Fouquier. So the carts went off, with Hanriot's sans-culottes thrusting aside the people in the streets and threatening the more demonstrative with their sabers. No "big game" in the carts this time, however; their occupants were nearly all of them humble folks, shopkeepers and women, including one poor widow. "Merely the daily quota."

In the last cart, one of the pinioned inmates muttered blasphemies between his teeth. "A ci-devant Baron, called Linio," somebody recognized. One struggled against his bonds, and cut the air with his screams and curses. Everybody knew him, pointed, laughed. "Taking your own medicine, eh? How do you enjoy it—Spartacus?" One in the dress of a priest looked about him sanely, even placidly. Once, to his calmer companions, he spoke in clear voice the words of absolution: *"Ego vos absolvo ab omnibus censuris et peccatis."*

Beside the cart, at length, there pushed a man, André, forcing himself near to the priest. "Oh, Father, Father, the General would die for you if he could, but he belongs to-day to France. He would tell you that the tyrant is toppling, to-night he must be overthrown. By to-morrow the Terror will cease."

The face of Father François became beatific. "I depart in great joy, good André. Take my blessing to all my children."

.   .   .   .

Five o'clock.

Higher the waves. Fiercer the tempest. Orator after

orator lashing the Convention. Every crime of Robespierre, every imagined crime of Robespierre, the evil he had done, the good—flung into his face. Like the signal of a ship in distress would clang the bell of the President when, in transports of passion, the deputies seemed nigh to dissolving into a seething mob. The atmosphere of the hall was reeking, while outdoors the sun was sinking into a fiery haze, and distant thunder growled through the sultry heat.

The Incorruptible had sat under the lashing, growing whiter, whiter. St. Just was now beside him, Couthon, Lebas, a very few more. Oh! for one champion with the physical presence, the great voice of Danton, to seize the tribune, to defy the Convention, to cow the deputies. Not one of them possessed it. And Tallien, again on the rostrum, delivered at last the theatrical blow which betokened the beginning of the end. "I have trembled for my country. I have watched the formation of the new Cromwell's army for the new dictator. Behold the dagger for his breast if the Convention has not the courage itself to accuse him." And above his head he flashed a bright stiletto.

But courage was not quite at the striking point. The Convention voted the arrest of Hanriot, of his chief lieutenants, of Dumas, the bloody judge, but not yet of the Incorruptible.

Robespierre himself it was who forced the final scene. Overwhelmed by the volleys of abuse, astounded by the silence of the galleries, conscious that his tried friends looked to him to play the man, again he staggered to his feet, pushed himself toward the tribune, despite the chorused *"A bas le tyran!"* and the incessant clangor of the President's bell. Whereupon a demand rang out from Louchet, another foe, who had just gained the rostrum. "Arrest!"

"Arrest! Arrest! Arrest!" pealed back from seven hundred throats.

At the foot of the tribune Robespierre at last raised his voice to a piping whistle, which penetrated even the rending din. "President of Assassins! For the last time, will you give me leave to speak?" Instantly his enemies pounced upon his words; he had insulted the President, he had insulted the Convention. "A vote! A vote on the arrest!" rose the demand from all the benches.

The Incorruptible turned at bay. In his agony, his small form swelled almost to commanding height. He faced the neutral deputies of the Center; the timeservers whom he had intimidated and despised. "You pure men! You virtuous men! Give me the right to speak which these cutthroats refuse!"—Stolidly they sat before him, answering with their "Arrest! A vote! Arrest!" He went up and down among the aisles, appealing to this man and to that. Silence and repulsion everywhere. He drew near to a vacant seat. "Keep away," roared a voice, "there's where Vergniaud you guillotined used to sit."

Then, in supreme effort, he turned again at the foot of the tribune, tried to speak above the tumult, lost his words, stumbled.

"*The blood of Danton chokes you!*" came from high up among the substitute's benches, from the seat of René Massac.

The President, white-lipped and stammering himself, rose to put the vote. At last he was heard through the hissing, stamping, cheering. *Voted* that Maximilien Robespierre should go before the Tribunal as conspiring against Liberty. *Voted* that his blameless and insignificant brother Augustin, also a deputy, who had bravely said, "I will share his fate," should be arrested also. *Voted* arrest for St. Just, Couthon and Lebas, as earlier for Hanriot and his aides.

The Incorruptible fell in his seat with a gesture of despair. "The Republic perishes, the scoundrels triumph," some heard his exhausted mutter. Then, with his friends, the ushers forced him to stand at the foot of the tribune while the formal accusation was read. The five under arrest still were as men dazed, who knew not what had befallen; only St. Just sometimes raised his head and flashed his wonderful eyes, like a Hermes silently gathering strength to confound his blasphemers. Then the ushers led them away.

The deputies rose, cheered, began to scatter. The deed seemed done. Lungs, nerves, linen alike were exhausted. In the reaction there was more thought of the cool sherbets in the Rue Honoré cafés than of the deliverance of France. To-morrow could settle the procedure before the Tribunal. Adjournment, therefore, till seven o'clock.

But when René Massac reached the lobby, a deep, grave voice sounded close behind him: "Do you think that we have finished?"

"*Ma foi*," vowed the young general, "how am I to know, Commissioner Carnot?"

"But I think we have not finished. You brought up two companies for guards this morning. Now bring up the whole demi-brigade."

CHAPTER XLI

CONVENTION or Commune, which was the ruler of France?
"Paris" had humiliated the King, had deposed the King,
had beheaded the King, had beheaded the Girondist moderates, had beheaded Danton. Now would it behead the
very Convention *en masse*?

What had happened as the nearer thunders rolled?

Hanriot had heard of the scene in the Convention with
explosive fury. Unfortunately for steady action, he had
been lunching congenially in the Faubourg Antoine and
had returned to his normal state of drunkenness. Certain
ushers from the Tuileries had, with premature courage,
gone off to arrest him and his lieutenants; whereat Hanriot,
with a roar of oaths, defied them, called to his sans-culotte
followers, "Kill!" and flung himself upon his horse. Hatless, under a torrid sun, he dashed about the plazas by the
Hôtel de Ville and the one-time Palais Royal, bawling
"Death to the scoundrel deputies!" and haranguing the excited spectators. In so doing, however, he galloped too near
the Tuileries, and certain men of the Twenty-second pulled
him from his horse, and clapped him safely into the rooms
of the Great Committee.

But the Tuileries was no jail, and the accused had been
ordered away to prison. Of the friends of the Incorruptible,
only a few of the leaders were under arrest, and the "Revolutionary Army" was already in the streets, wrought up by
rumors, ready for any bloody suggestion. Coffinhal, vice-

president of the Tribunal, a man after Fouquier's own heart, knew the value of prompt action. With two hundred gunners, he advanced toward the Tuileries, and found Hanriot being taken thence under a very small guard. Instantly he was rescued, and Coffinhal gave him counsel that might have changed history:

"Turn the cannon on the Tuileries; rush the Convention."

But the brandy fumes were befuddling his commander's wits; Hanriot was unwontedly hesitant.

"Back to the Hôtel de Ville," he ordered; "my brain won't work until Robespierre and St. Just are with us."

Robespierre and St. Just, in fact, seemed close to passing from the victims of conspiracy to the chiefs of victorious insurrection. In their behalf, the Commune, the city council of Paris, had met that evening and militantly defied the Convention. Fleuriot, the mayor, openly insulted the usher who brought the mandate of the deputies. Hanriot, recklessly bold again, being a little sobered, shouted after the usher (garnishing with the vilest oath): "Tell those maggots that we are planning to blot them out!"

The Incorruptible himself was being taken by his guards from prison to prison. He had announced himself to be of Spartan resignation; doubtless the Tribunal would acquit him; if otherwise, "the death of one just man is less harmful to the Republic than an example of revolt." The coach presently drew up at the gate of the Luxembourg, but the jailors (trembling at the howling in the streets) declined to receive him. Nowhere else would the prison guards receive him, and the perplexed gendarmes at last drove him to a small Section center, a government building and a technical place of arrest. Here (into the custody of actual friends) they deposited him, and drove off, happy to be free of so dangerous a charge.

But even this captivity was not for long. The Commune

was in action. The Commune would show what Paris thought of those "betrayers of the Republic" who now usurped the Tuileries. Its agents, with strong bands, were speeding out to every prison which might venture to detain the "friends of the Nation." Lebas they took triumphantly out of LaForce; St. Just from the old "Scotch College," a temporary jail near the University. Couthon, Augustin Robespierre they rescued speedily in turn. And as each released prisoner was brought across the Place de Grève, and carried shoulder-high into the Hôtel de Ville, the cheering from the close-packed square again made the pinnacles of Notre Dame to quake.

Maximilien Robespierre they brought in last. The Incorruptible had retained his intelligence. As yet he was only accused, not convicted; the Tribunal was still packed with his friends; to-morrow they might acquit him as they once had acquitted Marat. He could return then to the Convention, triumphing over his enemies. Only let him keep within the law; let him not break technical arrest. He could have fled from the dirty hall; instead he sat in the sultry darkness of the guardroom, beside a single smoking lamp, while outside the thunders alike from the populace and from the now ebony heavens grew louder.

"I obey the law," he said, lifting his head solemnly to the friends now pressing around him; and the ardent failed not to liken him to Socrates, who chose to suffer death rather than break his prison.

But the clamor increased; new champions thrust in; the outcry, "To the Hôtel de Ville," grew ever louder. How could the "sacred right of Insurrection" be asserted without the sustaining presence of the Incorruptible? Hanriot was free; Lebas and Couthon were free, the city (they urged on the First Deputy) was rising. But he stirred not until a tall figure at length darkened the portal of the building. Robespierre rose from the hard bench.

"At last, Antoine Louis."

St. Just's eyes were flashing with the fire of mortal excitement. "At last, my master! You alone now are necessary. Fate is avenging us. Your defamers have destroyed themselves. All can soon be regained. The perfect Republic of our dreams after all is about to triumph."

"Let us go then," and Robespierre took his disciple's arm.

They passed down the narrow street, over the old bridge leading from Notre Dame, across the Place de Grève and so to the Hôtel de Ville. Darkness had closed in, dense, murky darkness. Lightnings were flashing, thunders were rolling, but as yet not the least rain. Men glancing upward to the sky were muttering, "It'll be a fierce one when it comes!" Scores of torches now were waving, and lights were gleaming from all the tall windows of the enormous city hall. As the red flicker fell over the two men advancing side by side, many voices joined the cheering.

"The Incorruptible! The supreme patriot! To the guillotine with the deputies! The Red Mass for all of them!"

Hanriot was still prancing about on his horse. In the shifting light he was like a hideous centaur, continually flourishing his sword above his head, and shouting aloud, "Kill! Kill! Rip up the deputies!" But there was no generalship in the man and Robespierre had the wits to know it.

"We need a leader; none of us are military leaders, Antoine Louis," the grasp to St. Just's arm was tightening. "We ought not to have alienated Massac."

"He was tender-hearted, my master, therefore he became impossible."

"Yes, yes, Antoine Louis. The Republic of Virtue can only triumph by sublime ruthlessness."

Then, amid a last burst of uproarious triumph, they went
up to their confederates in the great hall of the Hôtel.

. . . .

The Hôtel raged, the Tuileries shivered. The deputies
who had wetted parched throats and returned for a routine
evening session, comforting for frayed nerves, were pale
and quavering when the President's bell called again to
order. But deeds were deeds. There could be no revoking
of the act of that afternoon, and the war with the Incorruptible must be implacable. "It is his life or ours," was
the general whisper, as deputy looked on deputy, while
the great galleries for once were vacant and silent as the
grave.

One substitute was not in his seat. René Massac had
sent Arnaud with his orders to the Invalides. He himself
remained with his two companies. As became a soldier, he
now cursed roundly enough those nice scruples of Carnot
which, "lest the Convention should seem dominated by the
military," had prevented that morning bringing up the entire
demi-brigade. The ushers and gendarmes of the Convention, hustled and hooted by the mob, were shrinking inside
the gates. By Massac's orders, all of these, but a single one
in the center, were now closed in the faces of hulking villains, who were bellowing, *"Vive Robespierre! Vive Hanriot!* To the knife with the deputies."

Fortunately, this mob as yet had no leadership. The
General drew up his own two companies, a thin enough
barrier, but yet a barrier with claws and teeth. His men
obeyed him perfectly; they would follow him to the death,
and he knew the Tuileries would be entered only over their
bodies and his. Not without fierce irony he recalled that
less than two years earlier the Swiss Guards had stood in
their red, where now he posted his infantry in blue, and he,

René Massac himself, had led up the attack from the Carrousel.—So far had swung Fortune's wheel! Westermann, Desmoulins, and ah! greatest of wraiths, Danton, were they now laughing down from their Elysium at the plight of their one-time comrades?

Messengers from the hall brought out relays of news to Massac.—Yes, the deputies were proving very brave. They were urging one another, "Let us die here like men!" They were naming Barras, a member of some military experience, as their war chief, dictator for the instant. They were naming delegates, men known and trusted by the less violent parts of Paris, to go forth into the city, to denounce the rebels, to raise the loyal National Guard to the rescue.

Could they have time? Could the almost naked palace hold out?—Suddenly through the stifling air and amid the increasing rattle on high of the thunder, there pealed a bell —the tocsin. Insurrection was again flinging wide its appeal to the mob spirit of Paris. Never since 1789 had the tocsin called to that spirit in vain. Always had authority crumbled. Would it be otherwise this night? Had they reached the climax of the Revolution?

The tocsin sounded, a thin, clear note from the Hôtel de Ville, whence the lords of destruction flung out their challenge. Would it be answered once more from twenty other steeples? Did it speak now the voice of Paris? Or only of the insurgent Commune? Massac and all near him understood, waited. St. Germain, near at hand, let out a hesitant stroke; then died abruptly. St. Antoine, far away, sent out a summons barely audible. St. Roch, much closer, boomed a few times, lapsed into silence. But the "Temple of Reason," profaned Notre Dame, could not find its great throat, and no others spoke at all. Presently St. Antoine died. Only the Hôtel de Ville continued speaking.

Massac's heart beat the calmer. It was not Paris, but

merely the Commune that marched against them. This insurrection was not to be like the others.

But now, under the flicker and toss of torches, hundreds of dark forms came trampling along the quays and the avenues, pushing aside the howling bystanders, forcing their way into the Place du Carrousel. They had pikes, muskets, and behind them rumbled their cannon; they were Hanriot's men, heated in the wine shops for the final thrust. It was the crisis, and Massac looked on his scanty hundred and fifty. They knew perfectly the numbers against them, but their contempt as veterans for the jangling mass now advancing was superb. With an ear cocked for the eastern bridge and for the gardens, their leader stepped out before them. They were too proud to bar the central gate, but stood an unflinching human barrier before it.

Massac had donned his complete uniform; the great plumes nodded above him. He had drawn his sword.

"Only a moment more, my men. Do not fire unless hard pressed. Our comrades now are near at hand. I can hear them. Before us are not Austrians, but Frenchmen. We must save Liberty without another slaughter."

The insurgent hosts rolled across the darkened Carrousel and came to a sudden standstill before the bayonets of the Regulars. "Way there, you fools," many attackers began calling, "or we'll chop you up for carrion."

As effectively they might have flung their demands against men of ice. The bayonets flinched not, and the torchlight showed the grizzled countenances of the campaigners who had flung dice with death. Not their numbers, but something stamped upon their opponents' faces made the sans-culotte masses hang back.

"We don't like this. They're the real thing," the front ranks began excusing to the files behind them.

Under the torchlight René Massac stood forth. He sent his voice far out into the tossing shadows of the square:

"Fellow citizens; Frenchmen."

"Aside aristo, or be hacked in pieces!" came voices from the rear.

"Listen to me first, before you strike down a representative of the Republic. Be not deceived. You are patriots. Patriots are obedient to the law. The law is made by the people, through their deputies. The deputies, I am just told, have passed a decree which you, I, all of us, must obey. They have declared Robespierre, St. Just, Hanriot, all who sustain them outlaws. Those who assist them will be outlaws. Disperse quickly then. Do not sully your patriotism."

Hoots, curses, loud demands, "Forward!" But also questioning; angry debates and a prolonged delay. "Outlaws does he say? Outlaws?"

"I said 'Outlaws,' citizens; because they have defied the Convention. Do you doubt me? I will bring Citizen Barras to confirm this to you.——"

But by this time a thunderous chorus advancing from the quay beside the palace made its dark copings shake, it was the song that had never failed in hour of need:

> Allons, enfants de la patrie!
> Le jour de gloire est arrivé!

And even while Hanriot's myrmidons blinked, an army of dark specters of living steel swung platoon on platoon into the area, pushing aside the demoralized sans-culottes with their gun butts rather than with bayonets; and the five full battalions of the Twenty-second demi-brigade spread out, setting themselves as a rampart unbreakable before the Tuileries.

The senior colonel saluted formally. "The Twenty-second is at command, *mon* General."

René gestured with his sword toward the mass of sans-culottes fleeing like sheep. Rain now was falling fiercely, and the thunderclaps were incessant, but all his men knew he was giving an indescribable laugh.

"Will you follow me to the Hôtel de Ville, comrades?" he demanded.

"Yes, yes, into the jaws of hell, if you wish," joyously from all the companies. And from the Massac village platoons rose a loud, exuberant *"Vive le Chevalier! Our Chevalier!—An* end to this long devil's dance! Enough of horrors! Let's terrorize the Terror!"

Disdaining a horse, René's long strides led off the columns of bayonets under the pelting storm. The troops advanced shouting and singing down the now black and empty streets, as their leader swung his sword toward the inky heavens. "Forward," he ordered, "to bring the sunlight back to France!"

.   .   .   .

In the great hall of the Commune, men swore and raged. No plan. No leadership. No obedience.

The bell in the cupola above was still flinging out its summons to Paris, but Paris was not answering. For the first time since the convening of the States General, insurrection was not wholly popular. Hanriot's sans-culotte companies came drifting back from before the Tuileries, shivering and grumbling. "The troops of the line are there, so many devils. We can't face 'em." The unorganized mobs that had ranged the streets since dawn were tired, hoarse, and beginning to take panic. The uneasy feeling was getting abroad that the Convention was about to strike back, and that a very safe place for honest men was in their beds, well away from the rain.

Hanriot was still galloping about the Place de Grève, lashing about with his sword, shouting his insensate *"Vive la Commune!"* but even his lieutenants had ceased to heed him. The city artillerymen hooted him as they abandoned their cannon under a deluge. "Go to a tavern, drunkard!" they told him; "sleep it off!"

Within the great Hôtel, however, where lights flared in their sockets, there continued the running to and fro of persons in an increasing frenzy of despair. In the main hall Robespierre and his rescued disciples sat at the long table, along with the chiefs of the city government. "Proclamation?" "Yes, there must be a proclamation." "Appeal to the people?" "Yes, an appeal to the people."—Then the bubble of the uprising instantly burst. In whose name? For what cause? How justify the open revolt against the chosen deputies of France, the one body which lay between the Nation and anarchy?

Words, words, and yet more words; while the Incorruptible himself, pitifully bewildered at the tempest he had evoked, quibbled, hesitated, raised difficulties. There were still thousands of armed men around the Hôtel de Ville. A leader, a Danton could have fired them into irresistible action. Ah! where was Danton?——

St. Just sat for hours at that table regarding his companions with a look, hard, fixed and still. Up to this crisis his fanatical soul had never wavered in its intense conviction—that the perfect Republic was about to be. Even the agony in the Convention had not shaken it. His rescue, his triumphant return with Robespierre, had momentarily confirmed it more firmly than ever. But as the slow clock ticked off their fates; as Hanriot reeled past in his regi-

mentals and cast himself upon a settle; as the tocsin rang
and rang and was not answered; as the thunders rolled and
the rain trampled, St. Just's face betrayed increasingly its
Golgotha.

His master was failing him. Confronting this crisis that
called not for high-pitched speeches, but forthright deeds,
Robespierre sat as helpless as a child. More than any other
one person, he was responsible for sending twenty-five hundred fellow mortals to the guillotine in Paris alone. Now
he balked merely at signing a resolute proclamation. The
paper, setting up a new provisional government, and doom-
ing Carnot and countless others "for placing the best of
patriots under arrest," lay before him. He would not touch
the pen. Still the thin lips questioned, theorized. The
greenish eyes groped with pathetic uncertainty.

St. Just had said what he could, as had Lebas, Couthon.
Then for long St. Just sat with folded arms, listening to the
sorry debate. His grip on realities told him that the
golden moment for martial action was passing forever; and
Hanriot, their one general, was lapsing into a drunken
sleep!

Suddenly a hand touched the young man's shoulder. St.
Just looked up and saw a person of about his own age, in
the dress of an agent of the Public Safety.

"A private word, Citizen St. Just. A trifle this way."

St. Just did not recognize the stranger, though a cast
about his eyes instantly reminded him of René.

"I do not know you, Citizen," he began as they stood
apart.

"You certainly do not, Citizen St. Just. Yet have the
goodness to answer this one question—where is Virginie
Massac?"

The insurgent chief almost caught the questioner by the
throat, but a hand stronger than his own fell on his wrist.

"Do not startle. This is no place for a scene, though I'm quite capable of making one. I know she was not lawfully arrested by your man Laclos. The patrol that took her yesterday was not authorized. Hanriot's regular men came later with the formal warrant and sought her vainly. I have traced down that much. I know that your feelings for her went beyond friendship.—Does 'pure patriotism' demand the carrying off of an enemy's wife?"

"Silence, if you want to live!" whispered St. Just, raising his free hand to cover the other's mouth.

"Faith," returned the stranger, "you and your friends all do their best to make living alike unpopular and uncomfortable.—Stay—I will ask Vernet. He's joined your conclave, and must have already smelled out your motive. He's pleading now at the table with your Incorruptible, who looks as befuddled as a bumpkin at a fair."

St. Just literally dragged the other to a distance, then delivered himself with intensity: "It was to save her from Sanson, whatever her husband's fate. After that—but how in the Fiend's name, for Fiend there must be, even if no God, did you track me down? Who are you?"

The stranger's laugh was boyish and reckless. "Call me your best friend. Call me the man who will save Antoine Louis St. Just from a deed that his worst foes in the Convention never fastened on him. What takes place in the next three hours you know as well as I, and you can judge the fate of Virginie Massac and her child if you perish and leave her in the hands of a cutthroat like Laclos and the villains he's had to employ."

St. Just looked at him like a man possessed, but his answer came with a certain calmness: "You are right. I was driven to bay and Laclos was the only refuge.—You seem to be a man of honor. I recognize the features, you must be——"

"For your Republican peace of mind, don't press that. Only tell me quick where they've taken her, or she and her child can be lost."

"Wine shop Mucius Scaevola Rue des Cordeliers." St. Just ran all the words together.

The stranger thrust out his hand and crushed the other's fingers. "You aren't all bad, you Jacobins. Take an aristocrat's thanks; the thanks of a viscount. And with that—adieu!"

St. Just gazed after the unknown as he vanished, and his lips shaped a protest, and even the outcry "Arrest him." But the other was gone, and the weary debate at the table had been resumed. St. Just went back nearer to his companions.

The Incorruptible was weakening to the demands of Fleuriot, Payan and other heads of the Commune. Never before had he, the pedantic, provincial avocat, taken the lead in defying the law. All the preceding great days that demanded deeds, not words, had found him shut in his study. Now he was required to pick up the gauntlet, to sound open defiance, or to perish himself, along with the Republic of Virtue, the Utopia of his dreams.

"Never in my life," the pale lips protested, "have I committed illegality."

"Illegality; what now is illegality?" burst from the frantic Lebas. "What is unnerving you, my master? Barras and his aides are raising the anti-patriot sections. They have more than six thousand men. Massac's janizaries of the Twenty-second are already advancing along the quays and Rue Honoré. They are driving our friends before them. Without a leader, without a pronunciamento we are lost—we and the Cause forever."

"Let me study the paper," pleaded Robespierre wearily.

From the table beside him there rose, at this juncture, a dapper figure in black, that glided over beside St. Just, who had not reseated himself, but who now stood at a little distance with folded arms and bowed head, surveying the sorry scene.

"My first miscalculation, Citizen St. Just"; Vernet's hands seemed going through their eternal washing without soap; "I surely thought that the Incorruptible would betray slightly greater energy. That's why I joined your party. My first error in a lifetime!—Well, what's our best wisdom at present? Is it not 'Save who can'?"

"You can decide best, Citizen Vernet," said the younger man, out of his gloom.

"After all, Monsieur St. Just (this 'Equality' game's about up, and I'll drop back to the old titles), for us two the case needn't be quite so desperate.—Yes, I know about Laclos and the pretty Madame. We have all had our spies on one another.—Now, if we can at once slip out of here, and you'll put the matter in my hands, we've still time to hide her better, then use her and the child for hostages; parley for safety with her husband.—Of course, Massac'll seem an Alexander or Hannibal to the Convention after this. For us he can do anything——"

"I've thought of no such escape, Citizen Vernet," spoke the other sternly.

"But I most certainly have. While our friends yonder have talked, my wits haven't been idle.—Thank me, then, for a smart turn that can save us both. Trust me to manage excellently.—And once clear of Paris, why I imagine you've been as forehanded as myself. You've surely not been on the Great Committee all these months, and not smuggled your snug rouleaux of louis through to Switzerland? Even I, with my humbler chances——"

The flickering shadows hid St. Just's menacing frown. "Then you have used your opportunities, Citizen?" was all he said.

"Naturally, not being an entire fool. A good half million's now to my account in the Banque de Berne. None of your rotten new assignats, but good old-time gold."

St. Just carefully drew from his pocket a small pistol. "No time for jesting, Citizen," he observed in tones at which even Vernet chilled.

"Dead earnest, Monsieur, and no boasting. Why the mask's off now; we're all talking freely. Once in Switzerland—Saints and angels, what are you doing? Of course I jested.—Put up that pistol! My nerves are jumpy."

He started sideways toward the nearest door. St. Just was there before him, clinched his arm, pressed the pistol against his breast.

"You have betrayed the Republic." St. Just's whisper was deadly. "You are viler than any whom we wished to guillotine. You would fly with the gains of infamy.—Now your lot shall be ours. Go back to that table. Sit still. If you rise, I kill you."

"Are you insane, man?" faltered the blenching Vernet. "Think. The last chance to save your own life. I'll help you carry her off. I'll divide my pickings. I'll——"

"Not insane, only awakening. Do not make me shoot you. She would have nothing of me. Now I may have destroyed her. Pray Heaven (if there be a Heaven) that she's about to be rescued for her husband. Sit down. I don't demand your blood."

Vernet shuffled into his seat, his face becoming ashen. When Couthon addressed him he barely muttered some reply. St. Just slowly approached the table and stood over him, heedless of the fact that the others cast wondering glances at his weapon.

Outside the rain now was pelting, the storm was raving. The deluge had cleared the streets and the Place de Grève, as effectively as grapeshot, and scattered to their homes almost the last of Hanriot's demoralized followers. The tocsin in the cupola had ceased its vain clamors, but through the rain and the thunders came now the steady tramping of thousands, nearer and ever nearer; and at length through the brawl of the elements the mighty chorus of the song going forth to battle, the bugle blasts of the Marseillaise.

Robespierre's hands went out haltingly toward a pen. "Well," he faltered, "since you demand it."

At the foot of the pronunciamento he had written one letter "R" [1] when a crash below told that the Hôtel's portals were being forced. Terrified clerks and custodians ran about aimlessly through the ill-lighted corridors. As they did so a pistol report sounded from the room nearest the great hall. Lebas had seen the Convention troops pouring into the building and had shot himself dead. Augustin Robespierre, the always incompetent brother, leaped from an open window, falling the height of the high porch. The soldiers picked him up with both legs shattered. Hanriot staggered upward from his plank, cursed, gazed wildly about him; whereat Coffinhal, beside himself with disgust, seized him bodily and flung his lumpish carcass through a second window into a pile of ordure. "Lie there, sot!" cried Coffinhal. "You are not fit to defile the scaffold."

But still the Incorruptible sat at the table, the pen poised in his strengthless hand. The greenish eyes were fixed upon the entrance; the white lips showed their puzzled smile. Then the door opened without resistance and the hall filled with bayonets, dripping shakos, swarthy ferocious men. A gendarme's hand was outstretched, another pistol shot resounded and Maximilien Robespierre's head dropped on

[1] This document, signed with the single "R," exists to-day.

the green cloth and the paper before him began to redden, his jaw shattered by the ball. Couthon struggled hideously to rise on his withered limbs ere they seized him. Of his companions, some were captured in their chairs, some as they scuttled in blind panic toward the well-guarded doors.

General Massac entered the hall just as his men were pinioning the writhing, inarticulate Vernet. St. Just had cast his pistol, undischarged upon the table, and stood quietly with folded arms, never of greater marble beauty. Involuntarily the eyes of the two one-time friends met, and the soldier momentarily recoiled.

"Do not hesitate," commanded St. Just. "The dream was beautiful. The awakening is horrible. There is no place left for me in the world."—And so they took him away.

CHAPTER XLII

THE LAST TUMBRILS

THE prisoners were taken to the Tuileries at gray dawn. Two men carried the helpless younger Robespierre; Maximilien, his brother, even more helpless, was borne on a litter by four gendarmes, his face covered by a handkerchief steeped with blood. St. Just, bareheaded and gazing proudly about, walked beside him. His own hands were pinioned behind him, otherwise he seemed to go voluntarily. From time to time he would glance at the litter and the red handkerchief. Sometimes his lips moved, and once the nearest guard heard him mutter, "So the end of the perfect Republic, the Utopia, the golden vision of a world set free—is this."

The Convention had sat all night waiting to learn its fate. Now the theater rang with the cheers of the sleepy deputies, as the great announcement was made; bravos for Barras who had roused the loyal sections, bravos for Meda who had shot down the tyrant, bravos from men gratefully delivered, for General René Massac and the Twenty-second demi-brigade that had stood between the Representatives of the People and destruction.

"They are conveying the recreant Robespierre and the other outlaws to the Tuileries," declared the exulting President; "shall they be brought in?"

"No! no!" from many voices, "to the Place de la Revolution with them as quickly as possible."

But although "outlaws," deprived of trial by their overt

521

treason, certain formalities for the prisoners remained. René Massac, despite the hard summons of military duty, tried to mitigate their last anguish as much as possible. In the anteroom of the Tuileries the Incorruptible lay for hours. A surgeon had dressed his shattered jaw and had bound it with a proper bandage, and Robespierre rested now upon a hard table with a wooden box for a pillow. He was alive and conscious. From time to time he wiped at the blood with a cloth case for pistols. Once when René was in the room, he saw the prisoner reaching vainly for his garter as if it cramped his leg, and the officer made haste to loosen it. "Thanks, Monsieur," struggled from the swollen lips. Those were the last words ever spoken by the High Priest of the Terror.

St. Just sat upon a stool by his companion; his arms had been loosened, he rested his head constantly on his hands. Despite the guard stationed to protect the prisoners from mob violence, the door of the room became crowded by figures hooting, mocking, reviling. St. Just seemed never to hear them; though other prisoners near him shrank and raved.

At length René made his way to him. The strong soldier was shaken to the bottom of his soul by the surrounding scenes, and barely was he keeping back the tears.

"Why do you wish to weep?" demanded St. Just suddenly. "If you had been condemned by the Tribunal you would not have wept. You would have gone on to the end carrying your head high. You would have said that you were dying for France and for humanity. Should I prove myself weaker than you?"

"Anything? Anything within my duty that I can do for you?" pleaded Massac.

"Where are Virginie and her child?"

"Virginie and Henriette are at Rue de la Démocratie.

Laurent, my cousin, and Olympie Durand found them at the wine shop just as Laclos and his villains were debating their murder lest their own crime be discovered. They are safe and well. Virginie sends you this message. 'Tell Antoine Louis that I wholly forgive him. I knew that he was not sane. In God's Heaven he shall return forever to a nobler mind."

"No," answered St. Just slowly, "I was not sane; but who among mortals is? ANANKÊ, Inexorable Necessity, is it not that which drives on all of us?—Heaven? I've no great wish for that. So many there one would have to meet!— All the hundreds, the thousands who went to the Red Mass, not because we loved their destruction, but because it seemed the price for building the eternal Republic of Virtue—yet it could not come to pass that way."

He put down his head heavily upon his hands, and then spoke wearily once more: "Tell Virginie my last thoughts shall be of her. No other woman has entered my life. I could never understand them. And my love for her I knew from the first was impossible. You had made her absolutely happy.—So many things that I cannot understand."

. . . They took the prisoners to the Conciergerie for legal identification. Fouquier hurriedly checked off the names of the intimates before whom he had cringed one day earlier.[1] It was four o'clock when the tumbrils started through the most crowded streets of Paris, for the guillotine had been restored to its old station in the Place de la Revolution. Women, young girls, old men, all who had feared, had lost, had agonized, were there to pour out exultation, ribaldry, fury upon the death carts. The gendarmes pointed with their sabers to the helplessly sodden Hanriot, to the struggling, gibbering Vernet, "the apostate priest," and above all

[1] Fouquier was removed himself from office almost immediately and was executed within the next year.

to the barely living body of "The Tyrant," as it swayed, bound to the rails of the wagon. Only for St. Just, standing tall, beautiful and unafraid, there were fewer curses and perchance even a little pity.

At last the roaring square, the merciful swiftness. Twenty-three times the Red Engine crashed. Twentieth was the Incorruptible.—And then one awful shout from tens of thousands of throats, strangers casting themselves into each other's arms, ecstasy, wild dancing. The sky had cleared. Cool evening sunlight was streaming across the Champs Elysées, while from the Bois de Boulogne to the faubourgs by Vincennes went spreading, tossing a single cheer, "The Terror is no more!"

. . . .

11th Thermidor, July 29th, 1794.

How quickly Paris had calmed! The Opéra was selling seats for "Armide"; the Opéra Comique was putting on that most harmless of pieces, "Paul and Virginia"; only on the door of the Théâtre des Sansculottes hung a placard not without significance, "No performance." The great heat had departed and likewise the storm. The afternoon was advancing, clear, balmy and beautiful.

Virginie Massac sat in the little garden behind her own house, with the old chestnut rustling above her with its clear monotonous music. In her little bed, set out by André, Henriette lay in absolutely peaceful slumber. René sat beside Virginie. For some time he had been holding her hand, speaking no word.

Laurent had quitted them an hour earlier. Probably Carnot had had his suspicions when General-of-division Massac came with the request "Kindly endorse this passport"; but for all that he had promptly signed. Laurent was on his way to Switzerland. "Stay in France. We can easily get you a pardon," his cousins had urged; but he had answered "My wife, my parents are beyond the frontier. Your Republic is a queer place for me—as yet"; then added, as if with a kind of after-thought, "but never again will I fight against France."

Major Arnaud Fargeau also had left them. He reported that the Twenty-second was almost over-seas to a man, drinking the health of their adored general in honor of his last promotion.

Olympie also had left them. Without any betrayal on her own part she had been delivered from an utterly uncongenial spouse, and she was extraordinarily reconciled. She had not yet decided whether to take Spartacus' dearly-earned assignats and open her own wine shop in Ard, or to attempt a similar venture in Paris nearer to her White Bird and to Henriette.

At last René remarked, "They are flinging open the prisons. The innocent suspects are being sorted from the real enemies of the Republic. Even the most guilty will have fair trials. All the news from the armies is good. The Republic has fought all Europe and has triumphed. The King of Prussia has just sent us his hints of 'Peace.' The other kings at length must follow.—And we are here—together."

After that neither he nor Virginie spoke again for some time.

Presently Virginie broke the silence: "My beloved, how long is it since the States General gathered at Versailles?"

"It is not yet five years and three months."

"Five years? Did you not mean to say five centuries?" Virginie's eyes looked straight upon the bed of flowers, but her husband knew that she was seeing none of them. "Oh! I feel old, old, old. Through what have we not lived!"

"But by God's mercy at least *we have lived*—is there not something in that, my dearest?"

Virginie's white fingers moved before her face slowly, as if she were dispersing cobwebs or a fine mist.

"Of what did we dream? Of a world set free by mild philosophy, enlightenment, knowledge. Of privileges crumbling at the first behest of reason. Of kings and queens cheerfully abdicating. Of liberty, equality, fraternity becoming the universal law.—All without bitterness, all without war!"

"We were children," answered the strong soldier beside her. "We imagined in a year|to undo the errors, the ignorance, the iniquities of two thousand years. Like other children we have paid our price. Now, as taught men and women, we must begin again, slowly, painfully, undauntedly to build that better France, that better world that shall pass down to the Ages of Ages."

But still Virginie's hands seemed trying to disperse the mist. "Shadows," she said, "the garden is becoming full of them."

René too could see the shadows.—Men, women, nearly all of them young or in the prime of life; figures noble, figures villainous; some in silk and velvet, some in felt and fustian; smiling or sad, courageous or trembling. Who were they? Whence came they? Why would they not depart?

Louis XVI, Marie Antoinette, Dreux-Brézé, Desmoulins and the gentle Lucile, Manon Roland, Danton, Robespierre, St. Just. These were a very few. And those other figures who had touched Massac's own life for blessing or for ill— Father François, Thibaud, Vernet and many another——

The garden seemed full of shadows. Their presence oppressed him, and his own voice sounded hollow and far away when he heard himself repeating, *"Five years and three months."* And then again, "WE HAVE LIVED."

Suddenly all the shadows took flight into the green and gold of the sunshine. With a rippling laugh, Virginie was taking his hand and pointing to the little bed. "Oh! look, what can be so enchanting her? Henriette is smiling in her sleep!"